The
Brahmadells

Translated from
the Faroese by
Kerri A. Pierce

The

Brahmadells

Jóanes
Nielsen

OPEN LETTER
LITERARY TRANSLATIONS FROM THE UNIVERSITY OF ROCHESTER

Library of Congress Cataloging-in-Publication Data:

Names: Nielsen, Jóanes, author. | Pierce, Kerri A., translator.
Title: The Brahmadells / Jóanes Nielsen ; translated by Kerri A. Pierce.
Other titles: Brahmadellarnir. English.
Description: Rochester, New York : Open Letter, 2017.
Identifiers: LCCN 2017027998 (print) | LCCN 2017034673 (ebook) | ISBN
    9781940953731 (e-book) | ISBN 1940953731 (e-book) | ISBN 9781940953663
    (paperback) | ISBN 1940953669 (paperback)
Subjects: LCSH: Families—Faroe Islands—Fiction. | Faroe
    Islands—History—Fiction. | BISAC: FICTION / Literary. | FICTION /
    Historical. | FICTION / Sagas. | FICTION / Cultural Heritage. | LCGFT:
    Epic fiction
Classification: LCC PT7599.N54 (ebook) | LCC PT7599.N54 B7313 2017 (print) |
    DDC 839/.6993—dc23
LC record available at https://lccn.loc.gov/2017027998

This book is published with the support of the Mentanargrunnur Landsins,
The National Cultural Foundation of the Faroe Islands

Printed on acid-free paper in the United States of America.

Text set in Dante, a mid-20th-century book typeface designed by Giovanni Mardersteig.
The original type was cut by Charles Malin.

Design by N. J. Furl

Open Letter is the University of Rochester's nonprofit, literary translation press:
Dewey Hall 1-219, Box 278968, Rochester, NY 14627

www.openletterbooks.org

The
Brahmadells

PART ONE

The 185th Birthday

EIGIL TVIBUR SHUT the cemetery gate behind him and, as so often happened when stepping into the shadow of the great oaks, his mind eased. The trees were among the city's oldest living residents, and thanks to their age and their beauty they were treated with enormous respect. When the municipality first installed drainpipes and sidewalks along Dr. Jakobsensgøta in the 60s, it proved necessary to move the stone wall on the south side somewhat further in. That left two of the trees standing just outside the cemetery, and in order to protect them, attractive iron grills were placed around the trunks.

The spruces farther up the yard were also a pleasure to behold. A good century back, Gerd, the wife of the businessman Obram úr Oyndarfjørði, transported some root cuttings back to the Faroes in a tub. She had been to visit her family in Bergen, and the tub spent the entire trip back from her old hometown securely fastened to the ship's deck. Perhaps it was the act of defying storms from sky and sea that had implanted something joyful and proud in the trees' souls. Eigil, in any case, had the feeling that one bright day the spruces would burst out singing that patriotic Norwegian hymn: *Yes, we love this land . . .*

The rowanberry trees, for their part, were gaunt and grew best on the cemetery's west side. Some had even been planted outside the yard. Indeed, a true penchant for experimentation had swept that part of Tórshavn, or Havn, as it was often called, right before World War I. The trees had grown quickly, and the beautiful crowns with

5

their conspicuous light-green leaves had provided pleasure to almost five generations of west-side city inhabitants, not to mention to the countless starlings and sparrows that had sat singing in the branches throughout the years. Now the trees had stopped growing, something that was obvious from the topmost branches, which were leaf-less, barkless, and brittle. Green and reddish carpets of moss grew up the trunks, and when the sun was shining, golden light beams seeped through their loosely woven crowns. In truth, the trees had come to resemble the people over whom they watched. And that was not so strange. The roots had long been absorbing their bodies and, eventually, you are what you eat.

The gravel crunched beneath his boot soles, and like always, when Eigil reached the nameless children's graves, he stopped. He knew nothing of their history. Presumably, they were stillborns or newborns seized by a sudden, devastating death. The graves looked just like the zinc laundry tubs women used, but bottomless and tipped upside-down. There was also no cross at the head of these graves. In the months of June and July, buttercups and orchids grew on the gravesites, yellow and reddish-blue summer flags waving from their slender stalks.

Eigil continued to the grave of Napoleon Nolsøe, a former *Land-kirurg*, or country surgeon. His hatred of the man had once been so great that on New Year's Eve, 1980, he had defiled Nolsøe's grave. He had been convinced that Napoleon Nolsøe was the prototype for modern Faroese nationalists, and that it was on his account that the cultural aspect of nationalism in particular had developed into an epidemic.

And if only Eigil had kept his mouth shut about defiling the grave, nothing would have happened!

Yet in December 1992, when Eigil was up for re-election on Tór-shavn's city council, his crime appeared in the newspaper *Sosialurin*. The man who had represented the Self-Governance Party on the city council for four years was hung out as a gravepisser! The newspaper wrote that he had disgraced an honorable man's grave in the same way the Nazis and anti-Semites had when they painted their spiteful slogans across Jewish graves. Or worse: Whereas the anti-Semites' paint came from a can or bottle and could be considered impersonal, urine was not.

With only the hallway lamp lit, as he stood and spoke into his floor-length mirror, he had justified his actions by saying it was the fault of that man of letters, Ole Jacobsen. In volume six of *From the Faroes – Úr Føroyum*, which the Danish-Faroese Society had published in 1971, and which Ole Jacobsen had edited, the scholar had succeeded in convincing the reader, or at least Eigil Tvibur, that Napoleon Nolsøe had broken the Hippocratic Oath in 1846. And it was not just a hard accusation—it was enough to destroy the man's legacy.

In 1846, the Faroes were ravaged by the measles; in Tórshavn alone, 50 out of 800 inhabitants died. Doctor Napoleon Nolsøe, whose practice was then located in Nólsoyarstova, was asked by Pløyen, the *Amtmand* or Prefect, to travel south to Suðuroy to help with the crisis. He was promised 50 rigsdaler a month. Yet Nolsøe refused to travel.

A few years after Eigil read Ole Jacobsen's article, *Bókmentasøga I* by Árni Dahl was published. In volume one of the literary history, it was clear that Dahl greatly respected Nolsøe. Page 75 featured a large photograph of the man, which was accompanied by a short biography followed by a few snippets composed in Faroese by Cand. med. & chir. N. Nolsøe.

This woke Eigil's fury. The brand of nationalist who claimed to love native verse but couldn't care less about the country's inhabitants had always disgusted him. As composer Regin Dahl put it: *Love the country, hate the people.* Or maybe it was the opposite. Eigil could not stand that kind of catchphrase. But that was more or less how Ole Jacobsen's article described Napoleon Nolsøe: He loved

Faroese folk ballads, but in 1846 he had turned his back on his dying countrymen.

If Eigil had his way, a man like Napoleon Nolsøe would never appear in Faroese literary history. He simply had no place there. Not that Eigil was against giving authorial villains their just due in histories or reference works or even naming streets and ships after them. Not at all. One of his great skaldic heroes was the Nazi sympathizer Knut Hamsun, and without authors such as the Marquis de Sade, Céline, and Jean Genet, the French literary mouth would be lacking much of its bite.

But Dr. Napoleon was no Genet, and had done nothing worthy of literary acclaim. He may have contributed to the development of Faroese orthography, but that was about it. The man had recorded a large number of folk ballads, but he had not actually composed anything himself, and what he did record had already been collected and documented by others. Napoleon Nolsøe had transcribed transcripts, that was his great achievement, and to fill literary history with copyists would be both unfitting and ridiculous.

At a meeting of the Writers' Association, Eigil had declared that the names appearing in Faroese literary history were just as randomly chosen as the names appearing on the Association's membership roster. One belonged because he had translated two or three minimalistic children's books a quarter century ago. Another had participated in a short story contest launched by well-meaning pedagogues as many years back, and where the result had been purely sentimental pedagogical drivel! And a third might have edited a festschrift for some alcoholic sleepwalker at the Academy. Such largely formed the Writers' Association membership roster. The few authors who actually deserved to be there had been branded the "cultural mafia" in the media.

The danger here was that when another Árni Dahl decided to write a new literary history in half a century or so, that person would turn to the association's membership roster in search of suitable representatives. People who were undoubtedly skilled with the copier would be called significant bearers of Faroese culture.

Eigil could see only one reason that Dr. Napoleon was honored with a place among the Faroese full and half gods: He had the right DNA profile! The doctor was the son of the old business agent Jákup Nolsøe, and therefore the nephew of poet and national icon, Nólsoyar Páll. It was for that reason and none other that Árni Dahl had smuggled him in through the back door of his literary history.

When Eigil reached Napoleon's grave, he put down his bag. It was August 26th, and today exactly one hundred eighty-five years had passed since Napoleon's birth. Eigil placed a hand on the headstone and wished Napoleon happy birthday, and as he had done so often before, he also asked Napoleon's forgiveness for having sullied his sleeping bones.

On the other side of the cemetery path was a concrete basin with a water tap. Eigil ran some water into a bowl, screwed the lid off the cleaning solution, and added the strong liquid to the water. He did not immediately notice when some of the rinse splashed onto his coat sleeve, and when he finally saw the spot, it did not disturb him. Truthfully, it fit his overall appearance. He had neither washed nor shaved in several days, and his bright brown eyes sought the source of every small sound, be it a rustle in the newly fallen leaves or a bird suddenly bursting into song. Compared to his body, his head was noticeably small; he was a huge man, and the grimy coat made him look even more massive.

Eigil had thought to clean the entire headstone, and also to scrape off the moss and the lichen, but that would only disfigure the stone. Yes, the patina would certainly vanish. He knelt down before the gravestone and with a little screwdriver began cleaning the engraved letters of debris. And there were 128 letters in total. But Eigil had plenty of time, and when he finished his cleaning, he took a paint-brush from his bag and began to brush and wash each individual letter with the cleaning solution.

Like a scoured corpse, Eigil thought, and a giggle broke through his lips. Exactly, a scoured corpse. Like a skeleton protected by dry skins, or as Eliot wrote of the whispering voices:

> . . .
>
> *Quiet and meaningless*
> *As wind in dry grass*
> *Or rats' feet over broken glass*
> *In our dry cellar.*

Stay calm, Eigil, stay calm, he told himself.

A rose branch twisted around the marble plate. It had been neatly etched into the gray material and a little soft moss grew in the concave stone leaves.

Smiling, Eigil asked himself whether it would have bothered Napoleon Nolsøe that Nils Tvibur's great-grandson was sitting here painting the letters with silver-bronze.

Eigil and Karin had planned to drink a birthday toast at the grave-site, and his bag held a bottle of Chablis and two glasses. He uncorked the bottle, lit a cigarette, and considered the freshly scrubbed letters:

HERE LIES BURIED
RETIRED LANDCHIRURG
NAPOLEON NOLSØE
MARCH 3rd 1878
THIS STONE ERECTED
BY HIS FRIENDS IN REMEMBRANCE
OF WHAT HE MEANT TO THEM
IN HIS DAY.

Yet Karin did not come. They had agreed that she would be here at four o'clock, and now it was nearly half past five.

He blew smoke past his lips; he didn't usually smoke, but it calmed him to have a cigarette between his fingers.

Shit, could he have offended her?

His mind turned to the Dusty Springfield song "You Don't Have to Say You Love Me." He had played it over and over during the wonderful week they had spent together.

It suddenly occurred to Eigil that perhaps they had not set a date after all, or that perhaps they had only done it in his mind. He had planned to invite her to eat at the new restaurant in Nólsoyarstova. The building had been Napoleon Nolsøe's childhood home. Later on he kept his medical practice there, and when he married Henrietta Løbner in 1874, she had moved into Nólsoyarstova as well.

The perfect setting for a cozy meal.

Could all the hell he was catching from the Self-Governance Party have ruined that plan?

Something was off.

The history of oppression on this island, its failures, the violence. The family histories that he had so immersed himself in. All of it now repeating itself through him.

Eigil felt how his hand shook as he poured wine into his glass, and when he glanced toward the cemetery gate, he dropped the glass altogether.

There stood his mother. The face of the person closest to him in the world was far too anxious, and she was clutching her hands together as if she were afraid she might lose them. She stood in front of the open cemetery gate, two policemen at her side.

The Orange

THE PASSENGER SPRANG from the cutter. His coat spread around him like a sail, and while he hung in the air with both arms outstretched he looked just like a bird.

Though the sight was neither unusual nor ridiculous, Tóvó still covered his mouth, biting his fingers to keep from bursting into uncontrollable laughter. There were three travel trunks onboard the cutter, each holding medicine and various instruments for minor surgeries: scalpels, scissors, amputation saws, and a copious amount of gauze. Also: alcohol, camphor, laxatives, quinine, opium drops, and mercury ointment.

Farther out lay the three-masted schooner *Havfruen*. They had enjoyed a good wind from Copenhagen. The first day they beat to windward, but after they were free of Skagerrak, the wind had blown from the south and the southeast. The voyage was made in seven days at full sail, and at midnight they dropped anchor in Tórshavn's harbor.

Finally, the trunks were unloaded and the passenger turned to Tóvó. Immediately, the amusement left the boy's eyes, and the passenger discovered the laughter-prone person was a six year old who had come to the dock to watch. The passenger had friendly, but searching eyes. He took an orange from his coat pocket and handed the boy the odd reddish-yellow object. Tóvó did not know Danish, but he understood enough to know that *en appelsin* was something you could eat.

Manicus and Panum

ONLY TWO WEEKS had passed since newspapers in the Danish capital had published an account of the measles epidemic ravaging the Faroe Islands. The article first appeared in *Fædrelandet* on June 17, 1846, and even though the article was unsigned, it was a given that Dr. Napoleon Nolsøe was the author; or conversely that, inspired by Dr. Napoleon, it had been written by Niels C. Winther, or "Doffa," as his friends called him. The *Berlingske Tidende* reprinted the article, and the news was considered so alarming that the Finance Chamber immediately took the initiative of sending medical aid to the Faroes. Two doctors were asked to assume the task.

One was twenty-six-year-old August Manicus. His father, Claus Manicus, had been Landkirurg on the Faroe Islands from 1820-28, so August had spent his childhood in Tórshavn and had been the playmate of Venzil Hammershaimb and Doffa.

The second doctor, the man with the orange, was better known as Peter Ludvig Panum.

For five months the two traveled the islands and administered medical aid. On top of that, Panum thoroughly examined living conditions on the Faroes. He studied factors such as housing, hygiene, the Faroese diet, and how food was prepared. The smallest detail made it into his notes. He also described the clothing, and how the weather affected the general health of both body and soul.

His results were published in the medical journal *Bibliothek for Læger* in the spring of 1847.

But what no one, not even Panum himself, knew before June 17, 1846, was that his treatise would prove one of modern epidemiology's great breakthroughs.

Manicus, too, documented his sojourn in the Faroes, and even though his report, which appeared in the medical journal *Ugeskrift for Læger*, was not as comprehensive as Panum's, he had a sharper eye for the connection between medical complications and social living conditions. He writes: *Bøigden Sumbø was one of the sites where the epidemic claimed the most victims. The poverty of its inhabitants, the poor housing conditions, and the fact that measles suddenly gripped the larger part of the inadequately nourished population—who, moreover, were susceptible to any sort of remedy—explains this.*

Manicus further added that the disease: *. . . spared nearly all of the Danish families and was significantly milder among the well-to-do native inhabitants.*

In a footnote to her doctoral thesis *Knowledge and Power*, which was published in 2006, Beinta í Jákupsstovu writes: *The mid-1800s was a period characterized by strong ideological currents; Manicus might have sympathized with political ideas surrounding the promotion of social equality or with Faroese nationalism.*

She admits, however, that no sources exist to support this idea.

Mogul

MOGUL RESTED HIS head in Tóvó's lap. He yawned deeply, and when the boy began to pick the sleep from his brown eyes, he did not resist, and he also swallowed the puss-ball that the boy rolled between his fingers and placed on his long tongue.

The dog probably knew that Tóvó was the reason he was still alive. He was twelve years old, and as sometimes happens with an old dog, he could snap at people. He did the same with other domestic animals, and one day, after he had mauled one of Frú Løbner's hens, Martimann said Mogul's days were numbered.

Tóvó did not know what numbered days actually meant. He could count to nineteen, and he knew there was such a thing as "counting the days of Christmas," which referred to a Faroese dance tradition, but that was surely not what his father meant. But when Martimann tied up the dog and went for his muzzleloader, it was clear to the boy that Mogul was about to be shot. That was what numbered days meant.

Tóvó began to sob. He said it was the chicken that had started it. That bird had crossed Mogul so many times. It had been sent by the Devil, and at night, when everyone was sleeping, Tóvó was going to set fire to every chicken in town.

Martimann was astonished by the strong words. He had also never seen Tóvó stomp and shake his fists like that. The boy was only six, but at that moment he resembled a raging dwarf. Tóvó put his arms around Mogul's neck and said that he would never let go.

For a moment Martimann considered the situation. He knew how much the boy loved the dog, and if he shot it, his son would undoubtedly consider him as an enemy for a long time to come. He could give Frú Løbner some fish in exchange for the mauled hen, she would probably accept that. And it was such a sweet picture: Tóvó sobbing with his arms around Mogul's neck, while the dog sat there inquiringly.

Martimann untied the rope, but to show that he still had a bit of authority, he gave the dog a kick that sent it spinning across the yard.

But Tóvó continued to cry. He hated his father. Hoped a whale would bite his arm off, or that a stone would come flying through the air and strike him right between the eyes.

The Little Wandering Church

ALTHOUGH IT WAS a regular weekday, Havn was a ghost town and had been for several weeks. Not a hammer stroke was to be heard between the houses, not a single woman washed her clothes in the river, and no playful children rolled barrel hoops in the alleyways. The city, which could normally man 16 eight-rower boats, could hardly man a single boat in May or June.

From a bird's eye view, the thatched houses resembled giant limpets stuck to the rocks with no sign of life.

The situation was so dire that the Dean Hans of the church bought several barrels of grain with poor relief funds. One large pot sat on the stove of the midwife, Adelheid Debess, another hung over a hearth belonging to an old married couple up on the hill. A few of the sick were able to fetch their own soup, but households where every family member was coughing and vomiting needed others to bring them their meals, and in some cases also to feed them.

One of the selfless souls caring for the sick was Old Tóvó. In his younger days he had been known as a skirt-chaser, but women still let him slip his hand beneath their necks and lift their heads while he gave them water or soup to drink. He inhaled their sweet, feminine aroma, and, indeed, he confided to a female relative from Bakkahella that he always liked it when women were sick, because they were so compliant. She tried to smile, saying he had always been a blowhard.

No one entered the church. Ever since the measles had seized the city, the church opened its doors only to the dead. Up to eight coffins at a time stood on trestles in the choir and down the center aisle. Protocol dictated that in cases of disease the coffins should be tarred on the inside, and the smell of tar and rot filled the church with a boundless despair. The dead were whisked from their homes as soon as possible, and they were neither washed nor prepared in another way before the cart retrieved them. One old tradition was to bind the big toes together so that the dead could not walk again, but measles had undermined most traditions. And who knew if the dead even wanted to walk. Why should they? In May and June, death in Tórshavn was about as bare as it could get. Ghosting around as autumn storms were shrouding the city in a salt-sea fog was not to be recommended either to living souls or to spooks.

Adelheid dried her tears and smiled. It must be a bizarre coffin flotilla indeed, she thought, setting a course for eternity's waters. The sails were the garments people were wearing when they died: nightgowns, loose pants, shawls, and tattered shifts.

Sure, sure, answered her husband, Ludda-Kristjan, and shrugged his left shoulder. He was one of those short-fused folk from Kák, but he could not do much against his wife. He did not dare tell her to shut her damn mouth and stop all this pretentious nonsense. However, that was how the flock around Dean Lund talked. Their sentimentality was disgusting.

One exception was the Norwegian Corporal Nils Tvibur, or Muhammad, as he was called. On The Feast of the Cross, back at the beginning of May, he was in Ludda-Kristjan's workshop and he said there was no point in wasting good wood. Given the circumstances, it was enough to make every coffin a foot high, and if the epidemic continued, they would have to reassess the situation.

Ludda-Kristjan asked if he was thinking of a mass grave, and that was exactly what Nils had in mind. Once a mass grave was dug, the dead would have to be wrapped in linen and lime sprinkled over the corpses.

Among Fort Skansin's soldiers, Nils Tvibur was the one Amtmand Pløyen trusted the most. The Corporal meant what he said; the man was no sycophant. The soldiers were responsible for unloading the ships that came to trade, and it was this trade that funded operations at Skansin; as corporal, Nils was the obvious choice for foreman. And even though he could be hard on people, even on his own men, he was good at getting things done.

Nils's Christian name was Selleg, and he came from the Sveio peninsula in Hordaland. No one ever called him Nils Selleg, though, and in the fort's log he always signed as "Nils Tvibur." He was called Tvibur because he was a twin. But since he had been born second, it was his older brother who had inherited the farm.

Nils Tvibur, though, was not one to shy from work, and when the gravedigger succumbed in May to the measles, Nils took up his spade, and he also drove the horses that pulled the cart. If a corpse was too tall to fit in the coffin, he broke the neck so he could nail the lid shut.

"Damn," he said one day after Dean Hans had blessed a man from Hoyvík whose neck he had just broken. "He looks like he's listening to something I can't hear. So long as it's not the footfalls of Iblis."

Dean Hans blanched at the name of Iblis. "Don't you go saying the name of Muslim Satan in a Christian church," he said, crossing the corpse anew.

"Of course," Nils replied.

There were few days that the corporal and the pastor did not cross paths, and one day Dean Hans asked why Nils was so infatuated with the Muslim faith.

Nils responded that religion in general did not really interest him. Neither the Muslim nor the Christian religion, nor Judaism for that matter. But last year a man had died whom he had greatly respected, the newspaper editor Henrik Wergeland. Nils said that he had not read the man's poetry, but the things he had written about religious freedom—those were manly words indeed. It was Wergeland who had opened his eyes to Muhammad, or the great Desert Captain, as Nils liked to call him. Since then he had tried as much as possible to follow the Muslim way of life. He knew that the Muslim people lived next to the high mountains where Noah's ark was stranded. Their cities spread south toward the Persian Gulf, and Muslims also lived along the entire North African coast. They were not too stingy to give alms to the poor, but they were also fearless warriors.

It was the general state of emergency that prompted Pastor Hans to make an unusual decision. Since the church only had room for the dead, he decided to sally forth and take hymns and prayers out to the townsfolk.

In the beginning, he walked alone, making brief stops at Bakkahella, at Doktaragrund, up by the library, or simply whenever he saw a door ajar. He prayed an Our Father, blessed the household, and then sang a verse.

After he was joined by Anna Sofie and Henrietta Løbner, who were mother and daughter, other poor souls turned out as well. For the most part, they sang "Fare, World, Farewell" by the Danish hymnodist Thomas Kingo. They sang it to the saraband melody, and their swaying steps made the group look solemn and strange.

No poet, of course, has made a greater impact on the Faroese national spirit than Thomas Kingo, and when Professor Christian Matras translated "Fare, World, Farewell" into the Faroese in 1929, he walked, humming, the same narrow streets as Pastor Hans did in an effort to instill the verses with Kingo's unique musicality.

The group also sang Oehlenschläger's more contemporary and milder hymn, "Teach Me, Oh Wood, to Fade Glad Away", and when they passed the Geil family house, Tóvó sometimes stood at the door, watching and listening to the little wandering church.

Tóvó's Flies

THAT MORNING TÓVÓ'S mother woke him. During the last two days she had been up to his room a few times, but she had not said a word. She was not her usual self, and now that the measles and its side effects no longer gripped her, she sometimes broke into such heartrending sobs that Tóvó had to cover his ears, and when that did not help, he simply left the house. He had no idea these crying spells heralded a budding insanity, and that in the coming years his mother would earn the nickname Crazy Betta.

In his *Observations*, Panum wrote: . . . *there is hardly any other country, or indeed any metropolis, in which mental diseases are so frequent in proportion to the number of people as on the Faroes.*

Tóvó's brother, Lýðar, and his sister, Ebba, were still confined to their beds, and their grandfather had placed a vomit bucket on the bench in between them. An old home remedy suggested that tidal seawater had curative powers, and so their great-grandfather often made the trip to the little promontory of Bursatangi to rinse out the bucket. He covered it with a lid to keep the flies out, but nonetheless they buzzed around this interesting wooden container. Sometimes they sat on the rim, and as they cleaned their shiny legs, Tóvó struck. Most flies he killed as soon as he caught them, but others he tortured to death. He would place the prisoner on its back and feel the faint buzzing of the fly's body as a tickle against his forefinger and thumb, and before the tiny heart would beat its last, he'd have the fly's plucked wings and legs arranged on the bench. Other flies he drowned in a quart measure-pot. Like a ship with no oarsman, the fly would sail around and around the small, tin-lined sea. The fly tried reach the edge, but every time it had almost gotten two or three legs beneath it, it would be mercilessly shoved away again, until eventually it gave up fighting for its miserable life.

The tobacco tin, which Tóvó had stashed behind the Heergaard stove's clawed lion feet, often contained nineteen dead flies. A piece of twine was wrapped around the container, and when Tóvó removed the lid, it smelled slightly of rot, but mostly of chewing tobacco. The flies that had not been tortured to death lay with wings pressed tight to their bodies and skinny legs curled up. Like they were begging forgiveness for their very existence.

Whether tortured, crushed, or drowned, the flies all had one thing in common: they were victims in the war Tóvó single-handedly waged against the measles. From what he understood, measles were a kind of fly. One single glance from those itty bitty measles-eyes and people immediately went feverish and began to cough and rave like mad. Some also sang like mad, a humming mixed with guttural sounds, until they were either exhausted, asleep, or blue in the face.

Still, Tóvó did not understand why the measles flies had not beamed their rays in Great-Grandfather's direction, or why Mogul was unaffected. A few cows, on the other hand, definitely had measles, the way they were behaving.

Here is what the cows should do. They should go up to the small lake, Hoyvíkstjørn, and out onto the Konmansmýri marsh, where they could eat grass and clover and thyme, and where their calves could frolic so they sprang straight up into the air. Sometimes the cattle grazed way up near Svartifossur, and one sunny day last summer, when Betta and her children went there to pick berries, they saw several white ravens and a heron fishing in the falls.

Svartifossur was not as high a waterfall as Villingardalsfossur, and it was also lower than the streams that cast themselves over the cliffs at Kaldbaksbotnur, but Svartifossur was still the most beautiful of the waterfalls. The rocks were dark, and when the sun shone they were wonderfully warm when you touched and sat on them. Small red flowers glinted among the plants growing along the stream and hanging from the rocks, and in the rocky crevices you could see whole bunches of yellow roseroot. According to Lýðar, the high rushes that grew north of the waterfall were called "grass knives," because they were so sharp you could cut yourself on them.

Their mother said rainbows also loved Svartifossur, and her children believed her. Svartifossur was where the rainbows' colors were mixed, and after that, proud and beautiful, they would straddle the fjord across to Nólsoy. Sometimes a rainbow would hit Heimistova, where their paternal grandmother and grandfather lived, and sometimes a rainbow would reach all the way north to Eystnes on Eysturoy. Svartifossur was a paradise for all berry lovers, their mother said, wiping red berry juice from her small daughter's lips. Lýðar lay splashing in the stream, and when he came out again, his mother wrapped the naked boy in her shawl.

Now everything was different. There was no one left to milk the cows, which had gone mad and bellowed through people's doors.

The fact Mogul numbered among Tóvó's worries was due to the reaction he had had against his father the day Martimann was going to kill the dog, but the boy dared not tell anyone that, not even his great-grandfather.

However, he did ask Great-Grandfather why he did not get sick.

Old Tóvó replied that, fact of the matter was, he had already had the measles when he was a child, back in 1781 when the measles had last swept through the island, and you could not get the disease twice. That was also why he was not afraid to visit people and help them. And perhaps the old man sensed that something else was bothering the boy, because he added that foul-breathed dogs could not get the disease either.

Tóvó asked if the disease really did come flying through the air. His great-grandfather explained that a ship had come from Denmark on Annunciation Day, and that that ship had brought the disease to Tórshavn.

Tóvó had heard of Denmark and he knew that a prince lived there. He had even seen the prince when he had come to Havn in a warship two years ago. Suddenly, he frowned and asked: why would the prince send a ship full of measles-flies to the Faroes?

Old Tóvó suppressed a smile when he looked into the boy's serious and lovable face. He had not been as fond of his own children as he was of Tóvó. And the boy was so clever. The journey between thought and question happened in the blink of an eye. His great-grandfather knew about all the dead flies Tóvó kept in that tobacco tin, and one day he had watched the boy drown one poor creature in the quarter measure-pot. However, he said nothing, just waited outside until the deed was done.

Now he explained to Tóvó that, of all the castles in the world, the measles castle was the hardest to conquer. Only the most cunning of princes could sneak through the gate and raise the flag of victory.

Grandma Pisan

THE CART STOPPED for the first time in front of the Geil family house on Pentecost. Great-grandfather opened the door so that Nils Tvibur and another man could enter and retrieve Pisan, or Grandma Pisan, as the children called her.

Pisan was from Hestoy, and when Farmer Támar's oldest son got her pregnant and she gave birth to a daughter, she took her own child's life.

That was what Old Tóvó told his great-grandson several years later.

Pisan gave birth to her daughter in a peat shed up on the island of Hestur, he said. And the child was healthy. She smelled so freshly of the womb, and Pisan could feel the warm breath from the newly inflated lungs against her neck and cheeks. She said that the breath coming from the tiny nostrils and mouth was like a storm, the most violent she had ever experienced. She put the baby to her breast, and when the child had nursed its fill, Pisan did what plenty of other unmarried mothers did back during the years of the Slave Law, which forbade anyone who did not own land from marrying—she killed her own child. With the little nape resting trustfully against her palm, she pressed her thumb to the baby's throat, and when its breathing had stopped, she wrapped it in the lined shawl on which she had given birth, bundled it up, and then sank her unbaptized daughter in a small pond south of Fagradalsvatn.

Old Tóvó stroked his great-grandson's hand. He could tell him one thing: If the Hestmen decided to drain that pond someday, they would find a mass grave of newborns swaddled in lined shawls. Of course, Pisan would have to answer for her deed on the Last Day. But so would the island's lechers. And the Devil give them what they deserved!

In *Saga Hestoyar*, Pastor Viderø writes: *A multitude of tears have been shed here on Hestoy, but God transforms them to the most beautiful rainbow.*

Pisan was never able to see the pastor's rainbow. Or rather, one might say that, with a freshly knitted shawl and her feet encased in leather shoes and clogs and with a bundle beneath her arm, she fled the rainbow over the fjord.

For many years, Pisan earned a living working on different farms throughout Sydstremoy, and then she moved into a garret near Sjarpholið in Tórshavn, where she, among other things, spread fish to dry on Rundingen and helped in houses where women were giving birth. And what she could not settle with money, she settled with her flesh.

One of her long-time suitors and friends was Old Tóvó, and when she grew old, he pitied her and took her into the Geil house. And it was there she was taken by measles.

The cart arrived for Pisan on the Eve of Pentecost. Little Tóvó was sick with the measles just then and did not fully comprehend what was happening. He saw only Pisan's bluish face as they lifted her into the coffin.

Here it should be added that Old Tóvó became a widower in 1822. Ebba, his wife, hailed from Venzilsstova in Kaldbak, and they had two children. Their daughter, Gudrun, was usually called Gudda. At 11 years of age, she became maid to Argir hospital's tenant farmer. Later, in 1820, Claus Manicus was appointed Landkirurg, and in the years he worked on the Faroes, Gudda served as his maid. When the

Manicuses left the country in 1828, they invited Gudda to come with them to Denmark. She served as their maid for 13 years, and died unexpectedly at the age of 49.

Old Tóvó's son was also named Tóvó. The younger Tóvó and his wife, Annelin, lived in the Geil house. Annelin was pregnant when her husband sank with the *Royndin Fríða*. She gave birth to their daughter, Betta, in 1810. Shortly thereafter, Annelin married Finnur á Kirkju, a farmer from Kirkja north on Fugloy, and she left Betta, to be fostered by her first husband's mother and father in Tórshavn.

Sorrow and Rhyme

SIXTEEN DAYS LATER the cart again stopped outside the Geil house. To Tóvó's mind, it was as if a stick had been stuck between the spokes of both wheels, and when he later thought back, it was as if the cart had stood there his whole childhood, digging and hewing itself deeper and deeper toward his soul's very bottom.

Nils Tvibur and a man with a mask set the empty coffin on the floor. The mask tapered into a beak that held a mixture of dried moss, caraway, and horseradish. The smell supposedly prevented contagion.

The Geil house had become quite nice. The floorboards were new. Martimann had laid at least half the floor and installed the stove before he contracted the measles. The disease's progression had been as expected. His eyes and cheeks had swelled up and for a week he had suffered a high fever. When he was feeling better, however, and his cough was somewhat improved, he thought there was no harm in occasionally nailing down a floorboard. There was no one else to do it, and he could not make himself ask Old Tóvó. The old man had enjoyed an excellent reputation during his years as a shoemaker, but as a carpenter he was not worth much. As a result, Martimann got out of bed; progress was made with every board he nailed fast. He saved the widest boards for the area around the door; these were up to eleven inches in breadth. The boards had been sawed from a piece of driftwood his father had given him, and on a sunny day last summer they had dragged the tree trunk to Tórshavn and got it up into the boathouse's loft to dry.

It was that ill-fated, short trip down to the boathouse to retrieve the boards that proved too much. Martimann grew damp and cold, and when he lay back down in bed, he fell victim to all the complications Old Tóvó had been constantly warning him against, and which strong Martimann simply could not imagine.

His intestines felt like they had a life of their own and were writhing like worms in his gut. Sometimes they squirmed up into his throat and made him vomit, or retreated down to his rectum, spraying filth onto the blanket Old Tóvó had placed beneath him.

Old Tóvó tried to coax him to eat. Boiled milk was somewhat satisfying and was good for combating diarrhea. However, the mites that lived on *skerpikjøt*—well-aged, wind-dried mutton, a specialty of the Faroe Islands—were said to be even better at stopping diarrhea. The only problem was they had no dried mutton. Out in the storehouse were some dried fish, and also a barrel of salted pilot-whale meat.

Martimann had been the anchor of the Geil house ever since he and Betta had married. For many summers he sailed with the Scottish sloop *Glen Rose*, and much of that income went to renovating the dilapidated house. He laid new birch bark on the roof and asked Ludda-Kristjan to build a double window, which he himself installed. The house sat on rocky ground, and Martimann built a chimney in the northwest corner. He covered a small piece of ground in front of the chimney with stones, and that is where he placed the new stove. The smoking parlor was converted to a kitchen, and the daylight streaming through the new double window quite literally heralded brighter days.

Once the floor was finished, the plan was to install a kitchen table where Betta could sort clothes and attend to other household tasks.

Martimann was a driven man, and during the years he lived in the Geil house, they wanted for nothing.

By the end of this year, however, the coffers had run dry, and Old Tóvó could hardly go to Landkirurg Regenburg or to Doctor Napoleon empty-handed and ask them to look at Martimann.

Nonetheless, Old Tóvó did speak to Napoleon, and the doctor told him that good care was all that could be done for the disease's complications. "I know what I'm talking about," Napoleon said. "Good wishes and devoted care, there's not much more in our power."

Old Tóvó did not expect an educated man like Napoleon to hold home remedies in high esteem, and so he did not dare ask the doctor for any *skerpikjøt* mites.

Indeed, he felt his only choice was to do what Tórshavnars did when the German privateer, "Baron von Hompesch," plundered Tórshavn's trade coffers in 1808: go out begging.

The Húsagarður farmer had meat, of course, but Old Tóvó didn't have the courage to go knocking on a Sunman's door.

However, Old Tóvó quenched his shame and made the trip to the Quillinsgarður house where the former Amtmand's wife, Anna Sofie von Løbner, lived. He told her his errand while standing in the doorway, and for a moment, while she tapped her knuckles with her fingers, she looked at him in surprise.

Old Tóvó could well remember when Anna Sofie had been one of the Húsagarður farmer's milkmaids. Her father was a cooper, so she was known as Anna Sofía hjá Bøkjaranum, or the Cooper's Anna Sofie. She was a shapely woman, and thanks to her round figure, she was asked to play one of the maids in Holberg's comedy *The Lying-in Room*.

Letters, however, were not Anna Sofia's strong suit; she needed someone else to read aloud her lines so that she could memorize them. And that other person turned out to be no less than Commandant Emilius von Løbner. He was patient and kind and read well, and he never failed to light a fire in the Bilegger stove so that the room where they sat was cozy. Sometimes these readings lasted well past midnight, and during their breaks Løbner would offer the budding actress sweet wine and even sweeter words. And she let herself be enticed by his mature charms, became giddy, inviting, and compliant.

"Just call me Emilius," he said, placing a candy on her moist, pink tongue. She let him bathe her with expensive soap, and he told her this was how aristocrats enjoyed themselves in the King's city. He placed the dish of warm water on the table, kneaded soap into the wet washcloth, and received permission to wash her face and neck and along her hairline. Nor did she protest when he untied her blouse, washed her beneath the arms, and carefully dried the sweat off her heavy bosom. She enjoyed this intriguing midnight game, allowing him suckle her breasts and making no objection when he loosened her skirt. He said "hopsasa," and she lifted her rump while he spread a towel on the chair to keep the plush dry. The towel was so large that he also folded it over her pubis, so that she would not feel too exposed. While he washed her toes, one after the other, he caressed and patted her thighs, which he called love's white columns. And just like the Bilegger stove, Anna Sofie purred with contentment.

"Just sigh," he whispered. There was no harm in sighing aloud when you were enjoying yourself.

By the time the comedy was performed in Fogedstova during September 1813, Anna Sofie was pregnant. The couple married in January 1814, the same day Frederik VI signed his name to the document dividing Norway from Denmark. In April, Anne Sofie delivered a stillborn male child. Three years later she was pregnant again. She gave birth to Ludvig, named after his Danish grandfather, and in

1825 she gave birth to Henrietta Elisabeth, named for both her Danish and Faroese grandmothers.

Why Løbner left the Faroes the same year that his daughter was born remains uncertain. By then he was in his sixties and his health was poor. In particular his sight was failing, and he often said that his eyes could not tolerate the raw Faroese climate.

There were also some complaints about how he conducted his office, but precisely how serious these complaints were remains unclear. In the second volume of Tórshavn's History, Jens Pauli Nolsøe and Kári Jespersen attempt to shed some light on the man: *To his credit, he compiled Løbner's Tables in 1813. They provide a valuable description of Faroese society and are actually the only precise record we have of economic conditions in Faroese rural society. For Tórshavn it was important that [Løbner] allowed Álaker field to be added to the city in 1807, which nearly doubled the area then belonging to Tórshavn.*

Much of Løbner's life remains in the dark, however, and it is perhaps for this reason that a number of Løbner's descendants have tried to envelop the man in mystery. Among other things, it has been suggested that the insane monarch Christian VII was his father. In that case, Løbner's mother became pregnant when Christian was still a prince. Løbner was born in 1766, the same year that Christian VII was crowned king, and it is conceivable that the prince visited his relatives at Augustenborg Palace the preceding year. Løbner's father, Jakob Ludvig, was a chamber lackey at Augustenborg.

There is also a lack of information concerning what Løbner did during his final years after he returned to his homeland. There is some indication, however, that he lived with Caroline Wroblewsky, who for several years ran a private school in Copenhagen. Wroblewsky adopted a young girl, Emilie Christine, and in 1858 she took over her foster mother's school. *The Biographical Encyclopedia of Danish Women* states, among other things, that: *In 1850 [Emilie Christine] changed her name to Løbner after her adoptive father, the former prefect of the Faroe Islands, Emilius Marius Løbner, who died the previous year.*

What is certain, however, is that Løbner spent a quarter of a century on the Faroes, and that he was around 60 when he departed. One reason for this lengthy sojourn was the major changes introduced by the Napoleonic Wars. Denmark, namely, had not fought a war since the Great Northern War ended in 1720, and in the extended stretch of time that followed—which historians term the Florissante Period—Copenhagen transformed itself into a European trading capital. During and despite the various wars plaguing Europe, the Danes sailed the seas under a flag of neutrality, an extremely profitable undertaking for both ships and maritime trading companies. The Danish-Norwegian trading fleet was the second largest in Europe, and aside from overseeing Danish colonial interests, the fleet sailed the globe, exporting and importing wares.

The Florissante Period ended in 1807. Fearing what might happen if the Danish fleet fell into Emperor Napoleon's hands, the British attacked. 30,000 soldiers were put ashore at Vedbæk north of Copenhagen, and a mighty armada besieged the capital. From September 2-6, Copenhagen was bombed and burned, and the British seized the entire Danish navy and every transport ship they could find.

However, it was not just Danish economic development that was stalled. All of Europe suffered a period of stagnation that lasted until around 1830.

When Løbner returned to Copenhagen, he was well past his prime, and in that respect he was no different than his homeland. Denmark had been transformed to a half-blind geographical bagatelle located on the Øresund. The Swedish had taken Norway, and even though Frederik VI's jurisdiction still included a region extending south toward Eideren, people were already clamoring for both Schleswig and Holstein to join the new German Confederation. As such, it remained a question of time how long Jutland could call itself a Danish peninsula.

A smile tugged at Frú Løbner's lips and for a short moment she resembled her strange nickname: Sildahøvdið, or Herring Head.

"I recognize you," she said, placing a hand on Old Tóvó's arm. "You're Tórálvur í Geil."

She gestured to the door and told him to follow her. On the far side of the path was the Amtmand's yard, and within it stood the storehouse. She kept the padlock key on a cord around her neck, and when she opened the door, Old Tóvó put his hand to his heart. What a beautiful sight! Several handsome barrels of salted meat stood on the floor. Besides whale meat and blubber, she also had lamb and brined guillemots. A trough held some lightly salted mutton wrapped in white cloth, and on the shelves were several jars in which Frú Løbner had preserved berries and rhubarbs and also mussels. Particularly inviting was the smell of two smoked pork sides. Some smoked trout were also hanging there.

The best smell of all, though, came from the dried mutton. Frú Løbner inspected the legs and found one that was sufficiently hairy. She untied the knot, wrapped the greenish leg in a cloth, and told him not to say another word about it. She also gave him a jar of rhubarb jam, saying that it would undoubtedly do Betta some good.

That evening the Geil household had bread and *skerpikjøt* to eat. No one, though, had much of an appetite. Martimann was unable to eat anything solid, only managing a couple of spoonfuls of warm milk. He was so weak that Old Tóvó had to press the scraped-off mites against his molars, and Martimann tried his best to take some strength from the Løbner storehouse's gift. His cough was somewhat diminished, the sound emerging from his throat now was more like a weak wheeze.

While Old Tóvó sat and watched over Martimann, he did as he had so often done before and hummed his homemade verses. He did not know if Martimann heard him, but little Tóvó lay perfectly still on his bed and listened.

Great-grandfather sat there rocking with his arms crossed over his chest. And it was difficult for him, especially when he recited the old Catholic lays against *syftilsi*, the illnesses produced by witchcraft. However, he also sang about Grandma Pisan, and then his voice grew small and meek.

> March, the mild month, has two hands
> searches in the raven's nest.
> Pisanhead from Hestoy came
> pisanhead from Hestoy went.
> Behind an old man sits.
> Tread hard, grip fast
> magic days seven.
> *Noves buba turra*
> *persia gif dissia*
> *nissia gif dissia.*
> Searches memory with two hands.
> Tread hard, grip fast
> ravens shriek in the fells.
> Little pisan went.
> Behind an old man sits.
>
> The Christmas sun, the bell ore,
> rings in a sea-washed heart.
> The Sweet One in a manger
> the manger in a stable
> the stable of stone
> the stone of earth.

Mother and father and whale oil
grandma and grandpa and tanned-leather shoelaces.
The shuttle sings in the loom
the shuttle sings in the loom.
Fish swim in tears
tears salty as the sea
the sea deep as sorrow.
Oh, you Sweet One
grant us winter cod
oh, you Sweet One
spare my tears for Martimann.

January, the peeking month, its mild sun
timid heavenly eye.
Holy Birgitta feeds gentle doves
they fly over gleaming ridges.
The days in blood
the blood in eggs.
Delights curse the harrow
Delights curse the plough.
January's mild sun
dries the dew on the cheek.

The Master Barber

THE CART ARRIVED for Martimann on St. Botolph's Day. The effect of the disease on his face and throat had been so severe that the soft and blood-rich parts had turned dark blue and black in places. The white of his eyes were bloodshot, and his right eye had nearly popped out of his skull. Now that he was dead, his eyes were somewhat sunken, but his Adam's apple was still rigid, and his mouth was slightly open, as if he were going to speak.

Betta sat at his side and stroked his face. Occasionally, she cried and shook his shoulders.

As soon as they had set the coffin on the ground, Nils Tvibur sensed that they might have some trouble here. He cleared his throat and said rather awkwardly that it was against the Landkirurg's directive to frequent death's domain himself.

Betta looked up at him with her astonished gemstone eyes. She said a Muslim had no business prattling about death's domain. Regenburg could go to Hell with his good advice, and he could take his temple rat of a wife and every last soldier and all the confounded birdfolk in this despicable town with him.

Nils knew there was no point in responding to her deranged words. For many years, he had been infatuated with Betta, but even though Martimann sailed with the Scottish sloop *Glen Rose* every summer, he had never managed to catch her in conversation. He had only seen her about the town, usually holding a child by the hand or in her arms. True, she might occasionally bid him good day and smile, but her smile had nothing behind it.

Sitting next to her husband now, she resembled an enormous insect; her long, full hair was the net she threw over his beloved body. She said it was the driftwood from Nólsoy that had finished off Martimann, and that the wood was cursed. Everything to do with Nólsoy was cursed. Heimistova was a witches' den, and it was witchcraft that had sunk the *Royndin Fríða*. Nólsoyar-Páll died there, and she had lost her father while she was still in her mother's womb.

Betta pointed to the coffin in terror and said that the coffin was black-tarred, just like Hell, though at the word *Hell*, she smacked her mouth, crossed herself, and said that she had not meant it.

Old Tóvó sat next to her, but he did not dare to touch her arm. Perhaps she might hit him or say something she did not actually mean. He simply remarked that Martimann's soul had departed long since, and that wherever he was, it was a good place to be.

"Would you shave Martimann for me?" Betta asked suddenly.

Her voice was weak and broken, and the request struck Nils's heart. After that, she began talking about the Shoemaker from Jerusalem who wandered the worlds' streets unshaven and filthy, and no one opened their door to him. The Shoemaker had not meant to be so disagreeable when Jesus had asked him for water, he was just so afraid of the Roman soldiers, and that was why he refused to give Jesus something to drink. Indeed, it was inconsiderate of Jesus to ask him for water, because he knew full well that he would be putting the man in an unnecessary bind.

And then Betta mentioned Hell again, and this time she was unashamed. Her hair and hands trembled as she said that the Geil house was a place in Hell, and that fire would soon shoot from the bay, and that no one would need to shave then because Satan, the Master Barber himself, would fix the problem.

A coughing spasm interrupted her terrifying words, and even though it seemed fruitless, the old man tried to comfort her. He also told Tóvó to come and tell his father good-bye, but Tóvó refused.

The boy also couldn't bring himself to ask where his father was going, even though he knew that the cart took the dead to the church, and from there to a hole in the cemetery.

Tóvó was terrified, that was what. He had wished his father ill, and God, who heard all, had heard that terrible prayer. It was his fault his papa would never wake up, and so he could not tell Martimann good-bye.

Tóvó bit his fingers, not knowing whether it was laughter or tears that filled his throat.

Betta looked at her son, and the fact that he refused to bid his father farewell subdued her.

Hr. Hans had paused in the doorway. Now he slipped inside, and he was so tall that his head touched the ceiling beams. Softly he asked the Lord to watch over this sorely afflicted household, and when he had said amen, both coffin bearers went over to the bed. Nils Tvibur gripped Martimann under the arms, the masked man gripped him beneath his knees, and then they lifted him into the coffin. As they were bending to lift the coffin and depart, Nils suddenly hesitated and asked where the shaving things were.

Old Tóvó sprang quickly to his feet. He found the light-colored cloth in which the shaving knife and soap were wrapped, and he also carried a small basin with water over to the coffin.

Nils looked at Betta. "May I have the honor of shaving the honorable deceased?"

Betta was so stunned by the unexpected question that she could not speak. Nevertheless, she nodded.

Nils passed Old Tóvó his cap, and while he wet Martimann's face and rubbed soap into the well-grown stubble, a reverent hush fell over the kitchen.

First he shaved Martimann's upper lip, and the scraping of the knife sounded oddly ceremonious. It was a tiny sound, but it reached every ear. Then he shaved both cheeks, taking pains not to cut the skin, even though Martimann's face was already cold. Although he was down on one knee, still he did not want to risk shaving the throat, because it was so difficult to reach with the blade. He also scraped the stubble from Martimann's chin, and when he was finished, he wetted the light-colored cloth and carefully wiped the dead man's face.

When Nils got to his feet, he was obviously affected. The others in the room also sighed in relief; they had more or less held their breath while Martimann was prepared.

Old Tóvó thanked Nils, and after that the two men lifted the casket and left.

Later Nils Tvibur remarked that if anyone had earned a royal sign of respect during the weeks that the measles raged, it was that old Brahmadella, or whatever the fuck the Havnarfolk called him.

It was only when the bearers had successfully finished and departed that the old man burst into tears. Suddenly, he was ancient, the oldest man in the city, perhaps in the city's history. He was the same age as the Shoemaker from Jerusalem, and all the world's sorrow stood written on his gray, unshaven face. He sat bowed, as he had on the night that he had watched over Martimann. In the Catholic lays against sickness, he had invoked the Angel Gabriel and the Holy Birgitte. Those mighty words had fallen like a cleansing cascade from his lips, he had been nearly out of his senses while he prayed and read, but still the words had been too weak.

At that moment Old Tóvó did not just hold the pain of humanity. His soft weeping also carried the fear of a wounded animal: The moment the coalfish lays with clapping gills on the shore, no clue where the sea has gone; the moment the poor lamb pisses in fear before the butcher's knife slices its throat. And Pisan had died the same way as her newborn, with a rattling throat and a blue face.

Old Tóvó gasped for air. He had lost his wife and both his children. Poor Gudda had gone to work at 11 years of age, and her grave was in another country. Nor could he visit the grave of his son. Suffering was a form of vengeance, that was what. Whatever you did from carelessness, recklessness, or conscious malice, or by simply letting things alone, everything came back to roost, and if you were not ready for it, it would knock you to the ground. Whether it was Heaven or Hell taking its revenge, he did not know. Vengeance had no source; all you felt was the pain of it grip your heart, and that grip was firm and cold.

When the cart had departed and the crunch of its wheels in the gravel still hung in the yard, he sat with his cap in his hand and wept.

The days following were not any better. He was incapable of shouldering Betta's sorrow, and he could get no words from her either, and when she cried, it was as if the heavens had broken and fallen over the house. He could not tolerate being there, and when he went for a walk or to visit someone, it was a comfort to have Tóvó with him.

Tóvó, though, wanted to be led by the hand, and that in itself bothered his great-grandfather. It was as if the boy had lost faith in his own feet and eyes. He had become as helpless as the flies that he drowned in the quart measure pot.

They slept in the same bed, and one evening Tóvó asked in a whisper why his great-grandfather had cried so horribly when the bird man and the corporal left with Martimann.

"Oh, my sweet child. Our family is dying. The Brahmadells are disappearing."

"Was Grandma Pisan also a Brahmadella?" Tóvó wondered.

"Oh yes, certainly she was," the old man replied.

"Then Father was a Brahmadella, too," Tóvó said happily.

Before his great-grandfather had turned over to answer him, the boy was fast asleep.

The Story of a Nickname

TÓRSHAVNARS CALLED HIS great-grandfather Old Tóvó or Tóvó í Geil, though he was Thorolf Thorolfsen in the parish register. The strange thing, however, was that when the boy's name was entered into the parish register on August 3, 1769, the pastor, Johan Hendrik Samuelsen Weyhe, added the nickname of his own accord, writing that the male child was *of the Brahmadells*. The pastor's handwriting, too, was visible after the names of the child's father and paternal grandfather, where it was noted: *of the Brahmadells*. The reason for the addition is difficult to pinpoint. However, it was simply done in the moment and not out of malice.

In a letter exchanged with William Heinesen, the Danish ethnologist H. P. Hølund pursued the Brahmadella question further. There was no tradition, he knew, that allowed pastors to write nicknames in the parish register, and he thought there was something threatening or ominous in the words *of the Brahmadells*.

To place the matter in a larger context, Hølund referred to the book *Faroese Yeomen of the King, 1984-1884*, where the Faroese national archivist Anton Degn, among other things, wrote of the pastor: *Hr. Weyhe was seemingly a talented and, especially when it came to oriental languages, a much admired man, and far exceeded his time in knowledge.*

As Degn continued: *In his latter years, [Hr. Weyhe] succumbed to the weakness which back then was common among clergymen in Norway and Denmark: "finding happiness in a bottle"* . . .

Hølund believed that Pastor Weyhe himself was the origin of the nickname, and that the name itself originated in a drunken act.

Hølund attempted to clarify or interpret the name and referred to ancient India, where the Brahmins were the highest and most learned caste, and observed that a fitting translation of the word *Brahma* could be *supreme god*. However, why Pastor Johan appended the Italian preposition *della*, which signified "from" or "of," onto *brahma*, which was a Sanskrit word or a Sanskrit name—that was something of a mystery. Indeed, properly speaking, the preposition should precede the nickname, but in Pastor Johan's ears "dellabrahma" had probably sounded flat, eclipsing the orientally shaded allusion.

Hølund's conclusion was that Pastor Johan had probably argued with either Old Tóvó's father or grandfather, and in the pastor's drunken state, the disagreement had become something distorted and unwholesome, causing the pastor to dare to record his frustration in the parish register.

The seventy-plus-year-old nickname had followed the family ever since.

The fact that the Brahmadella name truly did inspire fear was shown one day when Pastor Hans was passing the Geil house with his singing church. The man's following had substantially increased in the last weeks, and they were so pious now that they did not so much walk as sway. With faces turned heavenward and arms crossed over their breasts, they sang the Oehlenschläger hymn "Teach Me, O Forest". Frú Løbner's soul had also continued to slip its earthly bonds, had grown increasingly freer of the earth, and weightlessness enveloped her as she swayed in the wake of tall, skeletal pastor.

Pastor Hans was so skinny that people jested about his remarkable appearance. Ludda-Kristjan, who could be quite droll among friends and acquaintances, had dropped the remark that Pastor Hans was only susceptible to two diseases: blackheads and osteoporosis.

When the pastor saw Old Tóvó standing in the door, he lifted his right hand and made the sign of the cross. The pastor's smile was so disgustingly sweet and self-righteous that Old Tóvó slammed the door.

It was not just the pastor who saw what happened. Frú Løbner took Pastor Hans carefully by the arm and told him not to mind Tórálvur í Geil. She said the Brahmadells had no piety and were therefore incapable of appreciating good deeds.

Old Tóvó stood cursing in the hallway until the flock had passed.

Intemperate devils, that's what they were. Out taking a Sunday stroll through poor people's misery and sorrow! All the years he spent repairing their shoes and boots, just so they could to walk dry-soled through this diseased city.

It was the last pastor, Pastor Niels, who once tried to pay for a boot repair with some self-calligraphied scriptures. His bunions, which had ruptured the boot leather, had grown so big that they looked like budding horns.

And Old Tóvó told him that. He looked the pastor in the eye and told him that Hell was growing from his foot soles.

The Telescope and the Opium Drops

BETTA STUCK HER feet out of bed. Her hairy legs were well-formed, and her toenails were neat as tiny shells. She was wearing only a shirt, and while she wrapped the big shawl around her shoulders and beneath her heavy breasts, her toes sought out her clogs. She was not accustomed to the new wood floor, though, so when she found the clogs and started across it, it made such a racket that she kicked the shoes off again. There were some thick wool socks in the bed, and when she had pulled these on, she went over to the clothes chest. She unlocked the chest, lifted the lid, and took out the telescope bundled in a dark-red silk cloth.

As Betta walked to the peat box, she glanced at Mogul. Tóvó shrank back, certain his mother was about to kick the dog. Instead, Betta's eyes took on a look of anxiety. She seemed to fear the dog and gave him a wide birth before sitting on the peat box.

For a moment, Betta closed her eyes, and then she asked Tóvó to come and sit beside her. Carefully, she untied the ribbons, unfolded the cloth, and for the first time in his life, Tóvó saw a telescope.

"P. N.," she said, pointing to the letters engraved in the brass. "This telescope used to belong to Nólsoyar Páll. Pappi got it after his first tour aboard the *Royndini*. I want you to go to the Nólsoyar house and tell Doctor Napoleon that this telescope used to belong to his uncle, and tell him that your mama wants a bottle of opium drops in exchange for the telescope."

Tóvó longed for her to say: *Oh, my fortune's child*, or *Mother's little foal*. She had such sweet words, and not just for him, but also for Lýðar and Ebba. But not today. She was not in a tender speaking mood. And she also did not notice her son's loving gaze, or how his fingers fondled a corner of her shawl. He had the orange hidden beneath his sweater, and even though the Danish man had given him the strange fruit, he had decided that his mother should have it, but that he had better wait to give it to her. It made Tóvó happy simply to hear her voice, the fact that, in spite of everything, she still talked to him.

He did his sheepskin shoelaces, but once he was outside, he turned back around. "Opium?" he asked.

His mother nodded and her little foal galloped away, telescope in one hand and orange in the other. He raced straight across the road, a full meter between each glad step, only the tips of his shoes flinging the sand grains up. The bright bay quivered beneath the sunshine, and just like back then, back when everything was as it should be, dabbling ducks and eiders rummaged on the water's surface.

Doctor Napoleon's house was just beyond the river's mouth, and it was the largest house in the city, full of windows that drank in the sun. No, the second largest, because the largest house in the city was the church; that was where God and all his angels lived, or nineteen angels at any rate. The big coalfish net hung from the church ceiling, and during the fall, when the bay simmered with coalfish, the whole city was there. The net was dragged through the east gable opening and was grabbed by 20, sometimes 25 nimble-footed men. The net was around 30 fathoms long and crept, worm-like, along Húsabrúgv, down though Bringsnagøta, then farther along Gongini, and when it had emerged on the tip of the headland, a line of the net was rowed out to Krákusteinur.

Martimann had been one of the most enthusiastic netmen, but Tóvó did not want to think about that at the moment.

Opium drops, he must not forget the name. Mama said the drops made the pain go away. Yet where did pain go? Maybe it had wings like measles flies? Or maybe it crept away like woodlice under rocks? Maybe pain lived with the Jóvóvamaður up by Svartifossur. Great-grandfather said that Jóvóvamaður was half-human, half-plant. The human half was little more than a finger in height, the rest of him was roots extending far beneath the earth. He said the Jóvóvamaður was the Fly King, the Maggot King, and the Beetle King, so why could he not also be the King of Pain? Maybe it was Jóvóvamaður who sent pain to the city in the evenings? Oh! Woe to the poor soul who had left a door or window wide open!

The Amtmand's House was also large, but not as tall as Doctor Napoleon's. Still, if you counted all the additions and outlying building, the Amtmand's House covered a substantial area up toward Glaðsheyggjur hill.

Húsagarður was also large, or maybe it was just all the people living on the farm there that made it feel big. Lots of grandfathers and grandmothers lived there, and women and men and also children whom Tóvó knew and with whom he played.

And of course the Royal Trade Monopoly buildings in Tórshavn were even larger.

Then there was the doctor's house. Or rather, the house that belonged to his father, Jákup Nolsøe. Jákup was an old, robust man with broad hips and sideburns not unlike the corporal's goat. Sometimes children bleated after him—*mæææ*, they said—but the old man ignored it.

Jákup Nolsøe believed the Faroes needed to prepare itself for the new era, and the fact he had great expectations for his son was shown by the forceful name *Napoleon*.

The famous historian from Gjógv, Hans Marius Debes, explains Napoleon's name in his book, *Stories from the Old Days*:

During that time Napoleon Bonaparte was victoriously marching across

Europe, and Nólsoyar Páll so admired him that people said he was completely insane for Napoleon. When Marin Malena was about to give birth to their second child, Nólsoyar Páll decided that if it were a son, he would be named Napoleon. And yet it was a daughter. Nonetheless, the name Napoleon was given and Nólsoyar Páll decided to call her Napolonia. Yet the pastor refused. He said Napolonia was no proper name, but that she could be called Apolonia, which came from the Greek god Apollo, and as such she was baptized.

Debes continues:

Since Nólsoyar Páll was unable to give the name Napoleon to one of his own children, he convinced his brother, Jákup Nolsøe, who was a trade envoy, and who was married to Onnu Katrinu Petersdatter Skeel, to use the name Napoleon. And so it was. They called one son Napoleon Nolsøe. And that was undoubtedly the first Faroese to be named Napoleon. In any case, he was the first practicing doctor.

A few low wooden steps led to the door of the man who was named after an emperor, and as Tóvó entered the small apothecary, which sold opium drops and small bundles of sugar candies, licorice, and French brandy in bottles with glass stoppers, the doctor snapped a wet rag on the counter, spraying droplets.

"Shut the door, hurry, hurry! I don't want any more of those black beasts in here!"

Tóvó saw some enormous flies against the bright window. They looked as big as candy sugars. Or maybe it was just the sun playing tricks. That was probably it. Sometimes you saw something that was not real, and sometimes you dreamt things that were not real. The sun teased people, that was what it was. Everything it touched shone so beautifully and it could run away with the senses. And especially on a day like today when Mama was back on her feet and might even fire up the stove. As long as the fire stays out of my fly can, Tóvó thought, squinting his eyes so that the window flies were reduced to tiny buzzes.

"What do you need?"

Carefully, Tóvó placed the telescope on the counter, and with his forefinger against the dark red silk, he pushed the telescope toward the doctor. For a moment, he could not remember if he was supposed to get Napoleon drops or opium drops, but then he said that Mama wanted a bottle of opium.

"Does your mother think that this is a Jew shop?"

"My sister and my brother are coughing so bad."

"Everyone in this blasted hole is coughing, and if I were to fill my shop with your junk, I'd be ruined soon enough."

Then the doctor snapped his rag and took out two flies at once "Stay there, you black harbingers of summer." The words slipped from his mouth.

Suddenly, his eyes glinted. He repeated his words: *black harbingers of summer.* He repeated his words again and again, and his narrow lips relaxed into a wide smile. It was like he was tasting them.

Napoleon had the same sideburns as his father, but while the old man had retained his dark hair and youthful hairline, the son was white-haired and balding.

The doctor set down the rag and loosed the ties around the red silk.

"Mama said that my grandfather got that from Nólsoyar Páll. She wants a bottle of those drops in return."

"Hmm," said the doctor, "so Gudda í Geil is your great-aunt, and you're one of the Brahmadells." Head tilted, he considered Tóvó: "The smallest Brahmadella in the city, no doubt."

"I'm bigger than my sister," Tóvó replied.

"Of course you are. Forgive me, my friend. But a poet's glass! Paris 1791. P. N. Very, very interesting."

Then Napoleon saw Tóvó's orange and asked where he got it.

Tóvó said that a man in a big coat had given it to him, and that the orange was for his mother.

Napoleon laughed appreciatively and went over to the window.

"And here I thought Old Tóvó was your grandfather," he said, as he polished the telescope's lenses.

"My grandfather died on Nólsoyar Pall's ship. Mama said the ship was cursed, and that Nólsoy is full of ghosts. But Nólsoy might not even be real. Mama said that too. The island is only a dream, and maybe it'll sink someday, then all that'll be left is a stupid clog floating on the water. Do you believe that? Can dreams sink?"

Napoleon glanced at the boy. The world held some strange things, he said, putting the telescope to his left eye.

The houses on Krákusteinur nearly leaped into the apothecary, and he remembered how he and other small boys used to dance around burning bird beaks to the east of those houses. That was back when there was a beak tax and men between the ages of 15 and 50 had to render up bird beaks to help control nuisance birds, things like crows, ravens or skuas, or face a fine. He wanted to ask Tóvó if he had ever experienced the *nevtoldansa*, the beak tax dance, but then realized the amusement belonged to a bygone age, back before the beak tax was abolished. Besides, the boy would find his own fires to dance around.

Napoleon figured the boy was the Martimann's son. Still, Napoleon did not want to ask. Having a child's desperate sorrow cast onto his counter would completely ruin the day. And he did not like this conversation either. The boy was too small to speak so grimly and wisely.

Later that night, Napoleon spied after the schooner. He had woken up around midnight from the sound of the anchor chain rattling through its hawseholes. Although he kept out of sight of the visitors, he watched the men as they passed by the office somewhat later. Amtmand Pløyen and that crude Nils Tvibur accompanied by the newly arrived doctors, and he heard his name mentioned as they passed his front door.

The Uncle's Big Mouth

ONLY FIVE DAYS ago Doctor Napoleon and Landkirurg Regenburg had met together with Pløyen. They had no idea at the time that medical help was on the way from Copenhagen. On the table in front of them, Pløyen had placed the map of the Faroe Islands drawn by the commandant of the Tórshavn garrison, Christian Born. He pointed to those areas where measles was raging, and said that the disease had also been confirmed in the town of Trongisvágur south on Suðuroy.

He sighed and glanced up at Regenburg. "I pray to God measles is a miasmatic disease."

"The science is unclear on the matter," Regenburg answered.

Pløyen turned beet red. "I'm not talking about scientific measles. I'm talking about a disease that kills! Do you understand me? I'm talking about all the corpses Nils Tvibur has been hauling away in his damned cart!"

Doctor Napoleon brushed some lint off his shoulder. He could certainly understand Pløyen's heartfelt sigh, but he really disliked hearing the man yell. Pløyen had lost most of his upper teeth, and when he became angry, he could control neither his lisp nor the saliva that sprayed from his open mouth. How disgusting, Napoleon thought—and the stench that came from the man's mouth was rancid. Other people like the Norwegian corporal or the officer aboard the *Havfruen* could bark like that, but not the king's deputy! And Pløyen was also Napoleon's patient. Twice in the last year he had snipped Pløyen's hemorrhoids, and the fact that the man's upper and lower orifices were equally repugnant nauseated him.

And all this "miasmatic" talk was so backward and peculiar. Napoleon himself had not been entirely clear what the word meant and so had to look it up. *Miasma* was a Greek word meaning "to pollute," and in a medical context, it meant "airborne pollution" or "airborne contagion." Yet in reality, how the measles spread was meaningless. The real question was how to stop or further prevent the outbreak. But that was typical Pløyen: filling his big mouth with fine words, which turned out to be completely irrelevant.

One Sunday afternoon, as they were playing Ombre at the Club, Napoleon stated that deep down Pløyen was nothing but an incarnate plebeian snob. That was the real foundation for his clumsy ballad, *Grindavísan,* which was written in honor of the Faroese pilot-whale hunt, and to which authority-loving Faroese danced exuberantly.

At his table was an old shop assistant, a half-drunk farmer from Velbastað, shouting "Long live the Sunmen" at steady intervals, and the seventy-five-year-old Pastor Schrøter in his leather corset. The pastor's left hand had been dead for years, but he could make use of it by placing the cards between his thumb and forefinger.

Pastor Schrøter was actually half-doctor, and that served him well on Suðuroy. Otherwise, he was learned in many ways, and knew several modern languages. All the educated men who came to the Faroes visited him and received knowledge, both oral and written. So wrote Christian Matras in a newspaper article for *Oyggjaskeggja* in 1952.

Schrøter had been a friend of Nólsoyar Páll and had owned a share of the ship *Royndin Fríða*, and during the Napoleonic Wars, up until the 1820s even, he had been as much smuggler as pastor.

Now he peered over the rim of his lorgnettes and asked Napoleon to explain his allegation.

"It's not an allegation," Napoleon answered. "It's a fact."

They were sitting in the reading room, and the rustling of newspapers suddenly ceased. Astonished eyes peered from behind the pages, and abruptly it was so still that they could hear the firewood sighing in the tall black Bilegger stove. And what exactly was the wood sighing about? Perhaps it sighed: I'm burning, I'm burning, I was a forest. Or: I'm burning, I'm burning, once I housed songbirds.

The waiter stuck his head into the reading room and asked if everything was okay. And it was. When Napoleon was in his element, the world was bright and festive. He asked if a hymn to pilot-whale blubber might rank as high poetry? Or if pilot-whale meat would make a suitable poetic subject—if, that is, it did not drip too much?

"What would a poet like Lord Byron, who squandered his precious gifts on the Greek Revolution and died in a tent on the front lines, have said about the bard of the pilot whale hunt? Or what would that venerable erotomane, Aarestrup, have said about the strophe, *Quick lad, pilot whales to slaughter, that is our pleasure*? Of course, on the Flatland they don't kill pilot whales anymore, so translated to Danish the lines might be: *Quick lad, pigs to slaughter, that is our pleasure*."

Napoleon shook his head. It was only on the Faroes that a barbaric hocus-pocus man like Pløyen could be taken seriously.

Schrøter stroked his chin, and when Napoleon announced that he had a riddle, the pastor took a mouthful of gin.

Could anyone tell him, Napoleon asked, what kind of creature could convince Faroese peasants that Danish tyranny was the absolute synthesis of European statesmanship?

Schrøter swallowed his gin the wrong way, his double chin swinging as he coughed, and while the half-drunk Velbastað farmer slapped him between the shoulders, the words gurgled out of the pastor's throat: "Anyway, you've got your uncle's big mouth."

The Honorable Official

PLØYEN WAS NONETHELESS a popular man, perhaps the most popular government official who had ever worked in the Faroes. And there are solid reasons for that.

In the book *The Faroese Country,* which was published in 2001, Professor Hans Jacob Debes awards Pløyen this praise: *The most energetic and constructive effort to pave the way for material progress on the Faroes was carried out by the respected government official Chr. Pløyen.*

Deeds for the land on the east side of the sound between Streymoy and Eysturoy, and also in Hvítanes, where outlier towns would be built, bore his signature. Added to Pløyen's list of achievements was the introduction of longline fishing to the Faroes. The man also spoke flawless Faroese.

In 1991, communist and author D. P. Danielsen published a novel on the outlier population of Hvítanes, the Nesmen, where Pløyen achieved nearly sacrosanct status: *And if the Nesmen had no idol to which to turn, if they thought their true God was damnably slow at answering prayers, now they had found one. After that day no one under the sun could say an ill word about Amtmand Pløyen in the presence of a Nesman.*

No roses without thorns, however. In the jubilee publication written in connection with the 100th year anniversary of the Faroese National Library, the academic M. A. Jacobsen gave Pløyen, or rather, an incident in which Pløyen was featured, a different evaluation:

The bank directors (Pløyen, Lunddahl, and G. F. Tillisch) set aside 100 rigsdaler as a prize for whoever was able to produce the best Faroese grammar. However, the bank wanted to remain anonymous, and therefore the private archivist Finnur Magnusson was asked to place an announcement in the newspapers. We know that V. U. Hammershaimb, who took the official's exam in 1847, intended to win the prize. He wrote a letter to Rafn from Tórshavn dated August 16, 1847 (printed in "Breve fra og til Carl Christian Rafn", pub. B. Grøndal): "Since I've come to Thorshavn, there has been much unrest. Two Danish warships have anchored here and the officers swarm around constantly. Now a farewell celebration has been held for the Amtmand who is leaving us; I am, therefore, far from finished with the Faroese grammar, but do you not think that Etatsråd Magnusson would accept it, even if it arrived a little after the specified day, as long as no one else has submitted something?"

The deadline expired on September 23, 1848, and no grammar arrived. Whether Hammershaimb submitted his too late we do not know—it was not printed until 1854, and Finnur Magnusson died Dec. 24, 1847. In 1849, however, 100 rigsdaler were paid to Pløyen's estate. He had already permanently left the Faroes. We know that Lunddahl had requested the funds, but he received no answer. The bank directors, Lunddahl and Tillisch, decided in a meeting on March 8, 1849 that the Library should receive the money.

According to the available accounts, the money was never repaid.

In other words, the honorable Pløyen was the man who stole the award meant first for the father of the Faroese written language, and after that for operations at the Faroese National Library. And 100 rigsdaler was no small sum. As a comparison, it can be noted that in 1846 the monthly salary for a sergeant in Tórshavn's garrison was 12 rigsdaler, and that a barrel of barley cost 10 rigsdaler.

Angelica archangelica

THE SAME DAY that Doctor Napoleon—or Pole, as he was known by those close to him—met with Pløyen and Regenburg, he ran into Ludda-Kristjan on the street. They had been childhood playmates, and as in their boyhood days, Ludda-Kristjan's left shoulder twitched when he got excited. He whispered out of the corner of his mouth that the evening before last he had seen two riders heading west over the river, and that one rider had been Amtmand Pløyen and the other Nils Tvibur. With an air of mystery, Ludda-Kristjan asked if Pole had any idea where they might have gone.

Napoleon shrugged his shoulders, and Ludda-Kristjan continued whispering that the Amtmand had lost his faith. He was the king's highest representative in a country that seemed to have been forsaken by God, and that was why he had traveled to Skælingsfjall on the longest day of the year.

"So what?" said Pole.

"Shh, not so loud. Have you forgotten that the yokel farmers meet on Skælingsfjall on the longest day?"

"I remember, now that you mention it," Napoleon replied.

"Those heathen devils are praying to the sun! That's why they gather on the mountain every year. They're Sunmen! The sun is the landowner's old god."

Napoleon recalled this as he looked at Pløyen's angry red face. It was one thing to govern the Faroe Islands in peacetime, but now that the country's timber was being devoted to coffins, the ground was shifting toward the old traditions. When family fathers in their best years were being mowed down by the measles, there was every reason to shake the dust from one's mourning garb and set about praying to Jesus Christ in Heaven, not to mention the sun and Nils Tvibur's great Desert Captain, to preserve the Faroes. The newborns did not trouble Napoleon too much. If social circumstances truly shaped one's personality, then having the measles stop the heart of predisposed scoundrels was a good way to avoid grief. Maybe the infant would have become a drunk or unwed mother, a burden on the poor relief fund? Tórshavn had yet to hatch any painters like Rafael or playwrights like Oehlenschläger, so instead of cursing the measles, perhaps it was better to bow one's head in thanks for the harsh renovation that mercilessly cleansed every foul corridor.

Napoleon also had his doubts about the miasmatic idea, or rather: He had not given the word much thought in years, and the word was all but absent in the new medical works coming from the Edinburgh school and from Germany. The miasmatic viewpoint had to do with an older understanding of illness, in particular fever-related diseases, but thanks to that idiot Regenburg the officials and their wives were walking around saying "miasma, miasma," as if it were some industrious spirit blasting people with its devilry. Plenty of people also went around in those beaked masks that supposedly warded off infection, and encountering a flock of the bird people in some gloomy corridor was anything but pleasant; it was unclear whether these eerie creatures had invaded and conquered the city, or whether one simply had found oneself in a nightmare.

It was Ludda-Kristjan who made and sold the masks, and he explained to his old playmate that the masks were like medicine: if you believed it helped, then it helped. The masks especially sold like hot cakes among the members of the singing church. Ludda-Kristjan, however, could say with absolute certainty that the masks were not solely donned to prevent infection. Some of the singers feared the ill, plague-like wind coming from Frú Løbner's backside.

Napoleon subscribed to the Danish medical journals *Bibliothek for Læger* and *Ugeskrift for Læger*. He had read about the tiny creatures mainland doctors were studying beneath microscopes. In general, so much was happening within medical science, especially when it came to surgery and pharmaceuticals, that Harvey, indeed Edward Jenner, were almost outdated. Despite new instruments like mercury thermometers and stethoscopes, however, there was always room for error.

The first measles outbreak on April 7th or 8th was diagnosed by Regenburg as rheumatic fever. And although there were certain similarities between the two diseases, for example, high fever and fatigue, the Landkirurg's diagnosis was a complete disaster, particularly when one considered the consequences.

Doctor Napoleon tried to calm himself. He was well aware his own roll deserved no applause. He had made his share from selling morphine, not to mention various oils and salves into which he mixed ambergris, cinnamon, and anise. Still, however willing people were to pay handsomely for a few grams of ground senna leaf—or for an outright lie, really, just so long as it was written in Latin—there were boundaries for how much you could swindle people.

That is what he was thinking when he advised that farmer out in Húsi on Koltri to eat flowering angelica to prevent complications from the measles.

"Angelica?" the farmer repeated dubiously. "You must be joking."

"No, my good man," Napoleon replied. "The Crusaders ate *Angelica archangelica* when they fought against the heathens in Jerusalem, and it was the Archangel Gabriel himself who, lantern in hand, guided the wounded knights to the plant."

When the farmer realized that angelica figured in sacred stories, and that it was respectably baptized in Latin, he gave up protesting. He was not convinced, however, but scratched his beard and mumbled: "Hmm, I see, I see."

And Napoleon knew what lay behind the words: "Hmm, I see, I see." He glanced at the farmer and felt sympathy for his distrust. The man was a product of what had enabled the Faroese people to survive for nearly a thousand years in these northern latitudes, and part of his spiritual burden was doubting everything he heard and also most of what he saw.

Napoleon, however, could not very well tell him that there was no medical cure for the measles. It would be like denying his own profession. It would partially decimate the status medical science had finagled itself over the last centuries. Yet that was the bitter truth. Once the disease had taken hold, there was nothing to do. The incubation period was typically two weeks, sometimes shorter and sometimes longer, and then came the fever and the coughing and the outbreak over the whole body. However, if the patient was in tolerable health, he could usually overcome the measles. Good care was the most important thing, and so a bit of *Angelica archangelica*, dipped in cream and sprinkled with sugar, was nice on the tongue.

The corner of Pløyen's mouth twitched. He reminded the doctors of the high mortality rate in Tórshavn alone, and the fact that the epidemic was not diminishing. True, Dean Andreas had various remedies squirreled away in his rectory down in Leirar, but fighting the measles required more than Hoffmann's drops and old Faroese home remedies, not to mention the witchcraft practiced by that quack, Pól á Miðgerði, south in Akrar. Their twelve-hundred fellow citizens living on Suðuroy both wanted and needed a doctor's skilled hand and wise council.

Pløyen showed Doctor Napoleon a letter that Dean Andreas had written concerning the situation down south, and while Napoleon perused the text, Pløyen remarked that his office was prepared to pay him 50 rigsdaler a month. Rather sarcastically, the Amtmand added that even though the Suðuroyars had sold most of their horses to the British coal mines, some four-footed beast could be found to carry the doctor between towns. Otherwise, the island was overflowing with boats, eighteen hundred or so, according to Løbner's tables.

Pløyen talked as if Napoleon had already agreed to the request, and he reminded the doctor of the numerous relatives he had on Suðuroy with whom he could stay. The Amtmand was irritated that Napoleon had even paused to consider.

"Tell me, is 50 rigsdaler a month not sufficient, when your countrymen are, quite literally, in mortal peril?"

"The people here in Tórshavn and Streymoy are also my countrymen," Napoleon replied. "I also have to think about my clients here in town and can't simply from one day to the next shut my door and sing, like Dean Hans: *To the world, farewell.*"

"Regenburg can take care of your patients," Pløyen said.

Doctor Napoleon brushed a piece of lint from his arm and turned to Regenburg.

"I suggest, sir, that you travel to Suðuroy. You are the Landkirurg, after all, and Suðuroy falls under the your jurisdiction. In the meantime, I can attend to the patients in the north fjords and otherwise cover whatever medical duties arise here."

A heavy silence descended on the room.

Deep down Pløyen was forced to admit that Napoleon's counter proposal came as no surprise. Napoleon Nolsøe was an enigma. His attitude toward civil authorities, a class, moreover, of which he was a part, could be utterly juvenile. He continued to be infatuated with student life in Copenhagen, and had assumed the roll of a kind of rebellious grand seigneur who mocked authority while also trying to cultivate it in the stubborn Faroese soil.

And Napoleon also knew full well that Regenburg despised travel. It was no secret that you could hardly get him out of town, and that he especially hated long boat trips. Napoleon had obviously realized that the Landkirurg was the driving force behind the Suðuroy proposal. Nonetheless, given the current state of things, Pløyen still could not understand Napoleon's pig-headedness.

Regenburg knew essentially nothing about the Faroe Islands when he assumed the office of Landkirurg two years ago. He knew that the hospital had been built in 1828, and he knew what his salary would be, but not much more than that. In his ignorance he thought that sick patients could simply be brought to the city, or that he could travel to sick patients along relatively safe roads, if not by wagon then certainly on horseback. Yet that the mountains could be so precipitous, and that some roads considered passable were in fact narrow sheep paths along vertical cliff faces—that he had not suspected. Had he known the truth about traveling the Faroes, he never would have sought the post.

The shortest way to get between towns was by boat, and if the weather was good in the summer, a boat trip could be nice. But summers were short, the routes across the sound and the fjord were perilous, and there were no piers. Even the trip to Suðuroy seldom took less than ten hours. Regenburg loathed these long journeys, and simply the thought of being away from his family for one or two months, or however long his medical duties would require it, filled him with anxiety.

Pløyen walked over to the cupboard, poured himself a glass of brandy, and drained it. He tried to control his dislike for this upstart shopkeep. Who the devil did he think he was? How could a doctor treat the Hippocratic Oath so irresponsibly? And he had let this arrogant man snip his hemorrhoids! At the thought, Pløyen's anus contracted, and he pointed at Doctor Napoleon with the empty glass in his hand.

"It's vile to refuse to help your countrymen, now that death literally stands at the door. It's vile. Do you hear me? V-i-l-e! There's no other word for your refusal!"

"This isn't a trial," Napoleon answered icily. "However, I will state that on April 17th, when the honorable Landkirurg here thought measles was rheumatic fever, I had already reached the correct diagnosis, or in any case, I was certain it could not be rheumatic fever. I also advised you both we should think about isolating the city. Truly, I did. But you told me to calm down. The country's highest authorities said calm down!"

Napoleon also reminded them that the people of Víkar had gone ahead and isolated their town. The town gates were shut to all travelers, both those coming from north and south, and no one in a boat made landfall either, and the result was a measles-free town.

For his part, all Pløyen did was prattle about miasmatic diseases. His problem was a bad conscience. Eight years ago measles had been crossed off the list of dangerous contagions. It happened while David Vithusen was Landkirurg. And the decision was understandable, at least if one lived in Copenhagen. It was royal decree that declared the disease killing off the Faroese people to be innocuous. Indeed, in Denmark and further south on the mainland, people had also developed resistance to the various contagions the spring typically brought with it. However, the Faroe Islands were not Denmark. Conditions in the two places were not the same. Yet that was exactly the point that various officials apparently failed to grasp.

"In terms of consequences," Napoleon said, "it is my belief that a lack of courage from your side and all the miasmatic nonsense on the part of Landkirurg Regenburg bears the brunt of the responsibility for the fact that measles now flies on wings."

Pløyen had already opened the door and bade Doctor Napoleon farewell.

The Lapsed Prayer

TÓVÓ WALKED SLOWLY across the sand. His shoe prints followed him. A few steps to the right, then an arc to avoid some seaweed, then a few slow steps left, none of them more than a span apart.

In his pocket was a paper bag containing the small opium vial for his mother. His left hand held the orange and his right a piece of sugar candy that the doctor had kindly given him for free. Tóvó felt happy. The lumpy brown candy tasted good, and it was delightful to slide his tongue across it. Yet he was crying, too, and that is what confused him. How could someone be both happy and tearful? You could not be both sad and happy. That made no sense. Perhaps it was like when you both pooped and peed. And piss was also a kind of tears, a little yellow stream you could aim at a spiderweb or at the head of some stupid chicken trying to pull a worm up from the dirt.

And he had also learned two new words that day: opium drops and orange. The orange looked like the sun, it was gold and round. The skin was uneven and rather like whale-skin blubber, but the odor was different, sweet and mild, just like the old evenings at the Geil house when Mama baked bread in the embers and everyone was happy. That was before they got the horrible lion-footed stove. He hoped that one morning the stove would work itself free from the chimney, walk outside, and never come back.

And the sun had been shining all morning. The smell of dried seaweed rose from the hot rocks, it hung like an invisible fog around the Bird Tax Bridge and drifted all the way down to their boathouse. Tóvó sat at the boathouse door and longed for his father. He missed him so terribly it made his chest hurt and his head pound.

Here is where his father made boards from the driftwood. At the gable end of the boathouse was a large door, and while one end of the tree trunk rested on the boathouse floor, the other end was placed on a large sawhorse. Ludda-Kristjan pulled and guided the saw blade up, while his father stood below, his hair and body white from the sawdust. Hour after hour they dragged the blade up and down, and the boards that finally emerged were slightly reddish and smelled nice. Mother had brought everyone hot tea and a snack, and she spit on a rag to wipe the sawdust from her husband's eyes. Oh! How beautiful she was that day, all her handsome teeth glinting, she was light of foot and happy as a lamb. Mogul also took part in the merriment, he swam several meters after a stick that Great-Grandfather cast out toward Bursatangi. Later as they cut tongues and grooves into the boards, Tóvó and Lýðar collected the shavings into bags, since there was nothing better for lighting a fire.

Tóvó stretched out on his stomach and blew some sand off a flat rock. Then he dribbled some spit onto the surface and used a corner of his sleeve to wipe the stone clean. For a moment he wondered if he should place the sugar candy next to the orange. But the candy tasted so good, and who knew if God even liked rock candy.

He folded his hands and shut his eyes tight.

He had not meant all the awful things he had wished on his father that time Mogul mauled one of Frú Løbner's stupid hens. Whales could not even bite, and rocks certainly did not rain from the sky. Not in broad daylight. Well, maybe in Denmark, but not in Tórshavn. He had not meant what he had said, and if God wanted the orange, he was welcome to it.

Tóvó sat for a long time with his eyes closed. He clenched his teeth and his head pounded more fiercely than ever. Each time he was about to open them, he made himself count to nineteen. Finally, he could take it no longer. In agony of suspense, he peeked.

The orange was still there.

A Daguerrotype

WHEN AUGUST MANICUS returned from Suðuroy in September, he stopped by the Geil house.

"Perhaps you don't remember me, sir. I was just a small boy when I left Tórshavn," he said to Old Tóvó.

"But of course, it's like you were cut from the same cloth as your father's. And Claus was kind enough to send me a letter when poor Gudda died. I had Frú Løbner's Henrietta read the letter to me. I don't know why, but death seems to love the Geil house."

August gave him a daguerreotype of Gudda's grave. He said that his father had had it made and asked August to bring it, along with many greetings, to Old Tóvó.

Gudda was buried in Assistens Kirkegaard in Copenhagen, and on her gravestone was written:

GUDRUN THOROLFSDATTER
FROM TÓRSHAVN
LOVED AND MISSED

PART
TWO

Carl Emil and Pole

AROUND ST. GREGORY'S Day in 1851, Amtmand Dahlerup encouraged Napoleon Nolsøe to take the new post of landkirurg on Suðuroy. A doctor's house was going to be built near the Royal Danish Trade Monopoly branch there, and Dahlerup added that his office also wanted to move the district sheriff's office from Hvalba to Suðuroy. He said the place would eventually become a new Faroese center, and he had talked to Provost Jørgensen about moving the church from Froðba to Tvøroyri, as the new town was being called.

For his part, Dahlerup liked the name *Tvøroyri* well enough. He saw why they'd chosen it. A river called the *Tvørá* ran onto a gravelly beach, an *oyri,* located fifty fathoms west of the trade buildings. A more attractive name, however, would be to call the place *Oyri,* or *Suðuroyri.* North on Eysturoy was a town called Oyri, and on Borðoy was another town of the same name. Havnarfolk, of course, called the Oyri on Borðoy *Norðoyri,* and that also was a logical and pleasant word combination. *Tvøroyri,* in contrast, was linguistically inferior. He went so far as to brand the name a contradiction and hoped it would not color the character of the eventual residents.

He himself had planned to honor Countess Danner by naming the new town after her. Perhaps the idea was too daring, though. It would hardly have found fertile soil among the National Liberals in the Danish capital. The countess was an illegitimate child and had been a dancer in the Kongelige Ballet; she was baptized Louisa

Rasmussen, and that someone like her, with no family name, had moved into the royal residence—that rubbed many people the wrong way. In the meantime, she was the one who looked after Frederik VII, and she was trusted by His Majesty. And that was worthy of every respect.

Because of this, Dahlerup had entertained the names *Dannerbo* or *Dannerfjord*. But he had missed the boat. The hopeless name Tvøroyri had already taken hold.

The fact that such significant plans were in the works was due mainly to the large coal deposits in Oyrnafjall mountain. In his book *Færøerne*, which Jørgen Landt published in 1810, the author states among other things that: *In 1777, the directorship of the mines asked Assessor O. Henkel to examine the coal beds. According to his report, the beds are about 6,000 cubits in length and about 2,000 cubits in average width. The pure coal height is about 2 1/2 cubits. As such, the beds contain 30,000,000 cubits or 240 million cubic feet of coal, which amounts to 48 million barrels, 2 2/3 million loads of black coal, assuming the beds are everywhere as robust.*

Assessor Henckel's analysis was met with great interest. The mining operation stalled, however—and the reason was the Napoleonic Wars. The humiliating Treaty of Kiel in 1814 also decreased Danish enthusiasm for the North Sea, and the Faroes were unable to mine their coal alone.

Dahlerup and his fellow officials, however, knew that industry on the southern mainland was coal-hungry. It was only a matter of time before miners started boring into the mountains above Rangabotnur, and the huge cargo ship riggings would appear in the mouth of Trongisvágsfjørður.

This, in conjunction with the fact that the fjord was the best ship harbor in the isles, was the main reason that the district physician's office was being relocated to Tvøroyri, and that the sheriff's residence, along with the rectory, would also soon be built there.

As far as the salary negotiations and other employment conditions, Dahlerup could be quite generous. He asked Napoleon if he would take it upon himself to draw up the plans for the doctor's house. After all, he would be living and working there—and Pole was not in disagreement.

His dream was to build a stone house, and he explained to Dahlerup that within the Finance Chamber's archives in Copenhagen was a work that the Miðvágurin J. C. Svabo had written in the 1780s, where, among other things, the author reflected on Faroese building practices: *Much, I think, would be obviated on public and private buildings in the Faroes if examples, encouragement, and, in certain terms, mandates existed with respect to learning the art of stonemasonry. True! This building practice would still require quite a bit of wood, but much would be gained through the structure's permanence.*

Although the Faroes did have experienced stonemasons, putting together a capable team would be difficult. The main reason for this was that the men lived scattered across the islands, coupled with the fact that they had to farm their land throughout the spring and summer.

One possibility was to travel to Shetland or Orkney in search of stonemasons. These southern neighbors had been erecting beautiful and remarkable stone buildings for centuries, and simply walking the streets of Kirkwall gave one the feeling of being inside a massive stone edifice.

But all that fuss surrounding wages, back and forth trips, and finding accommodations for the men prompted Napoleon to abandon the idea of a stone house.

Nonetheless, the Faroese love affair with timber buildings was a mystery to Napoleon. It was illogical, or in any case strange, since the country entirely lacked trees—well, apart from the berry bushes and dwarf trees growing in the gardens of various officials. At one point, his father had suggested converting Koltur to a wooded island,

and although people found the idea intriguing, so far nothing had come of it. Despite the tree shortage, however, Faroese still insisted on saying that "the sun set behind the trees." It was undoubtedly the Norwegian settlers who had brought the tree-happy turn of phrase with them. The words harbored an ancient yearning, and Napoleon labeled the expression *the ABCs of Norwegian local patriotism.*

The Faroese aversion to stonemasonry, however, had another, more traumatic origin. Only once in a thousand years had the Faroese people taken steps to build something remarkable, and that was the Magnus Cathedral in Kirkjubøur. Or course, smaller and larger Magnus churches were scattered across the Nordic countries, the obvious architectural crown being the Nidaros Cathedral in Trondheim. The people of Orkney also set out to build a cathedral in Kirkwall, and in 1137 the red sandstone building was finished. Napoleon had visited the stunning church twice, and, as far as he knew, there were a good hundred years between the structures in Kirkwall and Kirkjubø.

Yet the Faroese cathedral was never completed, and to this day it was still half-finished. The work stopped because Suðuroyars boycotted the construction. They had nothing against the Church, the priesthood, or all the sacred finery—they just did not want to foot the bill. As a result, they took their weapons out, sharpened them, and under the leadership of Hergeir, the heathen Akraberg farmer, the Suðuroyars launched the one and only civil war in Faroese history.

Damned yokels, Napoleon thought. The Akraberg farmer managed to kill the bishop. Construction was halted, and since that time the cathedral has stood empty, a monument to the miserly and barbaric Suðuroy soul.

Of course, a Faroese architectural exception was the Látra building up north in Eiði. Naturally, it took the farmer and his farmhands quite a while to collect all the stones. But the outcome was truly beautiful, the joints between every single stone perfectly cut. The

Látra building was famous throughout the country, and when Crown Prince Frederik visited the Faroes, he stayed with the Látra farmer.

Napoleon gripped his head when he thought about the prince's visit. His Majesty had made himself a laughingstock. When he was on Vágar, he ordered that the hundred-fifty-fathom-high basalt spire, the *Trøllkonufingur*, or the Witch's Finger, be renamed the King's Scepter. The Vágamenn could only say yes. The King's Scepter, however, was never anything but a joke. When it came to naming, the prince had better luck on Nólsoy. When he was *Uppi í Skip*, or up in the ship (a place on the mountain where the locals once hid from pirates), His Majesty had the untimely, but natural urge to relieve himself. He had quite a few Nólsoyar royalists in tow, and these quickly surrounded the hard-pressed prince. So honored were the people of Nólsoy by this event that they built a four-meter-high cairn over the royal shit pile and dubbed the mound King's Heap.

Doctor Napoleon told Dahlerup this story one evening when the Amtmand had stopped by for a visit, and the Amtmand was loudly amused. Dahlerup did not enjoy the popularity of his predecessor, Pløyen—quite the opposite. He made little effort to win people's favor, and that in itself smacked of contempt.

Still, he and Napoleon got along well enough. Besides both playing Ombre at The Club, Dahlerup dropped by Nólsoyarstova from time to time, often with a flask of cognac in his coat pocket.

It was Dahlerup who brought the first hares to the Faroes, and on that festive August day, when the hares were set to be released, Napoleon was among those who helped take the cage up Kirkjubøreyn.

Dahlerup's maid had packed a basket with food and wine, and before the cage was opened, the group expressed well wishes for the animals that had been captured on Kragerø in southern Norway, and that must now survive and, hopefully, multiply on Kirkjubøreyn.

Dahlerup himself opened the cage door, but the hares did not budge. He made whistling noises and said both *fitse fitse* and *diddle diddle*, but they ignored him.

Napoleon won some laughter when he suggested Dahlerup sing some verses from *Grindavísan*, Pløyen's pilot-whale ballad, as that would undoubtedly send the hares fleeing.

The treeless mountain steppes probably seemed strange and perhaps also frightening to the hares, and at least the cage provided shelter and food. There were three pairs, and since Dahlerup did not know any other appealing sounds, all he could do was lift one end of the cage in the air and tip the hares carefully onto the grass.

Yet even with the dry heather beneath their hind legs, they did not scamper off. Instead, they remained sitting erect, and the last that Napoleon saw when the group headed home with the cage was twelve small ears trying to catch wind of any welcome sound.

One of Dahlerup's winter hobbies was making starling houses. The houses were attached to man-high poles in the gardens surrounding Quillinsgarður. The round roofs were covered with copper plates, which he cut and nailed fast to the small rafters, and in the middle of each roof was a flagpole sporting the Danish flag. The walls were made of selvage about a span long, and each house was smartly divided into four living compartments. The entrances were right beneath the eaves, and every opening was surrounded by a decorative frame.

According to Frú Løbner, who fed the starlings, the bird families were thriving within their Carl Emil pavilions, as she termed the starling houses with a sweet smile.

The doctor and the Amtmand were on such good footing that Napoleon felt comfortable telling Dahlerup about his nickname.

"Out with it, out with it," said Dahlerup.

Even though nicknames might seem unrefined, if not outright vulgar, they were actually keys to the countless doorways leading into Faroese self-esteem, or one might also say: into the lack of that very self-esteem.

"Yes, yes," Dahlerup said, narrowing his eyes. "Get to the point."

"I'll put it this way," said Napoleon. "I feel sorry for those without a nickname. They've been weighed and came up short. On every scale, the political, the scientific, and the cultural. They're like dust swept away by the wind."

"Now you're just annoying me," said Dahlerup. "Out with it."

Napoleon said people called the Amtmand *Pinn í lorti*—Stick-up-the-Shit.

Dahlerup could not believe his ears. He was offended, as Napoleon immediately saw. To blunt the Amtmand's anger, he rattled off a list of old, familiar nicknames: Kriss the shoemaker was called: Come Again Next Thursday. Then there was: The Brahmadells, Mouse Ass, Muhammad, the Goat—the latter being his own father. Then there were Murlamurla, Herring Head, Yellowish.

Dahlerup interrupted him, curious to know what Napoleon's nickname was.

Napoleon smiled. As far as he knew, he had no nickname, but he did not want to admit that. Out of sheer compassion for Dahlerup, he made up a nickname. He said that, as the Goat's son, his nickname was already predetermined: *Pinkubukkur*, or Goatlet.

Stick-up-the-Shit, though? No, it wasn't possible, Dahlerup kept repeating. In a depressed voice, he asked if something were maybe wrong with the stiff-legged way he walked? He made several passes back and forth across the kitchen floor and inspected his legs.

Abruptly, he stopped and stared at Napoleon. "It's those Faroese nationalists. They're the ones behind that nickname. The way I walk is the way I walk, and they can call me whatever the fuck they want.

But no one calls Mother Denmark a shit!"

Heh, laughed Napoleon. He loved conspiracies, he said. They were "sleepwalkers along steep cliff faces" and also "the soul's inscrutable arithmetic."

But Dahlerup did not share his amusement. Indeed, to the contrary, a set of odd traits began to emerge. Some were dictated by wounded nationalist feelings, while others had their origin in what Napoleon termed the Amtmand's physiological constitution. He rapidly blinked his eyes, bit his upper lip, and repeatedly stamped the floor with his heel. He refilled their glasses and reproached Napoleon for transforming serious subjects into laughing matters.

"Not at all," Napoleon answered. Danish officials were simply not accustomed to the fact that a native could prove their equal. Indeed, he would venture to say that it actually wounded a Danish official's self-esteem to realize a native was not only his equal, but even his intellectual superior.

"Take my father," said Napoleon. "A brilliant mind, the brightest in the entire country. The man is an exceptional poet, plays violin, and speaks and writes both English and German. As a supervisor, he could've worked in Bergen or Hamburg as well as in Copenhagen. Yet the man has become a diabolical grouch who carries one of the most ridiculous nicknames in town. And why is that? Because it's unbearable, almost a nightmare to be the only Faroese among Danish officials. In addition, he's self-taught, he's scrapped together all his knowledge himself, while his Danish colleagues are academic, well-structured officials."

"What, are you trying to make me cry or something?" Dahlerup shouted.

"I'm trying to tell you that my father reeks of an inferiority complex."

"Nonsense!" Dahlerup replied. "Your father is a proud man and he knows his own worth."

"I know that my father is a proud man, but being Faroese means standing lower on the cultural ladder. And the king still hasn't found it worth his while to name him a Knight of Dannebrog."

Napoleon laughed, but his heart was not in it.

They emptied their glasses and Dahlerup said it was high time they took themselves across the river and home.

The Doctor's House in Tvøroyri

DOCTOR NAPOLEON AND Tóvó stood at the front starboard shroud as the crew aboard the *Glamour* reefed the mainsail. The foam spray from the bow receded to nothing, and they dropped anchor thirty fathoms from land. The anchor flukes caught on a seaweed-covered knoll, and the *Glamour* slowly turned behind the line.

"There's our new home," Napoleon said, pointing toward the new Doctor's House. Construction was nearly finished—all that it lacked was turf on the birch-bark roof.

Tóvó nodded and was pleased to hear Napoleon used the word *our.*

He was wearing a blue English sweater, which his brother Lýðar had given him, and Great-grandfather had had Kriss the cobbler sew him a pair of wood-soled leather boots, because, as the old man put it, no Brahmadella should leave Tórshavn looking like a ragamuffin.

Napoleon pointed toward the yacht approaching the ship and said that the man at the oars was his cousin, Jóakim. He also said that Jóakim had grown up in Tórshavn and had been confirmed just after the family moved south to Tvøroyri in 1836.

Jóakim, it turns out, was a jack-of-all-trades. He and a man from Froðba had jointly dug out the area for the house, and had laid the foundation over the winter. On St. Gregory's Day, Ludda-Kristjan and a young journeyman, Obram úr Oyndarfirði, traveled south to begin the construction, and by St. Olav's the Doctor's House was finished.

Jóakim rowed the yacht against the ship's side, placed a foot on the sheer-plank, and swung himself over the railing. His jacket was open; he was a man of medium height, and his brown eyes seemed so hard and cold. As such, it was strange to see a grin playing around his lips, an unruly smile, as if the man at any moment might break into irrepressible laughter. His face reminded Tóvó of the cakes baked by the Trade Monopoly's new baker: dried plums on top and pudding below, or maybe it was the opposite. In any case, his presence made Tóvó uneasy.

Suddenly, Tóvó longed for home. He turned away from Napoleon and Jóakim, not wanting anyone to see how wretched he felt.

Jóakim tied the yacht fast to a belaying pin and asked about their trip south, and how his uncle was doing. That was a typical question among the Nolsøe clan. Jákup Nolsøe was the family's patriarch. Not because he was particularly agreeable or accommodating, not at all. He carried the crown because he was powerful, and given that the Faroe Islands was on the brink of significant change, he was a buoy to which both the younger and older generations could cling.

When he retired last year and handed over his keys to the Royal Trade Monopoly's new director, he had served the enterprise for 56 years, and had been top man since 1831. He knew every room and drawer throughout the Royal Danish Trade Monopoly's many buildings. He knew the location of every single ware, too, from darning needles to birch bark, from tar to slate pencils and blackboards. He was familiar with every agreement, both oral and written, and he had informants who relayed conversations from the Monopoly's various branches. In short, it paid to be on good terms with Jákup Nolsøe. When the Monopoly opened a branch in Tvøroyri in 1836, he appointed his brother as envoy, and the branches in Vestmanna and north in Vágur were also filled with his relatives and acquaintances. He seldom overstepped himself, though. No, he was far too clever for that. Whether the Amtmand was named Løbner, Tillisch, Pløyen, or

Dahlerup, Jákup Nolsøe was always the same faithful steward of the King's property. He knew what people across the country owed the Trade Monopoly, and although taking them to court was unusual, the Trade Monopoly calculated their outstanding debts in terms of goods, things like sweaters and trousers, and they went after people mercilessly.

The Royal Danish Trade Monopoly was established in 1709, and Jákup Nolsøe knew everybody who had been with the enterprise since day one, as well as their families. When the stairs beneath his old legs creaked and that surly goat-head emerged in the hatch, every hand was busy.

Unlike his brother Nólsoyar Páll, the trade director was by no means beloved—a fact that did not bother him at all. Popularity was fickle. Respect and dignity, on the other hand, had deeper roots in the human soul.

Medicine chests, apothecaries' weights, book cases, not to mention the old chaise longue from Pole's student years in Copenhagen were loaded aboard the yacht. He had also considered bringing his father's old piano, but he was afraid to do it. The piano was cumbersome and delicate, and barely tolerated a trip to The Club when there was a celebration, so it certainly would not make the trip south across Skopunfjørður and Suðuroyarfjørður. And just think, what if it were lost during the unloading process? Imagining the piano at the bottom of the sea covered in barnacles and whelks made him ill.

Jóakim manned the oars, and while he rowed them toward land he asked who the young man's family was.

Tóvó was kneeling on the bow's thwart. He heard the question, of course, but did not know if Jóakim was talking to him or to Napoleon. It was also the first time that he had heard anyone asked that question, since in Tórshavn most people knew him. Tóvó glanced back and saw that Jóakim had cocked his head inquiringly, like he was waiting on an answer.

Suddenly, Tóvó's heart began to pound. What in the world could he say? He could hardly tell Jóakim that Havnarfolk knew his mother by the terrible nickname Crazy Betta. His father had probably been forgotten by everyone; after all, six whole years had passed since he had died. Jóakim, of course, had probably heard of his great-grandfather, Tórálvur í Geil. People who knew anything at all about Tórshavn had usually heard of the Brahmadells. But Jóakim might laugh at him if he introduced himself as Tórálvur í Geil's great-grandson. He might as well say that Abraham, Isaac, and Jacob were his ancestors.

Tóvó was agitated, he bit his fingers, and he was eternally grateful to Napoleon when he said that the boy was from the Geil house and that he would be Napoleon's servant.

"And can your servant not answer for himself?" asked Jóakim.

"Of course," Napoleon answered. "His time will come."

The answer unsettled Jóakim somewhat, but he did not ask any more questions.

It took the yacht two trips to fetch all their items, but before Jóakim and three other helpers continued unloading the *Glamour*, they carried the chaise longue and the heavy book cases down to the Doctor's House. Napoleon and Tóvó took charge of the rest.

A bucket of Rangabotnur coal stood next to the stove, and Tóvó, who was used to lighting the fire back home, soon had the heat going. Napoleon asked him to also light the stove in the living room.

Tóvó had the attic room in the west gable. Beneath the eaves stood a bed, at the foot of which Ludda-Kristjan or his journeyman had built some shelves.

Tóvó put what clothes he had away. The nicest thing he owned was a linen shirt sewn by his mother. You fastened it with small buttons, even around the wrist, and as something extra special it had a breast pocket.

Tóvó sat on the edge of his bed and pressed his cheek to the shirt, which still smelled like his mother.

He was sorry that he had lied about the *Glamour*'s departure time. It meant not saying a proper goodbye, and for that he could not forgive himself. He just had not wanted to have his mother standing at the dock and waving. That was the problem right there. Being around people often caused her to lose control, she would start talking nonsense or singing loudly, and many times these displays were strange and even vulgar, and Tóvó could not bear to see the ridicule and even repugnance in strangers' eyes. He was ashamed of his mother, that was what, and the pain of that fact hounded him all the way south to Tvøroyri.

He placed the shirt on the shelf, and abruptly he longed for the sweetest person he knew, his sister Ebba.

Napoleon, who had often observed the siblings out the window, had told Tóvó before they left that, if he wanted to, he could ask Ebba to come visit him in Tvøroyri next summer.

And those words had gladdened Tóvó. Ebba would have her own pillow, he would see to that. And she would also have her own blanket and mattress to put on the floor. No, he would sleep on the floor, so Ebba could have the bed all to herself.

He remembered the day they had gone out to the harbor at Bursatangi. The sun baked down and he had sat on the hot rocks with his feet in the water. Clear droplets clung to the dark red leaves of the seaweed churning sluggishly on the water's surface, and the sound and smell of the sea was strangely calming.

Tóvó said that drowning could not be the worst possible death. It was just a little seawater, after all, flowing into your mouth and throat and lungs. After that, everything would get still and cold and you would float silently off into the blue depths.

It frightened Ebba to hear her brother speak like that. She asked if he had ever looked into a seal's face.

Tóvó said that seals had human eyes.

"That's right," said Ebba. "You shouldn't laugh. Do you know why they have human eyes?"

"Because seals are people who have drowned," Tóvó said, mimicking her voice.

He had done no more than say the words when he felt a hard slap across his cheek. The blow was so unexpected it silenced him. All he saw was his sister's back as she ran home crying.

Starfish, Sheep Droppings, and Dead Birds

THEY HAD BEEN in Tvøroyri all of a week when Tóvó asked Napoleon if it would not be a good idea to outfit the Doctor's House with a *tarakøst*, a seaweed compost heap, or midden. His voice, as he pronounced the word, sounded manly. He said *tara* with a rolling *r* and his chin thrust forward.

Napoleon was rather surprised by the question. He knew that Tóvó used to fill Nils Tvibur's seaweed middens, and when he spoke to Old Tóvó about taking the boy to Suðuroy, the old man had said that Tóvó was not a complete novice when it came to farming.

Napoleon knew that already. Besides, the boy had helped him numerous times. Sometimes when he was called to a patient, out to Kirkjubøer or Velbastaður, say, he would ask Tóvó to accompany him, and he would give him a dried mutton shoulder or some other little thing in return. Tóvó had also given him a hand in the apothecary. He was quick with the mortar and had such a good understanding of the fine weights that he could be trusted to weigh out whatever Napoleon wanted. The boy was a little odd, to be sure, but certainly not pathological.

But here in Tvøroyri there would be so many strange things for the newcomer to take in, or so Napoleon had assumed, that he had not given Tóvó any significant tasks. But if the boy wanted to make himself useful, Napoleon would certainly not object.

Tóvó grew enthusiastic when he realized his idea might become an actuality. His shoulders trembled and his eyes blinked rapidly. He pointed down at the beach and said that he had found at least two good places. He just was not sure about the surf.

"Tell me," Napoleon said, "do you like it here in Tvøroyri?"

Tóvó thought a minute. Then he told Napoleon what Corporal Nils used to say: it was not a question of like or dislike. Instead, a person should do what was asked of them and eat the meal set before them.

"That's right," Napoleon answered. "But don't you miss Tórshavn?"

Tóvó gave himself some time to consider this before replying rather dryly that he slept well up in the west gable, and that he liked the brown sauce that Napoleon made to go with the meat they ate on Sundays.

Napoleon clapped him on the shoulder and asked Tóvó to show him the places he had found for a midden.

Inwardly, however, he sighed. It would probably take quite a while before Tóvó became a typical and well-rounded young man.

He had never liked the Corporal, whom it appeared had crammed his Norwegian barracks mentality into a susceptible boy's head.

Building the stone wall around the seaweed midden was Tóvó's first independent task in Tvøroyri, and everything he came upon that could possibly rot he also tossed onto the heap. Seaweed, obviously, but also starfish, dead birds, sheep droppings, and cusk. The toilet pail was also emptied into the midden, and before the hens got to them, Tóvó carried their dinner scraps down to this sacrificial stone bowl, consecrated to future potatoes and root vegetables.

Tóvó's most important job soon became cultivating what later came to be known as the the Doctor's Field. It was something he had done before. Between Skansin and what Tórshavnars were beginning to call Penapláss, the Lovely Spot, was Nils Tvibur's field. When Pløyen had ceded it to him, the area was still a heather-choked outfield used for grazing, and for many years, right up until the time

87

that Nils got married and moved to Sumba, Tóvó had followed at the Corporal's heels. Nils had taught him to cut seaweed and to collect what the surf washed ashore, and he told the boy to fill both middens before St. Clement's Day in November, because without seaweed for fertilizer they would never coax potatoes or root vegetables to sprout.

By 1850, Nils had given Tóvó his own plot to work and the boy tended it well. He was proud of the ground he had plowed into neat long rows. The plants were also a continuous source of satisfaction. Their green stems were tall and thin, rather like the umbrella under which Frú Regenburg sometimes sat, and buzzing flies rested on their swaying leaves.

His great-grandfather told him make sure he took care of Nils's field as well, saying that it was only shirks and scoundrels who refused to show gratitude to a benefactor.

Napoleon asked his cousin to appraise Tóvó's work, and Jóakim immediately saw that Pole's young servant was capable and skilled. With quick motions he dug up and flipped the turf, and then further broke up the clumps, so the sloping, fathom-wide field looked nice and smooth. It was also clear to Jóakim that the boy was neither mute nor otherwise handicapped, despite his nervous twitches, which could be quite pronounced. The problem was the boy was just extremely shy.

Pole had explained to Jóakim about the tragedy that had befallen the Geil house, and Jóakim knew enough about Tórshavn to have heard of the Brahmadells. The boy, it seemed, came from a family of sorcerers, or, as the saying went, *from people who knew more than the Lord's Prayer*, so he would turn out alright.

Pole told Jóakim about July 1, 1846, the day he met Tóvó. The reason he remembered the date was that the *Havfruen* had come into Tórshavn that same day with Doctor Panum and August Manicus on board. That very afternoon the boy had walked into the apothecary at Nólsoyarstova carrying a telescope, which Nólsoyar Páll had given his grandfather, wrapped in a red silk cloth. Pole had showed his father the curious treasure that evening, and he imitated how the old man had adjusted his glasses on his nose and inspected the telescope from all sides. He thrust his chin critically forward, bared a row of worn yellow teeth, and made a series of bleating sounds. Pole's imitation of his father was so good that Jóakim roared with laughter.

"Yes, indeed," his father had said, "typical brother Páll." No doubt he swiped the telescope from some Frenchman whose name began with the letters P and N. Well, this much Jákup Nolsøe could tell his son the doctor, Mr. Hernia and Bladder Specialist. In 1791 his brother was still going by the name Poul Poulsen, so P. P.! "What we have here is stolen goods," the old man said. "Stolen during those brief, flamboyant years when that blabbermouth simply lived and died by the French whorehouses, and you're an idiot to let yourself be fooled by some weeping Brahmadella spawn. Well-educated man that you are, you're afraid of magic. That's why you didn't have the nerve to deny the boy his opium drops. To hell with the telescope, and learn to take real money for curatives!"

If problems arose, Jóakim tried to teach Tóvó how to solve them. One day when he was standing in the field he pointed to a large rock that Tóvó had been eyeing. There was no need to drag the stone from the ground, he said. Jóakim asked to see the boy's spade. Then he dug a hole next to the rock, pushed the rock in, and covered it with dirt.

That was how it was done. He also advised the boy to keep a whetstone on hand, since a sharp spade made the work that much easier.

Jóakim also taught the boy another trick. He showed Tóvó how to work rocks loose with an iron bar, and to put something beneath the bar while doing it, since that allowed you to lift many times your own weight.

And he constantly warned Tóvó against unnecessary effort. The trick was to work calmly and systematically. There were too many heroes here in the south who liked to pretend they were figures out of Faroese folk tales, like those giants of legend, Jansaguttar and the Harga Brothers. The result was crooked and misshapen spines.

And then came the wonderful day that Jóakim brought the rock bores and wedges—oh, how much more interesting Tóvó's life became. The smaller of the two bores was a foot in length, and Tóvó quickly caught on. The large hammer sang down onto the bore's head, and every crack that was split produced a little dust. Tóvó twisted the bore slightly, split another crack, and another, and every strike drove the bore a little deeper into the stone. Sometimes he also hammered two, even three times in the same crack or groove, and he noticed this caused the tip to disappear further, but could also damage the bore. So, a slight twist of the bore for every strike, and even though less emerged, the smaller strikes produced the desired result.

Diligent and happy, Tóvó sat boring rock, and from the ringing iron came snatches of songs and sometimes fragments of the witty and strange ballads his great-grandfather liked to hum.

Words like *rock king, chisel master,* and *hammer prince* also showed that Tóvó himself was no stranger to fancy.

He bored rock for his sister Ebba and for Great-grandfather and for his brother Lýðar, who had sailed again this year with the *Glen Rose*. He bored deep holes for his mother. Maybe he would reach that diseased place in her heart where insanity, like a starfish, had suctioned on. He bored for the sun and the moon and for the Tears of St. Lawrence. And last but not least, he bored for Pole, who could get so enraged he snapped his pipe between his fingers.

So absorbed in this simple iron music could Tóvó become that he completely forgot people might be standing and listening. A 700- to 800-pound rock split with amazing ease, and from there Tóvó eventually moved onto even bigger stones and the longer bore. The thrilling moment was when he pounded the wedges into the hole. Watching cracks spread through the hard material was always a true pleasure. A rock that was too heavy for a man to lift, and which he could not even have pulled on the rock sled, suddenly lay shattered at his feet, perfect wall material. Conquering rocks calmed the mind.

A Visit from Froðba

ONE DAY AN old man from Froðba, a town to the east, stopped by to see how work was progressing. He could hear the hammer singing clear out to Torvheyggjur, he said, and one thing he knew for certain: good things were happening here, both when it came to farming and to wall-building.

Tóvó explained that Doctor Pole took care of the all really heavy rocks. The big rocks on the wall's north and west side were ones the doctor had put in place.

The Froðbinger found a rock and sat down. He had light-blue eyes, and when he spoke, he tended to tilt his head. He said, yes, building a wall did take strength, but tilling new ground and making it as smooth as Tóvó had done also took strength, not to mention skilled hands and a trained eye. The old man had a dog with him, and while he talked he scratched the dog beneath the chin.

The words of praise gratified Tóvó. He had cultivated two separate plots, each around 20 fathoms long, and he had started on a third. Right now, though, he mostly bored rocks. That gave him material for a wall around the field and also let him clear the ground east toward the Tvørá River.

Tóvó smiled to find himself sitting and talking just like other people did. He asked the Froðbinger why rocks were made of such different material. Some were like glass and could be shattered to pieces, while other rocks took a whole day to bore through.

"I don't know exactly," the old man answered. But no doubt it was all part of God's plan. However alike dogs and wolves seemed, they were also different. The birds of the skies were different in color and song as well as wingspan. Or take fish. Halibuts were flat and had both eyes on the gray side, while the ling looked more like a worm. Could rocks not have the same variety? A place in Sumba had a green rock layer he had heard Pastor Schrøter call *jasper*. People said Charlemagne's armband had the most beautiful green pearls, and in Revelation it was written that God's glory is like jasper and sardius. And then the Froðbinger pointed toward Rangabotnur and said that the mountain was full of coal, and that coal was also a kind of rock. "Maybe everything in creation is so different," he said, "so that men can admire and praise creation."

The old man took up a wedge, weighed it in his hand, and then said an odd thing: "I'll tell you this, Tórshavnar. A wedge's strength and a woman's wiles—they're both unpredictable forces."

Tóvó grew anxious. Abruptly, the comfortable moment was shattered. Why did the man say women were unpredictable? Could he be referring to Tóvó's mother? Had rumors of her insanity traveled south? In that case, both Froðbingers and Trongisvágurs would know that Tóvó was the son of Crazy Betta.

Tóvó had the sudden, desperate thought that maybe the old man was not even human. He had never seen the man before, neither in the shop nor those times Pole sent him to Froðba with medicine. Plus, the man did not cast a shadow, but just sat there, a small, bearded figure with a dog, which also had not made any sound. That, too, was suspicious. Perhaps the dog was no ordinary dog.

Tóvó felt dizzy. He was sitting here talking to a hulda, that was what he was doing, and underworldly forces had stripped the dog of its bark.

A bank of clouds had blocked the autumn sun, but Tóvó did not notice. He was conscious only of the goose bumps rising on his arms, and how everything suddenly felt cold and unsettling. The old man was still holding the wedge, and suddenly Tóvó remembered you were supposed to strike huldas and other underworldly beings hard enough on the nose that blood flowed and they lost their power. But he dared not strike the Froðbinger, he had such lovely blue eyes, and when he thought back, the old man had done nothing wrong. Nothing at all. He had just sat and rested and spoken rather strangely about women and wedges.

Tóvó glanced west toward Rangabotnur, wondering what would happen if all that coal caught fire, how many years the mountain would stand burning out in the Atlantic? Would they see it all the way to Kirkwall? Or what if rot crept into the jasper in Sumba? Perhaps the mountains covering all that green stuff would topple into the ocean, sending all those people and sheep and chickens and even Corporal Nils's farm into the depths.

The dog suddenly lifted its head and as they looked into each other's eyes, Tóvó remembered the terrifying day his mother tried to kill Mogul. It was around St. Bartholomew's in 1847, right after the two Danish warships had left Tórshavn. With both her hands wrapped around the knife handle, his mother had driven the blade into Mogul's neck, drawing forth a spray of blood. The next thrust entered the dog's side, but after that Mogul was able to escape.

The dog had been whelped in Hoyvík, and probably because the animal sensed its end was near, it set a course for its birthplace. The wretched animal managed to drag itself to the town's south wall. And there it collapsed. It had no strength to climb the wall, partly because it had lost so much blood, but also because its insides were hanging out. A few ravens hopped around Mogul, the most enthusiastic hacking at the warm seeping flesh. Every time the dog managed to nose its guts back inside its belly a bit, the ravens went after its neck wound, and when the dog snapped at them, more ravens hacked at the unprotected entrails.

Mogul heard a man's voice and watched the vicious birds fly off. The Hoyvík farmer squatted down, spoke gently to the wounded animal, and immediately saw there was nothing that could be done.

With a quick motion he slit the dog's throat, and one day when he had business in Tórshavn he visited Old Tóvó and told him what had happened and how he had put Mogul out of his misery.

After the Froðbinger left, asking that Jesus be with Tóvó, the boy remained sitting, doubtful. He knew it was foolish, but he grabbed a handful of grass, picked up the wedge that the old man had touched, and placed the wedge in a puddle of water, where he let it lie awhile before retrieving it again.

My Sweet Lord

THE DAYS WERE getting shorter, and even though the ships tended to stop fishing in late November, Tóvó still watched the fjord mouth for sails.

For two years his brother Lýðar had sailed with the Scottish ship, the *Glen Rose*, and since the Trade Monopoly had opened a branch in Tvøroyri, it was usual for the Shetlandic and Scottish sloops that fished the waters south of Munken and all the way to the Bill Bailey Bank to put in for fresh water and supplies.

Jóakim said the Bill Bailey Bank had been named after a Welsh skipper who had invented a special net, which the Scotts called a *trawl*, around the turn of the century. The trawl was dragged behind the boat and could catch an incredible amount of fish, indeed, several skippunds at a time. However, fishing like that was dangerous because the ship relied on the wind for its required momentum. They fished at full sail and amid huge waves. A capstan was used to pull the trawl up and it was not unusual for men to be dashed overboard, a fact that pained Bill Bailey. Indeed, the drowned fishermen tormented him so much that finally all he could do was hang himself.

Tóvó asked if Jóakim had known Bill Bailey personally, but no, he had not. Tóvó said his brother was sailing with the *Glen Rose*, and that their father had been a permanent crewmember for about a decade. He did not want to tell Jóakim, though, that the Scottish fishermen were still regular visitors to the Geil house.

It was not too long ago, actually, that several crewmembers, along with the skipper, George Harrison, had visited the Geil house *to pay their tribute and to show their grief for a deeply respected man*, as the skipper put it.

The skipper, as it happened, belonged to a sect of church haters, and when he spoke, he continually exclaimed *Oh, my sweet Lord* in a hoarse, tear-filled voice.

Everyone in the Geil house knew the meaning of the English phrase, but their mother had made sure her children both feared and hated the words. She lay on her bed shouting *my sweet lord*, and that the Scots could go to Hell with their *tribute and grief for a deeply dead man*.

She changed the words according to her whims, and sometimes she invited the whole Scottish fleet to board her—she would show them the crushing force of a Brahmadella woman's loins!

Jóakim was familiar with George Harrison; he said that the *Glen Rose* had come into Tvøroyri several times for water, and to make Tóvó happy, he told him a little white lie. He said that he himself had once spoken to Martimann, and that the man was a fine fellow.

It was Jóakim who supplied the ships with drinking water. He steered his boat beneath the little waterfall called Sixpence, and when the water was almost up to the oar bank, he rowed it out to the sloop. The water was then hauled aboard by bucket.

It was the Scotts who had nicknamed the waterfall Sixpence, because that was the amount they paid Jóakim for the service.

Water was not the only liquid for which the ships came ashore. The fishermen also bought brandy at the Trade Monopoly, since in cities like Lerwick, Kirkwall, Fraserburgh, and Inverness, as well as the large cities along the north Scottish coast, brandy had either been outlawed or was so expensive that only the rich could afford a pint of the strong stuff.

A Faroese Hussar

ON CHRISTMAS DAY Tóvó was paid for the first time.

He and Pole sat talking at the round smokers' table in the living room, and when Pole had poured himself a second or third glass of port, he said that this last half-year in the wilderness had been one of the best times of his life. Living in Tórshavn had its advantages, of course. Not to mention Copenhagen, what with its wonderful taverns, its Kongelige Teater, and its newspapers that came out several times a week.

Still, in Tvøroyri you had this rare, primordial sense of being the first person on earth. Just stretch up your hand—look!—you've caught a bird. Go down to the beach, a merry little cod hops right into your pot. The world's best drinking water flows right by the house.

And then Pole suddenly sprang up from his red plush chair and pointed toward the white-decked mountains around the fjord, saying they were full of black gold, and that in fifty years Tvøroyri would be a thousand times richer than the old Catholic diocese Kirkjubøur ever had been.

He took a drink and said that Great Britain had wagons that ran on iron rails. You shoveled coal into a furnace, the fire heated the water in a big kettle, and the steam from the boiling water got the piston engine moving, which in turn caused the wagon's wheels to roll. Wagons like these were also coming to the Faroes, and Rangabotnur's coal was waiting on them. It would not be too many years before steam engines would drive ships across the sea, and then the name Tvøroyri would be writ large in the various logbooks.

Tóvó nodded. Pole had showed him pictures of moving trains, but exactly how steam engines worked was still beyond his grasp. Still, he liked it when Pole was rather tipsy, because he became so enthusiastic, everything was possible, and no matter how great the problems, they could all be solved.

"Fatherland," Pole said, his voice solemn now. "That's something that must be mined from steep, inaccessible mountains." And as always, when he said the word *fatherland* his eyes filled with tears. Yet his greatest delight during the last half year had been witnessing the way a miserable Havnar boy had transformed into such a pleasant young man.

He took out his pocket handkerchief, wiped his nose, and said he had not meant to cry on their very first Christmas Day. He poured himself another glass, lit a cigar, and each of his movements spoke a heartfelt content.

The fire roared in the Bilegger stove, and thanks to the snow, which blanketed everything from water's edge to mountain peak, the sky resembled a sea of white light. Pole cheerfully shrugged his shoulders, took the leather purse from his jacket pocket, opened it, and counted out one, two, three—five whole gold rigsdaler onto the table. His broad smile reached the finely shaved sideburns as he pushed the small pile of coins toward Tóvó.

He saw the boy's confusion, and to have a little more fun with it, Pole said that he even had a Christmas present for Tóvó. He reached around in his chair and handed Tóvó a good-sized package.

Tóvó had never gotten a Christmas present before, and so he asked if he should open it right away.

"As quickly as possible," Pole replied.

Carefully, Tóvó undid the string around the rough brown paper and opened the package. The first thing he saw was the horn buttons of a well-pleated maroon waistcoat. He held the coat up in front of him and a leather belt tumbled to the floor. And not just a belt. When he bent to retrieve it, he noticed the sheathed dagger attached.

For a moment, the whole thing seemed wrong and confusing. First the salary and now this magnificent gift. He had no idea how to properly express his gratitude. When he had been a little boy, he had kissed his great-grandfather and Mogul and also his mother. Probably Martimann, too, although he could not remember it. But he was too old for that kind of thing now. Painfully abashed, but also happy, he nodded to the kind man smoking in the chair across from him.

Pole told him to try on the waistcoat. A female relative from Trongisvágur had done the sewing and weaving, and the measurements were taken using one of Tóvó's sweaters.

The first thing Tóvó did, though, was to pick up the belt with its beautiful brass buckle and cinch it about his waist; having the sheath rest against his thigh thrilled him and made him feel grown-up. He inspected the knife—the edge was fine and smooth to the tip, and it was razor-sharp. The waistcoat also fit well, and Napoleon's eyes filled with tears. He threw out his arms and said that here was the embodiment of a Faroese hussar.

The Night Visit

DURING THE CHRISTMAS dinner, which was celebrated at the house of the Trade Monopoly envoy, the door opened and two men from Hvalba entered. The oldest said that his daughter was about to give birth to her first child, and that the midwife had sent them to Tvøroyri to fetch the doctor. The man's beard was white with frost, and he told them that the Káragjógv gorge was passable, and that it was a clear night.

"Yes, yes," said Napoleon, "a Christmas child is good fortune's child." He clapped Tóvó on the shoulder, stood up from the table, and asked the house folk to excuse him. While he fetched his bag and pulled on his boots, the Hvalbingers ate some hot soup, and as they left, they thanked the hosts for the hospitality and wished everyone a merry Christmas and happy New Year.

Shortly after midnight, Tóvó awoke when the door to his room opened. At first he thought it must be Pole returning from Hvalba, but then the doctor did not usually enter his room. Tóvó sat up, and in the pale light from the gable window he saw that it was Jóakim.

Tóvó leaped out of bed stark naked, ready to pull on his clothes, but Jóakim told him to calm down, the house was not on fire, no ship had been stranded, either. Climbing back into bed, Tóvó asked why Jóakim was there—was he drunk? The man shook his head. He perched on the edge of the bed and said rather cryptically that he had come with a request or maybe a question. Tóvó thought it must be a very important question, considering Jóakim had woken him up in the middle of the night. But he also had a feeling that something else must be going on. He recognized Jóakim's expression, the man had looked at him with those eyes before.

Tóvó waited in the greatest suspense, and then Jóakim asked in a whisper if he could see Tóvó naked. The silence in the room was so palpable you could cut it to pieces. Tóvó thought about asking why Jóakim wanted to see him naked, but decided not to. He already knew the answer. He was a bit scared, but what was happening was also exciting.

Deliberately, he pushed the quilt aside, and since he did not know what to do with his hands, he crossed them behind his head. A little hair had sprouted in his underarms, and he smelled his own sweat. He waited for Jóakim to say something. But what Tóvó did not know was that the man had been rendered speechless. The beautiful sight that opened before his eyes dried his throat completely.

Tóvó was more boy than man. He had even less hair on this crotch than he did under his arms, and his sex was unabashedly erect.

Jóakim carefully caressed the boy's thigh and his stomach, and even though Tóvó did not venture to say it, he hoped that Jóakim would also grip his erection. He did it often enough himself, and when he made a special effort, something exhilarating happened. The fact that a strange hand was only a few inches away, however, made him tremble, and he heard his heart pounding in his chest.

But Jóakim did not touch him there, not immediately. Tóvó observed him and nearly cried out when Jóakim's face neared his crotch. He sniffed like a dog and his nose slowly approached the stiff blue tip. It also explored his testicles, and suddenly Tóvó felt Jóakim's tongue on the soft skin between them and his anus. And then the man did something that Tóvó had never imagined possible. Jóakim gripped his penis, and the blue tip disappeared between his lips.

After Jóakim left, Tóvó still lay with his eyes closed. He was not entirely sure whether or not he was in a dream or some other place where all was peaceful and weightless. The anxiety that often plagued him was gone, and his hands were open on the quilt. And the strangest thing of all was that he saw the Geil house before him. He was awake, he was sure of that, and yet he saw the house hanging about a hands-width above the foot of the bed. Maybe he was having a revelation. The house stood where it should, with the view south toward Bursatangi. However, it felt as if it had grown large and cheerful. It was as if all of Tórshavn and also Tvøroyri were contained inside it. That was what was so strange.

The Ergisstova Farmer

ONE BEAUTIFUL SPRING day the *Riddarin* from Sumba lay moored below the Trade Monopoly. The group had just finished its errands and was preparing to row south again when the Ergisstova farmer, Nils Tvibur, asked the others to wait; he still had a couple of small errands.

As Sumbingurs often did when he spoke to them, they glanced crossly up from their beards and gave terse replies, and Nils was certain that as soon as his back was turned, they would mock and ridicule him. He had partially grown used to it, however; or rather, he recognized the behavior. The Sumbingurs were not unlike his paternal relatives in the Norwegian province of Hordaland. The same *je*-sound, which he recognized from his childhood, echoed again when Sumbingurs pronounced "girl" as *jenta* rather than *genta*, as it was spelled, "yesterday" as *í jár* rather than *í gjár*, or "to do something" as *jera okkurt* instead of *gera okkurt*. And sometimes they even said *gje-* instead of *je-*. Nils Tvibur's wife was named Jóhanna, but Sumbingurs called her *Djóhanna* or simply *Djøssan*.

Nils had known a few Sumbingurs before moving south to Sumba. Jákup Sumbingur lived right outside Doctor Napoleon's practice. He was a Skansin soldier and was known for his strength, but he was a gentle giant. His son was also a soldier, and aside from his soldier duties, he was also a bookbinder. Nils had always felt welcome in Jákup's house, and the old man confirmed that, indeed, that particular *je*-sound came from Hordalanders who arrived in Sumba 400 years ago and rebuilt their settlement after the Black Death.

Yet it was not linguistic similarities that Nils Tvibur focused on when it came to Sumba. No, he was more sensitive to things capable of inflicting pain or embarrassment. In his eyes, Sumbingurs were just as vindictive as Hordalanders, they both had long memories, and it would never occur to them to forgive or smooth over. And Nils had no problem with that. If you had an enemy, you nurtured that animosity. Nothing was worse than a sweet smile tightening your enemy's cheeks. No, what truly enraged him was the Sumbingurs' dog-like way of looking down while looking up. Soft necks, that was the problem. They were certainly not caravan leaders or desert captains like Muhammad. They better resembled the sheep thief Moses, as Nils had expressed it on more than one occasion.

Now he wanted to talk to Tóvó, because the news had reached him that the boy was Doctor Napoleon's servant. Nils had also decided to bequeath Tóvó his old house on Bringsnagøta, but that would remain a secret for now. What he wanted was to ask Tóvó to visit him on Sumba—that was why he was here, and he had no wish to betray it to his boat fellows. Whom he spoke with here in Tvøroyri did not concern them or anyone else on Sumba.

"Easy, Nils, easy," he told himself.

He took the bridge over the Tvørá and hastened up to the Doctor's House. A stone wall had been built along the path, and it continued farther up and enclosed a field that could have supported two cows.

Anger again boiled up inside him. He hunched his shoulders as he walked and his open hands seemed to be looking for a weapon. If the doctor gave him so much as half a lip . . . "Yes, and what are you going to do about it, Nils Tvibur?" he asked himself. He well knew it was an empty threat. He had no plans to quarrel with the doctor or any other public official. When Pløyen had left the country, he lost his guardian angel. That time he crippled Jardis av Signabøur, and also after the Granis Boathouse scuffle, it was Pløyen who had saved him.

Yet it was not without reason that he resented the doctor.

Three years ago, when rumor was circulating in Tórshavn that the Corporal was courting down in Sumba, he met Napoleon one day, and the doctor asked if it was an old Norwegian tradition for middle-aged corporals to fuck their way into landownership.

The question so shocked and embarrassed Nils that he did not know how to respond.

If they had been alone, he might have turned the question into a joke. But Jákup Sumbingur and old Michael Müller were also present, and the derision in the doctor's eyes had been obvious.

Yet Nils had sworn that he would never be so roughly humiliated by Napoleon Nolsøe again—or by anyone else for that matter.

Luckily, it was the maid who answered the door, and she said the doctor was out visiting a sick patient.

She was energetic and seemed amiable, and when Nils said it was Tóvó he was looking for, she leaned out the door and pointed left around the house. Nils partially allowed himself to feel desire for this unfamiliar woman, even thought his heart still pounded with rage. Her bare arm was shapely, one of her heels lifted from its clog, and Nils saw that her chest was pressed against the door frame while she pointed.

Tóvó was either out in the field or he was down at the midden, she said.

The maid thought she recognized Nils and asked if his name was Corporal Nils Tvibur. He said he was still called Nils Tvibur, but that he was no longer a corporal.

"Spring like a deer, plummet like a shit," he said and gave her a cheerful military salute.

He smelled the powerful odor of manure even before he rounded the corner. His nostrils flared; he could have found his way to the field with his eyes closed if he had wanted.

He surveyed the field with the discerning eye of a houseguest, and he immediately saw that Tóvó knew what he was doing. Two man-high boulders dotted the field, but otherwise the smaller rocks and debris were gone. The cultivated strips had the same beautiful slope as the ground north of Skansin Fortress in Tórshavn, or for that matter, the ground near Kelda on Sumba. Spring was approaching and the growing sprouts glinted like small green torches. They were not more than two inches high, tightly packed from the beach all the way to the north wall. There was an obvious difference between the rows that had been harvested last year and those that first would come under the scythe this year. And now it seemed Tóvó was also preparing a spot for potatoes.

Nils saw a young man with a basket on his back approaching over the rise, and the fact that the young man was Tóvó, his old friend from Tórshavn, filled him with joy. Nils helped him shed the fertilizer basket, and even though it felt light in his hands, he was glad the boy bore his burdens sensibly.

Boy? Tóvó was no longer a boy, but an attractive young man. His narrow chest had broadened, and there was stubble on his cheeks and upper lip. He had his great-grandfather's slender physique, and although his face was still inquisitive and serious, his eyes were milder.

Nils smiled, and an unexpected flood of tenderness gripped his heart. He wanted to tell Tóvó that he was proud of him, that there was no one dearer to him on this damned island, or any other place in the world, for that matter. He was not capable of such words, however, and he was also too moved to speak.

When Tóvó realized that Nils was close to tears, he gripped the corporal's arm and asked what was the matter. He had never feared

Nils—quite the contrary. When things in the Geil house had become so terrible that they were on the verge of moving, Nils had been like a surrogate father to him.

To feel Tóvó's hand on his arm and to receive such a heart-wrenching, indeed, such a childish question, was something Nils had not expected, and something for which he was totally unprepared. The question struck a vulnerable place in his heart, his shoulders began to tremble, and he could not stop the tears. He had the urge to sink down beside the basket and to forget for a moment the desperate, obsessive thoughts and all the hatred that had poisoned his feelings.

He had hoped to begin a new life south on Sumba, and he was no broke ass, either, when he arrived. He had a tidy amount stored away in the bank, and the Bringsnagøta house, which Tóvó would inherit, was in good repair. He had come south with gifts for both of his stepdaughters. Eight year-old Hjørdis got a slate pencil and writing board, while eleven year-old Adelborg got a small sewing box equipped with various needles, scissors, and embroidering thread. For his fiancée he brought an iron and several measures of white and dark-red linen.

Yet when it came to things of the soul, Nils was forced to take a pass. He was incapable of speaking sweetly, not to mention softly. Coming from his mouth, anything at all delicate ended up either twisted or, in the worse case, completely shattered. Even now, standing there with tears in his eyes, he was a baleful presence, as if he could explode at any second.

Nils said he had landed in a lunatic asylum for a town, and that balladeers hounded him *with nonsense and lies*, as he put it. The Sumbingurs were nothing like the worthy descendants of Muhammad, those sheep thieves were just as wicked as his relatives in Sveio.

These hateful words upset Tóvó, and suddenly he understood that Nils was not speaking to him at all. The Corporal's eyes had glazed, and his words resembled the continuation of an old, self-generated dispute. And this manner of speaking was familiar to Tóvó. It sent chills down his spine to hear Nils talk like this, because Nils sounded just like his mother when her dark mood was brewing.

Tóvó wanted to ask him to calm his anger, but he knew that such appeals were pointless. The rage did not merely flow from his mouth and gleam in his eyes, but came instead from his very soul.

And then Nils used the outrageous term *cowfuckers* to describe Sumbingurs, and Tóvó was saddened to hear such vulgar and shameful words from a rational man like Nils.

But the resentful tirade continued.

Suddenly, Nils said that if those cursed scoundrels aboard that Danish warship had not raped Betta in the Boathouse, maybe her mind would not have been so gone. Then maybe Nils Tvibur and Betta í Geil would be married today.

Tóvó had no idea his mother had been raped. Before now, no one had so much as hinted at it. And certainly not that her insanity could be connected to that rape. Of course, he had sensed that there was something between his mother and Nils. Still, so many revelations coming more or less in the same breath made his vision darken. Before he knew it, he was pounding his fists against Nils's chest: "What are you saying about my mother?" he kept repeating.

"I thought you knew," Nils whispered. He caught Tóvó's wrists, and his eyes grew mournful. "My boy, I thought you knew."

Admiral Bülow's warship had been anchored in the bay for a week, and as Hammershaimb put it in the letter to Rafn: *there has been much unrest.* To fully round things out, Pløyen decided to hold a large farewell dinner one evening. The officers' cook aboard the admiral's ship prepared the meal. A young bull was roasted on a spit in the Amtmand's garden, and the aroma from the parsley-and-thyme-seasoned giant floated through the little, flag-decorated capital.

Friends and acquaintances from across the country had been invited to attend.

Skraddar Debes gave this description of the Látra farmer's party attire: *"He was dressed in a traditional* stavnhetta, *a hat shaped like the bow of a ship, a cloak, trousers of black Faroese homespun, a black silk vest, red and blue fringed muffs, patterned mittens, light blue stockings, and Danish shoes with buckles. The Dannebrog Cross hung around his neck on a new, black silk ribbon. He had a Faroese mountain-staff in his hand."*

The Danish officers stared wide-eyed at this comical figure, who stood three cubits tall, and who, with his twelve-inch-high *stavnhetta,* towered like a giant before their eyes.

His wife, Anna Kathrina, was no less stately: *". . . she wore a black Saxon skirt with an embroidered silk apron, a corset that was a red, blue, and white, a flowered silk scarf held in place around her neck by twelve small glass-head pins, long white thumb gloves knitted from cotton wool. On her head was a flowered silk brocade bonnet, which was decorated on the cropped chin and neck band with gold braid."*

Among these Faroese dignitaries, Napoleon Nolsøe was notably absent, though the doctor lost no sleep over it. As far as he was concerned, Pløyen and all his set could go to hell. Nonetheless, his father had been invited, and after the higher officials and Admiral Bülow had spoken, the trade director tapped his glass with a knife.

By then the party was in full bloom. The guests were in high spirits, and a small ensemble started to sing and play drinking songs by Bellman. The trade director struggled to lift his goat's voice above the crowd, bleating about the great achievements that had been accomplished during Pløyen's eighteen years of governing the Faroese people, seven years as commandant, and the last eleven as both commandant and amtmand.

Some of the guests had trouble understanding his Danish, and when he sang three verses of *Grindavísan,* which was supposed to demonstrate Pløyen's poetic ability, the crowd began to laugh at the man rocking back and forth and singing with his elbows flapping.

The words praising Pløyen's achievements were also rather doubtful. How could anything great be accomplished in this hole? Tórshavn was just a north-European backyard, and one of the most miserable at that. There was no visible indication here of any great work! The true feat was that people could actually bring themselves to live in this hole, and the man with the flapping elbows was probably the backyard's aging clown.

Jákup Nolsøe was embarrassed. He was not used to being laughed at when he spoke, and the shame was crushing when Pløyen, with a small gesture and a gentle smile, asked him to be seated.

Pastor Schrøter related these events to Napoleon.

Nils Tvibur had not been invited either. As Skansin Fortress's watchman, he had had his hands full just keeping the boisterous officers in check. There were three more or less secret taphouses in Tórshavn, and for several days now there had been drinking and singing until the morning light.

Pløyen nonetheless had stopped by the Mosque, as Tórshavnars called Nils's house, to give the corporal a two-liter flask of Dutch gin and to thank him for a good collaboration. They talked for a good while, and Pløyen said that he regretted that he was unable to secure Nils farmland. He repeated his words and said that it was only on paper that he was the country's highest authority. He thought that the Faroes had been a theocratic chieftaincy under the Danish monarchy since the Reformation, and in only one respect had the theocrats followed the letter of the Scriptures, and that was to be fruitful and multiply and populate the earth. They had always managed to pawn their daughters off on rich farmers, and they had been no less efficient in securing good royal farmland for their sons. "I can tell you one thing, Nils Tvibur. Greedy clerical blood runs through all the lush farmland on these islands. If greed is still a deadly sin, then believe me, my friend, you won't get into Hell for all the pastors already there!"

At around two o'clock in the morning on the night of the farewell feast, as Nils Tvibur was passing the Granis Boathouse, he thought he heard a half-strangled shout in the dark. He noticed that the latch was undone, and when he glanced in, he saw several officers in the half-light. Two of them held the arms of a woman lying on the ground, and a third was on top of her. One or two long seconds passed by before Nils asked, "What the hell is going on here?" Even as he was asking the question, though, Nils had already grabbed the first officer by the neck, and his fingers were so long that his middle finger pulled back a corner of the man's mouth. With his powerful grasp he pulled the rapist off the woman, and the man, naked from the waist down, tumbled outside.

Now he saw that the woman was Betta í Geil. Just the other evening he had been talking to her in Óla-Pól's taproom, and he had warned her that the Danish officers had not seen a woman in months, that they were complete animals who only "thought of cunts. Go home, dear, they'll burst your ovaries." Betta had only smiled and said, "my friend Muhammad," and given the corporal's cheek a slight caress. She was still one of the most attractive women in the city, or more precisely, what she had was a dark, seductive magnetism. Yes, that was what she had. She had a Lapp woman's broad face, and according to Old Tóvó, one of their ancestors had been the Laplander Aslak Orbes, who was a barber in Tórshavn after the Reformation.

Now terror shone in her dark, gemstone eyes. During the brief battle that followed, however, she was able to creep beneath the boat's railing. Nils attacked the officers with unimaginable force, and although Betta could not see anything, she heard the blows and groans as the corporal's fists struck. Nils was undoubtedly one of the strongest men on the island, and when he was enraged, he became an absolute beast. The fight spilled outside the boathouse. The officer with the dislocated jaw and corner of his mouth ripped all way to his ear lay howling on the round timbers used to haul the boat up to the shed. However, Nils had two men in their best years against him; or more precisely, he had three men against him. A fourth had been standing further back in the boathouse, masturbating while the three others raped Betta by turns. Now he struck Nils with a wooden club, the kind used to kill seals, which he had found in the longline basket. The sharp spike on the end pierced cloth, skin, and flesh, ending with an audible sound at his shoulder blade. That only enraged Nils more. He bellowed with hot fury into the rapist's face. Grasping the officer by the throat and crotch, Nils lifted the man above his head and cast him with a heavy thud onto the timbers. And there the man remained, breathless and unconscious.

A couple of the longboats used to row the officers back and forth from the ship were located outside nearby, and when their crews became aware of the fight, and the fact that their own men were caught up in the fray, they jumped up and sprinted across the beach. Three officers lay wounded and unconscious on the ground, and the fourth was huddled into a corner making a terrified attempt to defend himself.

Nils howled at the boatmen, said this territory was under his jurisdiction. If they wanted they could step into the boathouse, and there they would find a woman these monsters had murdered!

The boatmen finally succeeded in calming Nils. Adopting a friendly tone, they said that they understood the situation, but that Nils must also recognize the necessity of getting the officers to a doctor. In any case, the man with the torn mouth and the onanist, who looked like he was convulsing.

Nils had no idea he was crying when he returned to the boathouse, although it was not humble tears of remorse that wet his beard. They were the tears of a Hordaland berserker. Hoarse sounds came from his throat and chest, and he did not bother to reflect that if the boatmen had not intervened, he would now be a murderer. As a Skansin Fortress soldier, it was his duty to protect the city's inhabitants, but it was also his feelings for Betta that had made fury erupt from the white-hot forge of his soul. Protecting the Brahmadella woman was one thing; however, that did not give him the right to beat her attackers bloody.

When he finally found Betta, she had crept up into the boathouse's gable and was pressed against a longline basket. "Sweetheart," he said to her, "come to Muhammad." She did not reply, however, and was unable to stand. Her blouse was shredded and her naked breasts heaved. She smelled of brandy and sweat and semen. Nils slipped his arms around her knees and waist, and she made no protest when he lifted her. He carried her so carefully her head came to rest against his shoulder, and the fact that she found his shoulder a worthy support filled Nils with an unexpected tenderness.

They had been together a number of times since Martimann's death, but Nils had always thought that what they had was lust. But now that he felt the weight of her wounded body against his, he wondered. Perhaps this beautiful, unhappy woman loved him.

When he reached Geil, he told Old Tóvó what had happened, and asked the old man to fetch Doctor Napoleon or the Landkirurg. Old Tóvó found a cloth to dry Betta's face, saying that they had no money for a doctor, but that maybe it would be a good idea to speak to Midwife Adelheid, she was always so helpful.

Nils's wound had begun to throb and when he removed his jacket the sleeve was full of blood.

He said he knew there was no money since the measles had taken Martimann and that old woman from Hestoy. Tonight, however, the doctor would come and the Danish fleet would foot the bill.

The Dream of Landownership

NILS HAD ALWAYS had the ability to form quick decisions, and that was true not only in daily life, but also when it came to momentous decisions that would affect his life's course. Among other things, the decision to leave his family farm, Sellegsgård, was one he made on the run, as was the decision to come to the Faroes in 1837.

For several years, he served in the Akershus Fortress in Norway, and one night when he was on watch with an older officer, the man said that Tórshavn's fortress needed a cannoneer. The older officer was from the era when Norway and Denmark still belonged to the same kingdom, and he added rather scornfully that the Faroes was not a country that attracted young people, so Nils could be certain of getting the position if he applied.

That remark wakened Nils's enthusiasm. A country that did not attract young people might be the very place to realize his dream of landownership.

In reality, the course of Nils's life was pre-established, and he was well aware of this fact. As a result, those quick, momentous decisions were critical only in the sense that they fit a pattern already formed in childhood. Landownership was not just his dream, it was his life's purpose, and decisions that were somehow connected to his becoming a farmer were not difficult to make—in truth, they made themselves.

He began to tire of daily Skansin life, particularly after the Granis Boathouse incident. He had often remarked how wrong it was to pattern one's labor on a schedule that ranked the man-made clock over nature's great clockwork.

The real way to live was to rise at the rooster's crow and to pattern one's work after the changing seasons. It was no coincidence that winter was the best time to fish. The inquiring kittiwakes and terns called to the fisherman: Come here, come here, fish beneath our wings! Potatoes and other root vegetables should be planted in April; and to ask the sun for a reprieve because the sheriff needed to be rowed to Nes, or because thirty barrels of whale oil needed to be loaded onto some cargo ship, that was ridiculous. Turf had to be cut and dried while the sun shone warmest. That was how it had always been, and that was how it would always be. It could vary slightly when exactly the sheep were driven together in the spring, but one thing was certain, sheared wool was a necessity for all the activity that took place place in living rooms during the dark fall and winter months. Every detail of creation fit harmoniously, and it gave a person a sense of security to work according to a schedule that went unchanged year after year.

The Sunmen

ONLY ONCE IN his years at Tórshavn's fortress did Nils Tvibur climb Skælingsfjall to greet the sun on the year's longest day. It happened during the measles epidemic. His actual mission was not to greet the sun; in truth, he had no clue what he and Amtmand Pløyen were doing up on the mountain that night. Pløyen had told him to bring a pistol and some ammunition, and when Nils asked if he was planning to shoot targets at the sun, Pløyen responded that even a modest ethnographic expedition should be armed.

Nils did not bother to ask what the *ethnographic expedition* was. He trusted Pløyen, just like he had always done. Undoubtedly, the men who rode to Medina with the Prophet Muhammad did not know their leader's objectives. They trusted the man, and therefore they followed him and his worthy steed Buraq.

And the evening was so bright and beautiful around them, it was so delightfully melancholy to listen to the golden plovers whistle while their horses ambled north across the island. It seemed as if the little birds were deliberately trying to calm the riders, as if they had realized that Nils Tvibur and Pløyen were plagued by all the deaths down in Tórshavn.

The closer they got to Skælingsfjall, the more riders they caught up with; they greeted one another courteously, and no one seemed to be in much of a hurry. Pløyen told Nils that these other men were called Sunmen, and who knows, maybe they were Christians who simply shed their Christianity this one night in order to pray to gods older than Christ himself.

Nils grew alarmed and asked if they were heading up Skælingsfjall to study heathen devils, but Pløyen simply smiled and did not answer the question.

Having almost reached their destination above, the men dismounted and left the horses to some servants. The last hundred fathoms or so were made on foot, and when they reached the flat peak they formed a circle.

The group sang the *Gudbrandskvæði* by Jens Henrik Djurhuus, also known as the Sjóvarbondin, and the old poet, who was also present, joined in. He was over seventy, but his aging voice was confident as he greeted the sun with these comely words:

> *If you will see the true God,*
> *gaze upon his work!*
> *Turn your eyes to the east,*
> *there comes his strong servant.*

Nils counted about a hundred sixty farmers in the circle. They had arrived from all over Streymoy, but he also saw men from Eysturoy and Vágoy. The journey up the mountain was one they had made every St. John's Eve for many, many years. Their fathers and grandfathers had also been loyal Sunmen, and Pløyen said that in 1777 it was pressure from the Sunmen that prompted the old parliament to adopt the unfortunate Slave Law, which forbade marriage to anyone who did not own enough land to support a family.

Pløyen tried to draw Bjørgvin, a farmer from Válur, into conversation. But the man bore his words as an offering to the old gods, and did not like that a Danish official with a Norwegian corporal at his heels had come to this holy mountain to snoop.

Among the farmers was also young Skeggin Pól from Leynar. He was only about as tall as a dwarf, and his eyes glinted above his full beard. An arm emerged from from the tangled wool and gave Nils's coat tail a tug, and the man asked in his gruff voice if there were many flies in Hordaland. His presence made Nils uneasy. He feared the hairy dwarf and kept his left hand on his sword hilt. Pløyen, however, had instructed him not to act without orders.

Pætur úr Kirkjubø was more friendly. He and Pløyen had met on many festive occasions, and the farmer had brought his two sons.

Otherwise, the men were subdued and introspective, and some were undoubtedly affected by their country's plight.

Regin, a farmer from Hvalvík, was not among the aggrieved. Like many who lived in Sundalagið, he was dark-skinned—a tint some people believed was due to the enormous quantities of mussels they consumed up north. Sundalagið's women looked outright southern, and their dark, luxuriant pubic hair was a frequent topic of conversation.

Hvalvíks-Regin said that farmers had long since forgotten that a farmhouse should be built on the farm's eastern edge. That showed Her Majesty the Sun that one of His own lived there. He also believed that Tórshavn's many new graves proved His Majesty was still capable of making difficult, but necessary judgments.

The smith Arnhjún stepped forward and recited several lines out of "Hávamál" from the *Edda*. A dagger in a finely worked sheath hung from his leather belt. As he said:

> *Where you meet evil,*
> *call it evil indeed,*
> *and give your enemies no peace*

he was applauded by the men, who were clearly moved.

The east side of the mountain's peak glowed red now, and as the sun slowly rose it was as if the blood of the indigent was sacrificially spilling in streams down the cliff's edge and hammer. A deep red light and a dark blue sky. The air was thin and pure and not a breeze stirred. The Sun was the guest of honor, and it was welcomed with reverence and with befitting silence.

The birds, however, had no restraint. Cheerfully and boldly, they fluttered up into the bright morning, intent on nothing else but being alive in this blessed hour.

Although midnight arrived with unusual solemnity, no one offered a sacrifice, nor was there any stone altar in sight. The farmers were husbands and fathers and ordinary Faroese men, but on this night they claimed their place in the great solar system.

Before they descended off the mountain, they broke their fast. Some had brought *skerpikjøt* and bread in a rucksack, and others had dried pilot-whale meat and blubber, but none of them ate potatoes. Only a few years had passed since a Norwegian pastor's wife had introduced that particular scourge to the country. She believed potatoes were an excellent food supplement for the poor. However, those present on Skælingsfjall were not among the needy, and no one, certainly not a Norwegian pastor's wife, was going to pollute this holy ground with potato peelings. They ate quietly, as befitted Sunmen, and occasionally someone would lift his right hand and say, *Oh, Mother Sun*, and continue their meal.

The only thing that was strange was seeing the old poet, the Sjóvarbondin, pouring drink from a horn. A smile played about his broad face, but what exactly was behind that smile, whether it was disdain or warmth, was difficult to say. He was bare-headed, and his long hair was the color of bark. The solemn face resembled a rugged cliff, and Pløyen thought his smile was as old as the mountain they stood on. His beard was also bark-colored, and as he served them, he skipped no one, not even the two inquisitive guests. The horn was decorated with carvings and silver inlay, and before he tipped it the Sjóvarbondin spoke three words: *sun, earth, eternity.* That was the password, and then the horn was emptied.

Even though everything on Skælingsfjall was calm and collected, the experience had been a terrifying one for Nils Tvibur. Not that he would ever consider telling that to anyone. He would rather break his own bones or thrown himself off a cliff than to so shamefully admit his distress.

What made the Skælingsfjall experience so terrifying was that it was familiar. His father, Gregor Selleg, had said once—no, not just once—the words on Walpurgis Night in 1827 when Nils was nine-teen years old. That evening his father had said that the sun was the yeoman's old god. The sun blessed their crops and animals, whereas poor men, not to mention those church-hating Haugeans, had to make due with the carpenter from Nazareth. And that Nazarene was probably no prize-winning carpenter either. If so, he would have stuck to his trade and refrained from gallivanting around, preaching and unveiling, since the god he called Father was even incapable of helping him in the end.

His father's words struck Nils as hurtful, and he asked why his father did not sacrifice to the Sun then. His father replied that most of what he said was meant as a joke.

Nils, however, did not take kindly to such jokes, and he did not interpret his father's words as such. Gregor Selleg's tone had been far too solemn.

Nils demanded to know if his father had taught Øystein, Nils's older twin brother, to worship the sun since Øystein was going to inherit the farm and all.

Gregor Selleg tried to calm Nils and put a hand on his son's shoul-der. But Nils was in no mood to be pacified. He ordered Gregor to remove his yeoman's hand.

His father did not obey. Instead, he put a second hand on his son's shoulder and said that Nils needed to learn to control his anger. Everything had a purpose, including the fact Nils had been second born. Anyway, Nils was too hot-tempered to run a farm.

Close to tears now, Nils repeated his words. "Gregor, my father," he said, "remove your hand, I beg you."

His father's derisive smile caused the muscles in Nils's neck and throat muscles to tense; his forehead struck his father's face like a hammer blow.

The old man staggered, blood running from his nose and mouth, and then he collapsed and lay still in the yard.

That same evening Nils left the Selleg farm, and had not been home since.

Of course, he had no desire to tell Pløyen any of this as they rode back toward the capital.

Some Words Concerning Kristensa, Eigil, and Karin

THIS STORY, OR rather, this short episode in Corporal Nils Tvibur's family saga, was related to Eigil Tvibur years later by his mother, Kristensa. She gave birth to Eigil in Tórshavn, and he had been a small schoolboy when she married the printer Ingvald Sivertsen. Even though Kristensa took Ingvald's last name, and though the two daughters they later conceived were baptized Sivertsen, she allowed Eigil keep the old Tvibur name.

Eigil belonged to an earlier period in her life, or rather, he belonged to a world that had nothing to do with Ingvald and the girls. Kristensa maintained a connection to her own origin through her son; that was the nature of the beast. Selfishly and thoughtlessly, she laid the groundwork for what was later to prove Eigil's misfortune. The often-grim tales concerning both the corporal and the Tvibur family were things she discussed only with her son. They came from a place where time had stopped, a little mausoleum that held the coffins of some unpredictable and dangerous individuals.

Eigil was thirty years old when he published a volume of articles, sketches, and short stories based on the tales his mother told him, and the prosaic title on the cover was just that: *Articles, Sketches, and Short Stories*. The book was as thick as it was uninteresting—so wrote the literary scholar Kim Simonsen in an article on contemporary Faroese prose. The article covered eighteen years of literature, from *In Greenland with Kongshavn* by Magnus Dam Jacobsen to *Rules* by Tórodd Poulsen.

The scholar, however, did touch on one thing that attracted him, and that was the remarkable ruthlessness that inflamed and beat at the body of the text. The so-called "Grettir-pastiche" had a tone and tint that was not only singular, but was downright frightening. What Kim Simonsen could not know was that the pastiches were actually excerpts taken from the Eigil's own family saga.

When Eigil met Karin in June 1988 following the Norðoyastevna Festival, he had just published *Between Tórshavn and San Francisco*, a work that the same Kim Simonsen branded an absolute masterwork in contemporary Faroese prose.

Eigil had been to the festival and had attended to some work-related errands in Klaksvík, and he was on board the *Ternan* back to Leirvík when he caught sight of Eyðun Winther, the translator of *Grettir's Saga*. The man was wearing a jacket and hat, as well as a woven scarf about his neck. He bore obvious signs of the illness that would send him to his grave a few months later. And the man knew he was living on borrowed time. His wife was a doctor at Fuglafjørdur's public health department, and she was seated at the table next to him, along with a younger woman, who turned out to be Karin.

Eigil greeted them and introduced himself, and the translator and his wife politely responded.

The younger woman told him to drop the false humility and take a seat. We know who you are, she said. Nations know their great sons, she added, her laugh revealing her teeth.

She was wearing a white blouse with red polka dots. Even though her breasts were not especially large, the dots made Eigil think of delicious strawberries.

She opened her purse, and while she carefully worked the stopper from the whiskey bottle she had concealed in it, Eigil noticed her delicate fingers. And then it happened. He had not been thinking of anything below the navel, or wherever it was that desire was situated, but within the two to three seconds he watched Karin's fingers play along the neck of the flask and stopper, he got an exceedingly hard erection.

She poured the whiskey into coffee cups and offered Eigil a drink. He brought the cup to his lips, smiled at Karin, and suddenly noticed her heavy eyelids. They were so heavy that on a plane she would have to pay an overweight baggage charge.

Eigil later told her that and they often laughed at the thought.

For Eigil, *Grettir's Saga* had been a pure revelation. And he said as much to Eyðun Winther. He said that 1977 was a good year for two reasons: Jens Paula Heinen's burlesque novel *Beachcomber* saw the light of day, and that same fall *Grettir's Saga* appeared in its handsome Faroese dress.

In his translator's introduction, Winther had written: *I have heard that when rural folk came to the Royal Danish Trade Monopoly in Tórshavn to do business and stayed on a while, the old director, Jákup Nolsøe, would stand at one of the shop's windows after closing time and read the Icelandic Sagas to them while they stood outside and listened attentively, and so well-versed was he in Old Norse that he could translate into Faroese as he read.*

Now Eigil asked if Winther thought Jákup Nolsøe occupied the place in Faroese history he deserved. Eigil also wondered if it was just idle speculation, or if it really was Jákup, and not his brother, who had composed *Ballad of the Birds.*

Eyðun Winther said he was familiar with the question, but was in no position to answer it. He said that it was certainly a tragedy that Nólsoyar Páll had died in his prime, but that when it came to tradition, a person's legacy was of great significance, so in that way one could say that Nólsoyar Páll had died a fitting death. He went straight from death into Faroese history, and he had reigned there ever since as a revered national deity.

Then Winther smiled and asked in what way *Grettir's Saga* had been a revelation for Eigil.

Eigil said he loved sweeping narratives and liked books less whose artistic merit was found in psychological descriptions. Grettir would not have sat well on Sigmund Freud's couch. And then Torstein Ongul, who murdered Grettir on Drangey, was himself murdered in Miklagarður. That 700-year-old saga had quite the unusual cosmopolitan streak.

What Eigil did not want to admit was that he saw the image of his great-great-grandfather, Nils Tvibur, in the outlawed giant.

Karin had sat and listened to the discussion and suddenly asked Winther why these ancient authors had been so reticent when it came to descriptions of a good old-fashioned fuck—*um gott gamaldags mogg*, as she expressed it

Winther responded that *gamaldags mogg* was not precisely correct, but rather *gamaldags moggan*, old-fashioned fucking, or perhaps *moggan í gomlum døgum*, fucking in the old days.

Suddenly, Eyðun Winther grinned and then burst into laughter. His laughter was fresh and clear as rain, and his face opened and shone like a light-hearted schoolboy's.

If one wanted to be truly antiquated, one could say *forn samlega millum kall og konu*, olden-day intercourse between man and woman, or why not *kynjanna aldargamla troðan*, the ancient coupling of the sexes.

He wiped the unexpected smile off his lips with the back of his hand, and while the laughter still shone in his eyes, he said that he was no writer, just an old school-teacher, and so he was not the one to answer her question.

He nodded politely toward Eigil, and his wife and Karin turned their faces in his direction, all three of them smiling.

All at once Eigil was the focus of a conspiracy initiated by those six inquiring eyes.

Karin again filled their cups and told him to wet his throat; Eigil followed her suggestion.

"Would you be offended," Eigil asked, "if I told you I wanted to lick your beef?"

Karin had to laugh at this tactless remark. She said that mainly the question caused her to wonder about his dining habits, since one did not usually lick beef.

"Okay," said Eigil, "But if I had looked you in the eyes and said: My dear, I want to fuck you, and for 'fuck you' I'd said *mogga tær*, using the second-person dative familiar, wouldn't you have felt offended? Wouldn't you assume I thought you were a cheap slut? Hand to your heart, wouldn't you hit me with your purse?"

Karin's face was suddenly serious; it was obvious she was insulted.

"I don't hit people," she replied. "And I, for one, have never been a killjoy."

The *Ternan* had docked at Leirvík's ferry, and the passengers were making their way to the door leading onto the deck. Eyðun Winther and his wife also stood and took their leave, clearly irritated at the unexpected turn the conversation had taken.

Eigil put his hand on Karin's arm and apologized.

"For what?" she asked.

"I don't know, exactly," Eigil answered. "But I didn't mean to be a killjoy."

Karin made her way to the door and Eigil followed her.

"How should I know what ancient authors were thinking? The man who wrote *Grettir's Saga* was probably a monk. Most of the Icelandic Golden Age writers were monks, and those guys can't describe good, old-fashioned fucking. But I wasn't trying to offend you, believe me. To be honest, you make me dizzy. And you have beautiful hands."

"Hands?"

They had reached the gangway when Karin suddenly stopped, and Eigil did not know if she was angry or about to burst into laughter.

"Is that the best thing you can come up with, to tell a woman you've insulted that she has beautiful hands? Fuck you, Eigil Tvibur!"

For a moment Eigil remained there on the gangway. Then he ran after Karin, who had reached the car belonging to the translator and his wife, the municipal doctor.

"Are you going to Tórshavn?" he asked Karin.

"We're going to Fuglafjørður. That's where I'm from. And you know, all the women in Fuglafjørður have such beautiful hands."

"Could we see each other sometime?"

She climbed into the backseat and the car door slammed shut, but Eigil got a neat little wave before the car drove away.

Eigil took the bus to Tórshavn, and it was a good thing he was wearing a coat because every time he remembered Karin's fingers, her teeth, and the marvelous disdain in her voice, he got another erection.

He mailed Karin letters multiple times that summer, but never heard back.

One day, however, the unimaginable occurred: a tidy envelope lay in his mailbox.

Eigil immediately guessed its sender.

The first thing he noticed was that the envelop was lined with light-pink tissue paper. If the color had only been a little darker, it would have been like staring into a woman's sex, and the fact she so charmingly expressed her womanhood almost knocked him off his feet.

The letter itself was on a regular sheet of paper, and she concluded her letter with the perfect line: Even a ferry ride between Leirvík and Klaksvík can be the start of an adventure.

Eigil answered her the same day, and in the months that followed it was not unusual for Eigil to write her one and sometimes two letters a week.

He asked questions like whether or not she still had any sweet childhood tendencies like sleeping with a doll, and the fact that such questions crossed the mind of a giant like Eigil Tvibur—that attracted Karin. He also told her that he had roasted a saddle of lamb, an animal that had made itself oven-ready on the slope of Blæing south of Sumba, and that he had set the table for two, but the woman who was supposed to sit across from him had missed the bus to Tórshavn. So he put *Songs from a Room* by Leonard Cohen on the record player and the evening had been almost perfect.

Later he ventured to ask if she slept naked or maybe in a nightgown. As a matter of course, he said it was not good for the circulation to sleep in both panties and a nightgown. If it were his choice, she would sleep only in a nightgown, preferably one whose collar was decorated with small embroidered flowers.

Eventually, he also sent her some small literary attempts.

For a while he had been writing prose pieces with the collective title *Cultural History*. One was called "The Cultural History of the High Heel," another "The Cultural History of the Kiss," and the one he sent Karin was entitled "The Cultural History of the Shit Dog."

It was not just for laughs, though, that he sent her two pages of rectum-related literature. Eigil wanted to test her. A woman who was all sweet and lovely, but who hardly cast a shadow, was not someone who could attract him.

Eigil, therefore, was somewhat distressed that Karin did not like "The Cultural History of the Shit Dog," and did not seem to understand that sheer decency was smothering Faroese literature.

Her reply was short and clear, she said every other word made her sick, and she hoped the story did not come from his heart.

The Cultural History of the Shit Dog

Canis Fæcalis, as the shit dog is commonly called, was notably very short and stubby-legged. Its most remarkable characteristic was its disproportionately large, pointed head that swayed atop a thin column of cervical vertebrae. So thin was its neck that one could in fact count the seven small vertebrae extending from its back on up. Yet not before it opened its mouth, and its long tongue either tumbled out or stuck straight into the air, did one understand why it so suited its calling of royal asslicker.

We are talking about the years leading up to the French Revolution, before running water was hooked up to the royal loo, when dirt was the mortar holding the Sun King's realm together: smegma, fleas, dingleberries, crabs, menstrual blood in pubic hair, hairline sweat and armpit sweat and sweat between the toes and scrotum sweat and asshole sweat, and black teeth stumps and food particles in beards, back when emptying the chamber pot out the window was a way to bid Paris good morning.

Young and old, women as well as men shit everywhere. Even in cemeteries, shit happened. Loo-shitting was a sign of rank, and having your own personal portable john at sea as well as on the road was a sign of the highest rank of all.

Ludvig's loo in Versailles was a long box decorated and adorned by the foremost artists. In a space to the right of the door lived Canis Fæcalis, and his job, as mentioned before, was to clean the royal asshole every time His Majesty had a bowel movement.

The shit dog, or the official canine, as he was also called, was blind. Not because he had been born with empty eye sockets, but because his eyes had been scraped out of his head. His teeth had also been chipped or broken along both the upper and lower jaw. This was not done out of malice, but in order to protect the King's genitalia, or the House of Bourbon, as Victor Hugo wrote in his memoirs. Canis Fæcalis was thus fated to live its days inside the royal loo, and not unexpectedly the most common cause of death was shit-poisoning.

On January 21, 1793, the people of Paris saw for the first time the creature that parents for centuries had used to scare children and about which horny monks had secretly dreamt. Fragile and blind the dog came hobbling across the Place de la République, and as word spread through the crowd what was happening, people silently made way. Occasionally the dog stopped and sniffed, and simply to see this beast, which had had such intimate contact with His Majesty, filled people with disgust, but also with a feeling reminiscent of curious sympathy. At the guillotine, where Ludwig the XVI lay in his white shift, waiting to be beheaded, the dog stopped, and it looked like the animal was hoping someone would make an effort and lift it up onto the scaffold. No one wanted to touch it. Only when the dog began to whine and scrabble, reared up on its hind legs, did an old woman finally take pity; removing her apron, she placed it over the dog's back and cast both dog and apron onto the scaffold.

Canis Fæcalis stood right behind His Majesty, and as the sharp blade came hissing down from the guillotine to slice the king's head off, his sphincter relaxed. As soon as Canis Fæcalis smelled that there was a need, he stuck his pointed snout beneath the shift and fulfilled his official duty. The strange thing was, the dog remained standing there. It seemed to wonder why His Majesty's asshole did not contract again.

And so this part of European cultural history came to a close.

Eigil and Karin saw each other between Christmas and New Year's Eve. It was a long meeting. Karin did not return to Fuglafjørður until the first week in January.

Patricide

THE MOST UNFORTUNATE event to come out of Ergisstova, which more or less affected all of the family, was the patricide on Misaklettur. It was from that cliff the Hordalander, Nils Selleg, commonly called Nils Tvibur, but also known as the Corporal, or Muhammad, fell to his death, and the person who pushed him was none other than Gregor, his own flesh and blood.

Father and son had been out on the Móanesfløta plain, and on the way home the snack-hungry old man had the idea of climbing down for some puffin chicks. Nils did not care that the people of Kálgarður owned the rights to the birds on Misaklettur. His palette craved puffin chicks, and the ancient yeoman's god shone on him as he climbed down among the colony.

Gregor sat on the edge holding a rope the old man was using for security, but the descent was easy, and when Nils had reached the grassy ledge, he let go of the rope and stood a moment listening to the din of countless bird beaks. Thousands of birds ate and shit here multiple times a day, and Nils loved the powerful smell coming from the rookery. Bird droppings were excellent fertilizer and a good defense, and the birds had their hollows all the way out to Misaklettur's point. The cliff was a giant heart beating to the heavens. Every hollow clamored, and the roar from Røstin Sound, which broke white and foaming in the intense afternoon light, reached the cliff's top.

Nils had killed two chicks and had his arm in a third hollow when he glanced up to see a large chunk of sod hurtling down toward him. Leaping out of the way was impossible. With his right arm still in the hollow, he grabbed onto a clump of dead grass with his other hand just as the lump struck his neck and back, knocking both legs out from under him.

Gregor carefully stretched himself over the edge, and he could not believe his eyes. About twelve fathoms below he saw his father's heavy shoulders shift, and for a split second he looked straight into his father's eyes. They glinted with shock, but also with a strange accusatory force.

The boy felt dizzy. This is not how it should have gone. His father should not be trying to get up. He should be dead. Dead as a rock! He should be smashed to bits, food for the ravens and jackdaws hundreds of fathoms below on the beach!

Gregor began to snivel and whine, just like he did when his father came after him back home with a rope. He considered running away, but where would he go? His father would find him in town, or if he headed north up the island.

Gregor tried to think clearly and to control his terror. At the moment he had nothing to fear, and it could be his father would not be able to climb back up. Maybe he had broken a leg or maybe even two.

A few rocks stuck out of the place where he had pried loose the clump of turf, and he used these to stone his father. He gathered every loose rock he could find, but the old man had already gotten his feet beneath him and was trying to take shelter beneath an overhang. His lower back and side seared; he probably had some broken ribs.

Perhaps he should try to calm his son down, Nils Tvibur thought, as he took shelter beneath the overhang. Perhaps Gregor did not mean to be so malicious. Perhaps it was just a momentary confusion that had seized him. It could happen. A person did not always have proper self-control. You could do things you did not actually mean. He himself had knocked his father to the ground.

Good God! Nils exclaimed. It had been half a century since he had left Selleg. Nonetheless, he had not planned that headbutt that felled his father. It had just happened.

"Shut up, Nils," he interrupted himself. What could he possibly do to calm his son? Gregor would never trust him. He typically subdued his son with a rope. And that right there was the great misfortune. Rope language was all that idiot understood.

Ah! Nils sighed, pressing himself back against the cliff. His son lacked the characteristics of a leader. The boy never let moonlight play in the full ladle before drinking from the water barrel. His own offspring had the miserable eyes of a sheep thief.

Nils had also rebuked Aksal, his brother-in-law, but that was with a mountain staff and had been several years ago. He had caught his brother-in-law mounting a heifer in a dark stall. And that damned sodomite was known among Sumbingurs as *the Wise One*.

True, his brother-in-law knew a lot, he read books in both English and Danish, but all these years he had instilled his venom in Gregor and now it was beginning to take hold. That was the way it all connected. First Aksal had turned his sister against Nils, and then he had done the same with her daughters, Hjørdis and Adelborg, or Hjørdis, at any rate. She was married and lived in Fámjins, and she rarely came south to Sumba for a visit. Adelborg was married to a drunk out in Keri, but she was one you could talk to. Nils had never been close-fisted with her or her household, and her children called him Grandpa. You could thank her for that.

Nils's eyes teared and suddenly he remembered Betta í Geil. That memory surprised him so much that a sound like a laugh escaped him.

He had not known many women in his life. He could count the Kristiania prostitutes with whom he had slept on two hands. He had only really gotten to know one of them. Her name was Mari Kolsbu, and one evening, when he went looking for her in the narrow streets of the whore district around Rådhuset, he learned she had run away. She had been caught up in Hans Nielsen Hauge's revival movement as the man traveled from town to town and farm to farm preaching the true word.

Yet it was only together with Betta that he had been happy, the way people ought to be happy when they truly desire each other or they truly care about each other. And Betta had also cried her bitter and exhausted tears on his shoulder. That had been before the rape, though. After that everything changed.

Nils was deeply touched at the thought of his old flame. They had had some good times together, in any case, she was the only woman he had ever made laugh. Sometimes when he thought of their relationship, he characterized their nights as two wild horses with blood on their hooves. He remembered Betta's terror when he came whinnying toward her with his terrible stallion cock. And she laughed when he said that there were few men north of Skagerrak who had his kind of equipment. The mere weight of his testicles would knock King Bernadotte silly.

Then the more troubled face of Djøssan appeared to him. She was clever and skillful, that she was, but he had never loved her. In all their years together they had never even reached an understanding, and it was rare that they even spoke. And if anyone had a long memory, it was Djøssan. Could she have brought their son to attempt . . . ? Nils could not bring himself to say the word *patricide*. However, the abusive words he had rained down on her person over the years were repulsive, and he groaned now just thinking about it. As a housewife and cook, he branded her the biggest poisoner on the island, and as a wife she was a bag of bones and stunk of ass at both ends. The blows he had rained down on her were also unpleasant to recall, but she had never complained. He respected her for that.

If any woman was fit to fetch water for Muhammad's horse, it was Djøssan úr Ergisstova.

Two more dirt clumps came flying from above, but Nils was able to press himself against the cliff and watch as they whizzed past and burst against Misaklettur. Perhaps he should have simply stay put. That was a time-honored strategy for wearing your enemy out. Yet he was not capable of it. Not Nils Tvibur. He felt the rage boil in his chest, clenched his teeth, and began to skillfully claw his way up. A rock from above bloodied the fingertips of his right hand, but he persisted. He had the devil in him now, and the pain in his side and his torn fingernails were like whale oil poured on fire, causing fury to flame up anew.

And he knew the terrain around the cliff's edge, knew there was not much loose material left to cast down at him. He began to taunt and ridicule his son, hurling curse words up at him; often it did not take much more than that to paralyze the wretch.

A few fathoms from the edge was a good-sized rock, and Gregor had just gotten his arms around it and was on his way back to the rim when he saw his father's battered head appear. The old man had just gotten his left knee onto the grass and was about to stand up when Gregor, with both hands and a heavy thrust of his hips, sent the rock flying, striking his father squarely in the chest.

It was only a brief moment, not more than two or three heartbeats, but for that length of time father and son looked into each other's eyes. And the Hordalander Nils Selleg, commonly called Nils Tvibur, but also known as the Corporal, or Muhammad, fell to his death. The Faroes had been his home for thirty-nine years, sixteen of those in Tórshavn and twenty-three in Sumba. He plummeted all the way down the cliff and died on the flat rocky beach, which today the Sumbingurs call Corporal Rock.

A Fucking Night
in Tvøroyri

DOCTOR NAPOLEON WOKE to the maid hammering on his bed-room door: "Pole, Pole," she cried fearfully, "There's someone at the door, they look half-dead." Then she began to cry. "You have to come down. I think it's Jóakim."

Shuddering at the idea of a dead man scraping against the door, Napoleon pulled on his pants and shirt.

It had been a miserable evening. The *Glen Rose* had arrived with a young man who had developed gangrene. George Harrison and the helmsman had followed him into the consultation room, and imme-diately Napoleon saw there was nothing he could do. The man's left hand and wrist were coal black and he had a high fever.

Napoleon asked the man to sit at the examining table and served him a tall glass of Hollands gin. He asked how far up the pain went, and the man pointed at his shoulder and said, *fuck*. He handed Pole the empty glass, was given another, and repeated his word, *fuck*.

Napoleon knew that some patients were more pliable when they saw the operation implements with their own eyes, and the young man seemed the sort who would rather lose his hand than his life. The amputation saw lay next to the scalpel, and the iron that would be used to cauterize the wound glowed red on the stove.

The consultation room was at the east end of the building, and double walls had been constructed and the space between them filled with dirt in order to soundproof the room. An additional layer of dirt above the ceiling filled almost the whole space between floors.

Suddenly the young man glanced at the skipper, his eyes glinting from spitefully narrowed slits, and with outright shamelessness he said: *fuck your fucking Jesus.*

Pole started and saw how these words surprised the skipper. George was a man of middle height with thick, round cheeks and friendly eyes. When he preached, he was easily moved to tears, and he tended to exclaim with arms crossed at his breast: *Oh, my sweet Lord.*

Meanwhile, the gin was taking effect, and the young man repeatedly said good-bye to his hand, lifting it to his cheek and kissing its scorching back. There was now a hefty variety of fuck-expressions. He also called Napoleon a *fucking butcher,* only the whites of his eye visible, but he did not resist as Pole bound a strap around his arm just below the bicep. Pole said *my good lad* and persuaded him to lie down. He placed a firm leather cushion beneath his upper arm and also bound his shoulders and arm fast to the table.

The skipper, who teared up easily, was now bawling uncontrollably.

He said the young man had cut himself on the trawl six days ago, but the wound was not serious. He had prayed for the man, indeed, he had earnestly prayed for him, but there must be some serious sins at work, because *the Mighty* had not listened.

George Harrison and the helmsman were told to be quiet, and with the scalpel Pole made an incision halfway around the young man's upper arm. The young man jerked and screamed, but fortunately he fainted as the saw blade began to draw white shavings from the bone. As soon as the arm was free, Pole took the branding iron from the stove, and its glowing red surface pressed against the wound with a *thiiisssss*. Although the flesh was rather crusted, he was nonetheless able to sew up the wound and bind the arm.

It was not until Pole had his pound sterling in his waistcoat pocket that he looked sharply at the skipper and told him that he prayed to the wrong god.

George Harrison asked what Pole meant.

Pole said in English: "You have been praying to the God that may gives fish to skippers, but who doesn't give a damn about young men suffering!"

A couple of hours after midnight, the *Glen Rose*'s anchor chain could be heard rattling through the hawsehole, and shortly thereafter it steered out of Trongisvágsfjørður at full sail.

Napoleon hurried down from the loft and found Jóakim in the yard. He and the maid each took one of Jóakim's arms, and when they had reached the hallway Pole told her to boil some water. Jóakim smelled strongly of alcohol and was more or less unconscious. However, whether this was due to drunkenness or his wounds was difficult to say. His face was bloody and swollen, but the strangest thing of all was that Jóakim was naked from the waist down. As such Napoleon did not ask for further help from the maid, but wrestled his cousin onto the table himself.

He closely inspected Jóakim's face and chest, and saw that one knee was open to the bone. It wasn't until he turned his cousin onto his stomach, however, that Napoleon realized that something was seriously wrong.

His thighs and legs were covered in blood, and the spot from his anus to his testicles was a bloody mess. At first Napoleon thought that was all it was, but when he began to wash the wound with hot soapy water, he realized that Jóakim's guts were hanging out. About five inches of Jóakim's intestine had been ripped out and hung like a clump below his groin.

Napoleon was so shaken that he retrieved the Hollands gin bottle and downed a glass on an empty stomach. The intestine was torn out and his anus ripped apart. That was the short, horrifying diagnosis.

"What have you done, you poor fool?" he whispered, and it soon became clear to him what had happened. Aside from being punched and kicked, a wooden shaft or something similar had been shoved up Jóakim's anus; the wood had not been smooth, because the intestine had been shredded as the shaft had been forced in and out, likely multiple times.

"Oh, God in Heaven," Napoleon sighed. The Great Sodomite had been at it again. That was how things were connected. And inflammation had already set in. Napoleon could feel an unpleasant heat from around the wound and could see it pulsing with his own eyes.

There was nothing science could do. Even the most skillful Edinburgh surgeon could not do anything in this situation. It was not even possible to set up a drain, and what would be the use of draining the pus away when the intestine itself was torn?

Nonetheless, Pole placed a kerosene lamp on the table and with a pair of tweezers he began to pick splinters from the wound. For a long while he tended to his cousin. He washed him, gave him morphine, stroked his hair, and covered him with a blanket. During the moments Jóakim regained consciousness, he tried to speak to him, and as far as he understood, Jóakim and a Scott by the name of Ronnie Harrison had been in the Trade Monopoly's boathouse located near Sixpence.

There was a sickroom as the west end of the house, but Napoleon did not want to call the maid and ask her to prepare it for Jóakim.

Pole felt exhausted and the incident itself was so shameful. Yet, right was right. He had sometimes thought that Jóakim might be a sodomite. There was something feminine about him, and suddenly he remembered that Tóvó once said that Jóakim's face reminded him of Baker Restorff's cakes, dried plums on top and pudding beneath.

Maybe that was a kind of code between sodomites? Maybe he had already made advances on Tóvó, maybe he had already ruined the boy? At any rate, they were good friends and had often gone boating or to the mountains together. Alone.

As Tóvó's doctor and master, Pole had warned the boy about the dangers of masturbation, but he had not thought that Tóvó had the particular characteristics of an onanist, at least not as Tissot described them in his classic, *L'Onanisme*. Pole, who owned the Danish translation, had told Tóvó what the French doctor meant when he wrote that the emission of semen caused a severe pain in the eyes, which afterward could result in sensitivity to daylight. The eyes also lose their luster, eventually causing those affected to become feeble-minded, especially when they have cultivated the habit early on.

In *Observations*, Panum also wrote about masturbation: *Among other examples, I can cite the instance of a mother who, when her son desired to marry, forbade him to do so, and taught him to practice onanism as a substitute. The unfortunate fellow carried this habit to such excess that his mind became weakened; and in his more lucid moments he cursed his mother with the most horrible oaths, because "she had wasted away his oil of life."*

Pole's medical experience gave him a certain familiarity with such dreadful occurrences, but the idea that he had an onanist beneath his roof filled him with loathing.

Tóvó? Tóvó was no longer his responsibility. He had made a man of the boy, at least as much of a one as he could. He had taught Tóvó to read and write, and there comes a time in life when everyone must stand on his own two feet. Pole himself did not intend to spend the rest of his life in Tvøroyri, and he had also made that clear to Tóvó. Last year a Danish merchant named Thomsen had bought the Trade Monopoly's old building, and it had not been much more than a year since since the church had been relocated from Froðba to Tvøroyri.

Significant changes were taking place all over the country, many of them not for the better. Pole regretted that Doffa, the political trailblazer, had left the country. Pole and Doffa were both among the parliamentarians elected to the newly reconstituted Faroese parliament, the *Føroya Løgting*, on June 18th, 1852. Pole sat for one term, but Doffa was reelected. The man was so shrewd and well-respected that he could have retained his seat in parliament until the world's end. And aside from serving in the Føroya Løgting, he also represented the Faroes in the Danish Folketinget.

Jóakim moaned in pain, but he had just been given morphine. Pole took his pulse and remembered the time he had asked Jóakim his opinion about the new Løgting. It was not without reason he had sought out his cousin in particular. Jóakim was so astoundingly bright and could, as if instinctively, evaluate extremely complicated matters.

Jóakim had responded that in order to vote a man was required to own three guilders of land. Each guilder was equal to twenty *skinn*, a skinn being the estimated value of a pilot whale measured eye to anus. Twenty skinn is equal to about 314.5 cm on this measure. Yet there was neither house nor any deed that bore the name Jóakim Nolsøe. All he had to his name was the boat that hauled water out to the sloops, nothing else. As such, he lacked voting rights. In his opinion, politics was something that officials and rich farmers used to pass the time. Over half of the men in the Løgting were Sunmen, and that sort did not begrudge their unlanded countrymen the shit beneath their fingernails. Yet Jóakim took comfort in the fact that Jesus had also been unlanded. If Jesus were registered in Froðba's parish, just think, the Almighty's son could not vote. So brilliantly had the Føroya Løgting been nailed together!

Napoleon was offended. No one was comparable to Christ, he said, and using worldly analogies when talking about God's son was pointless. Not only were such thoughts blasphemous, but they also simplified the matter's heart. However, to himself he was forced to admit that what Jóakim said made sense, indeed, a kind of terrifying sense.

And the Sunmen? He certainly understood why Dahlerup complained that in Parliament those damned meat-greedy asses tried to express pure rubbish and twaddle in their helpless Danish. Deep down they feared change. They wanted the Faroes to be governed like they always had been; they tended to ignore Doffa, especially when he talked about letting small folk cultivate fallow ground.

Without courageous men such as Doffa, the rocks of the Faroes would be cold and empty—that you had to admit, Pole had told his cousin.

"Maybe that's true," Jóakim replied. "But I have to say that I'm also a little sick of all this Doffatry. You can't have a conversation anymore without Doffa popping up. And I know him, as you're well aware. We used to play together before Hunderup brought him into the sheriff's office. August Manicus, Vesse Hammershaimb, Løbner's Luddi, Doffa, and me—we all stuck together in childhood. August died last year. He was a man I liked. I helped him on Suðuroy with the measles epidemic. I know you remember *that*," Jóakim taunted. "August said he was a socialist. I didn't know the meaning of the word and asked if that was a new kind of tar or tobacco. August said that Jesus was a Socialist, and when he rebelled and cleansed the temple he did it in the people's name. Doffa?" Jóakim shook his head. "The fact is, I knew every place name between Skansin Fortress and Boðanes by heart before he even knew the days of the week. But Hunderup thought Doffa was so clever. On Sundays he walked about in his sailor's suit, a fat kid in a sailor's collar. No, dear cousin. Doffa is not the man the Faroes has been waiting for."

Napoleon sputtered with fury. "I have no idea who you think you're waiting on here in the south. You all love August Manicus because he showered you with medicine he didn't even own. The

Danish Finance Chamber footed the bill. And then you all bad-mouthed the man behind his back. On Suðuroy all you do is bad-mouth honest people and then laugh like fools. And this is the island I'm supposed to care about. Lord help me!"

Pole sat in the kitchen for the rest of the night. He ate bread, picked dried meat from a sheep shoulder, and sipped gin. Several times he said *fuck*, and that desperate curse made him think of that poor, one-handed fisherman who was now on his way home to Scotland. Fortunately, the *Glen Rose's* skipper had taken the amputated hand with him. Otherwise, Tóvó would have probably tossed it onto the midden. Pole smiled at the thought, remembering how the boy had been so eager to toss anything capable of rotting onto his precious midden.

Pole sat on the peat box by the window, while on the table, wrapped in its dark-red silk cloth, was Nólsaryar Páll's old telescope.

Sometimes when he went into the mountains, Pole took the telescope with him. It was compact in size and was good for bird watching. Usually, it sat in the bookcase in the living room, and you could see yourself in the brass because Tóvó liked to polish the metal with tobacco ash and spit. He had considered giving Tóvó the telescope when they parted ways, but now he was not so sure.

At regular intervals he went to check on his cousin. The morphine was working. Jóakim whimpered with froth in the corners of his mouth, and once Pole kissed him gently on the lips and whispered: *good boy.*

The words brought tears to his eyes. However, when he suddenly remembered what Jóakim might have been doing with those lips in the Trade Monopoly's boathouse, he wiped his mouth with the back of his hand and whispered: *you stupid dog, you damned Sodomite.*

Tóvó had to leave the house. His decision was made. Pole was not Tóvó's father, after all, and God have mercy on his soul, thought

Pole as he stood up. No. Tóvó deserved no mercy, he decided, sitting down again. The boy had to go! He could well be an onanist. The diagnosis, of course, was not so easy to make. Still, he had the same low, degenerate forehead as Slavs, Lapps, and some Asian groups.

The boy was tough, though. Around two years ago Doffa asked in a letter how the young Brahmadella was doing, and Pole could well recall the satisfaction he had when he wrote back: *Whether it is old ancestral strength making its sudden appearance in the boy's mental constitution, or whether the climate here in the south is especially favorable, is difficult to say. However, our dear Brahmadella has acquired youth's hearty appetite for life, and he works like that warrior who in the early days planted the Babylonian gardens.*

He stood by the words. Tóvó truly had changed. He was no longer the distrustful milksop who peeked around corners thinking he saw the Devil in every other man's eye. Nonetheless, the Brahmadella would vacate the Doctor's House in Tvøroyri. The decision had been made, and the Devil take Pole if he gave that boy the telescope!

It was after six o'clock when Pole knocked on Tóvó's door. Tóvó had gone to bed early and did not know it was the *Glen Rose* that had anchored. His brother Lýðar no longer sailed with the ship, as he had married someone from Nólsoy and become a landsman.

Pole told him to hurry and fetch the envoy.

The Gentle Singer

NAPOLEON TOLD HIS uncle about Jóakim's condition in unusually harsh terms.

He said Jóakim was the victim of a crime and was going to die. He also said Jóakim was a sodomite and that this was the reason he was in this mess.

From what Napoleon had pieced together, the *Glen Rose's* crew had given Jóakim a strong drink after he had rowed water to them. One or two had come ashore with him, and they had continued the party in the Trade Monopoly's boathouse, where the terrible crime had apparently taken place.

Jóakim was going to suffer a painful death, Napoleon said and filled two glasses. The envoy, however, was not inclined to drink.

When the doctor had drained his glass, he offered in more neutral tones to write a report and give it to the sheriff. What his uncle had to realize, though, was that if the matter were brought before the authorities, it would quickly become general knowledge who Jóakim Nolsøe really was. The question to consider now was whether such a report would serve Jóakim's legacy, not to mention the family's reputation.

Napoleon had finally said his piece and he asked if they should go and see Jóakim in the consultation room.

The envoy stood and told Napoleon no. His voice trembled, but it was pure disgust, not sorrow, that shook his vocal chords. He said never before had such a load of shit been dumped on him and his house, and the words, moreover, came from a learned man, who was also his own brother's son. He said he was going to go home and transform the parlor into a sick room. Then he would return for his son. That way he could die at home among his family in peace.

"But I have a sick room at the west end of the house," said Pole. "Jóakim is in good hands when those hands also belong to a doctor."

"That might be true," the envoy answered. "But I also had no idea you were so self-righteous. Don't you think I know my son and his vices? I can't do anything about that, or couldn't, anyway, since according to what you said, it's only a matter of days until he meets his Judgment. But one thing you should know, Napoleon Nolsøe: I would rather be father to Jóakim the Sodomite a thousand times over than be in a family with a beast like you."

Tóvó helped the envoy bear his son home. They placed him on a ladder, wrapped a blanket around him, and carefully walked up the hill.

It took Jóakim six days to wrestle free of life. During that time, he naturally ate no solid food and a starling's throat could easily contain what he drank. His bowels became infected, and his stomach was hot to the touch and hard as a board. It was only on the last day that he was mostly unconscious. Most of the time he was lucid but taciturn.

Pole visited him once, sometimes twice a day.

The envoy's wife welcomed him quietly, said *my dear* and occasionally *blessed,* and opened the door to the parlor so he could be alone with her dying son. Pole brought morphine, and when he asked Jóakim how he was doing, he received only a shrug or a gesture in response. Pole tried to start a conversation, but it was difficult to find the words.

Sometimes Jóakim asked about Tóvó and that displeased Pole. He partly felt a sting of jealousy, but he was also growing increasingly certain that something aberrant had existed between his cousin and Tóvó.

And Pole was hurt that he had not been asked to watch over his cousin.

Tóvó, for his part, sat with Jóakim for two nights, and on the last night he learned what had happened in the Trade Monopoly boathouse. Or he at least learned what Jóakim remembered.

It was Ronnie Harrison, the skipper's nephew, who had come ashore with him, and it was not the first time they had been together in the boathouse.

Tóvó knew who Ronnie was, and he also knew that the man was a sodomite. Jóakim had told him that. Jóakim also told him that Ronnie was one of those famous gadabouts from Inverness. For four or five years Ronnie's uncle had taken him aboard the *Glen Rose* to make a decent man of him, and for longs stretches of time it could go reasonably well. They were not so dissimilar, Ronnie and George, or rather, they were like the rest of the Harrison clan, hard-knuckled priest-haters. Everywhere they went they heard the doors of evil creak and clatter; it was like an eternal blast of sin swept around their souls and deeds. George did seem milder, or in any case, he was more easily moved to tears. That was just on the surface, though. When he had a mind, he could be downright obstinate. The reason the *Glen Rose* had anchored at Tvøroyri was that there had been trouble aboard the ship lately. It had come to blows over the trawl, and the reason was that the skipper had refused to sail to land with the young man who had wounded his hand.

Jóakim talked slowly and sometimes it seemed he lost consciousness. He continued his story, though, and there was such great tenderness in his voice that it gripped Tóvó's heart. Yet he spoke so strangely, calling the Trade Monopoly's boathouse his *temple* and his *offering ground*, and saying that if he were not so bad off, he would dress it with Lebanese cypress or cedar wood. He said that the boat-house was located next to a fjord flowing high above the earth, and it was supported by basalt columns like those out in Bø.

"But what happened?" Tóvó asked.

Ronnie went berserk, Jóakim said. He was lying on his stomach when the Scott grabbed his head and started hammering it into the stone floor. Then he lost consciousness and had no idea how he had reached the Doctor's House.

Tóvó took the washcloth from the bowl and wiped Jóakim's brow. Jóakim said that a poor man was predestined to be a sodomite. If you owned nothing, you could offer no life to a woman or children. And now he was a joke and could only wait for the pastor to come and administer the Sacrament.

He told Tóvó about the time an American corvette had anchored at Hvalba for coal. They loaded for several days and the skipper said they needed a sailor. He had often regretted not accepting the offering and going out into the wide world. Flee, he told Tóvó. This was not a country for poor folk.

There were long pauses between the words sometimes, but Tóvó was patient.

He was sitting just as his great-grandfather had sat by Martimann's bedside eleven years ago. Tóvó had always been unable dwell on that terrible May night in 1846, but now he felt a call to follow Jóakim to death's door.

He held Jóakim's burning hand and asked if he was asleep, but Jóakim shook his head.

Tóvó asked if he wanted to listen to a couple of verses that his great-grandfather had taught him.

"What, now you're telling me you're a singer?" Jóakim whispered with a roguish grin.

The Christmas sun
in the bell's bronze
rings in a sea-washed heart.
The Sweet One in the manger,
the manger in the stable,
the stable of stone
the stone of earth.
Life and death and blackest sorrow
tell me you Sweet One in the manger
why the shuttle sings in the loom
why the sorrowful sing in the night.

March, the mild month, has two hands
searches the raven's nest
the kind man from Tórshavn came
the kind man from Tórshavn went
poor Tóvó sits behind.
Tread hard
grip fast
magic days seven.
Searches memory with two hands.
Tread hard.
grip fast
the sun beautifully reddens.

The Hour of Farewell

JÓAKIM'S FUNERAL WAS the first to be held in Froðba church since it was moved to Tvøroyri. Tóvó, two salesmen, and Jóhann Mortensen from Øravík carried the coffin down the path between the Tvørá and Doctor Pole's garden fence. Several boats lay at the bridge, and the Dannebrog flew at half-mast from the black-tarred funeral boat. Though the black-tarred boat was meant for ten men, that day six men rowed it, and between the stern seat and the last rower bank sat the coffin. They grasped the oars carefully, and the men in the other boats did the same. The small flotilla rowed slowly past Sixpence and Akurgerði toward the churchyard on Bø.

Pole was part of the procession that walked to Froðba, a journey not more than half an hour by foot. There was an occasional creak of the oars, but the rowers splashed water onto the wood beneath the oarlocks. Noise was not fitting at such a solemn moment. Pole appreciated the mythological notion of the deceased being rowed into a Froðbian realm of the dead.

Froðba was one of the most beautiful towns. In the sun the yellow fields waved right up to the infield fence, and golden plovers could be heard whistling from Torvheyggjur's green slopes. In *Reports from a Visit to the Faroes*, Svabo wrote: *Here one sees the best stone walls in all of the Faroes, not just because they are built from basalt, which Froðba has in abundance, but also because they have a correct height of eight to nine quarters.*

The landscape, however, was also a masterwork of nature. The sun shone most of the day here and the mountains stretching from Froðbiarnípa to Remberg provided good protection from the north wind. The town was located on two levels, so to speak, and from up on Hamar you had a view west toward the black coal mountains, while on the east side lay the great blue Atlantic.

But the most beautiful place in Froðba was Úti á Bø, and it was no coincidence that the old Froðbians had built their church at this precise location. A narrow waterfall plunged from the steep cliffs and ran white and babbling toward the beach. Rows of magnificent basalt columns stood on both sides of the churchyard, and as Pole walked by them, he genuinely felt that he was passing a forgotten shrine. That was exactly the sensation. The columns were reminiscent of a portal before a forgotten temple someone had raised to honor, well, he was not sure exactly what. Perhaps the dead or those dark, sublime feelings about which the Preacher sang.

Pole did not let it show, but it wounded his pride that he had been passed over as bearer. He could have chosen his words with greater care the morning he sent Tóvó to fetch his uncle, that he could have. But to punish a grown man in this way was simply ludicrous. Plus his family only had *one* educated man. He was the Nolsøe clan's intellectual jewel, and yet he was rejected in favor of two shop attendants, a young eccentric from Tórshavn, and a clodhopper from Øravík.

It was a strange funeral. Various rumors regarding the cause of Jóakim's death had leaked out, but no one knew whether his death was due to a tragic accident or to an outright murder, and they could not inquire. People did not know Ronnie Harrison nearly as well as they knew his uncle. George had shocked people one Sunday when the *Glen Rose* had come into the harbor with some other sloops for water. Several of the fishermen took the opportunity to visit the Froðba church, but George Harrison was not among them. Instead, he gave a speech on the bridge over the Tvørá, where he spoke the dreadful words that were repeated twenty-five years later by another priest-hater, namely, that the church doors were *the gate to Hell*. The subsequent priest-hater, William Gibson Sloan, founded the the Brethren Congregation on the Faroes.

Nonetheless, the large following showed Jóakim had been a popular man. Most Suðoroyingars knew him, at least those who had done business at the Trade Monopoly. And Jóakim was also hilarious, both when he imitated other people and, most of all, when he made fools of the authority. Still, that was not the kind of thing you said at a funeral. Nonetheless, a man from Hvalba, making his way home through the Káragjógv ravine, remarked that Jóakim was probably the only man on earth to ascend to Heaven with a ruptured anus.

When Tóvó and the maid returned from the wake, Pole was sitting alone in the living room smoking a pipe. Realizing immediately that Pole was in a bad mood, the maid hurried up to her attic room. Tóvó wanted to do the same, but Pole called him in.

He said he did not want anything in particular, just to ask how the young widower was doing. Tóvó did not grasp his meaning right away, and Pole did not wait for an answer. Instead, he continued that his good friend Dahlerup had entrusted this house to him five years ago. Next to the church, the Doctor's House or the Hospital were sacred, but whereas the clergy tended to the soul, it was the doctor's responsibility to look after the soul's vessel. One could say, therefore, that the Doctor's House was a holy place. In any case, it was a house governed by the Hippocratic Oath, and therefore moral purity ought to be held in the highest regard.

"Do you understand me?" he asked.

Tóvó shook his head.

"I'm asking if this house has been polluted by sodomistic debauchery."

"I don't know," Tóvó answered softly.

"If something objectionable did happen, I was considering asking Pastor Harald to come and drive the evil spirit away."

"You shouldn't talk to me that way," Tóvó said even more softly.

"What did the widower say? I couldn't quite hear."

"No one should talk to me like you are."

"Is that an order?"

"Yes, it is. I'm not a dog, and I'm not some rat or fly whose wings you can tear off."

"I didn't say that."

Tóvó stomped the floor with his foot. "Do you know who I am?" He approached Pole's chair. He circled behind it, watching the doctor's head as it appeared above the backrest.

"We've lived under the same roof for five years, and still you don't seem to know who I am. You could've been my father, but I could've been your forefather. You could've been the one to govern the Faroes, but I am the sea who fills the middens with growth. And why? Because I'm a Brahmadella.

"One day the Master Barber and Saint Birgitta will walk toward the rainbow, and they won't ask where Napoleon Nolsøe lives. They won't ask what herbs he has lying in his mortar, they won't count the number of opium vials standing on his shelf. They'll ask after me, the little chisel wight, and they'll want to know why so many tears are being cried in the mild March sun."

Pole put down his pipe, turned around in his chair, and told Tóvó to calm down.

And Tóvó was calm; he was so calm that it frightened Pole. He had the strange feeling Tóvó could see right through him and read his terrified thoughts. Pole also did not recall ever having heard such peculiar words before, and did not know whether they belonged to the realm of pathology or poetry. There was also a third possibility, but he dared not consider it. To mention the underwordly—the mythical, subterranean creatures of Old Norse folklore—was not something his heart could not have tolerated right then.

Pole grinned foolishly, and the laughter that rose in his throat sounded like a dry cough.

Tóvó came around to the front of the chair and looked at Pole.

"I was six years old the first time I spoke with you. Eight years later you took me with you south to Tvøroyri and I have been here for five years. Now it's time for me to go."

Pole nodded.

"I've had a good life here in Tvøroyri, and I have you to thank for that. I'm going to go to bed now. Good night."

"Good night, Tóvó."

PART
THREE

Death and Flight Dreams

HENRIETTA AWOKE TO the smell of blood and the first thing she thought of was her monthly cycle. She felt herself and sniffed her fingertips, but there was only the scent of her sex. For a while she lay in the dark, yawning and thinking back. When had she bled last?

Good God! It only just now hit her. It had been at least three years. She had not bled in the three years they had been married, and besides, the smell was never this cloying.

She lit the candle on the nightstand and lifted it toward Pole. That was when she saw that he was bleeding from his mouth and nose, and that the whites of his eyes were showing.

"Pole," she whispered, but he seemed unconscious.

She sprang into the attic corridor, shouted "my dear" to the serving girl, begged her for God's sake to fetch the Landkirurg.

When Hoff entered the bedroom not half an hour later, Pole was dead. Hoff said that his colleague and dear friend had died of an aneurism, and it was a comfort to Henrietta that she knew what an aneurism was. One of the large veins in his abdominal cavity had burst and the blood's characteristically dark color, already visible along his throat and the bridge of his nose, had spread like a dark growth around his eyes and forehead.

Hoff lingered in the corridor. His yellowish hair stuck straight up. His eyes were light blue and his unusually white teeth glinted in the half-dark hallway. He said that he wanted to relate a little event that happened in Tórshavn's Club on Twelfth Night.

Napoleon had tapped on his glass and, clearly moved, had told the story of a farmer in Nes on Suðuroy who had made himself a feather suit. His plan was to fly straight across Vágsfjørður, and so on a brisk, windy day he cast himself off the cliff's edge above the farm. The suit was equipped with a tail to steer, but after he was quite a ways over the inlet, he realized that he had too little control, and he was afraid the wind would blow him seaward. His sons sat in a boat below him, ready to help if anything should go wrong, and as he hung in the air he called to them in a terrified voice. There was nothing they could do, however, but watch him play bird twenty-five fathoms above the sea. Finally, the farmer was able to steer himself back to land, and man and suit took a head-over-heels tumble into the surf on the rocky beach.

A few years later, a young man from the Billhús in Sumba repeated the experiment. Instead of using feathers he covered the wings in red canvas, and instead of a tail he made it so the wings could move independently. He thought this would help him to steer better.

Like a giant red bird the man stood atop Krossjarðarhamar, and when he cast himself aloft, the whole town turned out to watch the courageous Billhús fool.

Proudly he floated over the house in Høggeil and over Ergisstova and down toward the cemetery. Occasionally, they could hear him shout—not cries for help, but the joyful cries of a flying chieftain.

His wingspan was a good ten feet long, and like a playful broom the shadow whisked away the heaps of anxiety time had deposited in the Sumbingur's consciousness. He had often told his fellow townsmen that people were made of both earthly and heavenly stuff and that one day he would prove it.

And now he sailed above the town, followed by gleeful and disbelieving eyes.

Suddenly, Hoff broke off his story and begged her forgiveness, saying that he did not want to exhaust Henrietta at such a time. The story was just so touching, its tone quite H. C. Anderson-esque.

Henrietta knew the story well, knew it inside and out, since it was one of her own. But she did not want to say that now. Still, it made her happy that Pole had been moved by it, and that his club friends had allowed him to tell it.

She had written several stories the summer her cousin, Fióla Kjelnes, lived with them in the Quillinsgarður house, and as she handed Hoff his hat, she remembered that the wind had swept the Billhús man away. Oh Jesus, she thought. The Billhús man had sailed around the globe. He had floated over forests where trees yielded oranges and other exotic fruit, and he had floated over cities that shone during the night. She told Fióla about bridges held up by iron cables as thick as your arm, and about churches built on high piles. She told the girl about red people who danced the rain down from heaven, and about yellow people who ate their food with sticks like the ones Faroese women used to knit sweaters.

She wove fragments from her scattered reading into her stories, and three or four were born right there at the bedside.

Personally, Henrietta liked the story about the seal woman from Agrar best. In her day there was a little circus on Suðuroy, and on Twelfth Night the circus clown hid himself behind some large rocks on the beach and watched the seal woman's delightful dance. It was not, however, the seal woman herself that interested him, but rather her sealskin, which she removed before she danced. Carefully, the clown removed his motley garb, including the red cardboard nose people always laughed at, and which ensured he was never truly happy. He did not want to be a clown anymore, so he slipped into the sealskin and swam away from the beach. The two children waited for their mother in the den, but great was their sorrow when they realized it was not their mother wearing the skin.

Fióla did not want to hear the rest of the story. She called the woman an impudent seal and would much rather hear the story of the Billhús man one more time. That story was tragic in just the right way, and he was so very high up in the air when he died.

For years he flew lifelessly around the world. Birds ate his flesh and laid eggs in his skull, hatching as cheerfully in the empty eye sockets as they would in Dahlerup's starling nest boxes. Storks and pelicans greeted the skeleton with their fine clattering when their paths crossed. When he flew past open town windows, people folded their hands and thanked God for angels. Museums in large cities offered huge rewards to anyone who could capture the skeleton, and clever artists attempted to sketch the unknown airman for the front page of major newspapers. Grass and moss grew between his fingers, and since up high it is always summertime, small beetles and berries thrived in the moss.

One morning the people of Sumba saw something floating at the beach's edge, and when they waded out with ropes and a dredge, they recognized the remains of the Billhús man.

The Sumbingurs were glad that their townsman had returned home at long last. Everyone who could walk followed him to the cemetery, and Fióla said that when she grew up, she would go to Sumba and plant flowers on the brave Billhús man's grave.

The Løbners and Michael Müller

LATER THAT AFTERNOON Adelheid the midwife helped Henrietta prepare Pole's body. They dressed him in the same clothes in which he had married two-and-a-half years ago. Ludda-Kristjan came to take his old friend's measurements, and the widow smiled when he said that a coffin was the second house he had built for Pole.

Ludda-Kristjan had often said that it was a real shame Frú Løbner had never allowed her daughter to live a normal life as a married woman. Adelheid did not disagree with him, but if she were to speak her mind, she understood Frú Løbner. She would not care herself to have a type like Pole for a son-in-law. It was that hole, Tvøroyri, that had taken his spirit, she said.

Ludda-Kristjan did not believe that Pole had lost his spirit, any more than people usually did over the years.

Indeed, Adelheid said, he was a complete pessimist when he returned from Suðuroy.

Ludda-Kristjan did not know what a pessimist was, and Adelheid, who liked to irritate the man, said that a pessimist was the opposite of an optimist.

Ludda-Kristjan lost his temper and told her to stop the pretentious nonsense and speak Faroese.

Pole was just so bullheaded, Adelheid said, that was what she meant. He always knew better than everyone else. And sure, he was entertaining, but there was usually a thread of devilry woven into his merriment.

Ludda-Kristjan and Adelheid were both familiar with the quarrel that had persisted between Emilius Løbner and Nólsoyar-Páll at the turn of the century, and all the years that had passed since the poet's death had not served to mellow Frú Løbner. In that respect she was a true Tórshavnar. She had no problem hating a family and everyone in it for five or six generations back, and if it had been possible to extend that hate into the future, she would have done that, too.

In *The Ballad of the Birds*, and especially in *The Ballad of Gorpland*, Nólsoyar Páll shamelessly belittled Commandant Løbner for cowardice, and the fact that Jákup Nolsøe had a hand in Løbner's belittlement was something she had heard from so reliable a source as the old skipper Michael Müller. The older brother composed the verses and the younger wrote them down, and wherever possible the younger mixed in even more wickedness. When it came to Nolsøe poets, Frú Løbner wanted nothing to do with them. Just seeing the trade director's surly and disagreeable face on Tórshavn's streets was enough to spoil her day.

And the director's son did not even know Latin, so Michael Müller had told her as well. And aside from being impotent, he had no other education besides completing the simple Civil Medical Exam. And if he appealed to rank, well, Frú Løbner could tell Napoleon Nolsøe that she had nothing of which to be ashamed. Not too many years ago she was the country's *Frúa*, the first lady, and mother to both of the Amtmand's children. Every Sunday for years she and Emilius had walked up the church aisle, and when Ludvig was big enough to sit still in the gallery, they started taking their son with them to church.

Michael Müller had been one of the Løbners' few friends, and he was also Henrietta's godfather.

Michael was a clergyman's son from Hvalba and had left the country as a young man. After the English bombardment of Copenhagen in 1807, he was among those who received a letter of marque from the king, and he captained several privateers as long as the Napoleonic war lasted.

Following the Treaty of Kiel, the English occupation of the Danish West Indies ended, and for a few years Michael sailed the isles. He was chief helmsman aboard the *Jakobs Stige*, and for a time he also captained the ship. Accordingly, he worked closely with Danish officials in Christianssted and Charlotte Amalie and saw that the attitude of these officials regarding slavery was not dissimilar to that of officials in Tórshavn. And he told the Løbners as much: "In your eyes, the riffraff of Tórshavn are like white negroes who don't have much use."

Michael later wrote a work characterized by Niels Winther as: "A flower amid the young Faroese national fauna." The work was extensively titled: *The Faroese Foundation for the Support of Spiritual Education, Useful Invention, and Helpful Organization on the Faroes for the Promotion of Young People Who Strive to Prepare Themselves through Education for Theological or Juridical Positions on the Faroes as Well as for Support in Other Scientific Disciplines and Prizes for Useful Inventions and Beneficial Arrangements, All of the Country's Inhabitants and Youth.*

Michael saw that Frú Løbner was not thriving in her marriage, and at a party one evening he said a few words that straightened her spine immediately. What Tórshavn's church needed, he said, was a Mater Dolorosa. Frú Løbner did not exactly know what that meant, but as Michael explained she sat still and listened.

He said he had nothing against the pastors taking helm and making necessary church-related decisions. However, the church's true authority did not rest with a bunch of distinguished gentlemen in chasubles and miters. The church ought to be more expansive than that and reflect life's source, and the name of that source was the Mother. He meant the Virgin Mary who had carried Jesus Christ beneath her breast, and had followed him down the terrifying road to Golgotha, and who was also there when her son was taken down from the cross. The road to Golgotha was named *Via Dolorosa*, and that could mean *the way of suffering* or *the way of pain*, and therefore Christ's mother had earned the beautiful and tragic name Mater Dolorosa.

Frú Løbner suddenly asked if Michael was Catholic; the question completely surprised him. As he surveyed the other guests in the living room, he said that one did not discuss such matters aloud in the Faroes, but since she had asked with a pure heart, he would answer her in the same spirit. Yes, he was a Catholic to his innermost soul! European history's greatest tragedy had been the Reformation. "In my eyes," Michael said, "Martin Luther was the Church's black angel." He had driven out the Virgin Mary, and in her place he set up a false nun by the name of Katharina von Bora, whom he had also married. The fact that *Bora* rhymes with *whore*, and brings to mind the great harlot of Revelation, well, that could not be a complete coincidence!

Frú Løbner sat straight as a candle. In that moment she could have kissed Michael. The words reached a barren place in her heart, and out of that desolation now flowed a small stream. That was how it felt. The sound of the stream was mild and peaceful, and it swallowed the feelings of inferiority under which she had suffered for years, ever since she and Emilius had moved in together. After they married, their relationship had changed. She never understood why, but everything was just different.

"What would you do in the King's city?" Emilius asked when she begged leave to accompany him to Copenhagen. She was obviously not capable of strolling in crinoline down Kongens Nytorv, much less conversing with anyone. She must not imagine that cultured Copenhageners were interested in hearing about her past as Júst á Húsum's milkmaid. Her place was in Tórshavn and there she must remain until her hourglass was run.

It is hard to protect yourself against such injurious words. She could not do much against her husband anyway, and when he left the country she was greatly relieved to escape his determined and callous denigration.

His departure, however, was not without a price. Frú Løbner was forced to surrender the privileges that came with being the country's Frúa. She moved out of the Amtmand's House and she lost her dignified seat at church. But most painful of all was that Emilius took little Ludda with him to Copenhagen.

That sorrow followed her her entire life.

Frú and Frúgvin Løbner

FRÚ AND FRÚGVIN Løbner, the mother-daughter pair, were a permanent city feature and every afternoon they could be seen walking down Laðabrekka and crossing the bridge toward Tórshavn. Sometimes they also made their way down to the old Nevtolsbrúgv, disappeared into Sandskot Alley, and then from Gongin they headed up Klokkaragøta and emerged onto Bringsnagøta.

Most often, though, their path followed the Havnará, and Henrietta had often remarked to her mother—in truth, she had repeated it hundreds of times over, sometimes while wagging a finger—that a city without a real river was worthless. London had the Thames, the Donau flowed through both Vienna and Budapest, and every morning ferries loaded with vegetables, fruits, and meat docked along the riverbanks in the French capital. The Havnará, of course, was smaller and in every way insignificant on the great world map. Nonetheless, the stream was useful for cooking and washing, and it fulfilled its civic duty with the same dignity as the much larger rivers.

Every day the women walked to Stóradamm to fetch water for their households, and in good weather they washed their clothes on the scoured rocks below the pool. Frú Løbner always bid them good morning and her daughter often said: "Good Lord, Mother, you can hardly walk you're so busy greeting people. One day you're going to trip and then who will roast fricadelles at Quillinsgarður?"

The mother patted her daughter's hand, saying that they were both among the luckiest inhabitants in the Danish kingdom.

Along the Havnerá, whose clear water ripples through the city, are gardens. These gardens are unusually attractive and well-kept. You especially notice the slender willows and golden chains, which during the summer and sometimes into the fall bow over the river, so that the large, yellow flower bunches brush and float on the water's surface.

This agreeable description is owed to the nostalgic Hanus Andreassen, and it was this very sight that met the Løbner pair every summer morning. Frú Løbner had planted some of those gold chains herself during her years as Amtmand's wife, and each tree had some small history, which Henrietta of course knew inside and out.

Emilius loved pot-roasted chicken, or coq au vin, as he delightedly called the dish. They planted their first gold chain the same year they got their hen house.

Of course, most people tended to dislike chicken; the meat was white and not unlike human flesh. Were it not for their eggs, none of these strange birds, which God has punished with flightlessness, would have made their way to the country.

The reference to human flesh had to do with the Dutch frigate *Edvin van der Sar*, which had been dashed against the cliffs by Mjóvanes on Suðuroy in 1743. Frú Løbner lamented that she was related to the Syðrugøtu Cannibal, as she called Líggja's farmer. He made cut halibut bait from the washed-up Dutch sailors, and it was rumored he had skinned one or two bodies and kept the salted meat in barrels. In any case, apparently the meat was both unusually white and just as dark as chicken.

Every time her mother brought up chickens, Henrietta asked why God was so cruel as to deny them flight. And her mother answered, as she had so often before, that maybe it was not a matter of punishment. Maybe when God created man on the sixth day, there was a little bit of white material left over, and from that clump he made a chicken and a rooster. Unfortunately, though, there was only enough material for two incomplete hopp-hopp birds.

Frú Løbner also knew that people on Mykines considered chickens to be foul-weather birds. In 1761 the Stovu farmer got a few hens from the cook aboard the French warship *Fleurs de Lys*. The ship had participated in the great American war and on the way home to France they bought a couple of oxen and some mutton from the Mykiners. And weather that summer and fall was the worst, since the Katla volcano had rained black ash over the islands. Once a northeaster brought a tornado roaring through town, and the Gallic poultry were swept up into the whirlwind, the hens left to live out their short and cheerless lives on Víkini.

When they reached the old secondary school, Frú and Frúgvin Løbner followed the river down toward Vágsbotnur, where they sat and rested on a piece of driftwood beneath Toku-Sigvald's boathouse before heading home.

Frú Løbner, who had once been a large and stately woman, had grown hunched over the years, and had lost most of her hair. The bones of her forehead and skull jutted out, and her aged skin hung in bags beneath her chin and cheekbones. Sharp eyes glinted beneath her red-rimmed and lashless eyelids. Her teeth, however, were intact, and she thanked God for that. At home she always wore a headscarf, but when she walked through the city with her daughter, she usually wore a bonnet, which she decorated with a cotton rose or perhaps with a fine feather.

Courtly Love

THEN CAME THE day when Frú Løbner realized that her beloved child and the director's son were more than friends.

The old woman tried to hinder the relationship, but her time as sole authority over her daughter had passed. Henrietta placed a forefinger against her mother's lips and, with a smile, said: *shhh, Mama.*

It was also what she did at Føroya Amts Bókasavni, Tórshavn's library, when half-drunk, foreign fishermen tumbled through the door, or when that sly sneak Skeggin Pól said that he had come to Tórshavn to woo *so fair a bride* to his rich farmland. Then she also said *shhh*, and she did it with such sweetness that the dwarf from Leynar sighed audibly.

Henrietta and Napoleon first met at the library, but the better part of a year passed before the acquaintanceship took a more serious turn. It also felt a little strange to be addressed as *Frúgvin Løbner.* It sounded so formal, almost ludicrous, but nonetheless it suited Henrietta. She admired the courtly form of address, which she recognized from literature, mostly from Walter Scott's historical novels, but also from the heart-gripping stories about the knight Don Quixote.

Of course, after they had gotten to know each other better, Henrietta recognized the few drops of sarcasm that pervaded Pole's courtly form of address. Pole, for example, thought that youth and the first years of manhood were romance's rehearsal years. Not before a man or woman was over 35 or 40 could one speak of real love. Only then did they realize that bodily fluids were the waters on which love's hopeful ships sailed their rough seas, struck bottom, and more often than not, smashed apart and sank. Mature love's job was to seek more mild, sun-warmed waters, and that task could only be accomplished by adults.

The Officer, the Godfather, and More on Courtly Love

HENRIETTA HAD ONLY been with one man besides Pole, and that was many years ago. It was the evening of Amtmand Pløyen's farewell feast. Henrietta was twenty-two years old and had danced with an officer from one of the warships anchored in the bay. Candles shone from the small glass containers hanging throughout the Amtmand's garden; they had danced several dances, and when her mother left for home, Henrietta agreed to take a stroll with the courteous gentleman.

They kissed and she enjoyed his warm caresses. She allowed him to touch her breasts, and she shivered with pleasure when he kissed and nibbled along the curve of her neck. He said he was a hot bull-seal and longed to swim into her cave. Henrietta was charmed by the beautiful words. The only problem was, she dared not open the cave.

When he unbuttoned his pants, she did as he asked, she took his hard erection between her fingers. His member was large and warm as newly baked bread. She took him in both hands and felt the veins pulsing against her fingertips. It smelled rather like shellfish, and she felt the urge to touch it with her tongue, but did not dare. Soon the blue veins began to pulse, she saw a hole open in the red head, and semen shot out onto her wrist and embroidered sleeves. The discharge was thick as cream, and in the cream there was a faint bluish stripe. But the officer was not finished, the semen kept welling out of him. He rode her hands like a dog, his knees buckled more and more, and his neck sank deep between his shoulders.

Afterward he begged her shamefaced to excuse his importunate desire. He dried her wrist and sleeve with a pocket handkerchief, saying that all the months at sea were simply unbearable.

With a polite nod, Henrietta accepted his apology, but the magic of the stroll had disappeared, and she simply wanted to go home.

No man had touched her body since that time. She had touched herself of course, during some periods quite a bit. But she liked walking barefoot in the garden, and when possible letting the wind touch her bare skin, and if having the wind caress her breasts qualified as a sex life, then her great lover had been the garden wind. She enjoyed washing the dirt from her toes and toenails at the river's edge, and she could sit for long periods of time watching her feet in the clear water. Foam pearls gathered on her calves, her light hair glistened, and her veins looked like thin blue lines beneath the skin. In the pool beneath Svartifossur, and also out on Sandá, she had ventured a couple of times to lift her skirts up around her waist and let the cool water embrace her underside, but only after she was sure no one was around.

No, that was not true. One other man had touched her.

Almost two years after her stroll with the officer, her mother sent her to Michael Müller's house on Undir Kjallara with two broiled guillemots. He had grown old and feeble, and when his goddaughter knocked, he was looking across the bay through the porthole he had built in the gable.

Michael was an exceptionally ugly man, and one time Jákup Nolsøe told about a ship he had seized, about how the sailers immediately surrendered because they thought it was the Devil himself come aboard.

Henrietta was convinced that his ugliness lay in the incongruity between his eyes and his mouth. His unusually large, brown eyes came down to his cheeks, and if his mouth had been equally large, people would probably have assumed he was of negro or Jewish origin. That was not so uncommon, at least not abroad. However, Michael's mouth was tiny, no bigger than a bunghole on a small barrel, and his lips were also narrow.

Now he talked exclusively about dying, said he probably would not last the year, and that he had already spoken to Ludda-Kristjan about building him a coffin. He had always loved life. His childhood in Hvalba and certainly his life at sea. He shrugged, and said Henrietta should recall he had sailed as far away as China for silk and tea, and that in the great city of Canton it was foretold to him he would see a marvelous sight before he died.

He cocked his head. His huge eyes glinted heatedly as he asked his goddaughter if she would be benevolent enough to fulfill his last wish.

Henrietta sensed immediately it concerned something special, and she asked what his last wish was.

Michael answered he would like to see her rosebud. He had no other wish on this earth than to be allowed to see the petals of her glory.

And the words were direct. It was as if the old skipper had readied himself for his final journey and so had no reason to mince his words. If luck were with him, he would be gratified; were his wish denied, then the hell with it.

For a split second Henrietta was profoundly confused and wanted only to toss the broiled guillemots to the floor and run. But as she looked at the old man, she was forced to shake her head, and with a smile she simply said: *oh, gubbi, gubbi.*

She sat on the bench before the fire, bent over, grabbed her skirt hems and pulled them, one after the other, over her shapely thighs. Like other Faroese women in the 1840s, she had no undergarments, and when she had hiked the last skirt up to her stomach, she realized her hands were trembling slightly.

Michael slowly crossed the floor. Rheumatism plagued him so that he could hardly walk, and he more or less skidded to the bench.

He braced his elbows against her knees and polished his glasses on one of her skirts.

Oh, how divine, oh how divine! he kept repeating while he enjoyed the sight. He was allowed to graze it with his hand. At that he closed his eyes and his whole body shook. He crept closer to the bench, pressed his bearded cheek against her tuft and inhaled, as if trying to fathom in which gardens she had walked.

That was all he could take. The old man began to cry. He said that the Chinese seer had been right, now he had seen everything he had to see in this life, and he was ready to depart.

When his goddaughter felt tears running down into her bushy crevice, she patted him on the head and said, that was enough, now he should go ahead and eat his guillemots.

Yet ever since she and Pole had started talking, she had begun looking at herself in the mirror. It was not something she had often done before.

Her forehead and cheekbones came from the Kjelnes folk, but her narrow chin and nose were her father's. Her lips were also narrow, and the corners of her mouth ended in a small smile. Or was she deceiving herself? Maybe it was just the first lines of spinsterhood that received the dubious honor of being dubbed a smile?

Some nights, when she heard her mother rummaging about in her own room, Henrietta took off her nightgown. And the peculiar thing that sometimes happened was that when she looked at her breasts in the mirror it was like looking at herself through a strange woman's eyes. She desired her reflection, that was what was so odd, and what set her blood aflame. The bristling nipple looked like the firm stamen of the mayweed growing in the gravel by the beach, and the thought of suckling the captivating nipples on herself or another woman made her dizzy.

She also explored the dark and dense growth of hair around her sex, and she liked the way she smelled. She imagined a lighter-skinned woman would have a milder scent, whereas dark-haired women had the powerful, sharp scent of the Valkyries as they tended to Valhalla's fallen warriors.

She also loved to coat herself in her own scent and lick her fingers afterward, just like when eating blubber or fermented cod head. She dreamed about being able to taste herself, or doing the same to another woman.

Desire terrified her. Her hunger was every bit as cannibalistic as her relative's had been when he ate that salted Dutch flesh. She spread her buttocks toward the curtains, shamelessly begging the underwordly to creep in from the great dark and ride her. If they wanted, they could also chew on her intestines, chew them like burdock leaves dipped in cream and sugar.

These attacks overwhelmed her after she and Pole started talking.

Clandestine Love.
Continuation of Courtly Love

ONE SATURDAY AFTERNOON Pole came into the library and asked if Frúgvin Løbner would be so good as to find him *Ode to a Nightingale* by Keats.

It was librarian Jens Davidsen who had asked Henrietta to keep the library open and to run it on Saturdays. She was one of the children whom he had taught to read and write in the thirties, and since he was so overburdened with other work he asked her to take on the responsibility. The library job was an unpaid volunteer position. Henrietta lit the stove, emptied the spittoons and ash trays, and kept the reading room clean and tidy. It was her mother who in 1928 had donated the plot of land upon which Farøya Amts Bóksavn was built, and so it naturally fell to her to mind the collection.

In the 1860s the number of books reached over 5,000. Most of them were donations from libraries in neighboring countries, but also from private sources, both in the Faroes and abroad. Due to the limited space, several hundred books were stacked in boxes up in the attic, while the rest were arranged on shelves according to subject: world history, literary history, theology, astronomy, and so on. Literature took up the most space; Henrietta knew this section by heart.

She told Pole that the library did not own a copy of *Ode to a Nightingale*, which was the truth, but she had a book of Keats's poetry and he could borrow her copy. However—she added this softly—if

Pole liked she would copy the poem out for him. He thanked her. He could not imagine a more beautiful gift than *Ode to a Nightingale* written in her own hand.

Next Saturday Pole was again at the library. He smelled freshly of shaving lotion, and his near exuberance revealed he had been looking forward to this moment.

He said that one evening this last week he had passed by Quillinsgarður and had seen a lovely nymph seated next to a petroleum lamp and writing. Rather teasingly, Henrietta asked why he had not simply come inside, and Pole sighed, saying that had he not been Nólsoyar-Páll's nephew and his father's son, he could not have resisted knocking on the window.

"The dead have too much power," Henrietta replied, and as she said it, she felt the blood rising to her cheeks.

"That's poetry," Pole whispered. Suddenly, he found himself admitting that he had stopped outside of Quillinsgarður many times; in fact, long before he left for Tvøroyri in '52, he had stopped on Laðabrekka and listened while she played piano in the living room.

And Pole was not the only one who paused on Laðabrekka to listen while she played. Other Tórshavnars stopped too, and for a time Laðabrekka was known Music Hill. Sometimes vicious youths played along by banging dried cod heads against the windows or eaves. However, Henrietta was not one to chase children down the street.

Suddenly, she seemed vexed, and Pole, rather confused, asked if he had perhaps said anything wrong.

"No," she answered. "Not at all. But remember, life is a gift, and fifteen years after you listened to me playing the piano in the living room, finally you tell me you enjoyed the music. I mean, why have you never said anything before? Why did it have to be so confounded, that a fifty-year-old quarrel between my father and your uncle prevented you from knocking on my window?"

She smiled and handed him the sheets of paper on which she had written *Ode to a Nightingale*. Their fingers met and two or three long seconds passed before she removed her hand. For the first time they gazed at each other with the rather forlorn eyes that characterize mature love, and when Pole saw that the verses had essentially been calligraphied, he again took her hand, carefully pressed his lips to her fingers, and thanked her.

Then he added in a faltering voice: "I'm an old man."

"We're both middle-aged."

He smiled and quoted the nightingale poem's final words: *Do I wake or sleep?*

"I don't know what you've been doing these last years," Henrietta answered. "But I've been sleeping, and I don't want to do that anymore."

Henrietta marked a new chapter in Napoleon's life. When he left Tvøroyri in 1858, and up until 1865, he held the post of Landkirurg. In 1865 the parliament members succeeded in driving Dahlerup out of the country, and since everyone believed Pole owed his position to Dahlerup, who had vacated the Faroes, Pole also felt the changing of the tide.

After his stint as Landkirurg, he resumed seeing patients in his old consultation room at Nólsoyarstova. He had become a solitary man who liked to wet his throat with gin.

Yet in the summer of 1869, the same year he turned sixty, he and Henrietta traveled south through Europe and stayed three weeks in Rome. Frú Løbner died in 1872, and although they followed old tradition and did not marry until the year of mourning was up, that year was the happiest of their coexistence.

They lived in their separate houses, but still ate dinner together, enjoying each other's company, and sometimes they spent the night.

Henrietta was an accomplished pianist and had taught herself to read music. Beyond the usual études, she had also tackled more complicated works, for example, Beethoven's *Moonlight Sonata,* and she could play some of Bach's simpler *Goldberg Variations.* Nonetheless, her favorite composer was Mozart and she owned all his operatic overtures transcribed for piano. Together with Traber, the violin teacher, and the young Dia við Stein, she occasionally held musical evenings at Quillinsgarður, small gatherings that Pole called a mild entry into the evening of his life.

When Henrietta sold the Quillinsgarður house to Sigrid and Poul Niclasen and moved to Nólsoyarstova, she took the Quillinsgarður piano with her, and so generous was Pole that he gave Nólsoyarstova's old piano to the talented Dia við Stein.

The House Altar

ACCORDING TO FIÓLA Kjelnes, Henrietta and Pole's relationship lost some of its warmth after they married and moved into the same house. For years they had been lovers beneath a narrow crescent moon, as she put it, and now that they had the full moon, not to mention the sun, it was as if the strong lightwaves washed away the shadows of mystery.

The first time Henrietta experienced Pole's terrible rage was on one of the first days of their cohabitation. Among the kitchen items and other things she had brought with her from her childhood home was a pastel drawing of her father. Of course, she thought the drawing might create some tension. She knew full well Pole had no use for "Hr. Amtmaður and Commandant Emilius Marius Georgius von Løbner," as he tended to call her father. But Henrietta and Pole were both adults, yes they were, and they could talk things through together.

Generally speaking, Løbner was held in exceptionally low esteem on the Faroes, and in the second volume of *Tórshavn's History*, Jens Pauli Nolsøe and Kári Jespersen offer a theory on why, historically speaking, he was so poorly regarded.

The year that Løbner took office was otherwise the year of an event that would prove exceptionally significant for the Faroes. For eighty years the

Danish king had not been involved in a true war, and that made it easy to become Commandant of the Faroes, but in 1800 everything changed completely.

As mentioned, Løbner came to the Faroes in 1801, and the animosity toward him, or perhaps one could say, the animosity toward Løbner harbored by Faroese nationalists, was essentially tied to 1808, the war year, when the British warship *Clio* came to Tórshavn and destroyed all of Skansin's defenses.

Everyone expected that there would be a general call to duty in order to resist the enemy with force, and people heard that lead bullets were being cast in Kaldbak for this purpose, but what was the Commandant doing while all this was happening? He was at Skansin, true, along with his regimentals, though these he had buried in a sack. Instead, he was wearing a rough, gray overcoat—which prompted the English Captain Baugh and his people to call him The Monkey. His command was: "Children, lay down." The enemy, who marched into Skansin without the least resistance, immediately hoisted the English flag, destroyed and nailed up the cannons, robbed the inventory of everything useful, distributed the goods to whoever wanted them, and finally blew up the powder chamber.

That, at least, was how Jákup Nolsøe told it. But Henrietta did not put much stock in her father-in-law's words. They seemed too frivolous and did not suit the solemn dignity that otherwise characterized the director.

Perhaps the Skansinmen could have damaged the *Clio*, perhaps they even could have sunk the 380-ton ship and killed the 200 soldiers on board; she had no way of knowing. Yet of this she was certain: No one who challenged the British fleet escaped unpunished. And the director knew that as well. In 1807, the British bombarded and burned Copenhagen. Why should Tórshavn not have suffered a similar fate?

Such thoughts passed through Henrietta's head as she held the pastel drawing. As long as she could remember, the drawing had hung in Quillinsgarður's parlor. In truth, the word *drawing* was something of a misnomer. Instead, it was the case of a small house altar, something to which she and her mother had turned throughout the years.

She had been very young when she learned who the man in the picture was, and she could not understand why her father did not just step out of the drawing. Other fathers talked to their children, and some told them stories or sung to them. One time she had cut a ladder from paper and glued it to the frame's rim, and with a child's hope, she thought her father could use the ladder to climb down. But it did not help. She repeatedly tempted the drawing with something sweet, but the same thing always happened. Her father remained enclosed in the frame, and every time she looked at him, she saw the same indulgent smile.

Finally, she accepted that hers was one of Tórshavn's silent fathers, a particular type of man who was only there when you remembered or dreamed about them. She knew there were other children in the city who had silent fathers. One had gone out to fish and never returned, and another was *útideyður*, that is, someone who had perished while journeying between one village and another, particularly due to the weather.

Sometimes she did dream about her father, and after such a dream she had all sorts of new things to tell the picture.

In short, daily life would lack something if her father's picture were not hanging up, and a man like Pole ought to understand that.

She hung the picture over the small sideboard in the living room and hoped for the best.

Yet hope became shame.

When it came to Emilius Marius Georgius von Løbner, Pole was just as viscious as her mother had been when denigrating those Nolsøe poets.

The devil seized Pole. He refused to have a portrait in his living room of the worst official to date the Danes had ever sent to govern the Faroes. The Commandant was a military and civilian zero. Did Henrietta know where zero came from? That right there was the Indian Brahmin's contribution to world culture. And we should thank them for it. Tórshavn had its own kind of Brahmin, the so-called Brahmadells, and when it came to morality and dignity, even the most witless of them was lightyears beyond the Commandant.

Henrietta struggled to pipe up with the fact that it was her father and, if nothing else, Pole ought to respect her feelings. Yet he refused to listen.

Pole called Løbner an ignoramus and asked, rhetorically, if she knew the distinguishing characteristic of an ignoramus who was both commandant and amtmand. It was that he lowered other Tórshavnars—yes, in principle the rest of humanity—to the absolute lowest possible moral state, namely, where the ignoramus himself existed.

There was only *one* hero during the Faroes' famine years, and that was his own uncle, Páll. And who made it hot as hell for him? Why, that genetically retarded whorehound, Commandant Emilius von Løbner.

In that context, he would like to remind Henrietta that she had a half-brother in Skopen. Of course she knew, it was Jens Winningsted, the shoemaker. Pole added, however, that she should be grateful that her family was dying out, because her grandfather, the king, was a psychopath.

"The king? What are you talking about?"

"I'm talking about Christian the Seventh, Europe's greatest psychopath. The woman you're named after let that monstrosity penetrate her at Augustenborg in 1765, and the result was the bastard, your honorable father. You're a carrier of royal insanity, that's what you are, and be thankful you never sent any children into the world. The result would've been a genetic, cerebral catastrophe."

For a while longer, he showered curses onto the unfortunate Løbner's head, until finally he pointed to the pastel drawing and ordered his wife to remove that shameful blight.

Henrietta heard his voice and saw his waving arms and his bright red face, but she had lost her nerve. She reached for her Italian handbag and clasped it to her breast.

Oh, Satan in blackest Hell, Pole thought, as finally he realized how severely he had lost control and how deeply he had wounded his wife.

He had seen her like this only one time before, on the day her mother was buried. She had sat in the parlor at Quillinsgarður and clutched the bag as if it were a life preserver.

Now she opened it up and began to take out the contents. She handled each object as if it were a precious artifact worthy of being examined and classified and perhaps put on public display.

Pole bought her the handbag when they were in Rome. The bottom and both end pieces were made of light brown leather, the sides were made of a woven black cloth, and the top could be closed with a long, handsome brass lock.

Carefully, she took out the coin purse and laid it on the table, but then she picked it up again, pressed it to her cheek, and tilted her head. In size the purse was no bigger than the back of her hand, and when it was opened, it divided into two compartments; the silk-covered divider had a thin leather strip on top. She kept a few coins in one compartment, the other held the white milktooth Fióla had given her and the ring her father sent as a confirmation gift in 1839. The tooth was a lucky charm, a Faroese scarab, and in church she often held the tooth and stroked it with her fingers. Now she kissed the ring and put it back in the compartment with the tooth. There were some hair clips and two silk ribbons in one pocket of the handbag, and the other had a comb, a powder compact with a mirror in the lid, and a nail file. When the nail file's old shaft had splintered, Henrietta had asked Ludda-Kristjan to make a new one. The new shaft was made from a whale's tooth and was kept in place by two riveted copper nails. She also kept a candy tin in her purse, and Pole liked to tease her about it, saying the tin was the typical handbag inventory of an aging, aristocratic spinster. Still, he was always glad when she offered him a piece, particularly when she placed the brown, glinting candy on his tongue and said that Pole and his father were the sweetest men north of the Elben.

In the latter half of the nineteenth century, women tended to bring handwork along when they visited each other. Henrietta was no exception to this rule. Yet whereas most women knitted sweaters and stockings for their husbands and children, she kept a crochet hook and some fine thread in her handbag.

However, the handbag's most valuable item was an address book. She did not really use it for addresses, however; in fact, addresses took up very little space. Instead, Henrietta collected proverbs, and her collection became the foundation for A. C. Evensen's *A Reader for Young Children* that was printed in 1906, the same year that Henrietta died.

When Pole returned home late that evening, he saw that the pastel had been taken down, and a vase of flowers set before the empty space.

At least once a week the vase received new flowers. Early in the spring it was meadow daisies, purple saxifrage, and soft lady fern.

In May and June, buttercups, fireweed, and mayweed stood in the vase, and sometimes also dandelions, whose white, sensitive wigs only barely tolerated her breath. As summer wore on, there were violets, geraniums, ragged robins, and forget-me-nots. The flowers brightened up the place and gave an almost supernatural glance to her father's memory.

Løbner in the air, she whispered. Løbner in the vase, she smiled. Life is Løbner, she said, shaking with laughter, as she decorated the vase.

Pole never mentioned the pastel again, and he had to accept that the vase had become Nólsoyarstova's new house altar.

When the hawkweed died in August and fall was at the door, Henrietta put heather clusters in the vase. From the reddish-green brush she hung small cutouts of animals and mythical creatures and of amusing flowers that bloomed only in her mind. The cutouts hanging from sewing thread were reminiscent of what people would later call Christmas decorations.

Torshavn's Workers Union

IN 1882, JUST before Easter, Obram úr Oyndarfjørði's schooner *Haabet* docked at Tórshavn.

Aside from cargo transport, Obram also ran a business in Tórshavn that had additional branches north in Oyndarfjørður and west in Sørgvágur. In his younger days, the man had learned housebuilding from Ludda-Kristjan, and he put in a bid to build the new Amtmand's House only after many long conversations with his old master. Obram got the job, but the work team now lacked building material: the thick, internal beams, as well as boards for floors, walls, and ceilings, not to mention the roof tiles, were all left aboard the *Haabet*.

Havnarfolk had long since baptized the half-finished residence on Glaðsheyggjur "Amtmansborg," or Amtmand's Castle. The building's high stone walls and gables, its various additions, and the square tower from which you could view the entire city, made it a true castle, at least by Faroese standards.

The window apertures in the tower and living room were appreciably larger than those in the church, and each one terminated in a point at a beautiful capstone and was surrounded by finely worked stone ornamentation.

The Danish architect Hans Christian Amberg had designed the castle and an Icelandic stonecutter was overseeing the construction. Otherwise, the work crew was Faroese.

The building stones had been excavated from Glaðsheyggjur. Holes were drilled and wedges placed, and hammer strikes sung throughout the city. Occasionally, large cliffs were blown up using black gunpowder, and a tipper wagon ran between the expanding quarry and the construction site carrying the finely hewn stone.

The children of Tórshavn had never seen a tipper wagon, and when the driver, Sámal á Kák, sometimes allowed two or three or them to ride the fifty fathoms between the quarry and the construction site—oh!, a technological journey of the rarest kind.

Most of the rocks could be carried by hand, but they were still too heavy to be lifted overhead. As a result, the construction site had a hoist system, and two men usually operated the pulley, heaving the blocks and rock fragments and other building material up to the men on the platforms.

Easter was only six days away, and Obram ordered the work crew to help get the *Haabet* unloaded before the holiday. The agreement was that the men would work Sunday and would receive a bonus in addition to their hourly wage, on the condition, however, that they emptied the ship before the holiday.

And the men threw themselves to work. Two old, refitted, and reinforced ten-men boats, as well as a thirty-eight-foot lighter, which they called the *Omba*, and which Obram had acquired in Norway, sailed back and forth between the ship and the unloading dock at Bryggjubakka. Whereas the ten-men boats were rowed, the *Omba* had sails and a rudder. She carried the planks and beams, and the majority of the items were unloaded by hand. The thirty-foot-long beams were heavy and unwieldy, but the ship's gunwale was equipped with rollers that could be used to roll the beams. The ship also had a capstan, and they used it to lift the lime tubs and barrels of petroleum, syrup, and brandy. The *Omba* transported the heavy materials, while the ten-mans took everything that could be carried by hand: flour and sugar sacks, birch bark for the roof, window glass, and other small items.

The unloading dock at Bryggjubakka had a tripod with a crane, and the boom could lift around two skippunds.

Sleep was scarce during the unloading. From the time the sun rose at six o'clock in the morning until it set six days later, there was perpetual traffic back and forth, and it was only after midnight that the items first stacked at the unloading dock were carried to the warehouse basement or up to the shop. The beams were simply stacked outside, though tarpaulins were spread over the better wood.

Despite everything, the men failed to unload the ship on time. The Easter holiday began on Holy Thursday, so on Wednesday night the *Haabet's* hatches were battened down and its storm lamps extinguished.

Obram was in a good mood that evening. He hung his silver-shafted cane on a nail in the warehouse basement and went around with a jug of gin and a glass, serving each man and also offering each tobacco. Two lamps gleamed from beneath the ceiling beams. Wash-tubs and a scale stood in one corner, and an enclosure held several skippunds of carved and salted winter cod ready to be spread on the rocks to dry.

Obram was now over fifty, and although he rarely took part in the actual stonework, he had a hand in all the preparations. Work was his life, and if everything was going well, then he was a satisfied man.

Even if they had not been able to empty the ship, the offer of a bonus still stood, Obram said. The bonus, however, would not be paid in money, but in goods. Most of the men understood this, and even if they did not understand, it was not common to object once Obram úr Oyndarfirði had spoken.

This evening that tradition was broken.

Sámal á Kák, who had been sitting on a lime tub smoking, suddenly spoke. He said that it was not right, after everyone had struggled through Friday, Saturday, they had even broken the Holy Sabbath, and then had continued Monday and Tuesday and Wednesday, and now that they had worked their asses off, they find out that they could expect their bonus in goddamned goods. That was no way to treat someone.

Sámal was Ludda-Kristjan's nephew and he was as short-fused as his uncle. He sat with his legs crossed and during his tirade he dropped his pipe to the floor.

"But maybe that's the new worker politics you and the bailiff and Løbner's salt-and-pepper cunt are trying to introduce," he said. "What fine people you are. On the morning of Good Friday 1800 years ago, the Romans beat Jesus, they blackened his eyes and kicked him in the balls, and on that same day you have the nerve to offer us goods mice have been fucking in all winter. Does every worker in Tórshavn have the word *idiot* written across his forehead?"

The boatmen and the work crew all stared at Sámal aghast, and they looked from him to Obram. Tobacco still glowed in their pipes, but they had stopped smoking. Over twenty men were present, and they had never heard such impudent words spoken, at least not in Obram's presence. And the speech was unrehearsed, that was what was so strange. Those stallion-hoofed words simply broke from Sámal's mouth.

Obram set down the gin jug and walked over to the nail where his cane hung. He felt insulted and humiliated; something like this had never happened before.

Still, such words were not entirely unexpected. Lately, Obram thought he had sensed a certain hostility directed toward his person. Not that people had held back or pussy-footed around before. Well, some people certainly did that, especially the father and son from Hvítanes, the father especially. The old man was probably consumptive, the way he coughed, and he more or less expected his son to do the work for both of them. The old man was Obram's informant, and when he repeated tales from the construction site, Obram always had to turn away on account of his fetid breath.

It was from the old Hvítaner that he first heard the work crew was thinking of demanding a higher wage.

The news was completely unexpected. Indeed, it shocked Obram to the core. He had come to Tórshavn in 1841 and still remembered what it was like under the Royal Trade Monopoly, when the fishing rod was a Tórshavnar's livelihood. Conditions had never been better than they were today, and twice a month he personally counted between twenty-five and thirty kroners into each worker's hand.

One evening Obram asked his wife if she had sensed any hostility from people.

Gerd was from Bergen, and although she had lived in Tórshavn for many years, she still spoke Norwegian. They met when Obram was working and attending technical school in Bergen.

At first Gerd was surprised to hear her husband ask such an odd question. It was unlike him. But since she thought his voice held an edge of true anxiety, she chose her words with care.

She said you tended to find in people whatever you were looking for. If you went looking for good-will and benevolence, you would find it. If you went searching for deviltry, there was certainly no lack of it. In her opinion, Tórshavnars were pleasant and orderly folk, and they were also sulky and difficult. In short, they were just as they had always been, at least for the years she had lived in Tórshavn. What she was trying to say was that they were *heiðursmenn*, men of honor. If something had changed, it was thanks to Ewald Hjøstrup, the young bailiff.

Gerd laid a hand on her husband's arm and told him to avoid

suspicion of those people the bailiff was out to get. Otherwise, before he knew it, he would be seeing trolls in broad daylight.

For several months, the bailiff had namely been working to found a so-called labor union. The idea was new to the Faroes, but it was not uncommon in Denmark and farther south on the continent. Old Europe was changing, and the battle for the soul of the steadily growing middle class intensified year after year. On May 5, 1872, Hjøstrup had participated in the famous *Slaget på Fælleden*, the Battle of the Commons. Well, more than participated. The twenty-seven year-old Hjøstrup stood at the head of the police force that arrested Louis Pio, Harald Brix, and Poul Geleff, the three leaders of the Danish socialist workers' movement. Although he said nothing about it, the incident filled him with a reasonably cold satisfaction. He had ripped the German-sown socialist weed from home ground, and he was proud of it.

And Hjøstrup was an educated man; he had a way with words, especially when equipped with a rapt listener like Obram. As he explained to the Oyndfirðingur, a new and ravenous class of worker beasts had already gotten their teeth into Europe's roasted bacon. These demanding units sprouted from the noise and soot of the continent's factories. These beasts ate, slept, and bred in port-city hovels, signed aboard schooners and modern dampers, and their hands shoveled coal into the burning jaws of locomotives, which connected the continent from the Baltic Sea to the Bosphorus Strait.

The new Europe had already made its appearance in literature and Hjøstrup took that for an ill omen. He had closely read the scandalous novel *The Red Room* by the young Swede August Strindberg: *And the day will come when things will be worse; on that day we shall come down from the White Mountains with a great noise, like a waterfall, and ask for the return of our beds. Ask? We shall take them! And you shall lie on wooden benches, as I've had to do, and eat potatoes until your stomachs are tight as a drum and you feel as if you had undergone the torture by water, as we . . .*

So threatened the Swede with his quasi-Biblical wording, and Hjø-strup told Obram it was just a matter of time before Faroese workers walked the same path as their fellows in neighboring lands.

Hjøstrup, together with Obram, invited some reliable residents to a meeting, and they had only one agenda—to found Tórshavn's Workers Union. Among those invited were the bookbinder, Hans Niklái Jacobsen, young Pastor Ewaldsen, the doctor's widow, Henrietta Nolsøe, and Sheriff Müller. The Sunman, Pætur úr Kirkjubø, also received an invitation, and he showed up to the first meeting wearing a *stavnhetta* and with a mountian staff in his hand.

The bookbinder wanted to know why no actual workers had been invited, considering the subject was a labor union. Hjøstrup told him that the union's purpose was to produce good and faithful citizens, a task that was best handled by educated people. And Frú Nolsøe was a shining testament to the fact that there was truly a modern-minded leadership here, with women's emancipation also on the agenda. The workers would be enlightened and cultivated, yet it would take time to encourage roses to grow in the outfield.

The Tórshavn's Workers Union saw the light of day in July 1882—the very same union Sámal á Kák had mocked that evening in the basement cellar.

Afterward Sámal á Kák wondered where his audacity had come from, if audacity was even the right word. His tongue was rather loosened by a combination of rage, exhaustion, and gin. And perhaps he also wanted to show his brother-in-law, Tóvó, that he was no weakling. Sámal was married to Ebba and they lived in the old Geil house.

After Obram had set down the jug, he walked slowly toward Sámal. He had taken his cane down from its nail, and the way he gripped the silver shaft made it look like he was about to strike a blow. He stopped before the lime tub and for a moment leaned with all his weight on the cane.

"Why do you have to be a candle-snuffer on such a joyous eve-ning?" he asked Sámal. "What have I done to you, that you're com-paring me to the Romans who bloodied Christ? Is it perhaps a crime to provide Tórshavnars an hourly wage? The city would've seen plenty of lean times without people from the towns and abroad to help you out. Do you see those stacks of fish? Go ahead, smell them. Don't you realize that's the smell of money and progress? Maybe we'll have good weather on Easter Monday, and your wife and chil-dren can spread the fish out on the rocks. Isn't that a good thing? Answer me, Sámal á Kák," Obram suddenly shouted, and his voice was so powerful that the basement's ceiling braces seemed to shake.

Sámal did not know what to say, and he had no time to speak any-way, before Obram shoved the handle of his cane beneath his chin.

"In the future, beware of using such strong words. It's doubtful your shoulders can bear the weight."

"There's nothing wrong with using strong words." The voice came from a gaunt man standing in the doorway. "If the words match the truth, strong words are not only acceptable, but it's one's duty to speak them."

Tóvó strode over to the lime tub to stand next to Sámal. "To be honest, I love strong words, and have ever since I learned my great-grandfather's rhymes. Not to mention since Doctor Pole gave me the Bible. For too long the working man has been like the dust beneath the broom of powerful men. I realize the condition was that we should empty the ship, but this week has been a hard slog. It would befit you to put money on the table."

The men looked at Tóvó í Geil in astonishment. He was the quiet sort who spent his days on a low footstool and bored and wedged. Sometimes you heard him sing about hammer kings, gunpowder barons, and wedge devils, and then a smile would light his otherwise serious face. Now he sounded almost like the Scottish preacher Wil-liam Sloan, who in his terrible sermon on the Kongebrúgv said that no one was born a Christian, and to insist upon it, like some pastors did, was to send people straight to hell.

For a second it seemed Obram was going to respond. Then he walked over to the first lamp, unscrewed the wick, and snuffed the flame. He extinguished the second one, bade the men a good night, and wished them a Happy Easter.

Maundy Thursday Dinner

ALL WEEK TÓVÓ had been looking forward to eating fermented cod heads. He had acquired twelve decent-sized ones from a fisherman, had torn off their gills and stuffed them in a sack behind the house, and for the past couple of days the right odor of decomposition had hung about the bundle.

Ebba and Sámal and their son Martin were coming for dinner, and on Maundy Thursday morning Tóvó took the cod heads down to the stream to wash them and rinse the slime off, and then he carried them back to the house.

Since returning home in 1878, Tóvó had lived in Nils Tvibur's old house on Bringsnagøta, which he now owned. The will Nils wrote when he took over the Ergisstova farm in Sumba made Tóvó heir to his house in Tórshavn. He had written the will in Havn, and ever since it had been kept at the bailiff's office. Tóvó had known nothing about it. Absolutely nothing.

He had been home a few weeks when one day he was summoned to the bailiff's office. Ewald Hjøstrup read the will aloud and then asked Tóvó if perhaps he were related to the deceased.

Tóvó told him the truth: they were not related, but he had known the corporal.

Hjøstrup asked if there was some concrete reason for the unexpected inheritance. Tóvó, however, said he could not think of anything. He had no desire to tell a stranger that thirty years ago Nils had taken him, a miserable boy, beneath his wing, and that his mother and Nils were lovers for a time.

As Hjøstrup spoke, or in the pauses between sentences, he would stroke his upper lip with his thumb and forefinger, and that irritated Tóvó. It was what the sailors did after they had been to the whorehouses on Paradise Street in Liverpool or Schipperstraat in Antwerp—they would lie in the dark of their berth sniffing their fingers. That was not how one should act in a public office, though, not in Tórshavn or anywhere else.

Hjøstrup asked if Tóvó knew that Nils Tvibur had died under suspicious circumstances. The news startled Tóvó, but he did not let it show, he just said, no, he knew nothing about it.

Hjøstrup also wanted to know what Tóvó had been doing out in the world. In fact, he was so impudent that Tóvó finally asked what any of that had to do with the will?

Nothing really, Hjøstrup answered, a bit surprised.

Tóvó asked if he needed to sign any papers, since he had no desire to stand here talking to a stranger about things that did not concern him.

Tóvó was furious when he left the bailiff's office. He was clearly older than the bailiff, but the man had not asked him to sit, even though two empty chairs stood at the desk. But was it the impudent questions that fueled his fury, or was it something else that caused his heart to pound?

No. His emotional turmoil was due to the keys in his pocket and the deed in his hand. His heart was beating as if he had just landed on the king's payroll. He had not expected this. Never in a million years! He had nothing but good things to say about Nils, but that he should inherit the Mosque? No, that Tóvó had never even dreamed of.

And so he wept as he walked back along Bringsnagøta, the tears running unabashedly down his cheeks. It was utterly inconceivable how a friendship between a grown man and a small boy could result in Tóvó being served, so to speak, a house on a silver platter, carried in from realm of death.

And then that arrogant police whelp, God knows where his sticky fingers had been.

Tóvó had another outburst, but this time it was not tears. He clutched the door and doubled over in laughter, and luckily he was alone. He covered his mouth with his hand, but the laughter gushed between his fingers. Finally, he got his merriment under control, was able to fit the key into the lock, and literally stepped into his new house laughing.

At dusk he heard a young seagull call from down the hill, and Tóvó immediately knew it was his nephew. That was how they greeted each other, with bird calls. Whereas Martin primarily sounded like a young seagull or a raven, Tóvó cooed like a dove or murmured like an eider, and occasionally he also clucked like a laying hen. Gentler sounds were his arena. The window was open, and Tóvó answered that playful shriek with a bit of middle-aged hen cluck.

The door led right into the kitchen, and beyond the kitchen was the room where Tóvó slept. In a sea chest at the foot of the bed was a Bible, a Norwegian geography textbook, an almanac, and a volume of poems by an American named Walt Whitman. The chest also held his sailor's tools: sailmaker's gloves, a grease horn with needles, and some stilettos, one made from a whale rib, two made from wood, and an iron one to splice wire with.

On the wall hung a painting he had bought at a little Paris shop. The girl in the painting was wearing a ballet skirt, and from a distance she looked like a flower. The painting was not more than two spans high and a little smaller in width. He had bought the painting for his mother, thinking she might be rather proud to have a pretty dancer hanging on the wall. But by the time Tóvó returned in 1878, his mother was already dead, and the painting remained in the sea chest until he moved into the Mosque. Someone named Edgar Degas had painted it, but Edgar was not in the shop the day Tóvó happened by. He bought the painting with the loose change in his pocket.

And Pole, too, was dead. That grieved Tóvó. They had parted coldly, and that had often plagued Tóvó. During the quarter century he had spent sailing around the world, he had written Pole at least ten letters, most of them in Danish. Pole had given him a Danish bible in 1858 when he signed aboard the Norwegian schooner *Rosendal*, and he found that biblical language suited him when he wanted to say something that came from the heart. Still, he liked Whitman's language even better, and in one letter he wrote in English, Tóvó repeated whole passages of Whitman's poems.

The conversation soon turned to the confrontation in the warehouse basement, and Ebba said that Obram had a long memory. Many days would pass before he forgot the harsh words that had been spoken.

"Perhaps you're right," Tóvó replied. Still, having a long memory was one thing, but being a louse was another. And that was something he had never taken Obram for.

Ebba was sitting on the peat box and had taken out her knitting. Although not yet forty, she was already a nervous woman, and sat and rocked and chewed her lips as she knitted. She had lost her lower front teeth, and while her jaw worked, her lower lip slid into the space between her remaining teeth, sharpening her chin like an old woman's. The corner of her shawl was frequently raised to the corners of her eyes, but it was not for sorrow that she cried. To the contrary, Tóvó's homecoming was the best thing to happen to her in many years. She knitted him stockings and sweaters, and during her evening prayers she thanked God that he had sent her brother home in one piece. No one else in Tórshavn, not one single person, invited her and her little household to dinner. She also thanked God for that.

The relationship with her older brother was not as warm. Lýðar had inherited the old Heimistova farm on Nólsoy, and during the summer Martin normally visited his uncle. He helped with the hay harvest and rowed out to fish with the old Geil boat, which had also ended up at Nólsoy.

Lýðar claimed that George Harrison was Ebba's real father, and insisted that she resembled the Harrisons both in mind and body.

Tóvó dislike hearing his brother talk like that. It was entirely possible, of course, that Oh-my-sweet-Lord had indeed been beneath his mother's skirts; there was little those Scottish baptists would not do once it had occurred to them.

Ebba's fretfulness, however, had more concrete grounds than traits potentially inherited from Fraserburgh. She was married to an alcoholic, and Sámal could be thoroughly unpleasant in a drunken bout. It had been a while, though, since the last binge. Ever since his uncle had gotten him a job with Obram úr Oyndarfirði, he had been as good as dry.

Ebba's foremost affliction had been her mother. In truth, it was a great relief when she died, and that is exactly what Ebba told the pastor the day her mother's coffin was carried from the church. And the pastor nodded. He added that God certainly had a plan when he filled Betta with black visions. His intention had been to test the compassion of her fellow man, and her daughter had stood the trial with the highest marks.

Ebba had also cared for Old Tóvó, in any case after he had gone blind. With him, though, it was completely different. He was so mild and obliging. In his later years, he had become what H. P. Hølund called: *En Thorshavnsk Shaman*. Young mothers visited the Geil house with their newborns and wanted him to lay his shaman hand on their babies' heads, and happy was the mother if he also took the child, laid it on his chest, and stroked his bearded face against the baby's soft chin.

And Tórshavnars were also fond of what they called his verses. And as often happens with valued or even loved words, it was not always easy to tell which were the author's words, and what others might have added or perhaps omitted.

When men sat with their fishing lines, they sometimes recited the verse that Hølund in his survey called "Winter Hymn":

> Fish swim in tears
> tears salty as the sea
> the sea deep as sorrow.
> Oh, you Sweet One,
> give us winter fish.

"Street Hymn" was also popular. *In reality,* H. P. Hølund later wrote, *it was a Tórshavn illiterate who unwillingly introduced a blend of poetic modernism and homegrown lyrics into young Faroese poetry.*

> Birds fly on the wind
> dreams hover in fog
> Wind
> fog
> birds
> dream.
> The heart beats in the bay
> the blood sings in the sky
> Geil swaddled in stars.

Ebba routinely accompanied her great-grandfather to the old pillory up on Kák, where he liked to stand. She often retrieved him after one or two hours, but it also happened that he carefully felt his way home. He knew every stone on Geil and around Kák, and if he fell he would just say that his childhood soil was welcoming his old bones.

But he could be fierce, if not to say terrifying, when he propped himself against the half-rotten post and, with the wind whipping his thin gray locks, shouted out over the housetops:

> Sarakka, Sarakka, Sarakka, Sarakka
> child in the sea
> the blue chick.
> Sarakka, Sarakka, Sarakka, Sarakka
> tread hard
> grip fast
> crumbling cliffs of a broken moon.

Tóvó worked the perforated ladle beneath the cod heads and tried to transfer them whole from the pot onto the wooden dish. They had shrunk in a bit, and their boiled, lopsided smiles seemed outright friendly. He served potatoes next, and Tóvó remembered his great-grandfather once saying that potatoes housed the light from fallen stars. In any case, he meant that the potatoes, which the Norwegian pastor's wife had brought to the Faroes, had a gentle and appealing spirit.

He had cut dried fat into a saucepan; and when Ebba suggested it was rather excessive to also melt the sheep tallow, her brother replied that during his years at sea it was the sheep tallow smell that came back to him whenever he remembered the Faroes.

Each ate with his own small knife, working savory pieces from the cheeks and dipping the potatoes in the melted tallow. Cod heads tend to preclude small talk, and Martin smiled at his mother and father's eager slurping, not to mention Tóvó's. Twice more Tóvó ladled heads onto the dish, and it was not long before the white bones began to emerge, seeming to have forgotten everything to do with their Atlantic origin.

The real dot over the *i*, though, was waiting in the fly cabinet. Earlier in the week, Tóvó had asked Baker Restorff to make a layer cake with pudding below and dried plums on the top. Whatever else went into it Tóvó left to the baker's ingenuity and his craft pride.

He and Restorff ran into each other regularly on the street and conversed on a variety of everyday topics. They always talked about long voyages and foreign customs, and when Tóvó came to pick up the cake this Maundy Thursday, it was no exception.

While Restorff wrapped up the cake, he suddenly said: "Be careful, Tóvó. Obram is a good friend to have, but he makes a terrible enemy."

"Hmm," Tóvó grumbled. "Obram needs to realize that the light of free trade doesn't just shine for him and other layer-cake princes. The light is also meant for workers and sailors."

"Well spoken again," Restorff laughed rather nervously. "I remember your great-grandfather. An excellent man."

Ebba smiled when she saw the beautiful cake. At times she baked crullers and periodically also fancy sugar-bread for special occasions, but she had never even approached such a fine cake. And she told her brother as much.

"Why do you think I asked Restorff to bake this cake?"

"To make your little sister happy, since she's become such an old woman," Ebba replied.

Sámal saw her wipe away a tear, but whether it was her brother's kindness, or perhaps the confrontation in the warehouse basement she had on her mind, that he did not know.

Sámal asked his brother-in-law if he remembered Sára Malena, the Skúvoy witch.

"Are there witches in the Faroes?" Tóvó asked.

Sámal filled his pipe while he told the story of Sára Malena, who a few years ago had been sent to jail, condemned for begging and for stealing knitting yarn. Her first night in jail, a strange thing happened: Judge Øverstrup's cow died. The next night the judge's wife went sleepwalking and took a tumble down the attic stairs, breaking one of her legs.

The judge immediately summoned Doctor Nolsøe, and while the doctor examined and bandaged his wife's leg, he also sent a message to the constable on duty at the jail. He wrote that Sára Malena had spent her last night in Tórshavn and that she should be sent back to Skúvoy as quickly as possible.

"And who do you think stood on the Kongabrúgv with a sack full of sugar, salt, tobacco, and flour for the departing witch? Gerd, Obram úr Oyndarfirði's wife. Obram had sent his wife with those gifts. Trust me. The man is full of superstition. He wouldn't dare to trip up a Brahmadella, and certainly not a Brahmadella's brother-in-law."

A Toast to Deep Respect

ON GOOD FRIDAY, Hjøstrup heard the entire story of the events in the warehouse basement. The two were sitting together in Obram's parlor. The evening red was reflected off one of the glass cupboard doors, and coffee cups and cognac glasses stood on the table. Cigarette smoke drifted slowly toward the cracked window, and the only sound to be heard was when the maid knocked, curtsied to the men, and refilled their coffee cups.

Obram and Gerd were childless, and shortly before the holiday Gerd had traveled north to Oyndarfjørður. Aside from celebrating Easter with her mother-in-law, she also wanted to speak to one of Obram's relatives about bringing the woman's daughter back to Tórshavn, where she would live with the Obrams while attending secondary school.

Obram told Hjøstrup how he had promised his workers a bonus on the condition they emptied the *Haabet* before Easter. They had not pulled it off, but in order to show the men that he valued their efforts, he promised them some of the goods from the store.

That was the heart of the matter.

Hjøstrup set down his coffee cup, wiped the corners of his mouth with a napkin, and said that he understood that kind of generosity. It was not his job to teach Obram his business, of course. Nonetheless, he was of the opinion that once an agreement was struck between two parties, it ought to be abided.

Not too many years from now, he said, parties in the labor market would enter into written contracts—the practice had already been instituted in other countries—and it was just a matter of time before it came to the Faroes. Of course, a man was a man, and his word was still his word. However, when it came to buying and selling, and that included the buying of labor, legally binding agreements were becoming a necessity. Modern times required it.

Obram repeated the coarse and rather blasphemous words spoken by Sámal á Kák. He knew that vulgarity was a poor man's delight, as he expressed it, and if the words had been spoken in a larger public space, the man could have expected a rebuke. Sámal was one of the town drunks, and aside from that, he was a member of the obstinate and hot-tempered Kák clan. That family had yet to produce any schoolteachers or church sextons.

These last words were spoken in a conciliatory tone, but the bailiff did not appreciate this kind of consolation.

Founding the Workers Union was only one piece of a larger plan to modernize the hopelessly backward Faroes. And he told Obram as much. All that talk about race and clan struck him as provincial, and he provoked Obram deliberately when he said that it also sounded a little Old Testamentish.

Obram responded with surprise. He viewed himself as a representative of the modern era—did the Old Testament now stand in the way of progress?

The bailiff answered that the Old Testament and Mosaic Law were interesting in a cultural-historical context. He stroked his mustache and asked if Obram had ever noticed that whenever more than two Jews put their heads together, be their names Marx, Brandes, or Lassalle, suddenly the resolute urge for a crucifixion hung in the air?

No, Obram replied, he had never noticed that.

Jews are book people, Hjøstrup continued. And as much as possible, book people ought to quietly lead their lives lost in their books.

The New Testament's message of love, as well as the civil laws that saw the light of day in 1849, these were the rails on which the modern man ought to lean for support. Not some squabble between long-dead Jews.

Although Obram did not have much to say about Tóralvur í Geil, it was actually the part concerning Tóvó that Hjøstrup found most interesting. He told Obram about the time he gave Tóvó the deed to the old corporal's house on Bringsnagøta. In the first place, Hjøstrup was amazed to see an ordinary Tórshavnar walking about in foreign clothes, and with the delicate hands that characterized the saints in El Greco's paintings. And Tóvó was reserved, but it was not for lack for words. Exactly the opposite, Hjøstrup said. Words were precious, and what was precious must be guarded, something a type like Tóralvur í Geil knew well. And the man was always so watchful, that was what was so strange, indeed, utterly suspicious. The thought had crossed Hjøstrup's mind, and he would gladly stand corrected, if he were mistaken, but he was convinced that Tóvó had the frightened eyes of a shrewd criminal. Hjøstrup raised his index finger, and his nostrils flared as if he had caught the scent of a lurking fiend as he added in a low voice that perhaps Tóralvur í Geil was one of the secret members of the International Workingmen's Association.

Even though Obram was irritated at the mention of Greco, and all the other foreign names Hjøstrup liked to insert into the conversation, he listened to everything the man said with great interest.

All that Obram knew about Tóvó were things other people had told him. He knew that Tóvó had left Tórshavn in 1852—he remembered the exact date because he and Ludda-Kristjan had built the Doctor's House in Tvøroyri over the spring and summer of that same year. Back then Tóvó was just a wretched kid, and since '57 or '58, and for the next quarter century thereafter, he had been away from the Faroes, at least as far as Obram knew.

Obram did not want to discuss Tóvó's family, and certainly not Crazy Betta. He remembered her well, though, from his apprentice year in Tórshavn.

Lunatics terrified him, and for that matter, so did imbeciles. You knew them by their dreadful words, which sent cold shivers down your spine. It was like their eyes saw right to your heart, that was what was so frightening; and if you had any stain of conscience on your heart, they knew it. Luckily, the Landkirurg had begun sending such people to institutions in Denmark. No, he had no wish to discuss Crazy Betta, and although he had nothing unfavorable to say about her son, neither as a stonemason nor a work companion, he had been shaken by Tóvó's schooled and hard words Wednesday evening in the warehouse basement.

There was a reason, however, that Obram tended to avoid the subject of lunatics. His whole childhood north in Oyndarfjørður, Obram watched how his father was plagued by what his mother termed the Gray Disease, and Obram still considered the nights when his father lay there screaming, with men from the town coming to tie him down, to be the worst period of his life.

He was thirteen years old when he left home; he would have left sooner if it had been possible. Ludda-Kristjan apprenticed him, and the fact that Ludda-Kristjan had pitied such a young, country boy was a kindness Obram would never forget. Therefore, he could not bring himself to fire the mudslinger Sámal á Kák.

Hjøstrup asked if the rumor were true, that the Brahmadells were some kind of local family of sorcerers.

Obram replied that the Geil family were reputed to know more than their fair share.

Hjøstrup digested the answer, then asked if he could pose Obram a personal question.

"Of course," Obram replied.

"Do you believe sorcery to be an actual force in society?"

Obram laughed. He raised his hands to his cheeks and rested his head in his fists. "I wouldn't discount the possibility, at any rate," he answered.

"Hmm," Hjøstrup said. "If it turns out that Tórálvur í Geil is an agent of the International Workingmen's Association, and that he is secretly planning to organize a strike, would you hesitate to exercise the authority given to you by the Penal Code of 1866?"

"No," answered Obram. "I wouldn't hesitate for a second. Nonetheless, I must admit that I have a kind of strange respect for these people."

"Isn't that a medieval mentality?" Hjøstrup asked.

"Tell that to the young mothers who take their newborns to visit Old Tóvó's grave. They recite his strange verses, and they take home a blade of grass or maybe a small flower from his gravesite. Talk to them. Do it. Hello, you there, yes, you, young lady. You're living in the Middle Ages. Tell them that. Or go the pastor and tell him that idolatry is being practiced in the Svínaryggur churchyard."

"Are you saying there's a Brahmadella sect here in the city?"

"Old Tóvó was 105 when he died, and even though he had a church burial and the pastor spoke over his body, people held another ceremony some time after that. I heard it from my old master Ludda-Kristjan. You can call it medieval or whatever else you want. But there's a deep respect surrounding the Brahmadells."

"Good," said Hjøstrup. "Let us toast to deep respect."

Their glasses met with a delicate sound. A trimming had been etched just below the rim, and while the lovely brown cognac wet their tongues and slid slowly down their throats, it occurred to Obram that the crafty devil had just tricked him.

The Strike and the Treacherous Crew Member

FOLLOWING ST. OLAF'S Day in 1882, two representatives from the work crew, Habba av Velbastað and Sámal á Kák, met in Obram's office. They had come to demand a higher hourly wage.

What neither Habba nor Sámal knew was that Obram was already well acquainted with their errand. He knew that the two spoke for the men in this matter, and he also had a reasonable idea who the crew's more tractable members were. The old man from Hvítanes, who informed on his crew members, had spoken quite candidly, but Obram thought he also had a good sense of the men who depended on him for their bread and butter. What Habba and Sámal could not possibly know was that their boss and the bailiff had already discussed it. And not only that. They had also developed a plan in case the men actually took the major step of going on strike.

After Habba had said his piece, Obram offered each a quid of tobacco.

The cordiality was unexpected, and before Habba knew it, he had accepted the offering. Obram asked Sámal how the Geil family was doing, and Sámal said it was business as usual. However, he quickly added that he did not see what his family had to do with the matter at hand.

Obram smiled and told him not to be so defensive. Then he stood up from his desk and accompanied the men outside. He looked at Habba and then he clapped Sámal on the shoulder.

"Go back to work," he said amiably. "I intend to forget what we've just discussed, and that's the message you can take back to the others."

They were utterly confused as they walked along the new Amtmansbrekka. Two weeks ago the rafters had been raised and laths installed, and it was now apparent how truly imposing the building was. Neither Habba nor Sámal said a word. In the face of that colossal structure, they realized their insignificance.

Before this meeting, the men had agreed that if the negotiations with Obram proved fruitless, work would stop. And after Habba had told his associates about the dubious and strange meeting with Obram, their resolution was set in motion.

Most men remained at the building site, though some went to help with the hay harvest in the outfield, and others made their way home. That was around nine o'clock in the morning. At about noon, however, a boy leaned out of an open window and said that soldiers were on their way. Two minutes later the stamp of boots could be heard in the yard, and then ten armed soldiers came tramping over the temporary floorboards with Hjøstrup at their head. The bailiff was wearing a long coat and had buckled on his saber. He took charge immediately.

In wartime, he said, it was fitting to threaten the enemy. However, there was no war in Tórshavn, and the city had not seen war since Captain Baugh and the Spectacled Man plundered the city in 1808. Hjøstrup ordered the men to return to work and to be quick about it. They should also keep in mind that Obram úr Oyndarfirði was no enemy. On the contrary, it was thanks to men like him that Tórshavn had entered the modern era.

Habba replied that it was not a crime to suggest that 18 oyru was too low an hourly wage. In Copenhagen, stonemasons received 32 oyru an hour for the same work. The salary demand was not unreasonable, when one took into consideration that they had large households to support.

The bailiff did not seem to hear his words. He simply looked at Habba, and saw before him only a great proletarian beast that filled the bucket every time it shit.

He signaled with his left hand, and suddenly the soldiers assumed position, their legs astride, rifles by their right feet, and hands on the barrels.

The bailiff said he was not here to negotiate. He was here as the highest representative of the law, and he wanted to remind the crew that disobeying him would be taken as a sign of insurrection.

Confusion seized the men. The bailiff's message had caught them off guard.

The first to yield were the father and son from Hvítanes. His neck bent, the son trailed his father across the supporting beams, and given the threat, a few others also returned to work.

The rest were conducted to Skansin's prison.

Even though Habba and Sámal had spoken for the crew and carried the wage-hike demand to Obram, they were not the ones brought into the guardroom for interrogation around ten o'clock the evening of the arrest.

Two soldiers retrieved Tóvó and shackled him. One of them was Laurits á Bakka. Tóvó was annoyed at the length of chain between the shackles; it was so short that it forced him to stand with his hands folded, as if the skackles had deliberately been made to make prisoners seem like they were begging for mercy. He asked Laurits if shackles were really necessary, and the answer he got was so unreasonable and unexpected that a short laugh burst from his lips. Laurits replied that Tóvó was just as crazy as his mother and that he belonged in shackles.

Hjøstrup was standing next to the Bilegger stove when the soldiers brought in Tóvó, and he immediately launched into a long lecture regarding what a dangerous organization the International Workingmen's Association was. The scribe sat at the large plank table beneath the window, and every time Hjøstrup paused to take a breath, the hasty scrabble of pen across paper could be heard.

The Association found its members in large cities, the bailiff said. And one should not underestimate them. Oh no. They were just as well organized as the zealots back in Jesus's day, and they were no less ruthless. Those zealots were just pathetic Jews who despised the Romans with the same fervor as the Association did authority in the modern era. And as strange as it might sound, it was the Jews who headed the Association, and the worst sort of Jews at that, the Ashkenazi. They governed the Association, and they spoke that hateful pipe-valve language, *ssszwwhh* sounds whistling between their ravenous jaws.

Labor strikes on the continent had become a real plague, and the men on strike had but one goal—power. The Danish politician Estrup knew it, and so did the Prussian Chancellor Bismarck, and as long as he, Ewald Hjøstrup, was bailiff in the Faroes, no one would escape unpunished for trying to demolish what men like Obram úr Oyndarfjørði and the modern Faroes represented.

Hjøstrup took a deep breath and then asked Tóvó how the International Workingmen's Association sent messages.

"I don't understand the question," Tóvó replied.

"I want to know who the courier is," Hjøstrup said. "Do you get your orders from foreign sailors or perhaps from visitors? Or does the Association simply have a local chapter here in the city that makes independent decisions? That's what I'm asking."

Tóvó tried to remember if he had ever heard Habba or Sámal mention the International Workingmen's Association. His brother-in-law certainly knew nothing about the organization. Habba, however, knew a thing or two about Danish affairs. Still, he could not remember the man ever mentioning the Association or anything that had to do with international cooperation.

He shrugged his shoulders, and said that no one was giving him orders.

"Are you trying to say that you don't know what the International Workingmen's Association is?" Hjøstrup inquired.

Tóvó said that he had heard about a labor union by that name, but he had no connection to any union. And certainly not the one organized by Hjøstrup.

Hjøstrup seemed to consider these words and asked where Tóvó had heard of the Association.

"I've been a sailor for many years," Tóvó replied. He might have heard the name mentioned aboard some ship or in some foreign harbor. He could not remember where, though.

Hjøstrup persisted. He asked if it had been in Northern Europe or maybe in some Mediterranean seaport. Or perhaps he had heard of the Association while sailing to New Orleans with weapons.

Even as Tóvó was wondering if he should start feigning ignorance, he was also curious as to why the bailiff had mentioned New Orleans. What was his endgame?

The American Civil War was over by the time Tóvó had first sailed across the Atlantic. He had often sailed to Hamburg, and also to Amsterdam and Bergen, so it was probably in one of those cities that he had heard about the organization. Was it really all that important?

Suddenly, he became angry and asked what the meaning of all this nonsense was anyway.

Tóvó did not know that a few months ago Hjøstrup had been to see the post master, Hans Christoffer Müller, and had instructed him to retain all correspondence that might come for Tórálvur í Geil.

The bailiff had also approached the bank director regarding Tóvó's finances, and was told that while Tóvó was not a rich man, he had more money in his account than most people did.

Hjøstrup was so obsessed with conspiracies that he had already decided that Tóvó was a man the authorities ought to keep their eye on.

The bailiff answered that it was his job to decide which questions were important and which were not. This was an interrogation, and perhaps there was some shred of insanity bound up with it, he could not rule out the possibility. Tórshavn, though, had suffered a strike, that was the real insanity, and everything to do with strikes immediately smacked of the Association.

Hjøstrup, who had been pacing the floor while he talked, now took a seat beside the scribe.

For a time he seemed preoccupied, now and then glancing at Tóvó. Then he reached for a piece of paper, dipped his pen in the ink bottle, and sketched the European and North American coastlines, after which he asked Tóvó to list the ships with which he had sailed and the ports he had visited.

A smile flitted across Tóvó's lips. It was the first time anyone had asked him that, and any answer he gave would only be used for, well, he had no idea for what, but hardly anything good.

He said that his life as a sailor began in the summer of 1858. That was when the Norwegian schooner *Rosendal* put in at Tvøroyri, or rather at Hvalba, since the ship wanted coal. He had been nineteen years old, and since then the bulk of his life had been spent at sea. He had cut his teeth on the Baltic Sea. The miserable dinghies unable to compete with the steamships sailed with timber and fish to Lübeck, Rostock, Gdansk, St. Petersburg, and whatever those other Baltic ports were called. Later he signed on with the paddle steamer *Håkon Jarl,* which had a fixed route between Bergen and Hamburg. In Amsterdam he got a berth aboard the *Thin Lizzy,* which sailed between Amsterdam and Newcastle with coal. He had sailed quite a bit between Alexandria and Southampton and also between Southampton and New York.

Hjøstrup interrupted him. Suddenly, it was as if all this maritime talk was beside the point. His expression turned startled as he said that, to his knowledge, there were three murders associated with the person of Tórálvur í Geil.

The scribe handed him a large envelope, and after rifling through the papers for a moment, Hjøstrup found the one he was looking for.

In 1858, he said, a man by the name of Jóakim Nolsøe died in Tvøroyri, and, according to Napoleon Nolsøe, various things pointed to murder. Hjøstrup put down the paper, remarking that the authorities had not done much in the matter, but that a Scot named Ronnie Harrison had been a suspect. He assumed Tóvó knew who Ronnie Harrison was.

Tóvó felt the blood drain from his face; his throat was suddenly dry, but he did not dare to ask for something to drink. He said he remembered Ronnie Harrison, primarily because George Harrison was his father, and Tóvó's own father and brother had sailed on George Harrison's ship, the *Glen Rose*.

Hjøstrup further rifled through the papers, saying that eleven years later, in 1868, that same Ronnie Harrison had been murdered in the basement of a Fraserburgh chapel. The murder shook the congregation, both due to the fact that it had occurred in a house of worship, and that the victim had been a Free Church pastor.

Hjøstrup said that he knew Tóvó was not in the Faroes when Nils Tvibur suddenly died—indeed, there were some who insisted he was murdered. Nonetheless, Tóvó had inherited his house on Bringsnagøta. So, how was all of this connected? Were all these deaths pure coincidence?

"Perhaps I ought to be a little more forthright," said Hjøstrup. "In truth, I fear you, because it stinks of blood wherever you go.

Do you understand me? Let's put it another way: A hundred years ago this list of names, Jóakim Nolsøe, Ronnie Harrison, and Nils Tvibur—not to mention the fact that you may very well come from a family of sorcerers—would have earned your miserable carcass a death sentence. That's why I'm asking if all these deaths are pure coincidence?"

Hjøstrup poured water into a glass. The water was the same pale color as the lamplight; he did not pick up the glass. When he was finished pouring, he simply left it to gleam on the table.

"And now the strike, is that also just coincidence? Why is it only now that you all went on strike?"

"I have no idea," Tóvó answered. "Ask someone else."

"Who else?" Hjøstrup asked.

"The jail is currently full of workmen."

"Why didn't you all strike in the autumn instead?" Hjøstrup insisted. "Back then you could've pressured Obram. Or why not earlier in the year, for example, right after the confrontation in the warehouse basement?"

At this point, Tóvó did something he should not have done. He went too far.

Or rather, he went too far in order to escape having to talk more about the murders, particularly the murder of Ronnie Harrison.

"I read in the *Dimmalætting* that the Amtmand receives a yearly salary of almost 6,000 kroner," he said, "and that you yourself receive around 3,600 kroner. Not only that, but you each get free housing and the use of a farm. In kroner and oyru, you're worth about ten times more than any workman under Obram úr Oyndarfjørði."

Hjøstrup laughed loudly. "Does Tórálvur í Geil mean to imply that a workman ought to be measured on the same scale as a royal official?"

"No! Not at all. An official is far too high and mighty and his office far too lazy. The Bible has nothing to say about employees of the Danish king. On the other hand, Luke writes that a worker is worth his wage."

"I believe I've struck a chord," Hjøstrup said.

"Do you truly believe that Obram úr Oyndarfirði pays his workers enough?"

"Tórálvur í Geil. Let me tell you something. My job is to maintain law and order in this country, that's the only reason I'm mixed up in this affair. I have no particular opinion about money matters. That's for the labor market to decide."

Tóvó reached out his manacled hands. "Why do I need shackles, then, when all you want to do is talk?"

Hjøstrup smiled. "As I said, I'm told you're from a clan of probable sorcerers. A man must protect himself."

The bailiff stood up from the table. He was half tempted to thank Tóvó for providing so much material for a fruitful report.

Now he was going home to have a decent meal. And he would take two guards with him. If the workmen were capable of going on strike, they were probably also capable of assaulting authority figures.

Perhaps it was Habba who stood behind the strike, him and that scoundrel Sámal. Habba just seemed so uncommonly stupid, though, and suddenly Hjøstrup giggled. He covered his mouth to conceal the laughter that bubbled up in his chest. The image he had had earlier in the day, of Habba as a great beast that filled the bucket each time it shit, returned to him. The man was nothing but a body, mouth, and bowels, and every time he beat his furry chest, he made the smaller beasts hop.

Hjøstrup pulled on his jacket and told Laurits á Bakka that he could release the prisoners in half an hour.

On his way out he stopped by the stool where Tóvó sat, and he began to sing inwardly: *brahmi, brahmadu, brahmaduff.* Cheerfully, Hjøstrup continued out the door.

The Fight That Changed It All

THE FIRST OFFICIAL event sponsored by Tórshavn's Workers Union was a presentation of Heiberg's musical comedy *King Solomon and Jørgen the Hatmaker*.

The play took place on February 3, 1883 in the old church built by Pastor Bauer, and at the small reception that followed, Hjøstrup asked Henrietta what she had thought of the performance.

Henrietta answered that Dia við Stein was a treasure on piano, and that many of the songs were heart-gripping. "But if that's a Danish classic, Heaven preserve me from the rest of them."

Around midnight she went home. Three hours later she woke.

Someone had been knocking at the door for a while, two small raps, three small raps, again and again, with short pauses.

Finally, she lit the candle, holding it in front of her as she carefully made her way down the stairs. She had no idea that she was walking straight into a modern drama, with a Brahmadella playing lead.

"Who's there?" she called.

"Tóvó. Tórálvur í Geil."

"Do you have any idea what time it is?" she asked after a long pause.

"All I know is it's pitch black."

She turned the lock and cracked the door open, then thought about slamming it shut when she saw his bloodied face. But Tóvó wedged his boot between the door and the frame, apologizing for the intrusion, but he had nowhere else to go, she had to let him in.

The first thing Tóvó asked Henrietta to do was to help him pop his left shoulder back into its socket. His voice was not particularly threatening, but she still dared not refuse.

Tóvó sat on a step, passed his hand and arm through the bars of the railing, and told her to grip his forearm tight with both hands, and he would put his arm back into place. The first attempt failed, and judging by Henrietta's expression, she was the one who felt the most pain. The second time went better. Tóvó counted, one, two, three, and while she held his forearm tight, he wrenched his upper body slightly, and the audible *click* confirmed it had worked.

Henrietta poured lukewarm water from the stove's hot water tank into a bowl and inspected his face. She said he would need stitches, his ear at least would require two or three, but she could not do it. The bright red flesh visible under the torn skin, and the hair caught in the wound nauseated her.

His nose also appeared to be broken, but she was so sensitive to even the slightest sound that she dared not touch it. The very thought of hearing the minute scrape of broken cartilage gave her chills.

Even though they were from the same small city, this was the first time Henrietta and Tóvó had been in the same room. She had seen him occasionally, and she had also spied after him from the kitchen window with the—oh Jesus, that old telescope was the connection between Tóvó and Pole. She had observed him because he was one of the few men in the city who wore foreign clothes. And now she saw that he was also handsome, and like many sailors he wore a gold ring in his earlobe, and his mustache was well groomed. She might have spoken to him when he was a small child, but she had no memory of it. Vaguely she recalled that the Geil family's dog had gotten into their henhouse once or twice.

The memory of Betta, on the other hand, was crystal clear to her, particularly Betta as a young woman. She had been so lively and nurturing, and she was widowed during the tragic years. Suddenly, Henrietta remembered that on that same August night in 1847, she and Betta had both feasted with the Danish officers, and she nearly burst into laughter when she again saw before her her own suitor, the one whom she had "assisted" in the garden.

For Betta, though, it had been more than a festive night. Those officers had ruined the woman, or what was left of her. Pole had told Henrietta that more than once.

Oh Jesus, Henrietta sighed, remembering the letter from the former Landkirurg Claus Manicus. That had been in 1840 or '41. Old Tóvó had asked her to read the letter aloud to him, and she remembered his quiet sobs as she read with a trembling voice that Gudda, his daughter, was dead. And then Henrietta's mother forbade her to return to the Geil house. Oh, Mama, Mama, she thought. Your dreadful snobbery.

Though Henrietta tried to keep a modest distance between them as she washed Tóvó's face and neck, his masculine scent was alluring. His skin was so hot that she had the urge to dribble a tiny, clear droplet of spit onto the pale skin, to watch the moist trail as it sizzled or burst, just like water on a hot stove.

Get a hold of yourself, Henrietta, she thought.

The most remarkable thing, however, were the tendons along his neck. Not that she was an expert in necks, but nonetheless she had never seen so nice a pair of tendons. She wanted to touch them, but held herself in check. The tendons, which looked like rope ends, could be used as a jump rope or a church-bell pull.

She retrieved the make-up mirror from her Italian handbag and gave it to Tóvó. For a moment he inspected his nose. Then he squinted his eyes, grasped the bridge between his thumb and forefinger, and very carefully moved the broken pieces back into place. For a moment he sat there with his eyes closed. Then he said that Pole used to deaden the pain with gin.

Henrietta clapped her hands and apologized for not having thought of it sooner. She hurried to fetch a port wine glass and fill it with gin. The first glass went straight to his heart. She filled it again, and as Tóvó again drank, he tested his teeth with his tongue. He smiled to find none broken. At the same time, he swished the gin between his teeth and along the gums.

Henrietta pointed to his ear and said she did not have the skill to sew it up. Tóvó said that was no problem. He had doctored wounds more than once aboard a ship.

While Henrietta was in the old consultation room hunting for needle and thread, Tóvó caught sight of Pole's old chaise beneath the window. Even though it had been reupholstered, he recognized the twisted legs and the rounded seat back. Just like home in Tvøroyri, he thought.

However, it was obvious that Pole's widow felt uneasy.

"I'm not dangerous," Tóvó said when she had returned to the kitchen with Pole's old doctor's bag.

"What else do you call someone who forces his way into someone's home at night?" Henrietta asked.

"Fair enough," said Tóvó, threading the needle. "I need to sew this up first, though. Can you hold the mirror for me?"

Suddenly, he smiled. "You were married to a doctor, after all, and thirty years ago that same doctor was my foster father."

Henrietta nodded and touched his cheek. For a moment, she considered telling him that she had also read the letters he sent Pole, and that they were both beautiful and curious. But he might resent her for that. He probably would. The letters were so personal that Pole had never even mentioned them. It was only after his death that she found them in a desk drawer. The stack had a red ribbon tied around them, and the fact that Pole had kept the letters hidden meant they had been important to him. Tóvó should have the letters, Henrietta thought, as she did what he asked and held the mirror so he could see where to put the stitches.

Henrietta buttoned her coat as she walked down narrow Klokkaragøta. The night air was brisk and cool, and it was good to get some distance from the events of the night. Night? She could already hear the loud-voiced fishermen over by the Boathouse, and when she paused, she could also hear the ducks and eiders down by the estuary. Man and birds, she thought. God, how good it was to be alive!

Abruptly, she noticed how dark blue the sky was to the north, while a golden layer was weaving its way into the lighter sky to the east. Tórshavn's church also had a blue vault over it, and seeing that image right at this moment gladdened her. The morning star had nearly vanished, and the moon hung unusually heavy and yellow over Konufelli Mountain. She was astonished how happy it made her that Tórálvur í Geil lay sleeping on the chaise longue in her kitchen. He had asked if he could lie down for an hour or two, and she did not have the heart to refuse him. Especially when she realized he would be spending his subsequent nights in jail.

When she reached Bringsnagøta, she saw that a light was burning farther up the street, and as she approached it, she realized it was coming from Nils's—now Tóvó's—Mosque. The blue door stood open, and a soldier stood on the threshold.

She wanted to turn around and go home, but in order to avoid suspicion she kept walking down the street, and when she reached the Mosque, she bid the soldier good morning. She recognized Laurits á Bakkahellu, and remembered that Fióla, her cousin, had once said that she and Laurits had played together as children, and their other playmate was none other than Tórálvur í Geil.

Laurits had also been the cupbearer at her and Pole's wedding, but this morning he hardly acknowledged her. His clay pipe was lit, and as she passed him, she could feel his probing eyes on her neck.

Tóvó's story had planted a seed of doubt in her, that was the thing, and the man certainly knew how to state his case. She thought she also recognized his writing style in his speech. Of course, the letters were written in Danish and occasionally in English, but the same dignified tone also lived in his Faroese words.

What he said about the fight that had taken place that night utterly terrified her. What he said about Hjøstrup and the Workers Union, however, was thorough and accurate.

As everyone in Tórshavn knew, there had been only one loser in the strike, and that was Tórálvur í Geil. Everyone but Tóvó was given his job back, and the very next day hammers could be heard ringing from the Amtmansborg.

And the worst of it was that the things Tóvó had said about the bailiff were things she already knew instinctively, but had never put into words. Perhaps she had simply lacked the courage.

But whom could she tell that she thought Hjøstrup was a dwarf-ish version of Mephisto?

Pætur úr Kirkjubø might know the story of Satan's lackey, but he was not someone who discussed important matters with women. Such things were beneath a Sunman's dignity.

The bookbinder, Hans Niklái Jacobsen, was trustworthy, that was for certain, but the man's reading material extended to his bank-book's credit columns and the Bible. Henrietta thought of Sunday dinner with lamb on the menu every time she saw him. Over the years his lower lip had come to resemble the spout of a gravy boat, and every time he talked, his words were dark and thick like sauce.

Nonetheless, she liked participating in the meetings surrounding the union, and she also believed it was high time a society had been founded whose purpose was to educate the common man. It was like an extension of the library's purpose. And education was also the purpose of the newly established weekly newspaper *Dimmalætting*. However, calling the union a "workers union" was like raising a false banner.

During one meeting, Hjøstrup had told her to read *The Red Room* by August Strindberg. He loaned her his copy, and judging by all the underlined passages and notes in the margin, the book had both been carefully read by and had provoked its owner. And *The Red Room* certainly made for difficult reading. But that also applied to *Oliver Twist* and *David Copperfield* by Dickens. Not to mention *A Doll's House* and other brand new dramas by Ibsen, the brilliant Norwegian.

When it came to realistic literature, the Danes were behind the times. And that was what she told Hjøstrup when she returned the book. Strindberg was a modern man, she said, and he described in detail what his searching and inquisitive eyes saw. One could not blame him if modernity in many ways was ugly and unpleasant.

In that context, she repeated the words that Brandes used to describe Danish literature: *It does not treat our life, but our dreams.*

"I can't stand that arrogant Jew," was Hjøstrup's only reply.

The King Is a Castrate

THE WINDOWS AND both doors of the former Catholic Bauer-skirkju stood wide open after the play and reception. It was as if the church had of its own accord opened itself to the night and begged the wind to purify it of ballads and Jørgen Hattemager's sarcasm.

The church was dedicated in 1859, and although the souls that Pastor Bauer managed to save from Purgatory's cleansing fires were fewer than the teeth in Pløyen's mouth, as Doctor Pole once put it, the church could still fill half its pews. This was on the Sundays when Belgian, Scottish, and sometimes even French fishing vessels lay at anchor in Havnervág.

The moon shone on the dilapidated garden as Obram úr Oyndarfirði sat on a pew by the south door, blissfully ignorant that his testicles would be ripped off this very hour.

It had been a while since the guests had left, and Obram and two women had collected the dishes, cups, and glasses, and had swept the floor. He told the women to go home, and he would turn off the lights and lock up.

Yet even if the windows and doors seemed to beg for a cleansing wind, not a breath stirred. The currant bushes, bare and silver in the pale moonlight, looked cut from the dark itself.

A sudden shriek startled Obram; the hospital was just a stone's throw from the church. He wondered if he had dozed off and was dreaming, but when he again heard the same shriek, he guessed that it was someone with the Gray Disease who stood cursing at the bars of the psychiatric ward. For a moment he considered going up the hill to see if anything was amiss, but he did not really want to. Nonetheless, he stood up, and when he reached the gate and unlocked it, he found Tórálvur í Geil right outside.

Obram made no attempt to conceal his dismay, and as they stood there staring at each other, the voice again began to shriek. It was a shrill woman's voice, but he could not tell how old she might be; the voice was as enigmatic as it was ominous. It came from one of the ward's windows, where the insane were kept, and Obram thought she was calling: *wet sweater, wet sweater*, which was the curse Sára Malena úr Skúvoy once used. The words' strength came from the belly and broke from the throat, exploding like a burst of gunfire.

Obram was the first to speak, and he asked in a low voice what a bird of ill omen like Tóvó was doing in this area at night, and as soon as the words *bird of ill omen* left his mouth, he regretted it. Inwardly, he cursed the fact that he could not better control his tongue, yet before he knew what he was doing, he had blocked the door with his cane, as much to say: I demand an answer.

Tóvó asked if the Workers Union's newest initiative was to require workmen to pay tolls to enter the city?

Obram replied that Havn would be a better place if the authorities had been better at weeding people out in time.

Tóvó asked him to name some people he thought should be weeded out, adding that, as far as he knew, Obram and his wife were both outsiders.

Obram replied that the only growth Havn had seen over the centuries was the green sprouting from the thatch roofs, and that was where hens sat and cackled and shit over the pathetic city. Now things had changed. Havnarfolk were beginning to stage plays. The sleep had been washed from their sluggish eyes. In Bergen, Leith, and Copenhagen, people now knew the name of a small, but promising north European seaport called Tórshavn.

And then he aggressively added that people who had no idea what duty was had no right to make demands.

"I'm not aware I'd ever wronged you," Tóvó replied. "It's a mystery why you and Hjøstrup, and whoever else the new heroes are, can't leave me in peace. Even Restorff has forgotten that Tóvó í Geil is his nearest neighbor. You ought to remember that my family has always lived in this city, and I certainly don't need lessons from you on duty. I've tried to make myself useful and hard-working since I was seven or eight. I have no idea why I'm being treated like a criminal in my middle age. And I would advise you to move your cane."

"I ought to give you a taste of it!" Obram replied.

Once again he regretted the fact he had lost control of his tongue. He wanted to assume a more amiable tone, but there was something about this damned Brahmadella that made him question—yes—his own virtue.

At heart he had always regarded himself as a philanthropist, and it bothered him that the strike in August had blemished his reputation among Havnarfolk. He had never stolen anything from anyone, and when someone came to his office to ask for an advance or a favor, it would never occur to him to show them the door.

His dignity was nonetheless wounded. A new and uncomfortable atmosphere existed between him and Gerd. He could not mention either the Workers Union or Hjøstrup without provoking his wife, and sometimes she expressed herself so violently that he was forced to laugh from shock.

She castigated the *fucking Dane* who was always going around sniffing his onanist fingers. Obram asked what the devil she meant, and she replied, no, she hissed, that Hjøstrup had a woman's eyes, and she would not be surprised if he had a cunt between his legs.

While these thoughts raced through his head, he remembered Sára Malena. Was everything so confounded that at this late hour she had actually come to the aid of a Brahmadella? He was attempting to brush away this ridiculous thought when the shriek came again, and that was when the situation truly spun out of Obram's control. He glanced toward the hospital, and at that instant Tóvó grabbed Obram's cane and broke it across his thigh.

And that was all it took. The next moment they were at each other's throats, an unexpected rage burning in their fists. The fight took them toward the river, and with every step and every blow Tóvó had to acknowledge that his grand plan of forgetting Havn's troubles was shot. The other thing clear to him was that he was fighting a better opponent. Tóvó had the advantage of speed, but he needed more than just speed. He realized this when Obram grabbed him by the collar of his sweater and the waist of his pants. He lifted Tóvó over his head and was about to throw him in the Rættará, when suddenly he lost his footing. Tóvó got a thumb in Obram's eye, and in the blink of a moment the man lay stretched out on the grass. However, he recovered quickly. Like a wounded bear he staggered back to his feet, and he fought and forced Tóvó to the ground with fierce blows.

Deep down Obram hoped the Tórshavnar would be smart enough to beg for a truce, and Obram would not hesitate even half a second to grant it, because he both feared and hated the situation in which they found themselves. Yet not a word crossed Tóvó's lips, as with clenched teeth he allowed himself to be beaten and thrashed, though periodically he did succeed in injuring his opponent.

Perhaps because they were so different in strength, but eventually the fight grew dirty. They kicked, punched, and bit. Blood dripped from Obram's chin—not because a tooth had been knocked out, but because he had bitten Tóvó's ear and torn the top part off. At one point, Tóvó was able to grab a fist-sized rock, and with bashed it into Obram's knee. While Obram was down, Tóvó did what some bird species do when threatened—he vomited onto Obram's face while trying to force open his mouth.

A moment later, while Tóvó lay groaning in the grass, the tables turned. Two kicks to the side had robbed Tóvó of air, and on the third kick, Obram's foot met Tóvó's shoulder, and he thought he heard the pop of the arm leaving its socket.

Obram was at that point on the verge of begging Tóvó to forgive him, because he could see the pain he had caused. It was also clear to Obram, however, that his actions had set him in a strange land ruled by foreign laws, and that he was now damned.

That is what he later told the Scottish preacher William Sloan. He said that when Tóvó rose from the ground with incredible strength, he was half man and half devil. That was the only way he knew how to describe what had happened. His handsome, bloody face, the jacket hanging torn from his shoulders, it was like he had stepped out of some terrifying painting—he could not remember the name of the painter, though, Greco or something—anyway, that bloody man stood there prepared to smash the hourglass of Obram's life that had started running in Oyndarfjørður fifty-two years prior.

With the Bauerskirkju's open windows still beckoning the wind, as the Rættará River flowed silently toward the bay and the moon hung brightly in the sky, Obram felt merciless fingers close around his testicles. He pleaded for himself. Shamelessly, he pleaded for his manhood, but the time for mercy was long past. Suddenly, he was a pathetic beast caught in a trap; in his mind's eye he could dimly make out the great plains where the herds mated, and could just catch the rutting scent of thousands of exhilerated bodies.

For the first time since he was a small boy, he lost control of his sphincter and emptied his bowels. He was still conscious, or at least he thought he was, when Tóvó's hand came free of Obram's body, and his testicles followed.

"You can own the most beautiful mountain fells. You can become the world's greatest man and fill the stars with sheep and cattle and lighthouses, which cast light upon your sublime name. But the king is a castrate."

Obram was uncertain whether he heard or dreamed these words before everything became hazy, and he collapsed to his knees and lost consciousness. Still, he vaguely remembered someone putting him on a stretcher, and being rushed to the hospital. It did not take long before Landkirurg Hoff figured out what had happened, and Hjøstrup the Bailiff was summoned.

God Will Give Thee Strength

A FEW DAYS before St. George's Day, 1883, Tóvó was found guilty. He was sentenced according to § 204 of the new Danish criminal code from 1866: *Should one person maim another, rob him of sight or hearing or visit on him any other injury such that hand, foot, eye, or any other equally important limb is rendered useless, or his powers of body or soul are weakened to the extent that he is incapable, permanently or for an indefinite period, to carry out his duties of employment or tend to the activities of daily life, he will be judged guilty, if he intended the injury or if it must be regarded as a logical and not improbable result of his actions, and will be punished with up to twelve years of hard labor.*

Hard labor is more precisely defined by § 11 of the criminal code: *Hard labor is either convict labor or correctional labor. A person is either sentenced to convict labor for life or for a period of at least two years and not to exceed sixteen years.*

Tóvó received the most severe sentence. He was forty-three years old, and for the next sixteen years the new prison at Vridsløselille, west of Copenhagen, would be his new home.

Laurits á Bakka told him that Vridsløselille was a new type of prison. The prisoners were forbidden from talking to each other, and the guards were also banned from addressing the prisoners. Being an inmate there meant total isolation. The Almighty was the prisoners' sole consolation. The prisoners also wore hooded cloaks to church service, and they occupied small, solitary cells. Laurits said the one chance a prisoner had to see his own face was to try and catch a glimpse of his reflection in the water of the tin cup from which he drank.

A strange event occurred while Tóvó was waiting to be transported to Denmark, which many Havnarfolk associated with rumor of the Brahmadells' sorcery.

One morning, the daughter of Obram's relative, the girl who had been brought to live with Obram and Gerd and attend school in Havn, was found dead in her bed. The couple had been planning to adopt her and they treated her like their own child. She had gone to bed healthy and happy, but never woke.

Obram was not well enough to attend the burial. His wife represented the household, and after the pastor had cast dirt on the coffin, the bailiff was among those who approached Frú Gerd to offer his condolences.

Gerd stared at him aghast. She glanced at his outstretched hand, looked at his face, but did not say a word. For two or three long seconds his hand hung in the empty air, but Frú Gerd refused to accept his condolences. Slowly, Hjøstrup's hand sank, as did his confused expression, and as he turned on his heel to go, his hand disappeared into his coat pocket.

Two days later the Scottish preacher William Sloan was in the bailiff's office, and he had come to ask permission to visit Tórálvur í Geil.

Hjøstrup asked why Sloan wished to visit the condemned.

Sloan replied that Tórálvur í Geil might want someone to pray with him, and besides, Sloan's wife and Tórálvur were second cousins.

There was also a third reason, but he had no desire to betray it to the bailiff or to anyone else in the city for that matter.

The bailiff sat a moment stroking his mustache. He liked the gentle spirit that radiated from the preacher, and the man had those striking blue eyes. He offered Sloan a seat and then asked whether he believed the Brahmadella clan was involved with sorcery.

Sloan replied that evil was certainly a real force.

Hjøstrup leaped from his seat. "That's not what I asked you. I'm talking about the Brahmadells."

"Evil doesn't dwell within families," Sloan answered. "Evil dwells in the individual soul."

"What do you mean by that?"

"One must repent and do good works, there is no other protection against evil."

"So how did Obram's niece die then?" whispered the bailiff, his eyes glinting with curiosity, as if he was setting the dignity of rank aside and simply asking the Scottish preacher to explain how things worked.

But Sloan simply listened. He had also attended the burial, but the churchyard was full of people and from where he stood he could not see what actually happened at the gravesite. However, he had heard that Frú Gerd had refused to take the bailiff's outstretched hand.

And it was true. The highest legal authority in the land had been publicly scorned.

By the time he had reached the cemetery gate at the funeral, Hjøstrup was convinced he had nothing more to do in this country; rather, he did not understand why he had ever sought a post in this anachronistic hole.

The hatred in Frú Gerd's eyes had been so dreadful it bordered on disgraceful. It was not his fault if that occult deviant had lightened her husband's weight by two testicles.

Yet there had been no compassion in the eyes of the other funeral guests either. The lack of a proper respect to authority was frightening. Right now everyone seemed to hate him. That was the truth of the matter. It was mob hatred he was up against, and there was no protection against such mass emotions.

"Of course, you have no idea how the girl died," Hjøstrup said, answering his own question.

He looked out the window while he talked. A daffodil bed was already sprouting in the yard and the first currant leaves were beginning to unfurl. He said it had occurred to him that death was an independent entity on par with God and the Devil. Sometimes healthy bulls died. Sometimes ships with 200 men on board sank, or a fire might consume an entire neighborhood. But what did God have to do with it? Or what difference did it make to the Devil whether or not a flower survived?

Sloan disliked these words, and did not know whether the bailiff was being serious, or whether he was simply thinking aloud. If they had been some other place, in the meeting house or perhaps in his own home, then he could have told the bailiff that there will come a day when Death and the Devil and human sinfulness would vanish like dew before the sun. But to instruct such a high official in his own office, that was not something he could do.

Now Hjøstrup smiled, and his smile was pleasant and encouraging. He said that he had almost forgotten Sloan's errand, but that the preacher could have half an hour with the Sorcerer of Geil.

He took a piece of paper, dipped his pen in ink, and after he had written some words, he blew on the text and then handed Sloan the paper, saying he could show it to the guards at Skansin.

Sloan thanked Hjøstrup for the sign of goodwill and they bade each other good day.

The three weeks during which Tóvó waited to sail to Denmark saw friendship arise anew between himself and Laurits á Bakkahellu. Though a better word might be *understanding*. Laurits saw how harshly the sentence had affected his childhood friend, and although Laurits could seem callous, if not to say small-minded, he had long comprehended that Tóvó had fought for his life, and that was the heart of the offense. A poor man had lifted his head too high, and although Laurits admired that kind of pride, he could not express those thoughts, certainly not in a workplace whose highest authority was Hjøstrup. For his part, Laurits did not have anything in particular against the bailiff, and he was not paid to have an opinion of the man. His post at Skansin put bread on the table. Nothing more to say.

Sometimes he let Tóvó borrow his pipe, and occasionally he loaned him a copy of the *Dimmalætting* to read. Now and then he said something amusing and there was usually a barb to it.

One day Laurits said he had heard that the Workers Union was about to announce a special musical evening featuring a castrate from Oyndarfjørður who planned to sing *The Ballad of the Missing Jewels*.

He also told about a spring day when the people of Nólsoy were leading their cows to the outfield, and a heifer had fallen into a bog from pure spring fever.

Tóvó knew the story well, but he liked hearing tales from his father's hometown.

Several attempts were made to drag the cow out, but the mire simply closed around the large body, and the poor animal sunk deeper and deeper. Some told the creature farewell, others suggested cutting the cow's throat to put it out of its misery.

One bright mind from the Stovu house came up with the idea of running home to fetch a half-pint flask of brandy. One, two, three, and he was back, tipping the flask into the cow's mouth and letting the brandy flow. Cows have several stomachs and, therefore, longer intestines—indeed, some claimed a cow's intestines were four times the length of its body—so it took a while for the strong drink to make it back and forth through the animal's system. What happened next was exactly what the bright mind was hoping for: The cow cast its head, gave its body several good heaves, and suddenly looked like it would free itself. If fact, it practically flew, and when it landed, its body was half on dry ground.

Laurits also said that he was the cupbearer at Napoleon and Henrietta's wedding, and that Hammershaimb, the provost on Nes, had come to Tórshavn to marry the couple. Everything had to be so damned Faroese, no Danish pastor was allowed to show his face. Nonetheless, Pole died two and a half years into their marriage, but that was another story.

At the wedding banquet, Hammershaimb told the strange story of a black ox, and it did not surprise Tóvó that this story also came from Nólsoy. Hammershaimb said he had heard the story as a boy in Havn.

It was during the autumn, and the sheep had been driven home for the winter. When they returned for the cows, they looked for the ox but it was nowhere to be found. The next day they searched again, but with the same result. The animal probably fell to its death, nothing more to say.

Around Christmas time, though, some men were out fishing east of the island. The day was bright and still, and suddenly they caught sight of something large and dark moving around the rocky beach at the foot of a cliff. They drew in their lines and rowed toward land. Maybe it was a large seal or a walrus taking advantage of the glorious weather to sun itself. However, as they neared the beach, they saw that the dark shape was the ox they had lost in the autumn.

How it had gotten to the beach at all was a mystery. The beach was as big as a good-sized field and it was backed by vertical cliffs rising fifty fathoms up. An agile man might have been able to make it down from the edge, but certainly not without a rope, and the animal could not possibly have gotten down that way. There was also no food. The black beach was surrounded by a wide belt of whelk and limpet shells, and kelp and reddish seaweed rocked on the water's surface with the gentle surge.

The real question, though, was how the men were to get the ox home. The ox also seemed so tame, which in itself was suspicious. They did not dare take it on board. They could tie down a sheep, to be sure, but hardly a large animal weighing 500-600 pounds. No one dared say the word *sorcery*, even though it is what they were all thinking. And it also seemed the ox understood human tongue. Its large brown eyes followed whomever was speaking, but there was no trace of a raging bull there. If anything, its eyes appeared questioning.

After debating the matter for a while, they finally decided to slaughter the ox. They cut its throat—its blood was more black than red—and then dismembered the body.

No one back home was pleased by the catch, but you ate what was put on the table. The strange thing about the ox was that its meat tasted more like fish than beef.

On the evening Sloan came to visit, Laurits showed the preacher into Tóvó's cell. Then he stepped outside so they could speak privately.

After Sloan had greeted Tóvó and taken off his hat, he asked if he could sing a psalm, and Tóvó had nothing against it. Sloan said he had written it himself, and with his beautiful voice he sang:

> *Trust today, and leave tomorrow,*
> *Each day has enough of care;*
> *Therefore, whatsoe'er thy burden,*
> *God will give thee strength to bear,*
> *He is faithful!*
> *Cast on Him thine every care.*

The song had several verses, but the words "God will give thee strength to bear" seized Tóvó's heart and he thanked Sloan for singing it. However, he did not believe Sloan had come just to sing a psalm to him.

Tóvó was suddenly reminded of the stories his great-grandfather used to tell of the mysterious Jóvóvamaður, the half-human, half plant creature that lived up by Svartifossur. He had never given much thought to how the Jóvóvamaður might look, but if he resembled anyone at all, that person would be Sloan. What with his huge white beard and wild white hair, he resembled a light-colored bouquet of flowers; Tóvó smiled at the thought that, in place of legs, Sloan's trousers might contain roots. Tóvó was delighted that the visit had triggered a warm childhood memory. Nonetheless, he asked why his guest had come.

Sloan told him that seventeen years ago a terrible thing happened in Fraserburgh. The preacher Ronnie Harrison was found murdered, but the killer's identity remained a mystery.

Tóvó replied that he was familiar with Ronnie Harrison. In 1858 the man had killed his friend, Jóakim Nolsøe. At the time, Ronnie was sailing aboard the *Glen Rose*, and in the autumn of '58, the ship had put in at Tvøroyri with a man suffering from gangrene on one arm. Since Tóvó was a servant to Doctor Napoleon Nolsøe back then, he knew the particulars. While the *Rose* lay at anchor, the men on board started drinking. Jóakim, who had delivered water to the ship, participated in the festivities. Later, he and Ronnie rowed to land, and went to the old Royal Danish Trade Monopoly's boathouse.

Jóakim was a sodomite, Tóvó said, and so was Preacher Ronnie Harrison. That was why they came ashore together, and it was not the first time they had been to the old boathouse together.

Sloan crossed himself, but Tóvó told him to calm down. The world was an ugly place, he said, and human bestiality knew no limits.

"And that is the message you can take to Hjøstrup."

Sloan winced. "Do you think that Hjøstrup sent me?" he asked.

"It wasn't so long ago that Hjøstrup told the same story you just did," Tóvó replied.

"I asked Hjøstrup for permission to visit you. That's all we discussed. Nothing more."

"So it's pure coincidence that you and the bailiff brought up the same subject?" Tóvó asked.

"I have no idea why Hjøstrup would be interested in Ronnie Harrison," Sloan replied.

"And I suppose you also didn't know that Ronnie Harrison was a sodomite? I'm not interested in small talk. You have to be honest with me."

"Perhaps I should have been clearer," Sloan said. "But first I'd like to ask you something, and I hope you'll answer my question."

"The first time I came to the Faroes was in 1865. For a few years I sailed between Scotland and the north islands, and also all the way up to Iceland. When we built Salin here in '79, I saw you and thought, I've seen that man before. I saw him in Fraserburgh in 1867."

Tóvó nodded.

"And since then I've feared you."

Tóvó felt his forehead burn. There was only one single person who knew that Jóakim had been avenged. In a letter to Pole, which he had sent from New York the summer of '69, Tóvó wrote: *He is avenged, he who died in the Temple of the Flesh. His avenger is neither pleased nor proud, but at peace.*

If the letter still existed, then Henrietta Nolsøe had it in her possession. However, Tóvó could not believe she would let anyone else read the letter, or rather letters he had sent Pole over the years. Even if someone else had seen the letter, how would that person know who the avenger was, or what the sender meant when he wrote *Temple of the Flesh?*

"It's good to lighten one's heart," Sloan said.

"True," Tóvó replied. "So I guess, that said, I could ask if you were ever a victim of Ronnie's advances."

The question surprised Sloan. He was so used to hearing others confess their sins that he himself had mostly forgotten the art of confession. Still, he answered that few had mourned Ronnie Harrison.

"But I also want to say something else," Sloan continued. "I'm convinced that the sentence you've been given is unjust. I'm not saying that to comfort you, but because I know what happened. Unfortunately, I can't say anymore. People turn to me in confidence and their words are hidden here." Sloan put his hand to his heart. "However, I might add: The sentence also harbors a kind of involuntary justice. That's the extraordinary thing! Because the punishment you'll undergo in Denmark is actually for the murder of Ronnie Harrison!"

"I've had the same thought," Tóvó said.

"That means you're a repentant man," Sloan said. "And he who repents is no stranger in the Lord's house."

Sloan kneeled and began to pray. Tóvó also kneeled, but he was silent. And he remained silent after Sloan had finished. It was not until Laurits could be heard unlocking the door that Tóvó took his guest's hand, thanked him for coming, and asked him to send his greetings to his cousin.

PART
FOUR

The Fools' Narrow Way

OVER NEW YEAR'S in 1988-89, when Karin was staying at Eigil's, they told each other a number of secrets. Karin said exchanging secrets was the essence of love.

Eigil was charmed by these words. He had never dared to speak so openly. Of course, he had read things that were just as charming or perhaps even more beautiful. But to see the fire in her eyes and watch her lips form the words, *exchanging secrets is the essence of love*, that endowed the words with a life of their own, so they took root and bloomed in the half-light.

One unexpected thing to seize Eigil that week was one of his reoccurring Dusty Springfield binges. Dusty's voice belonged to the music of Eigil's solitude, when he was craving depth of feeling, or for what was unfolding between him and Karin.

He owned an LP and two EPs, which she released in the latter half of the 60s; he had bought the records while he was studying accounting at the Handelshøjskolen in Copenhagen.

Karin was just a kid during Dusty's heyday in the 60s, and by the time she started listening to music and paying attention to names, Dusty's time was already past. Not that that bothered Karin too much. She thought Dusty's most unusual characteristic was not her voice, but rather her enormous beehive hairdoo. She did not say that to Eigil, however.

One night, Karin woke to the sound of Dusty's voice. The door had come open, and her voice crept into the bedroom together with a gray light. Karin tiptoed to the door and glanced down into the living room where Eigil sat listening to "You Don't Have to Love Me," again and again.

He was naked, and when he stood up to reset the record player's arm, she saw how truly powerful his body was. His shoulders were thick and muscular, and his back was incredibly broad.

When he returned to his seat, Karin saw that he was crying. His shoulders shook and for a moment he buried his face into his hands.

The sight frightened Karin. It felt overwhelming to see a man, whom she had essentially just met, sit there crying. And she did not go down to him. There was something awkward, yes, even repugnant about his tears. And besides, it was not fitting for a grown man to sit there blubbering to the sound of a backcombed 1960s slut.

Eigil told her that he had discarded his plans for a book on Faroese cultural history, and was now devoting all his time to a novel about the Faroese measles epidemic of 1846. He was also trying to work in some of his own family history into the book. Both during the epidemic, and in the years that followed, his great-great-grandfather Nils Tvibur had demonstrated some personality traits that were worthy of all praise. Nonetheless, Nils Tvibur had not been a good person, and, truth be told, Eigil sometimes suspected he was more like his great-great-grandfather than he knew.

Karin asked if he was being serious, and his answering shrug angered her.

"Why do you think I've spent nearly a week with you?" she asked. "Why do you think I answered your letters for almost half a year? I care about you, that's why. Don't say that you're a bad person, that kind of talk scares me. All it does is push me away."

Karin paused a moment and then almost shouted: "Is that what you're doing now? Is this how you're thanking me for a week in bed?" Eigil struggled to explain what he meant. He said that his

Sumba relatives were characterized by a rather pathological brutality. In saying that, he was not trying to make himself seem psychologically interesting, it was simply that he worried about what things his genes might be harboring.

He told Karin that his mother was mentally fragile and that he did not know for sure who his father was. He had a suspicion, that was all, and that suspicion occupied his mind quite a bit in the third and fourth grades.

He had asked his mother about his father, but she did not give him a satisfying answer. She said that Jesus Christ was his father, just as He was father to all children on earth. Another time she told him that the only father who counted was the one who put food on the table. The rest were good for nothing.

And that was an answer Eigil could live with. Sometimes people asked him who his father was, and he could earnestly call Ingvald his father, and say that he worked in the Bókhandil printing house.

The third or fourth grade was also when Eigil was viciously bullied. A punk named Evert, Evert hjá Tannlæknanum, was the ringleader. The boy was an excellent soccer player, and had a big mouth; one of his gang's favorite pastimes was to chase and tease the big, clumsy boy with the Suðuroyar dialect.

Eigil complained about them to his mother, said he wanted to change schools, that the bullies would not leave him alone.

His mother gave him a piece of sound advice: an eye for an eye. That was what Sterka Marjun did when her father tried to exact revenge after she married against his wishes, and that was also what her sons, those giants the Harga Brothers, did when they fought the sea-raiders. Kristensa told her son to wring blood from the dentist's shitbag son, and the rest would take care of itself.

And that was exactly what happened. One day after school, Evert and his gang had chased Eigil into the bike shed. They had been especially malicious that day. They had emptied his school bag, scattering his books and notebooks among the bikes, and one of his tormentors had stomped on his lunch box, which was made of tin and bound by a rubber band.

Before Eigil knew it, he had grabbed Evert, and he was surprised himself to see the boy fly into the bikes. And he was not the only one startled. All the boys were shocked at the considerable strength that had been so unexpectedly revealed.

And then the Devil blazed up in Nil Tvibur's great-great-grandson. All at once, he shoved the bicycles aside, and when he got his hands on Evert again, he tried to follow his mother's advice to the letter.

Sometimes Eigil went to the printing house after school on harsh winter days. It was so cozy to sit on a stool next to the radiator and read, and he liked the smell of the ink and all the sounds from the various printing machines.

Eigil had no idea that Ingvald was even more delighted by these visits, and that, as a stepfather, he considered them to be a kind of knighthood, honoring him with the role of father.

Eigil thought all of the printers working at the Bókhandil were cut from the same cloth. Perhaps this world of lead simply attracted scrawny men, a flock of linguistic skeletons who printed newspapers, funeral hymns, and books.

When Eigil began to write later, it was Ingvald who provided good literary advice. Among the books he had set were *The New Testament*, translated into the Faroese by Jákup Dahl, *Faroese Folk Tales and Fables*, and *Life Stories and Poems*, both by Dr. Jakobsen. And whatever Ingvald set and read, he remembered. With his thoughtful eyebrows raised, he could recite from memory how this or that author had expressed himself, and also which language usage was more modern or more antiquated.

He was a bachelor when he and Kristensa met, and after they were married he stuck to his bachelor ways.

His daughters laughed affectionately at their father when he saved the tags on the Christmas gifts he received. He was known to smooth and set aside the shiny silver candy wrappers, and part of his morning ritual was to roll three or sometimes four cigarettes, which he smoked over the course of the day. He bicycled to and from work, and his pant legs were always neatly fastened with bicycle clips.

However, Eigil never called Ingvald *father*, and Ingvald was also not the type to express such a wish. He obviously did not wish to intrude.

"You make it sound like not wanting to intrude is some kind of weird character trait," Karin said.

"That's exactly what it is," Eigil replied. "People who are passionate about something—whether you're talking about a child or an idea—are bound to be intrusive. There's no other way forward."

Indifference was also a terrible emotion, Eigil thought. Or rather, indifference meant that no other emotions were present. Indifference was a hole scoured by caustic soda and cleansed by fire. He also said he could not tolerate humility, because in most cases it simply represented a hidden inferiority complex.

"I'm not sure I follow," Karin said. "Do you dislike Ingvald?"

"No, I like him. But I like him in the same way you'd like an obedient dog."

Karin did not like these words. Although she did not know Ingvald, it dismayed her to hear Eigil compare his stepfather to a four-legged animal.

Eigil said that the Faroes were an extremely clannish society, and that one of the particularities of clan bonds was that they were based on smell. Those who lacked a father did not necessarily smell bad, but they smelled different. The connection between children and parents was essentially based on everyone smelling right. That was just how it was. One reason for this, of course, was that people in the same household ate the same food, so everything from visits to the john to sweat smelled similar. Families also used the same words and pronounced them with much the same intonation. What was genetically inherited and what was socially determined, that was six of one, half dozen of the other.

Nonetheless, he said he was an outsider in his own family. He did not smell of lead like Ingvald and both of his sisters. After a person left home, Eigil estimated it took three to four years to cleanse one's family from one's body. Only then could you be an independent individual.

What one could not cleanse, however, was DNA.

Eigil had a nagging suspicion that his grandfather's brother, Hjartvard Tvibur, was also his father. That was why he sometimes feared that he had inherited the violent nature that had probably entered the family with his Norwegian great-great-grandfather, Nils Tvibur.

Karin simply sat and listened to all this with a foolish grin, and when Eigil suggested they invite his family to dinner, she could not bring herself to protest. Or rather, she dared not protest. She had a headache and she regretted ever coming to Tórshavn. She lived with her mother alone in Fuglafjørður. In the mid-70s, Karin had studied nursing in Copenhagen, but when her father suddenly died, she returned home to her mother, and since then she worked in the municipal doctor's office in Fuglafjørður.

She told her mother about her relationship with Eigil Tvibur and that she had come to care about the man. That was why her mother read the book *Between Tórshavn and San Francisco*, and she paid enough attention to know that Eigil Tvibur was the star of the Self-Governance Party's Sydstreymoy branch.

And he also besieged Karin with letters. Some weeks two letters would come through the mail slot, and her mother would ask which it was she was in love with, the letters or the letter-writer.

Karin told her the truth: that she hoped the letters reflected the letter-writer. She was no longer a young woman, and could picture living together with a man and having a child.

And now she realized that Eigil frightened her a bit, and that the seeds of this anxiety must have been sown in their relationship already.

Eigil noticed her distress. Carefully, he took her hands in his and said that she had nothing to fear.

"You can be such a brute," Karin said. "Your words scare me. You have try and be a little . . ."

". . . nicer?" he suggested.

"Stop putting words in my mouth," Karin replied. "It's giving me a headache."

For a moment they sat in silence, and then Eigil asked if she thought it was a bad idea to invite his family to dinner.

Karin smiled. "Just promise me you won't be so savage and I'll be happy."

For a moment she was silent and then she asked why he had cried when Dusty Springfield sang.

"Were you listening?"

"You weren't in bed."

"I just feel sorry for Dusty," Eigil said quietly.

"Was that why you were crying?"

"I don't know exactly why. I don't usually sit and cry."

And that was the truth. What Eigil did not venture to say, however, because it sounded artificial or even like something borrowed from a book, was that deep down he was afraid of happiness. Excessively happy people were fools. They knew their way down life's narrow path, but the true life, the grandiose and the festive life, not to mention the life that crushed people, that was found on a broader road.

He was captivated by Karin, and she loved with a passion he could not remember having ever experienced. However, he already sensed that their relationship was entering the fool's path.

Two days later Karin met Kristensa, Ingvald, and Tórharda for the first time. Eigil's older sister, Svanhild, was studying to be a doctor in Copenhagen and had not come home during the Christmas break. She had not been home in nearly a year and a half. Svanhild lived with a Norwegian woman, and when she told her mother the truth about the relationship, Kristensa, suffering one of her attacks, had said that the wickedness from Ergisstova knew no bounds. Then she had gone into her room and locked the door, and mother and daughter had not spoken since that day.

Even though Kristensa had lived in Havn for the last thirty-five years, she had mostly retained her childhood dialect. For Saturday she said *leyvardegur* instead of *leygardagur*, and the *tje*-sounds were largely unaltered.

This was not the first time she had met one of Eigil's girlfriends; they came and went, and if she thought back, she could not remember any of them making a real impression on his life. Maybe Tóra av Sandi, but she had married a man from her hometown out of the blue, and that was that.

Eigil was too proud, and Kristensa told him that. Yes, he was an educated man who knew how to present himself, and she was proud that the boy she had borne and raised was spoken of with respect among the cultural elites. However, he liked the spotlight too much, both as an author and as a local politician, and that was a nasty trait.

When Eigil called to invite them to dinner, his mother could immediately tell by his voice that something unusual was afoot. Normally terse, his tone was lighter and more open. Eigil had not been to visit her in over a week, and even though she had called on New Year's Day, no one had answered the telephone. She immediately asked who else was coming to dinner, and he said that he had met a woman from Fuglafjørður named Karin, and that she would handle the potatoes.

And that quasi-cheerful tone characterized the first hour of their visit.

Tórharda was twenty-two years old and still lived with her parents. She had her father's face, but whereas Ingvald was taciturn and had small gray eyes, Tórharda was talkative and had the large brown eyes from the Sumba family line. She worked as a gardener and wanted to go to school for agriculture. Although she had not told her mother, she could imagine herself taking over the Ergisstova farm. Her mother's uncle Nils was in his early sixties, and neither his daughter Margit nor his son Jenis showed any interest in farming.

Eigil had fried a leg of lamb. Like many other middle-class Faroese, in the last four or five years he had started drinking wine with his meals. He owned large, bulbous glasses with long stems, and Kristensa thought it was contrived to sip at wine. If you could drink water or milk out of a nice ordinary glass, why could you not use that same glass for wine? And then he had also started cooking with garlic and parsley. He even used those terrible herbs with fish. She did not usually invite him to dinner anyway. It was as if fish balls, rissole, and whale meat and blubber were no longer good enough for his accountant's stomach.

On this early New Year's Day, he had placed pieces of garlic in the meat and sprinkled a blend of lemon zest, thyme, rosemary, and oregano over it. In the frying pan, he had poured a mixture of white wine and water, and the fine wine flavored the sauce.

Karin praised the meal, saying that she was not used to such fine food in Fuglafjørður.

Kristensa asked what she usually ate.

Fish balls, corned beaf, boiled cod in onion gravy. On Sundays she and her mother sometimes ate at Muntra, the local restaurant.

Ordinary food mainly, and then fermented mutton on Christmas Eve of course.

Kristensa said that this kind of sumptuous fare was not what Sumbingurs were brought up on in her day.

Eigil said the meat was from Sumba.

Kristensa tried to pretend everything was normal. She said that they had eaten meat on holidays, but that was it. However, she said it in such a strange way, then she set down her knife and fork and excused herself.

The bile was already rising to her throat as she stepped through the bathroom door, but she managed to get the door locked, and then, kneeling before the toilet, she surrendered the entire meal. All that meat from that hellhole known as Sumba, not to mention the potatoes cooked by that New Year's Slut. Angry tears streamed from her eyes, but she tried to vomit as quietly as she could, and she hated the stink surging out of her.

Afterward, she rinsed her mouth and face with cold water, and while she inspected her mournful expression in the mirror, she wondered how Eigil could be heartless enough to serve meat from Sumba.

When she returned to the living room, Kristensa settled into the large reading chair.

Eigil brought her a cup of coffee and asked what was wrong.

His mother answered that if you had grown up under a dictator, something was always wrong.

"Don't talk about Ergisstova on a day like today."

"Did you have to serve meat from Sumba?"

"Oh Jesus," Eigil sighed.

"Sure, call on Jesus. That's what Sumbingurs do, too. But has that ever helped that damned people?"

Ingvald had already stood up from the table.

"Come, dear, let's go home," he said.

He gave her his arm and led her into the hall. While Tórharda was also preparing to leave, she told Karin that her mother was "allergic to Sumba."

"Why didn't Mom say anything to me?" Eigil asked his sister.

"There was nothing to say," Tórharda answered. "Everything was fine when we left the house. These attacks just happen, and then you know how it is. No one can control them, least of all you and me."

City Council Politician
Eigil Tvibur

. . . *income must correspond to expenditures, that's the ABCs of basic eco-*
nomics. No matter the party or political tone, a banana costs one kroner sev-
enty at the SMS shopping center. It makes no difference if a Social Democrat
stands at checkout proclaiming his love for banana farmers in Paraguay.

Revolutionary agitation at the checkout is just a bluff.

A ton of inch-sized gravel stones from the Hundsarabotnur quarry, sixty
kroner.

Genuine Faroese gravel.

The fatherland in cubit measure.

The new incinerator on Hjalli, this twentieth-century midden with the
country's tallest chimney, a mini-hell charing the leavings of 18,783 modern
consumers, not to mention the packaging from all the Moloch-importers,
the smoke-ejaculating iron phallus, roasting oystercatcher chicks in their
eggs . . .

Thus Eigil could sit and scribble during city council meetings. The
meetings were not interesting. Every meeting since he had been
elected to the city council was dominated by checking off the agenda. The 1988 budget for Tórshavn's municipality was around 231 million kroner, the 1989 budget around 253 million. It took a decided
and detailed form of government to operate kindergartens, schools,
oversee road maintenance, pay salaries, and otherwise manage all
other normal municipal responsibilities.

The investments made in the 80s had been necessary, of course, but they had also been expensive. The indoor swimming pool, which came into use right before 1983, cost around 42 million kroner.

By the time the elderly residents moved into the Lágargarður nursing home in 1987, the price tag for that project had reached almost 70 million.

The Hjalli incinerator was also finished in '87 and cost around the same as the Lágargarður nursing home.

The water reservoir up in Villingardalur was completed the following year, and along with the treatment plant and the road leading up to it, the price reached 110 million kroner.

Midway through the 80s, the port undertook a major project east of the old breakwater, and when all was said and done, the project, which included space for warehouses and a modern container port, cost around 140 million kroner. The port authorities, who oversaw the city's maritime operations, had miscalculated and had to ask the municipality to assume a loan worth 70 million kroner.

The small port of Sund on Kaldbaksfjørdur was another thing entirely. The plan was that a Faroese-Icelandic industrial firm would build an ultra-modern fish-processing plant on the wharf, but when the wharf was finished the firm pulled out of the project. By then the municipality had expropriated most of the infield belonging to the Sund farm, and fighting the expropriation so negatively impacted the health of the farmer that it killed him. So aside from a dead landowner, Tórshavnars were stuck with a bill for 50 million kroner.

That sum rested on the shoulders of around 11,000 taxpayers.

Sports were also a major investment in the eighties, and one Eigil firmly supported. Unconditionally. Not because he was particularly interested in sports, or was trying to curry favor among young people. Not at all. In his eyes, Bjørn Borg, Maradona, and Mike Tyson were as brain-dead as the masses who worshipped their triumphs. Eigil had the same arrogant, nineteenth-century attitude toward the masses as Napoleon Nolsøe. He could understand Pole, who had shed no tears for dying babies during the measles epidemic. Like Pole, Eigil thought there was much greater cause to weep for an adult, especially if he had been a good person. People were okay individually, but as a mass they could be threatening and unpredictable. Eigil reasoned like this: A city is an artificial being wherein nature and culture are in constant struggle, and for culture to gain the advantage, it was necessary to keep serious threats in check. Anywhere 15,000 people were gathered was crawling with bacteria, and that was why, for example, sewers were dug in the ground. Sea travel required a certain control over the sea itself, and so seawalls were built. And it was also necessary to control the natural savagery harbored in youth. Therefore, it was sound political policy not to be stingy, but to provide young people with sports halls and playing fields. Athletes were not the ones who increased crime statistics. Exhausted soccer players were too tired to bomb people's eyebrows off. Table tennis players and volleyball players were asleep by midnight, not to mention all the heroes of boat racing. They did not trespass on private or public property or go stalking lone women to rape them in the garden.

Now the city council's majority was trying to get rid of deadweight. They privatized the bus routes and closed the quarry at Oyggjarvegur. Havn was also saddled with a large fleet of houses that were either in miserable condition or were poorly maintained. Among these decrepit properties were Nils Tvibur's Mosque, William Heinsen's childhood home, and Sloan's house. The latter two were deemed to have culture-historical value and were restored. The former ended on the for-sale list.

The Self-Governance Party had only one seat on the city council. The biggest ballot winner in the '88 election, and also in the '84 election, for that matter, was Poul Michelsen, who represented the People's Party. Before becoming mayor, he had controlled a rather large wholesale company, and Eigil soon realized that he governed the city council coalition in the same way. The man was democratic as long as the other city council members were of the same mind. However, when the other politicians shied from making unpopular decisions, or when they allowed committee matters to stew, wanting to hold special referendums on the smallest details, Poul Michelsen hung his democratic jacket in the closet and entered the council chambers in his despot's robe.

This was his third term as mayor, and aside from being clever, the man had an uncommon work ethic. And that was a trait Eigil respected.

One time when the two of them were alone after a city council meeting, Eigil said that it was unfortunate that an independent man like the mayor—in truth, he was a civil anarchist—did not break with his party and its organ, the *Dagblaðið*. The milieu in which the People's Party moved had become coarse and primitive. Eigil said he would go so far as to maintain that the lack of humanity had helped create a new breed of Faroese who feared culture and modernity, and who shamelessly pandered to the ultimate one-eyed brand of Christian sectarianism. Any problems the Faroes had were not religion-based; if anything was wrong there, it was that Faroese were too devout. What the people needed was an enlightened elite, both on economic and cultural planes.

Poul Michelsen listened until Eigil was finished. Then he asked who Eigil's political role models were.

Eigil's answer was short and sweet. The industrial miracle of California's Silicon Valley, and Japan.

"And how do you propose to unite Silicon Valley and Japan with the Self-Governance Party?" the mayor asked him.

"I have no idea," Eigil said.

"I won't hold it against you," the mayor responded. "The party has been a coffin since Jóannes Patursson left the Self-Governance Party in 1936. To be a member, you either have to be infatuated with political decadence or you have to be a sly devil with a hidden agenda."

After Eigil had sat on the council for about half his term, he decided to tell Kjartan á Rógvi, the manager of the accounting firm where he worked, that he would like to reduce his work week to twenty-five or thirty hours.

Eigil was quite certain that Kjartan would have no objection to this request. Most of the city's accounting firms had less to do now, and his time as number two in the organization was over. Since the firm's twentieth anniversary celebration, the air between them had cooled.

Amalia, Kjartan's wife, had come onto him. And Eigil viewed that with distaste. He considered it vulgar to become involved with the boss's wife. Indeed, Amalia had been so forward that Eigil had seen no other choice but to insult her. He said he did not have much interest in old vacuum cleaners, and besides, her bag was just about full.

For two or three seconds Amelia stood and chewed over his remark. When she could finally speak again, she whispered that this humiliation had been duly accounted for, and would not be forgotten.

The Rattling Keyring

ACTUALLY, IT WAS by complete chance that Eigil was chosen to be the Self-Governance Party's candidate. He no had previous ties to the party whatsoever. Neither his mother nor Ingvald were self-governance people, nor did he have any other acquaintances who voted for them. At least not that he was aware of. Karin was a social democrat and his few friends in the Writer's Association, or rather, the literary colleagues with whom he occasionally spoke on the phone, were far to the left.

During his university years in Copenhagen he had always voted for the Radical Left. Twice he had supported them. They were an elite group led by academics and old high school and college folk, and although the party was a little dusty, it was reminiscent of the Self-Governance Party, at least as the party had been back in its heyday in the 1910s and 20s.

When Eigil analyzed the results of the 1992 election, he nonetheless realized that perhaps the apparent coincidence was not all that coincidental. He was a politician at heart, as most authors were. His critical faculty sometimes prompted him to make harsh judgments, and as a writer he desired to be seen and heard. It was the exhibitionist impulse of his poetic soul.

As a result, when the Self-Governance Party's chair, Jens Julian við Berbisá, rattled his keyring, Eigil was, so to speak, ready to enter into politics.

It began with a long interview the *Dimmalætting* conducted with him following the release of his San Francisco book. In that interview Eigil called himself a cultural Faroese. He said that culture stood for humanism and for art, but also for the awareness of tradition. To be Faroese primarily meant that you were born here, and you should certainly tend the ground upon which your crib had stood. Yet to build an idolatry around said ground, which he believed to be the Republican Party's political slogan, was pure intellectual nonsense.

The Social Democrats and the Unionists preached fear, cultivating it among the retirees, who scarcely had the means to fill their gas tanks, and also among the church-goers, who were afraid of what would happen to the church if Faroese authorities took over.

The Social Democrats in particular were composed of double-dealing unionists. They wanted the Danes to support everything, even while they deluded people into thinking it was their political skill that brought public funds into the country.

The Unionists had no objection to being governed directly from Copenhagen. Lack of principle had always been their most notable feature. In truth, the party was a party of imbeciles. None of the unionist politicians wrote books, and you would certainly never turn to the party to find representatives of art and culture.

The People's Party worshipped Moloch, and although they seemed more honest than your average unionist man, they were also more malicious.

The Self-Governance Party was nothing to shout about, but it was still Kristin í Geil's old party, and they were still extremely open.

Immediately after the interview, Jens Julian við Berbisá called and said that he was impressed with the argument surrounding a "cultural Faroese." He said that the Self-Governance Party's current chairman was an ex-skipper, and even though he knew how to set and navigate a course, now more than ever the party needed cultural representatives.

He encouraged Eigil to run for city council in Havn. That would let them strengthen their weakened Sydstreymoy constituency and to more closely measure their metropolitan potential.

Jens Julian við Berbisá was one of those who had read most of the historical books from the time of Lucas Debes and Thomas Tarnovius, and up until Poul Petersen, the lawyer from Funningur. He had worked through *Varðin*, that excellent cultural journal, which contained a significant portion of the Faroese intellectual output from 1921 and until the present. The seventeenth-century Parliament books, which Einar Joensen had transcribed and printed, lined his bathroom shelves. When Jens Julian sat on the toilet, he often spent more than half an hour scrutinizing the three-volume work concerning old Faroese transgressions.

Jens Julian repeatedly said that he was proud to represent the same constituency as Niels Winther once had, and he reminded people that, even though the unionists were strong now in the towns surrounding Skálafjørður, it was nonetheless the people of Eysturoy who had once elected the first Faroese self-governance man into parliament. And what once was will be again.

Jens Julian was audible wherever he went. Not that he liked to loudly proclaim, *Look, here I am!* Not at all. He had a gentle demeanor and like many middle-aged men walked with a slight hunch. He shuffled more than walked, and his white nylon shirt was always buttoned to his throat.

What made him audible was the substantial keyring attached to his belt. Keys to his Opel Kadett, the cellar door, and the outer door. Keys to the sheep shed and the storehouse, to the home office and the office closet. Keys to the postbox on Strendur and to the party's postbox in Havn. Keys to the boathouse and, most of all, keys to the parliament house. All that jingling iron advertised the fact that the Self-Governance Party chairman was nearby.

Periodically, he dropped by the shops and the various wharf areas around Skálafjørður. And he did not just talk about politics—in fact, politics was what he talked about least of all.

In Hilmar's bakery in Skála the conversation might turn to the talented women on Strendur's StÍF handball team. He said the *sociocultural* significance they represented for the town's prosperity and growth was immeasurable. Slipping strange foreign words into a conversation gave him particular pleasure, and as the conversation continued, he would drink a Hawaii Dream soda and might eat a Twix as well.

To the school superintendent in Toftir he floated the creative idea about introducing chess as a school sport. The Russians had been doing it for years, and they showed the best results in chess tournaments throughout the world.

In the baiting sheds, Jens Julian could bait one or sometimes even two whole longlines, and he would often tell a dirty story. He referred to an old Tórshavnar who supposedly said that there were two things a married man should fear: The first was petty debts, and the second was an additional cunt in the house. And when the words left his mouth, he would often cross himself, and that in itself he found mighty amusing and folksy.

The Berbisás lived with their mentally challenged son in a three-story concrete house in Kolbeinagjógv. The house was built during the years Jens Julian had sailed with the Norwegian shipping company Lange, and its size showed that here lived a man with high social ambitions.

The Berbisá flowed through Strendur, and Jens Julian was also born and raised in that town. In 1973 he moved to Kolbeinagjógv with his wife, his son, and their new surname. Jens Julian reached the rank of chief mate and skipper, but still he came ashore because it was too hard on his wife alone with their son. And Jens Julian adored his child. The fact the boy was retarded did not stop Jens Julian from loving him unconditionally.

Once ashore, he began covering his house with yellow plastic siding, and soon finished the side of the house facing the main road. The other three sides remained bare. One comedian remarked the house reflected the Self-Governance Party under his leadership, and the description was not entirely without merit. The party was in many ways like a half-finished plastic project.

What made the house truly remarkable was the twelve-foot-wide steps leading up to it. The afternoon sun warmed the stoop, and the son liked to sit there and watch clouds and play with crane flies and sunbeams. At thirteen years old the boy was around six feet tall, and when the Berbisá family took their evening stroll north toward Morskranes, it was quite an unusual sight. First came the ample-bossomed mother, at her heels her ever day-dreaming son, and finally Jens Julian with his keyring.

At a meeting of the party's Sydstremoy chapter, Eigil let fall the malicious remark that their chairman was actually the custodian of a mausoleum where the country's best men were kept behind glass.

And the image was entirely fitting. First, Jens Julian við Berbisá had neither the courage nor the vision to set a new course for the party, and second, the most prominent feature of a custodian's uniform truly was a jingling keyring. It surprised Eigil, though, that the remark went further, and that such a small party would have even people who took it upon themselves to play the role of informant.

Judging by everything, the chair of the Parliament's smallest party felt threatened, and up until the 1992 election Eigil would continue to feel the discord that had arisen between himself and the party chairman.

The Eye in the Jewelry Box

WHEN INGVALD ARRIVED home for lunch on February 2, 1992, he found his wife lying on the kitchen floor. He immediately called for an ambulance, and the drivers had arrived and left with Kristensa before the 12:20 radio news had begun.

During the next week she hovered between life and death, and the family took turns watching over her, but when she had recovered enough to communicate, she wanted nothing to do with Tórharda, and when Svanhild returned from Denmark, she also sent her eldest daughter away. Only Ingvald and Eigil sat with her, and eventually she also wanted nothing to do with her husband.

The doctor explained to Ingvald that one very common result of a stroke was what psychiatrists called *acute psychosis*. The psychosis might last for three, maybe four months, and during that period his wife would suffer from all sorts of delusions.

Kristensa did not want to be alone, however, and constantly pulled the bell string and told the nurse to find her son.

Her left side was more or less paralyzed, which meant that she could not articulate all her words, and she was also not aware of the saliva gathering at the back of her throat. Words containing *f* and *l* sounds were particularly problematic, and when she could not pronounce them, she became irate, and a disgusting spray spurted from her mouth.

It was on one of the first days following the stroke, while his mother was still unconscious, that Eigil bought the Mosque. He offered

100,000 kroner for it and explained to Poul Michelsen that his great-great-grandfather had built the cottage in the 1830s, that it was in terrible condition, and that no one else was interested in the property.

Poul Michelsen maintained that 100,000 kroner was too low an offer and suggested they raise the price to 150,000 kroner. People would form opinions on such a low price, after all, and as a politician Eigil was bound to take people's opinions into account.

"The demon with the glass eyes, that's your father."

Eigil sat dozing by the sickbed and did not immediately comprehend what his mother was saying. He grasped the word *father*, though, and woke abruptly.

His mother said Hjartvard had raped her one evening as she was milking Stjernu, and when she said the name Stjernu, her eyes filled with tears.

She had often told Eigil about the Norwegian names given to Ergisstova's cows, as well as the fact that it was Nils Tvibur who had brought the names with them to the Faroes. Besides Stjernu, there was also Staslin, Dagros, and Litagod. Only one heifer bore the Faroese name Reyðflekka; Hjartvard had bought her off a Porkeri boatsmith, and Reyðflekka died that same year from milk fever.

Unfortunately, the luck the Norwegian names brought did not extend to the eighteen-year-old milkmaid. The milk pail and the stool toppled over, and Hjartvard defiled his niece in the gleam of the petroleum lamp. They lay half in the stall and half in the manure. That was what was so revolting: Her first child was a manure baby, and all her life she had been trying to overcome that shame. Eigil was her bitter love. He had also became her pride, but there was an ever-present fear that his life and work would somehow become polluted, or that he would somehow disgrace himself.

Even though she could not fend off her uncle, she managed to scratch his eye, and afterward the wound became infected.

Hjartvard was not the type to go pounding down a doctor's door, but he could not exactly look for help elsewhere either.

An old home remedy suggested rinsing the eye with stagnant puddle water, and that is what he did. He also sliced a hard-boiled egg in two, removed the yoke, and covered his eye with the egg's hollow side turned in.

None of it did any good. The infection throbbing beneath the scab steadily worsened. His left cheek turned black, but it was not before the area began to stink of rot that he capitulated and sought medical help.

But there was nothing to be done.

Hjartvard returned home from the hospital in Tvøroyri with a single eye remaining, and sometime later he got what the doctor called a prosthetic eye.

Eigil never saw his biological father, and they never visited Sumba while the man was still alive. But during the years when the infirmities of age began to make themselves known, Hjartvard tried to atone for his misdeed. Or rather, he tried to atone for a long line of misdeeds that he had accumulated from his years living and working south on Sumba.

Kristensa and Ingvald's house stood on Landavegur, not far from Kinabrekka, and in 1962 the roof suffered substantial fire damage.

One stormy autumn day that same year, the old man traveled north to Havn with 13,000 kroner for his niece. He hoped that she would be generous enough to accept the money. As it turns out, he had underestimated the power of her resentment. He did not get so much as a foot in the door, and had to shout his errand through the mail slot.

Kristensa told him to get lost, she wanted nothing from him, least of all money. Ergisstova's top psychopath could go to hell.

Hjartvard shoved the money through the mail slot and set off down the road.

At that point, Kristensa opened the door and shouted to him that if he did not come and take his money back, the wind would have it.

But he just shrugged his shoulders.

Kristensa grabbed the stack of hundred-kroner bills in her right hand and violently threw it after him.

Oh, that she-devil! Hjartvard sighed, as he saw the wind scatter his hard-earned money. Behind every bill stood lambs, ewes, and rams that he had tended and slaughtered, and whose bodies he had hung to dry in the storehouse. He felt a pain in his chest and leaned against a pole while he watched his riches flit away. Some bills stuck to neighboring roofs and houses, others ended in the brush out on Kinabrekka, and some flew over the Rættará River on toward the west harbor.

In 1964, Eigil went to Sumba for the first time and saw his father's glass eye—or rather, his great-uncle's, since in 1964 he was still ignorant of his biological origin.

His cousin Margit showed him the eye. She was two years older than Eigil, and she enjoyed showing her younger and rather awkward cousin from Tórshavn everything possible, including her budding womanhood.

The eye was kept in a small jewelry box in the sideboard. She unfastened the lid, lifted the light-red cotton square covering the eye, and told Eigil to smell it. He held back. She whispered in his ear that it smelled a lot like her pussy, and he turned away, feeling queasy.

He did not want to see an eye that had neither brows nor lashes. It was as if the eye could see through everything, even straight into the realm of death. This was what was so strange: his deceased great-uncle Hjartvard's glass eye in its jewelry box, surveying the living.

And the pupil was brown. Eigil himself had brown eyes, and so did his mother, and Margit. His mother said their brown eyes came from the Norwegian side of their family, and Eigil pictured a whole swarm of brown eyes setting forth from western Norway across the Atlantic and landing in Sumba.

Eigil asked Margit if she knew why their great-uncle had a glass eye. She did not. The Sunday school teacher in Betania had once said that whoever saw a nixie could be certain their eyes would rot out of their heads, so Hjartvard must have seen a nixie. Suddenly, she hesitated. She could not actually remember if the Sunday school teacher had said that a person would lose both eyes or only one.

Eigil was eleven years old that summer; it was his first time in Sumba, but it was like the place remained closed to him, at least the town that lived in his mother's stories did.

The sky reached high over Beinisvørð, and the two neighboring cliffs, Spinarnir and Blæing, looked nearly blue as Eigil stood outside the Billhús and observed their outlines.

Even stronger light streamed from the great sea, and the eternal sighing, which echoed along Sumba's entire rocky shore, out at Pollinum and east toward Sandi Lítlá, filled the townspeople with a sharp and mighty sound. Nowhere else in the country could you find such dancers and singers as there were in Sumba.

When it rained early in the morning, it was as if the entire town was covered in a layer of brightness, and the drops sprung cheerfully from the buckets or off the red tarp spread over Uncle Nils's mower.

But the light was not compatible with the dark brutality of his mother's stories.

Eigil was especially interested in the stories about his great-grandfather Gregor, or Gregor hjá Djøssuni, as the Sumbingurs called him.

Gregor was born in 1858, and by the time he was twelve was already helping the Sumba church-bell ringer. In truth, the bell ringer was not an old man—he was at most in his thirties, but he was not entirely bright. Like so many other Faroese during the second half of the nineteenth century, he had been ruined by drink.

Nils Tvibur told his son that it was the same in Norway. He told his son the story of Hans Nielsen Hauge, who tried to encourage the northmen to put the stopper back in the brandy bottle and put their lives in God's hands. However, his father continued, Hauge was no Muhammad, and the northmen did not have the Arab's strength.

Nonetheless, the words stayed with Gregor, but what pleased him most was that his father approved of his sexton work. With a happy heart he let the bell ring east to Bø, up to Kvíggjá, and all the way out to Hørg, and he felt like he had been called to wake the town from its sinful brandy-stupor.

Eight years after Gregor murdered his father, he married Susanne Krogh, commonly known as Sunkan, the oldest daughter of Pastor Krogh from Leirar. They were married in the newly built church in Bug.

In these years Gregor was considered one of Sumba's stewards. He was of slighter build than his father, but whereas his father Nils had projected something sinister, his son was said to have the most good-natured eyes. Aside from three cows, he was also responsible for the town's bull, and when children from "brandy homes" occasionally asked for something to eat, he never refused them.

However, beneath all the good deeds and humility lived a tortured soul, and as the years passed it became ever clearer that Gregor was an oddity. He talked to himself, and when his wife asked what he had said or whether something was wrong, he might say that as long as you were breathing, hope was ahead. And his wife could not deny that. He might also say that it was foam bulls you heard bellowing in the ocean currents, or that Sumbingurs only believed in the drying house and the power of grave-mould.

And it was true. Sumbingurs had the bad habit of stealing into the graveyard to fetch consecrated ground, which they then placed beneath the pillows and blankets of people they disliked. Yes, generally speaking, Sumba was a town where the underworldly kept a firm grip on the living.

However, Gregor's words were neither evocations, nor were they pieces of a conversation. The words came, so to speak, from nothing, and that was what terrified Sunkan. Bit by bit she was forced to acknowledge that her husband had locked himself away, and no matter how she tried to get through to him, it only got worse.

Gregor's most peaceful moments were up in the church tower on Sunday mornings when he could dream away uninterrupted.

Occasionally his father's ghost would visit, and the first time Gregor saw his father's head coming through the trapdoor, he was filled with terror. As he used to do as a child when the old man beat him, he crept along the tower floor saying he had not meant it, and if his father wanted, he was welcome to spill his blood.

It turned out that was unnecessary. The years spent on the other side had transformed and gentled Nils Tvibur, and eventually his father became Gregor's best friend. And that was what was most meaningful to Gregor. His father seemed to have forgiven him. And what does a son want more than his father's approval?

He also began making special trips to the tower during the week, and might sit and pick clean a gooseneck or some puffins while he waited for his father.

Sometimes the old man took off his shroud and showed his son his body. His rib cage resembled the small storehouses, known as meat safes, that people were beginning to hang in their houses. Yet this safe was empty and shattered; the birds had picked it clean while he lay on the beach with the large rocks looming over him.

His son told him that the place where he had been found was now called Corporal Rock, and he said that the Sumbingurs thought it was quite the accomplishment to make a fifty-meter freefall into death's literal embrace.

Gregor did not want to tell his father, however, that no one had mourned him. He had come to town an outsider, and had vanished into death just as much an outsider.

His son loved to hear stories about Muhammad, or the Desert Captain, as his father called him. His father also described the storehouses found in death's realm, the ebony doorsteps, and the pure gold hooks from which the drying bodies hung. No foam bulls burst forth to smash boats asunder, and mermen and nixies were best friends with the dead.

Gregor sat and listened, a foolish grin on his face. He could be so far away that he did not even realize someone was calling his name. It was outright bizarre to hear someone who wanted his cow serviced standing there shouting his errand up the church tower.

Sunkan never fetched her husband herself. She always sent Hjartvard, their eldest son, and he would bring his father home.

Not unexpectedly, some comedian composed a satirical poem about Gregor, and whenever Kristensa told Eigil about his great-grandfather's hallucinations, she would repeat a couple of verses from the poem she believed Pól Johannis á Øgrum had written:

> Gregor stands in the tower
> shouting to the bones:
> "Have you seen a Corporal
> buried in the sod?
>
> Have you seen a Corporal,
> who fell from a tall cliff?
> Some believe his own son
> broke his big fat neck."

In summer of 1907 Sunkan reached out to the young pastor Frederik Moe, and one Sunday after he had preached in Sumba's church Moe visited Ergisstova. He knew that Sunkan was the daughter of his predecessor, Pastor Krogh, and like others on Suðuroy he had also heard the rumors surrounding Sumba's patricide.

Sunkan had dressed her husband up, had combed his hair and beard, and her large, gentle eyes followed the young pastor as he prayed over Gregor.

The pastor told Gregor he was possessed by evil spirits, and that he had been for many years. That was why he had killed his father. It was also Satan who had commanded him to go into the church and disgrace God's house from within. Satan, namely, sought weak links, and a twelve year-old bell ringer did not always make the best churchwarden.

Sunkan saw that her husband did not understand Moe's words, but she paled when the pastor further insisted that Gregor had consciously married into a pastor's family, the better to spread his diabolical poison. However, she was not in a position to speak, much less protest.

Nonetheless, she crossed herself several times during the pastor's speech, and so great was her concern for her husband that she was relieved the pastor's words did not reach him.

Now and then a thoughtless smile lit Gregor's eye, and when Moe said Amen, Gregor echoed him out of old habit.

Thanks to Doctor Jørgensen, Gregor was sent to the Oringe mental hospital in Vordinborg around Midsummer's Day in 1908. He sailed to Denmark with the cargo steamer *Føringur*. With him on the voyage were Sunkan and both their daughters. Aksal, Djøssan's younger brother, was an old man by that time, and Sunkan asked him to look after both boys while she was away.

In 1908 Hjartvard turned fourteen, and his brother Heindrikur—Kristensa's father and so Eigil's grandfather—had just turned seven.

Unfortunately, Sunkan never returned to the Faroes.

It Happened on St. Olaf's Day, 1918

ONE SUNDAY AFTERNOON, while Kristensa was still recovering in the hospital, Eigil asked if she wanted to hear a short story he had written about Hjartvard.

His mother thought a moment. Then she said that a true story was always worth hearing.

Eigil nodded, set his glasses on his nose, and began to read:

"It happened on St. Olaf's Day, 1918.

Hjartvard had come north to Tórshavn with the ferry *Smiril*, and his plan was to stay with his relative, the bookbinder Hans Nikláa Jacobsen. Hjartvard's great-uncle Aksal, who had raised the boys after their mother left for Denmark, had often spoken of their educated kin in the capital, and thought it could be useful to establish direct contact with the bookbinder folk.

Hans Jacobsen's youngest son was the famous Dr. Jakobsen. Aksal claimed that this clever man spoke both living and dead languages. Hjartvard reasoned that a living language must be the language people spoke. But what a dead language might be was something he dared not ask his great-uncle Aksal, who sat with eyes half-closed as he spoke about Jakobsen. Hjartvard imagined that the doctor must have the power to communicate with dead kings and chieftains, which was how he had learned the languages of the dead.

He did not know as much about the bookbinder's middle child, Onnu. She was a teacher in Copenhagen, and Aksal maintained that her surname, Horsbøl, implied Danish nobility.

The bookbinder's oldest child was Sigrid Niclasen. She ran the family's business and was also educated. She had written the play *Jákup á Møn,* and Aksal said it was such a great work that it had been translated into both Danish and English, as well as a dead language called Norn or Nornia.

In the 1890s Sigrid Niclasen and her husband bought the Quillinsgarð house, and when Sigrid was widowed, she took her parents into her home. Her mother died in 1899, and by then the bookbinder was so deaf that guests had to announce themselves from the doorway by shouting.

Hjartvard introduced himself as the grandson of the Norwegian corporal Nils Tvibur, and said that his grandfather and the bookbinder's father had been friends. He also added that the Ergisstova siblings, Aksal and Djøssan, were second cousins to Jákup Sumbingur.

Hjartvard did not want to say that his father and the bookbinder were third cousins. His father was no longer on the Faroes, and he was also not a person one spoke about. Mental illness was a form of death; a person was still breathing, but it was a tainted breath, blown straight from underworldly bellows. Mental illness was an even greater blemish than the murder on Misaklettur, that is what Aksal said. Murder required courage, after all, especially when felling an angry Westland giant.

The bookbinder, who had just turned eighty-six, sat on a small bench by the stove, his upper body rocking back and forth. His underlip hung so low that you could see his gums and all his evenly-worn lower teeth.

He remembered the Corporal well, and the shouting man in the door was not unlike the scoundrel in appearance. He had the same hunched shoulders and strong jaw. He also knew that the Corporal had a son named Gregor, but he had forgotten what might have become of Gregor. If he took after his father, there was nothing more to say.

And then the young man tried to smile, and that is what terrified the bookbinder. Involuntarily, his old hands reached for the stove's edge, and he felt the urge to call his daughter. Something had suddenly twisted the lower half of the man's face, as if something had smashed his jaw and his teeth had been transformed into rows of razor-fine peaks. It was terrifying. His smile became a gateway to Hell, and the bookbinder, who had always tried to remain within the borders of the straight and narrow, had the deranged thought that Beelzebub himself had sent one of his minions to torment him.

In *Memoirs and Autobiography*, his contemporary, Sámal á Krákusteini, wrote that the Bookbinder was one of the city's funereal singers, and it is due to his place as a former singer for the dead that the Krákustein fellow has this to say: *The bookbinder N. H. Jacobsen escaped that particular duty after he demanded a kroner in payment; most often a person was invited to the funeral feast as compensation.*

Now the bookbinder shouted and pointed at Hjartvard with his gnarled hand: "Away, you Satanspawn, you who have come to sing over *my* sinful body!"

The shout surprised Hjartvard, and Sigrid, who heard it down in the cellar and stuck her head through the cellar trapdoor, immediately saw that her father was scared to death.

She too received a smile from the giant, but did not grow afraid like her father.

She let the trapdoor bang shut, and without greeting Hjartvard or inquiring about his family, said that her father was unable to receive guests that day.

In a more friendly tone, she added that they were in process of moving into the old secondary school, so he would have to excuse them.

Hjartvard had a dried ram haunch in his trunk, which he had intended to give to his relatives in Havn. The ram had grazed on the lush pasture of Skridnaland west of Beinisvørð, and when they slaughtered it, the body weighed 72 pounds. A shiny layer of fat glistened around the handsome haunch, and its greenish tint was reminiscent of September grass. But if these were the types of people he would be meeting here, they would get nothing from the Ergisstova storehouse!

At the outer door Hjartvard turned to Sigrid. He was too tall for the door opening, so he had to bend his neck and tilt his head to the side, and standing in this strange position, he said that greater respect had sometimes met a Sumbingur in Tórshavn.

Then he left.

Once you step into the Inn, you immediately enter the taproom, which was packed full of St. Olaf Day's guests. The Inn was black-tarred and three stories tall. It had extensions to the west and south, and stairs and hallways connected its great, staggering timber body. Chickens roamed the grass-sod roof, and if someone forgot to close a skylight or gable window, you could expect to discover a newly laid egg in a scarf or in a hat. The building had been mortised and nailed together, and when a couple offered up their love to Freya, or when the boisterous guests broke into song, or even when a strong southeasterly wind buffeted its walls, the partitions and French laps in the timber beams shook.

Despite the alcohol ban that had gone into effect with the 1907 referendum, people still smuggled strong drink from their hip flasks to their coffee cups, and Anna Katrina Djurhuus, who ran the Inn, pretended not to notice—it was St. Olaf's, after all.

Unsurprisingly, all the rooms were occupied. In many cases, people slept two or three to a room, and the maids had their hands full emptying the chamberpots, filling the washing pitchers, and heating water for the men to shave.

Anna Katrina advised Hjartvard to go to Gamla Danmark, where it might still be possible to find a room. Hjartvard thanked her for the advice and asked if she could tell him where a house called the Mosque was located. The woman followed him out into the yard, pointed up Bringsnagøta, said that the Mosque was located at the top of the hill and that the house was recognizable by its blue front door.

Hjartvard wiped away a tear as he looked at the Mosque. The smoking chimney indicated someone lived there. A tar barrel was boiling in the yard, but the front door was closed. Still, he decided not to approach the house.

Aksal had said that the Corporal had bequeathed the house to a Tórshavnar named Tórálvur í Geil. Aksal remember Tórálvur, or Tóvó, as the Corporal had called him, because Tóvó had sometimes visited Sumba. He was servant to Napoleon Nolsøe, the doctor in Tvøroyri, and it was said that the beautifully cultivated Doctor's Field was his work. A few years later he was sent to jail out of the country. He had instigated murder and arson in Tórshavn and supposedly ripped the testicles off some businessman. Around the turn of the century the man had returned home, and if he had been strange before, he was much more so now. People said he refused to speak his mother tongue, calling Faroese a *fucking corrupt language*, and if he heard people speak Danish, he immediately felt threatened and left. The little interaction he had with people was in English. That was the language he had used when he was out sailing the world.

Aksal thought there was sorcery involved in the Corporal's so-called will, and he often said that the Brahmadells in Havn knew quite a bit more than the Lord's Prayer.

Hjartvard eyed the Mosque. Perhaps the Brahmadells did practice magic, but it would take more than jailhouse sorcery to intimidate him!"

Eigil glanced over the rim of his glasses; he saw that his mother lay with her eyes closed and a small smile played around the corners of her mouth. He continued to read.

"Festively dressed St. Olaf's Day guests passed Hjartvard by, and only now did he notice the dried mud on his shoes. He was wearing a white shirt and tie beneath his coat, and before coming here he had gone to Magnusi á Gørðunum's boutique to buy himself a pair of Danish pressed trousers. He grabbed a clump of grass from the roadside, spit on the tips of his shoes, and wiped the mud off the black leather.

Hjartvard met two boys and asked if they could tell him where Gamla Danmark was. One boy said the café was next to Hans Bernhard Arge's forge, Utí við Grind.

Hjartvard said he did not know what *Utí við Grind* meant.

A sarcastic gleam came into the boy's eye. He pushed his lower lip out, creating an underbite that resembled Hjartvard's, and in Suðuroyar dialect he said that all you had to do was walk straight ahead, go three assholes to the left, and there was Gamla Danmark.

The boys walked away laughing, but their laughter stopped abruptly. It all happened so quickly. Before the boy knew it, a monstrous fist had closed over his shoulder, and the next moment his feet were dangling and he could feel the rural giant's breath hot on his face.

"I didn't come all the way here to be laughed at," Hjartvard whispered.

"I know," the boy replied, trying to hide his face in his hands.

"I don't give a damn which house is to the left or right in this city, but I do give a damn at being laughed at."

"I didn't mean it!" the boy cried.

Suddenly, there was the smell of urine, and a wet spot formed on the boy's pants. He had pissed himself, and he wailed so pathetically that Hjartvard instantly realized he had gone too far.

He sat the boy down, but the idiot stayed put; it seemed as if he had forgotten how to breath. All he did was inhale, and the small amount of air that did escape wheezed through his nostrils.

An older couple had stopped farther up the road, and the woman asked in a shrill voice what was going on.

"Get lost," Hjartvard told the boy. "Didn't you hear what I just said?"

But the boy did not seem to hear anything at all, and did not move from where he sat.

The older couple approached them, and it was only when the woman reached for the boy that he seemed to fully exhale. At that point he began to howl in earnest. And he did not stop, he just cried and cried, like he had been paid to do it.

The woman glanced up at Hjartvard and asked what had happened.

Hjartvard said he had no idea. But that the child was the spawn of Satan, that much he knew.

Hjartvard tossed his head, grabbed his suitcase, and marched straight-backed through the flag-bedecked city.

While he walked, he wondered at all the freshly trimmed grass sod roofs. Of course, if the birch bark was in good condition, the damp hardly reached the attic. Still, it was striking to see the city that was both trimmed and flag-covered. In the south the grass hung so far down it covered the windows, and now that he thought about it, it made the houses look as though they were drowsing, whereas in Havn everything looked so young and attractive.

But the low cliffs around the city were nothing special. And yet, Kirkjubøreyn and Húsareyn shot up like two long patches of turf and smoldered in the afternoon sun, and the higher slopes on Nólsoy also shone bright red.

Never before had he seen so many people gathered together in one location. At home it could be a little cramped in the sheep pens, as well as in the shop on Ólafløttur when the Danish weeklies arrived.

Hjartvard also remembered all the people who came together that time the loudmouthed Kirkjubø farmer came south to campaign for the telephone. The farmer insisted that speech could travel through a thin copper wire.

Hjartvard could not see that the man was lying—he thought the wire must be hollow, and some strange forces either pulled or pushed words through the gap.

In any case, it ended in laughter when an elderly Sumbingur asked the farmer if you could also fetch the doctor through the wire.

A large crowd had gathered in front of an open workshed, and Hjartvard heard several voices shout: "Come on, Berint, come on!"

When he could finally make out what was going on, he saw two men, each with a knife, sitting and eating sheep heads; by all appearances, they were competing.

One of the men resembled a heron. His long elegant neck stuck out quite a ways from his collar, and while his jaws worked, his Adam's apple quickly bobbed up and down. He had shoved his blue dress cap beneath his thigh, and a few thin strands of hair fell from his forehead onto his cheek. Hjartvard liked his appearance. The man was either a shipsmith or a schoolteacher or a parish clerk.

The other was definitely among the stoutest men, and Hjartvard heard someone call him Berint the Great Beast, from Oyrareingir.

He had a full beard, and chewed bits of food decorated the entirety of its woolly splendor. He had removed his coat and loosened his tie, and every time he reached for the beer bottle, people clapped, since a huge, hairy crack was exposed between his waistcoat and waistband.

Hjartvard could not count all of the picked-clean sheep skulls laying in two heaps on the table, but he overheard a woman who seemed to be rooting for the heron-like man say he had tallied at least nine and a half sheep heads.

Hjartvard moved on, and had soon reached a pretty stone bridge, in the middle of which people had formed a dancing ring. They sang a song about the Scottish rogue Sinklar, and although Hjartvard liked the ballad and had sung it down south, he was not one to join in. What he most needed was a stiff drink.

From the bridge one could see Tórshavn's tiny forest, which Aksal had mentioned and, on that subject, had said that during St. Olaf's the darkness there belonged to lovers.

The debauchery, at any rate, between those trees was infamous.

All Hjartvard wanted was a drink. What the Havnarfolk did with their evenings, if they wanted to go stretching each other's assholes, that was their business and also their shame.

In a little hollow across the river he loosened the cord around his suitcase, took out a triple half-pint bottle of gin, and took a seat. He closed his eyes while he drank three swallows, letting the liquid slowly run down his throat. The effect was immediate and he enjoyed the calm that descended on his mind. He was both cooled and reassured by a common snipe calling and the river's murmuring.

The last thought he had before his eyes closed was that he had promised his brother Heindrikur a bird rifle. And he should not forget that.

Adelborg, his father's sister, had scolded him more than once for treating his younger brother so harshly, and she said that Sumbingurs gossiped about the brutality in their home.

Hjartvard told her to hold her tongue, said that all Sumbingurs beat their children, and that it was written the Book of Psalms that: *Whoever spares the rod hates his children, but the one who loves his children is careful to discipline them.* That was what Aksal had said more than once.

Adelborg just shook her head.

And deep down Hjartvard knew she was right. Heindrikur was terrified of him. Sometimes when Hjartvard heard his brother crying in the night, he dragged him from his bed in a mindless rage, stared down into his face, and dared him to whimper again. Then Heindrikur sometimes admitted that he missed their mother. And it was not easy to resist such words. Sometimes both brothers broke down crying, and at moments like those Hjartvard swore to himself that he would be a better person.

Half an hour later Hjartvard woke up to find the landscape ablaze. To the southeast the sunset stretched blue and red toward Kirkjubøreyn, and to the northwest a fiery tongue lapped the more rounded head of Konufelli Mountain.

And he was ravenous. Adelborg, who had kept house for the brothers since Aksal died in April, had packed him a few rolls and a small lamb shoulder in a cloth, and as the dancers continued their song down on the bridge, he ate his fill and washed it down with small sips of gin.

At the very end of Tróndargøta, Hjartvard finally found the café with the unusual name of Gamla Danmark.

The building had been assembled using some large rocks the sea had washed into a heap, and out of the open, lit windows he could hear boisterous chatter.

Café-Jenny wiped up an unconscious man's vomit as Hjartvard asked if they had any vacancies. She asked him to excuse her while she tried to revive the drunk, and Hjartvard asked if he could do anything to help. She thanked him, and he lifted the drunk and carried him outside.

Hjartvard heard the sea surging and was tempted to dump the man down the rocky slope; surely he would wake when he hit the bottom. However, people were standing out in the yard, and Tórshavnars seemed so damn sensitive that a person was branded a criminal just for giving some Satan's spawn a little scolding. He set the man down, but could not help himself. Before he entirely removed his hands, he gripped the drunk's nose and squeezed hard enough that blood trickled from both nostrils.

After he came back inside, Hjartvard felt a tap on the back, and when he turned around he found an old man sitting there grinning, a silver-tipped cane in his hands. Whether the man was also drunk or just very old, Hjartvard could not tell, but it was obvious he had seen better days.

The man said good evening and asked Hjartvard if perhaps he was related to Nils Tvibur.

Hjartvard proudly replied that he was indeed Corporal Nils Tvibur's grandson.

At that the old man began to laugh. And it was no ordinary laugh. It was unusually shrill and importunate. The man had the high squealing cackle of a castrate, and while gleeful tears streamed from his eyes, he pounded the floor with his cane.

Café-Jenny said that she did not usually rent rooms, but that last St. Olaf's she had rigged up some bunks, and if he wanted he could have one.

Hjartvard glanced at the old man, then replied that the man who was too proud to sleep on a bunk while living did not deserve to sleep in his native soil when dead.

True, Jenny said.

Petroleum lamp in hand, she conducted Hjartvard up into a room in the attic.

On the lower bunk right by the door sat a man around thirty years of age. He wore red and green polka-dotted stockings, light-green knickers, and a waistcoat, jacket, and tie. He had a writing pad on his lap, and when Hjartvard entered, he looked at him over his glasses, said good evening in Danish, and continued to write.

Hjartvard gave his roommate a long look, then he sang a verse from the ballad of Svend Felding.

> *All my days I have heard*
> *Danish men are so pious:*
> *I thank Father God in Heaven,*
> *here must be one of them coming.*

The Dane smiled and unscrewed the cap on his fountain pen. He set his writing pad aside, stood up, offered Hjartvard his hand, and said that his name was H. P. Hølund and that he was an ethnographer."

Kristensa abruptly turned her head toward Eigil and asked who H. P. Hølund was. She had never heard of him.

Eigil replied that Hølund was a fictional character, someone he had made up.

"You can't just slip any random person into a novel," his mother said.

"Of course you can," Eigil replied. "The world of the novel has many doors, and obeys its own laws."

"Well, well," his mother murmured.

"Hjartvard placed his suitcase on a little table by the window. He had no idea what an ethnographer was. Perhaps an ethnographer bought or sold fish, or perhaps he worked for a newspaper. He was not an author; at least he did not resemble the great writer Saxo depicted in Aksal's Danish chronicles.

Hjartvard untied the cord and opened his suitcase, and immediately picked up the fine scent of his Skridnaland gin. A cup stood on the window seal, and after wiping it clean with the small tablecloth, Hjartvard filled it and offered it to the ethnographer.

Hølund thanked him, offered a toast, and then to his own surprise, emptied it.

After Hjartvard had also drunk, he presented himself as a King's yeoman from Ergisstova on Sumba. His kin had worked the farm since the days Duke Christian mixed blood with Martin Luther and started driving the papal spooks from Skåne, Norway, and Denmark, not to mention had had Bishop Jón á Hólum killed, and had made that hellion Jens Gregersøn Riber the first Lutheran bishop of the Faroes.

Hjartvard took a deep breath and continued, saying that Jens Gregersøn Riber did not have much good in him. He was one of those horny monks whom papal power had kept in check, and one of the first things the scamp did when he came to the Faroes was to knock up a woman from Kirkjubøur. It was true. But the worst thing about it was, the child was born with hooves.

"Wait, I didn't quite understand," Hølund interrupted him.

"I said the child was born with hooves. One was black like night, the other gleamed like moonlight on glass. And that tells me that Riber's seed was drenched in evil. That's why Kirkjubø folk are the way they are."

"Do you mean the Patursson family?" Hølund asked.

"Yes, I mean the family who even this moment are trying to sow doubt about the holy oath the Faroese swore in their day to King Frederick III. They're descended from that hoofed child."

Hølund reached for his writing equipment. "You said that one hoof gleamed like glass?"

"That's what Aksal the Wise said, the wisest man Sumba has ever produced."

Aksal the Wise. Hølund chewed on that name a bit. He wanted to ask the newcomer if he was a Christian or a pagan, because he remembered there was a place in Sumba called Hørg. He remembered it from the work *Faroese Folk Tales and Fables* by Dr. Jakobsen, and the story, or rather the trilogy he had liked best, and which was as much literature as history, was the one about the Laðangarður yeoman, his daughter Sterka Marjun, and her sons, the Harga Brothers. Dr. Jakobsen's work was one of the reasons Hølund had come to the Faroes in the first place. The fact that his half-brother was a pastor in Nes certainly did not hurt the situation.

In the same way that Knud Rasmussen had found a doorway into the Inuit culture, Hølund hoped during his visit to find an entrance into ancient Faroese culture. Such an entrance must exist, and if he found it, he could do his part to recreate an old identity, or at least contribute to the task.

One thing that had fascinated Hølund during the months he had spent at his half-brother's vicarage in Nes was when the Toftirmen and Nesmen sang psalms. He liked to stand at his open window and listen as they rowed south along the shore at dawn, and in his journal he described their singing as the most magnificent High Mass he had ever experienced.

While the mountains acted as altar walls, the stars played the role of candles in the choir, and Hølund believed that the power and beauty the song carried were not solely devoted to Christ, but were equally an attempt to come to terms with nature's might. The fishermen were trying to tame the sea with their song, and that was what was so precious and lovely.

Or put another way, the kernel of Faroese Christianity was a fusion of Jesus worship and pantheism. That idea was embodied in the mythical creatures particular to the Faroes, things like nixies, mermen, and sea monsters, beings that for centuries had existed side-by-side with the Old Testament patriarchs. There were other mystical creatures such as huldre and wights, but they could not be called distinctly Faroese, and anyway, they were associated with the dry elements. Hølund was also working on a thesis about Faroese Sunmen that he called *The North Atlantic Pagan Aristocrats*. The fact that Hølund was currently staying in Tórshavn, however, was due to the fact that he and his brother had quarreled. The pastor said that Hølund's ethnographic studies were pure escapism. He had fled from the great war south on the mainland, and he had also fled from Copenhagen, from their old and domineering mother.

And Hølund did not entirely disagree with his brother.

However, his half-brother the pastor added—and this was the root of the quarrel—that Hølund shamelessly stole from more serious men like Hammershaimb and Dr. Jakobsen. He also insisted that the very heart of his brother's academic ambitions was a veiled hatred of him and the church he represented.

Now Hølund was about to head back to Denmark, and by pure chance he had met a Sumbingur who perhaps knew a thing or two about sacrificial ritual sites.

He had not found any pagan traces in the Hørg trilogy, and he had to admit that it was due to simple laziness that he had not yet visited Suðuroy. However, he had several drawings of altars from throughout the Nordic countries, and perhaps this Ergisstova yeoman or Aksal the Wise could show him the remnants of a sacrificial site, or perhaps even several. Hølund remembered there was also a place on Suðuroy called Hov, which in Old Norsk meant "heathen temple" or "place of worship."

"You need to clear your head," Hjartvard said and emptied the rest of his flask into the other man's cup.

While Hølund took a sip and lit a cigar, Hjartvard told stories about his family. Hølund immediately recognized that some of what he said was pure drunken brag. However, he also felt the boasts contained a kernel of truth.

Hjartvard said his grandfather was descended from old Norwegian soldiers, that his great-grandfather and his brother had been stationed in Copenhagen in 1807, and that they had sailed with the low canon boats that sank so many British warships.

And the desire to perform heroic deeds had certainly been inherited. He told Hølund that it had nearly killed him on May 25th last year when German submarines sank nine Faroese sloops off of Føroya Banki. The day was foggy and silent, and the explosions that sank the sloops could be heard all the way to Sumba.

His mother's father came from a Jutlandish family of pastors, and he himself had thought of studying to become a pastor, but he said all that changed when his mother died in childbirth ten years ago. His wise uncle Aksal, his mother's brother, claimed that the Jutlandish Krogh branch of their family could trace its lineage all the way back to the giant Svend Felding.

Hølund remarked that Svend Felding was considered a mythological figure, and that the boundary between history and myth blurred, or completely disappeared, after seven generations.

Exhaustion had overcome Hjartvard, or perhaps he was just drunk. He dragged his shoes off his feet and flung himself onto the bunk.

Before closing his eyes, he said that whoresons and drifters might have trouble counting their family seven generations back, but that was no problem for a man related to the Desert Captain."

A Little Failed Family

THE 1992 CITY council elections fell on Tuesday, December 8th, and in the Friday edition of *Sosialurin* the lead story prior to the election had discussed the election with the term "Nepotism."

For most of its existence, the newspaper had long been oriented toward the pro-Danish community with an interest for "Things Near," as Arne Paasche Aasen's popular social-democratic poem expressed it. In the last few years the newspaper had tried to give its rather serious reputation a lighter bent.

This was reflected in its pronounced interest in trout and salmon breeding, and also in its preoccupation with billiards, that sport of happy drunks. The newspaper also had a skillful graphic artist: the former go-go dancer Hilda Poulsen. Aside from hating Faroese nationalism, she was said to be the editor's mistress.

Obituaries in the style of "has now rowed across the fjord" or "a noble candle has been blown out" had long filled the newspaper. The obituary writer was rarely named, and most of the newspaper's letters to the editor were also unsigned. The author of the lead story also remained anonymous.

In the famous Christmas Letter that the aging H. P. Hølund wrote to William Heinesen, he called the newspaper "opportunism's shithouse."

A significant portion of its news coverage was devoted to printing speeches or portions of speeches given by the Social Democratic Party's representatives both inside and outside the country.

The few times its columns grew somewhat louder was when the author Hanus Andreassen reminisced about dead Social Democratic heroes.

Eigil did not know if the editor himself was a social democrat. However, for his faithful role as the social democrats' unofficial propaganda minister, the party had voted him onto the board of the Landstrygd public insurance company. Unsurprisingly, Jens Julian við Berbisá represented the Self-Governance Party on that same board.

The author of the lead story wrote that the word *nepos* in Latin signified grandchildren or descendent, and in a tiny society like the Faroes it could hardly go unnoticed that one sometimes favored relatives and friends. Common decency, however, demanded that there be a limit. Yet the city council's finance committee chair, Eigil Tvibur, was by no means common, and the word *decency* was foreign to his vocabulary. Ten months ago he had purchased a house that was colloquially known as the Mosque, and he himself had set the sale price of 100,00 kroner.

The conclusion of the lead story was that such blatant nepotism was a threat to democracy.

Late Thursday evening Kristensa called and told her son to read *Sosialurin*.

Eigil asked if something had happened.

"Why do you think I'm calling?" his mother shouted. "Who else besides you have I worried about and prayed for since the glass-eye beast raped me?"

Eigil could hear her spit frothing as it half-forced its way out between her teeth, a flood of white foam. But he also heard anxiety.

"Dear child, I didn't know that you had desecrated a grave. As God is my witness, I didn't know. The dead own the graveyard. Don't forget that."

"What did you say?" Eigil asked.

"I said the dead own the graveyard. Go get a newspaper, and God be with you."

Eigil hurried to the little kiosk at the corner of Jóannes Paturssonargøta and Grønlandsvegur. There were some paper Christmas elves sitting between the packages of candy and cream cake in the little display window, and inside the old man who ran the kiosk was about to close up shop.

They had never exchanged any words beyond the few it took to ask for a newspaper or a package of coffee. Eigil did not know the man at all, just as he did not know the other people in the neighborhood. The man had a friendly and trustworthy face. As he handed Eigil the newspaper, he quietly remarked that everything had its time. The words were neither accusatory nor judgmental, he was simply stating an old truth, after which he said good night.

When the voting results were reported just before midnight on Tuesday, Eigil was among the toppled politicians. During the vote in '88, he had received three hundred thirty-seven votes. Four years later that number had sunk to fifty-eight.

And like the scorned candidate he was, Eigil stayed home the day after the election. For the entire weekend after, for that matter. He asked his sister Tórharda to go to the Rúsuna and buy him some whiskey bottles, and then he sat behind closed doors, unplugged his telephone, and drank.

Four or five times someone knocked on the door, and twice it was sharp, urgent raps, but he ignored it.

Only once did he plug in his telephone, and that was around midnight on Tuesday evening when he dialed the one Fuglafjørður number that mattered.

It had been over three months since he and Karin had last spoken, that is, not since she had learned he had had an affair.

The other woman was Marianne Bøge, a lecturer on Nordic literature at the University of the Faroe Islands. That relationship was also over. Marianne had said that he was one of those writers who too much resembled his disturbing characters, and that frightened her.

Karin's voice was friendly, if not partly anxious. She said she had called several times because both the *Dimmalætting* and *Sosialurin*, and also someone from the Self-Governance Party, were trying to contact him.

Eigil said he had not set foot out of the door since reading the *Sosialurin* last Thursday evening, and he hoped that his political downfall would not impact the novel he was writing.

Karin asked how his mother was getting along.

Eigil said that she could take walks alone now, and that Ingvald and Tórharda were both back in her good graces.

Karin asked if that grace also extended to Svanhild.

Eigil laughed at that. He said that his mother had mellowed since the stroke. Or maybe she was just thinking things through more. One day she had asked him what he thought about inviting Svanhild and her secretary home for Christmas, or perhaps next summer. Eigil thought that summer was definitely the best time to have guests, and that answer pleased his mother.

Mostly out of politeness, Karin asked how it was going with the new novel.

Eigil was not satisfied. He said that the best passages so far were his descriptions of Henrietta Nolsøe and Betta. And the reason for that was simple. He had had a living model on which to base both women. The intelligence that blossomed from Henrietta's mouth and the eros he had instilled in the Brahmadella woman were both inspired by one woman from Fuglafjørður, whom he knew very well.

Hmm, Karin responded.

She did not want to criticize him for the fact, but his literary characters had always been closer to him than any living person, that was just the nature of things, and if that had not been the case, he would not have been much of a writer.

Nonetheless, their love had cooled. In May of '91 they had spent two weeks in New York and there it cooled even more. That was when Karin first experienced the rage Eigil had so often spoken about, and which he called his genetic flaw from Sumba. The violent episode happened in their hotel room. He had thrown her across the room, and it had cost her two broken ribs and a sprained wrist.

Of course, it had happened while he was drunk and he had also begged for forgiveness and promised that it would never happen again, that he would rather tear himself to pieces. But Karin did not believe him. Eigil was far too ruthless. Even what he wrote lacked a trace of human warmth or empathy. It was the exact opposite: his characters shattered from internal coldness.

It was not until after they returned home that she discovered she was pregnant. She had already suspected it at the beginning of June, and she called the following months the most wonderful and beautiful of her life.

Finally, she was pregnant, and all the small changes happening to her body filled her daily life with a quiet satisfaction. The incessant bouts of morning sickness were simply part of it; afterward, she brushed her teeth and drank a sip of cool tap water.

She was usually a quiet and thoughtful woman, and these were the traits that unfolded, so to speak, for every gram the fetus grew. When she realized that her clothes were becoming tight around the hips, it was a pleasure to take up her sewing basket, pull everything apart, and let out the waistline on her dresses and pants.

Her breasts also grew, she changed from a C to an E cup, and she was delighted to feel the maternal heaviness of her breasts. The veins lining her stomach became more visible; the skin of her stomach resembled a map, it was like blue rivers ran down from her breasts, spread out over her midsection, and collected into an estuary well below her navel.

She knew that her little treasure, as she called the fetus, had already developed his own digestive system, his own heart, and his own eyelashes. She had a little dreamer in her stomach, and whenever he declared his presence, either with a kick or a movement of his head, she stroked her stomach in response.

Sometimes, when her mother brought her tea in bed, she had complained that Eigil so seldom came north to Fuglafjørður. At that point, Karin replied that both she and Eigil were creating life. He through his fictional books, while she was carrying *the real thing*.

On October 17th her water broke unexpectedly, and she miscarried in bed.

Karin asked her mother to photograph what she termed the little failed family. They dressed up and sat on the living room sofa, or rather, they perched on the sofa's very edge, she and Eigil and their dead baby boy. She had dressed the baby in rompers and a little hat that she had knitted.

The photograph was black and white, and since then it had hung in a glass frame over her headboard.

A carpenter in Gøta made the tiny coffin, and the baby boy was buried in the same grave as his grandfather.

Eigil did not want to tell Karin that the little boy had proven a strange inspiration. The coffin, which Eigil himself carried, and which he lowered on top of the grandfather's rotting coffin lid, had prompted him to rewrite the fifth section of his manuscript, a chapter he called "The Little Wandering Church."

They had been talking for half an hour when Karin said it was time for her to go to sleep since she had to work tomorrow.

Eigil thanked her for the conversation, but added that the choice of love versus writing was an artificial one. That mentality was rooted in the Romantic when authors were brilliant creatures who holed up in ivory towers.

Karin interrupted him, saying that she knew what he wanted to say, and that she did not want to hear it.

"Well, it's the truth," Eigil said.

"I can't take your truths," she replied.

"I would much rather have a woman than the world of words."

"Good night, Eigil. Sleep well."

The Gold-Rimmed Entrance to Death

WHEN EIGIL CLIMBED inside his old Fiat Uno on Wednesday morning, he did not immediately notice that the vehicle had been vandalized. It was only after the heater had been running a moment that he noticed the yellow spraypainted letters spelling "PISS" across the windshield. Both Ss in the word were reminiscent of the runes the Nazis used on their posters and banners.

Egil was deeply horrified. He sat shaking, his hands locked around the steering wheel, and before he knew it, he had ripped it off the steering column in a fit of rage. The large nut was all that remained on the column; he had torn off the iron plate at the wheel's base.

He was about to smash the wheel into the lit dashboard panel when he suddenly caught sight of his eyes in the rear view mirror. Or what he thought were his eyes.

They were red-rimmed, the whites yellowish, the pupils glinting with pure insanity.

He breathed through his nose for a moment and then carefully set the steering wheel aside.

Enough was enough! He had not bought the Mosque for personal gain, but because he was afraid of losing his mother. And even if he had bought the house for personal gain himself, what the hell did that have to do with anyone else? And the fact that a twenty-seven-year-old man on New Year's Day, 1980, pissed on the grave of a man whom *the very next year* he came to admire and respect—that just showed a capacity for strong emotions. And that was the kind of emotion that the *Sosialurin* needed more articles about!

Tucking his bag under his arm, Eigil began to walk with long strides home along Jóannes Paturssonargøta. He did not look right or left, and whatever thoughts the pedestrians and drivers entertained about him, or if they had any such thoughts at all, that was their business.

One thing was clear: If he began to view himself through the eyes of others, it meant he had already put himself in the defendant's seat, and then all Hell was loose.

A small sigh escaped his lips, and he was forced to smile; the last few days he had been doing nothing but viewing himself with what he imagined were the accusing looks of others, so Hell was already loose. Hell had ripped open; any minute now smoke would begin leaking from people's ears, and cloven hooves would be galloping through the streets!

He unbuttoned the top two buttons on his coat and walked along, slightly more relaxed. Traffic also seemed calmer, if not to say outright slowed. It was as if the drivers in their various vehicles did not care that this dark morning was the 343rd day of the year, that it was almost 9:30 in the evening, and that time itself just ran and ran without ever pausing to take a rest.

He heard the sleepy horn of a ship out by the pier, and what Tórharda said was right, that the city's pulse was significantly weaker since both the large banks had gone bankrupt.

But the full moon with its gold ring was lovely. The moon calmed the mind, just like pictures of the moon have always set people at ease, and just then Eigil noticed Kirkjubøreyn's snowcap.

When he had reached the old churchyard, he glanced out of habit down the graveyard's middle aisle. The maple and rowan trees were bare. If it had not been so dark, he could have made out Pole's grave.

On New Year's Eve 1980, the entire city had been covered in snow. He had had to force the churchyard gate open, and at some points he was knee deep in snow as he waded toward Napoleon Nolsøe's grave. He opened his zipper and a yellow stream sank into the white blanket of snow. And Eigil pissed and pissed. It was as if he had been storing up urine all Christmas for this one infamy, or as if his bladder was connected in fellowship to all those who had despised the loud-mouthed Nolsøe clan. When Eigil finally shook off the last drops, Pole's was the only black grave in the entire graveyard.

And in truth the image of that black grave had never left him. Not that he was plagued by nightmares. Not at all. But a gold-rimmed entrance into death, that image stuck fast in his mind.

The aversion he had felt against Pole had later been transformed, or rather it had been transferred eventually to Ole Jacobsen, the man responsible for the whole damned situation in which he found himself.

Eigil had not known Ole Jacobsen, not personally or professionally, and the fact that a complete stranger could cast such a dark pall over his life was rather uncanny.

Eigil only knew that the man was from Vágur, and that during the war he had gotten a doctorate in comparative literature. That information was in the preface to volume IX-X of *From the Faroes – Úr Føroyum,* which was published in 1983: *This final volume of* Úr Føroyum *was largely assembled by Ole Jacobsen, who unfortunately was unable to see its completion.*

So wrote the head of the Dansk-Færøsk Samfund, Aage H. Kampp.

An odd misprint in the preface indicated that Ole Jacobsen truly was deceased. *Føroyum* was spelled *Fóroyum,* an error that never would have escaped Jacobsen's observant eye.

Ole Jacobsen might be called a tragic figure, since it would be difficult to otherwise describe a man whose wife went insane and took her own life—and if that was not enough, whose daughter did the same, following her mother into death.

Eigil had learned those facts from Marianne Bøge. While study-ing in the Faroese department at the university, she had attended some lectures that Ole Jacobsen held in the 70s. She said the man was an amazing lecturer. Clear, sharp-minded, and with his big white Andy Warhol hair, also charming and seductive.

One of Jacobsen's lectures was on Christian Matras's poetry, and the story of Matras roaming old Tórshavn's narrow streets in order to find the correct rhythm for his masterful translation of "Fare World, Farewell" was also something Eigil heard from Marianne Bøge.

Jacobsen had also given a lecture on Karsten Hoydal's last two published poems. He thought that enough had been said about the poetry collections *The Red Dark*, *The Singing Stone*, and *Water and Light*. Jacobsen wanted to highlight "Bridges" and "Bamboo's Song," two great poems that demonstrated that the aging writer had attained new poetic ground. For strange reasons, "Bridges" and "Bamboo's Song" would prove to be Karsten Hoydal's last works. He died at the height of his craft, which guaranteed his remains would not be hauled out some literary back door and buried at the foot of a sickly tree.

However, Eigil was certain that Ole Jacobsen also had a hidden agenda when he published his eighty-seven page long essay in 1972 on the measles epidemic in the journal *From the Faroes – Úr Føroyum*. The man had sown hatred on Napoleon Nolsøe's remembrance, and had the hatred been just, there would have been a kind of brutal rationale about it. But Ole Jacobsen's hatred was irrational, and what sprouted from irrational soil was always unpredictable and most often abominable.

The professor could go to Hell, and that was probably where he went when he had died.

Laughter bubbled in Eigil's chest as he looked down into the churchyard. He pictured the professor strolling among the coffins in death's realm. Only a few strands were left of his Andy Warhol hair, and his burial shroud fluttered around his dry, rattling bones. Eigil also heard the coffin lids creak when the professor broke them open, and whenever he gazed into the gaping skull of a Faroese nationalist, curse words filled the halls beneath the piss hole.

True, Ole Jacobsen had succeeded in casting a light over a forgotten period in Faroese history, and he also correctly criticized the nationalistic approach that all too often colored regional history writing.

Yet the man did not just write about the measles epidemic. The essay could also be interpreted as a personal statement about the entire nationalistic elite from the 1840s until his own day, or at least up until the Klaksvík Rebellion in the 1950s, where the citizens of Klaksvík took an armed stand against the forced removal of a Danish doctor, thereby underscoring Faroese independence.

Jacobsen wrote: *There is a kinship between the aftermath of Panum's visit to the islands and the instincts it unleashed and the social mass- or group hysteria, not to mention the affect- and conflict psychology, which a century later came to a glaring outbreak during the doctor's affair in Klaksvík, and placed one of the islands' largest towns under a state of siege after the doctor's case became truly politically infected.*

Eigil found himself incapable of sketching a closer psychological profile of this man, who reverently wrote about cultivated Danes, especially Panum and Pløyen, even while he defiled Faroese nationalists.

And Marianne Bøge also never succeeded at the task. Or rather, the subject had never come up, and since they had lost contact, it also no longer mattered. However, Eigil had suspected her of being in love with the professor, and not only that, he was convinced she had been his mistress. The refined slut, who lived alone with two daughters, loved loud men, which is why she had been Eigil's nighttime companion. He could easily imagine that she was also the type who enjoyed hearing middle-aged men shout their pathetic ejaculations into the dark. And when you threw a spiteful Faroese anti-nationalist into the mix, she almost writhed with ephemeral desire.

Yet Marianne also believed the professor had had two faces.

She said that she and some other students had gone drinking with the professor, and Ole Jacobsen did not use gentle words when he criticized Christian Matras, the poet whom in his public lecture he had just praised to the skies.

Jacobsen thought that the academic exam in 1928 destroyed Matras as a poet, and that the man had been a *kíkur*, an inflated whale stomach, all his days. For a time the *kíkur* was filled with air from socialistic compressors. Then nationalistic hoses were connected. For a few years the *kíkur* had floated around with bishops Kingo and Grundvig, basking in the warmth of church hymns. He was a great consumer of Pan-Scandinavian, and at times Francophilic, air, and after returning to the Faroes in 1965 and accepting a professorship at Fróðskaparsetrinum, he was so full of every air imaginable that he practically hovered over Faroese waters.

Marianne claimed that deep down Ole Jacobsen suffered from the lack of that Mosaic yearning that prompted others of his generation to return home after the exile of the war years, and to begin rebuilding what was left of the Faroes. Instead, he remained in Denmark and created a safe bourgeois framework for his own life, whereas the nationalists undertook to modernize the old homeland.

On page 68 in Volume VI of the journal *From the Faroes – Úr Føroyum*, Jacobsen wrote that Faroese students studying in Copenhagen had once threatened to tear Panum limb from limb for the way his *Observations* described the Faroes. Jacobsen wrote: *If these details about Faroese reactions—which, after all, do not stem from popular, but from so-called intellectual Faroese sources—are not exaggerated, and, truthfully, one must say they are not, then one will perhaps ask whether these people and their insolent representatives truly were ignorant of all other possibilities. Or were the conditions that Panum criticized so provocative and insulting that, on the islands where he had healed around 1,000 victims of the epidemic, he could expect nothing more than censure and threats of a beating as payment for an accomplishment the rest of the world found admirable, and which was viewed as a sacrificial human effort and a great scientific achievement?*

What Panum actually wrote in his *Observations* was: ". . . I myself observed and treated about 1,000 victims . . ." His colleague August Manicus treated around the same number of patients, which means that about a fourth of the Faroese population was in their hands.

However, Panum did not actually say he healed 1,000 Faroese, as Ole Jacobsen claimed. And it was not out of humility that Panum so expressed himself, but simply because it was *not possible* to cure people once infected. Ole Jacobsen should have known that. The introduction, in fact, proves that he did know it, and yet failed to mention that fact.

Instead, he uses religiously charged words like *healing* and *victim*. He makes Panum seem semi-divine, and that is not because he loves men like Panum—irrational people seldom love. No, he makes the man seem godlike because he needs Panum's reputation to act as a stepping stone to: *"these people and their insolent representatives who truly were ignorant of all other possibilities."*

As Panum wrote in his *Observations*: *"The Faroe Islands would probably not have lost nearly 1,000 inhabitants if an edict directed against the introduction of measles had not been removed some years ago."*

These words cannot be interpreted as other than as a direct medical accusation against the incompetence that characterized Faroese authorities, particularly Amtmand Pløyen, and of course Landkirurg Regenburg. Yet Ole Jacobsen was also silent on this subject.

Fuck you, Ole Jacobsen, Eigil thought as he turned from Jóannes Paturssonargøta onto Dalavegur, patting the churchyard fence.

You Reap What You Sow

ELSPA TÓRA LAMHAUGE greeted Eigil when he entered the reception at 9:00 A.M.

He flashed her a peace sign with his left hand.

It happened before he knew it, the spreading of forefinger and middle finger. It was not something he usually did, and he regretted his assumed playfulness.

Peace signs, fist bumps, the extended right arm Nazi salute—none of those had ever attracted him.

Elspa Tóra, on the other hand, flirted with him every now and then, and sometimes she called him *my friend* or *my dear*. She was a woman barely in her fifties. When her children left home, she went back to work, and for the last seven years had worked the reception desk at the P/F Rógv accounting firm.

Today she simply smiled and said that the director would like to see him in the Inner Sanctum.

Eigil stopped at the desk and asked if she thought he looked strange.

She gave him a concerned glance and shook her head. She said she was sorry he had not been re-elected to the city council, but that it would take more than a headline in the *Sosialurin* to make her change her mind about the city's most handsome sheik.

Eigil was so moved that his eyes filled with tears.

She handed him her handkerchief, and while he dried his eyes, he said that she must bear with him, he was little fragile at the moment.

Kjartan á Rógvi had seen Eigil outside, and when Eigil entered his office, he was standing before a large wall painting by Ingálvur av Reyni titled *They Wait*, which meant the boss had something serious on his mind.

Kjartan liked having this particular painting behind him on the occasions he was interviewed for TV or photographed for some newspaper.

Eigil was convinced that what Kjartan lacked in natural dignity he borrowed from this great work, or from the visual arts in general.

Kjartan began by saying that his telephone had not stopped ringing all weekend, and added that what was printed in the *Sosialurin* was nothing less than a scandal.

The newspaper was on his desk. He flipped to the lead story, and then to the letters to the editor, and after reading several snippets aloud, he asked what the hell was going on. As the firm's director, he thought he had a right to know.

Eigil patted the leather chair and asked if Kjartan planned to offer him a seat.

Kjartan stared at him in disbelief, and then grew furious.

He did not give a shit if Eigil sat, stood, or lay down. That was beside the point. He wanted to know what was going on. Nothing more.

"Okay," said Eigil. "Should we talk about the article first, or is it the public urination you find more interesting? I don't know if you've heard, but pissing or spitting on graves is actually the most popular underground sport on the Faroes, perhaps in all the Nordic countries. And you know why? Because Northerners hate each other."

Kjartan á Rógvi walked over to the window, and when he had calmed down, he said that the matter was serious. The reputation of a well-respected firm was at stake, whose clients numbered some of the largest companies in the country, and in addition to legal advisers also had eleven full time employees. That a top employee had dishonored a grave was extremely concerning.

Eigil replied that the firm actually had ten employees. The eleventh had just quit.

Kjartan gripped his head. "I'm too old for this bullshit," he shouted. "You can't be so childish."

"If we were just talking about childishness, everything would be good," Eigil responded.

"I don't understand," said Kjartan. "You've changed."

"Maybe I have. But the fact of the matter is, I don't want to listen to such garbage so early in the morning. The most petty, bourgeois newspaper in all the northern countries has character-assassinated the man who used to be number two in this firm. That's what's going on.

"I've been hung out to dry, and you know what that means? It means, among other things, that people get to vandalize my car. They get to call me up and insult me. That's the real problem, not that your and Amalia's weekend was ruined."

"You reap what you sow," Kjartan replied.

Eigil's eyes filled with tears, but this time he simply let them run, while he whispered: "So you've finally gotten me into the catapult so you can shoot me to Hell."

Eigil saw sudden fear bloom in Kjartan's eyes, and in the same breath understood why. He realized he was holding up the leather chair, about to hurl it across the desk. He was so surprised he dropped the chair with a clatter. One of the back legs struck the floor and broke, and the chair toppled onto its side.

Kjartan tried to say speak, but could not.

"You can expense the chair leg," Eigil said.

He took his key ring out of his pocket, removed the keys to the building and to his office, and set them on the desk.

"I have some books and folders in my office. Elspa Tóra can pack them up." Then he said farewell and left.

PART
FIVE

The Mosque

ONE LOVELY DAY in March 1993, someone knocked on the Mosque's front door, and Eigil opened it onto an old man standing in the yard. He was wearing a Faroese hat and a long coat, and was carrying a leather bag in his hand. Eigil could see the man wanted to speak with him, and invited him inside.

The old man said that his grandfather was Lýðar í Geil, and that Lýðar had been Tórálvur í Geil's brother. He said he was aware of the friendship that had subsisted between the Norwegian corporal Nils Tvibur and his great-uncle, and added that he had thought a lot about Eigil since the *Sosialurin* wrote that he had purchased the Mosque.

But he had not come to visit just to talk about old friendships.

The man opened his bag and set a small bundle of letters bound with a faded ribbon on the kitchen table. He also set an American book called *Leaves of Grass* on the table; he said the book and the letters had been kept in his great-uncle's sea chest. Since Eigil was a writer and also the Mosque's owner, he might be curious about these things.

After they had talked a while, Eigil placed two glasses and a bottle of whiskey on the table, but the old man said he could not drink if he did not have something to smoke with it.

Eigil told him to wait two minutes and he would run down to Haldor's shop for a pack of cigarettes.

"If you're going to buy something," the old man called after him, "buy cheroots."

Eigil returned with a pack of Lucca, and while the comfortable smoke filled the kitchen, they sipped their drinks.

The old man was talkative and told Eigil about everything the sea chest had held. Besides the letters, there was a Danish bible printed in 1842, some awls, and also a photograph of a great-great-aunt's gravestone in Denmark.

The chest had also contained an amusing painting of a dancing girl. He could remember it well. Whether the girl's name was Edga or Edgar Degas, or if that was the name of painter, the man really could not say. A lawyer had liked the painting so much that he had bought it. Or rather, the lawyer had handled a matter for his father, and when it came time to settle up, the lawyer had said that instead of money his father could give him the painting hanging in the parlor.

Eigil asked the old man to repeat the painter's name, since he was not sure he had heard right. Again the man said Edga, or Edgar Degas.

Eigil tried to act casual. He was familiar with the paintings of Degas and other French impressionists, and he also knew that their paintings sold for millions.

But he could not bring himself to say this out loud.

Nonetheless, he asked for the lawyer's name, and the old man said it was Husted-Andersen.

In terms of the letters, the old man knew that Doctor Napoleon Nolsøe's widow, Henrietta Nolsøe, daughter of Commandant Løbner, had kept them after her husband died, and that she had given them to Tóvó when he returned from Denmark in 1901. And so generous was this Henrietta that she also gave Tóvó an old telescope that had once belonged to Nólsoyar Páll. He said that Henrietta had liked his great-uncle, that she had truly cared about him, and that Tóvó was sorely grieved when the sweet lady died in 1906.

They had finished about half a pint from the bottle when Eigil asked if it was true what he had heard, namely, that Tóvó refused to speak both his mother tongue and Danish when he returned from prison.

The old man replied that there was at least a kernel of truth there.

As he understood it, the many years Tóvó had spent in Vridsløselille had changed him. He avoided most people, which meant that only very few ever heard him speak.

However, the old man's father remembered Tóvó well, and all the times they had spoken together had been in Faroese. He could say that for certain, because Faroese was the only language his father knew.

Eventually, the old man pulled on his coat, saying that he had to catch the next boat out.

Eigil told him he would copy the letters and send the original back to Nólsoy.

"Nonsense," the old man said. He said Nólsoy had so many originals that, two or three more, and the long, narrow island would be in real danger of capsizing.

A Years-Old Autumn

LIKE SO MANY other houses in the á Reyni district of Tórshavn city, the Mosque had not been equipped with a toilet when Eigil had bought it. There was a dry closet behind a curtain in the bedroom, and in it a low shelf with a can labeled *Scented Disinfectant*. This chemical horror was mixed with water, and the first few times you sat on the pot, you could expect a green liquid to slosh up your backside, and if it happened to be a woman sitting there, *ahh*, Eigil sighed, *poor she-devil*.

He had searched the house thoroughly from the crawl space to the attic.

The space between the attic floorboards and the roof's crown was only a meter high; if Eigil wanted to go up into the attic, he had to crawl or squirm his way in. So he stood on the small white kitchen table, which he had positioned beneath the hatch, and with flashlight in hand he explored the attic.

The dark shapes visible between the roof timbers had to be birch bark, but a moment passed before Eigil realized that the threads hanging from the attic ceiling were roots.

The entire space above the room and also a substantial portion over the kitchen was a veritable root forest. The thickest roots were like the tip of a child's finger; from there they grew smaller, with the thinnest roots being fine as thread. In some places the roots had attached themselves to the attic floor, and when Eigil carefully blew into the forest, everything moved—dust swept across the wooden boards and the entire attic lived.

Eigil reached for a narrow box he also discovered there, and when he removed the dusty lid, he found several shoes and some cans of English shoe polish. He knew that a cobbler had kept his workshop in the house after the last war. The shoes were worn out, and judging by the battered upper leather and noticeable bunion marks, they had probably belonged to workmen who were either dead or who had not had the means to retrieve the shoes.

Unsurprisingly, woodboring beetles lived in the rafters. The tiny beasts had dug a countless number of holes, and in some places so little was left of the rafters that Eigil could scratch light brown dust out of them with his nails. There was little doubt it was pure habit keeping the roof up. He tried to find a word to describe the smell, and suddenly he realized it smelled like autumn. That was precisely it. A years-old autumn with long roots had overtaken the attic.

One of the last residents had mounted an oil burner in the old coal stove's combustion chamber, but it was difficult to say when fire had last appeared beneath its cast-iron rings. Nonetheless, the faint odor of petroleum permeated the kitchen floorboards.

And there were still houses in the neighborhood that burned petroleum. Haldor, who currently owned Restorff's old shop, was one of the last in the city to sell petroleum in cans. On still, foggy days, when the smoke barely crept from the chimney mouths, all of Høgareyn stank of petroleum. The thick fog slipped slowly between the tarred gables, drawing the petroleum smell with it and pressing it against the windowpanes. And it was like the smell had both color and shape; small bluish bubbles grew out of it and spread like scales over the thin glass. The smell hung in every blade of grass, and if someone had left a floor rag or a sweater on the clothesline, that too would absorb the smell.

To Eigil, the odor seemed so strong that a single match would be enough to set the fog on fire and burn down all the houses on the rocks.

And Høgareyn, and all of Tinganes for that matter, was little more than rocks. The only dirt to be found was on the furry house roofs, where grass and sorrel, and in some places even marsh marigolds grew as well, and on foggy days everything was enveloped in the miserable petroleum odor.

Besides the stove and sink and the small white table, the kitchen contained two stools and nothing else. Eigil bought a sofa, as well as a coffee machine and an electric oven.

He had sometimes toyed with the idea of traveling to Ireland or Denmark for a time to write, and the thought occurred again after the confrontation with Kjartan á Rógvi. But the plan was abandoned. As it turned out, this spartan kitchen was unusually well suited to the activity of sitting and writing. He could sit long days there with his typewriter, an electric IBM with a ball head, more or less as rooted as what was growing beneath the roof, and when he could not do any more, he extracted himself carefully from his forest of words and threw himself onto the couch, where he slept peacefully underneath a woven blanket.

He remembered a photograph of Gabriel García Márquez sitting shoeless at a small white table and writing, and the photo's appeal was that particular spartan element.

One of Leonard Cohen's nymphs appeared at a similar table on the back of the record sleeve from *Songs from a Room*. Her hands were on the keyboard of a little manual typewriter; behind her stood the obligatory bed, which Leonard Cohen had schlepped with him the last thirty-five to forty years, in case he should meet a Nancy, Marianne, or Suzanne.

The only thing Eigil did to the house was to hire someone to replace the dry closet with a working toilet. The people next door were kind enough to allow him to couple his toilet to their septic tank.

That kindness reminded Eigil of an odd ferry trip to Bergen on the *Norrøna* in 1986. He had bunked with a baker from Klaksvík and, although most of the passengers on board were partying, Eigil had turned in early.

He was fast asleep when the baker returned to the cabin around midnight, so drunk he barely made it into his bunk. As it turned out, the man had recently had a colostomy, and something happened that was not supposed to happen—the bag burst.

While sleeping it off, the poor baker began to shit. And it kept running out his side. All night. Brown clumps piled into a minefield of filth and diarrhea, and when Eigil woke up and discovered the source of the terrible stink, he could do nothing but leave.

The result of that strange experience was the prose piece "The Shitdog's Cultural History."

Ghosts and Tears

ALL WAS AS it should be in the Mosque, until one night Eigil woke to find an unfamiliar man standing next to the sofa.

The front door was locked, so he could not have entered that way. Eigil wanted to ask the stranger who he was, but could not get the words out, and then suddenly the man was gone.

Two months after the stranger's visit, Eigil experienced another bizarre phenomenon.

It was during the evening, and he was aware of Tórshavn's church clock striking ten. A second later it felt like there was someone inside Tóvó's old bedroom. Eigil stood up from the table, walked over to the bedroom door, and considered opening it, but was not brave enough. It was like all his courage drained away, it was all he could do to remain standing. It felt like a terrible pressure was being applied to the door, not so that it bulged, but a force so great that the door jam, the frame, and the door itself trembled, nearly bursting from the wall. And that force did not wish him well, of that he was certain. Suddenly, Eigil realized that it was pure evil pressing against that door. He felt that the Devil himself had arrived to Tórshavn.

Eigil stumbled to the typewriter, did not bother to shut it off, but just grabbed his coat and fled.

He did not want to tell his mother about these events because he knew how she would interpret them. And the fact that she was so sensitive, so mortally afraid, was strange, considering she had never shied away from telling stories about the underworldly.

Or maybe it was not so strange at all. Many Faroese blended questions of moral behavior with the supernatural. If you overstepped a certain moral threshold, you could count on the underwordly to come after you like tax collectors.

It was this idea that ensured parapsychology had not yet gotten the respect it deserved, and that was also why that pursuit of the supernatural had more of a gothic than scientific air about it.

It is worth mentioning here that Hjartvard Tvibur was apparently one of those individuals able to send messages from beyond the grave. Or so Margit, his cousin in Sumba, claimed. She and her husband visited Eigil one St. Olaf's Day, and she told him that Hjartvard had once appeared to her in a dream, complaining that his feet were cold.

She could never remember Hjartvard's voice being that afflicted while he was alive, and the dream would not leave her.

A few days later she went to the graveyard, and that was when she saw that a large hole had opened at the foot of Hjartvard's grave. Apparently, the coffin lid had caved in and broken, allowing dirt to spill and rain to fall onto Hjartvard's feet.

She had emptied three wheelbarrows full of dirt and sand into the hole and smoothed the grave's surface.

The great mystery was how Hjartvard, who was dead, could have gotten the message across.

Or maybe someone else had carried the message for him.

But then, why would someone else care anything about Hjartvard Tvibur's grave?

Kristensa did not find out about Eigil purchasing the Mosque until she came home from the hospital. Only then did he tell her that the Mosque was back in the family.

Kristensa did not reply. Still, she thought these last years had been too good to her son, and life was not generally good. Misfortune awaited everyone. But the idea that eventual tragedy might be connected to the Mosque filled her with terror.

Not until Eigil lost the city council election and had resigned from his accounting position did his mother break her silence. She called the Mosque a house of misfortune and told him to sell it or give it away. And in order to emphasize how fervently she meant her words, she said that, just think, Hjartvard had murdered poor Tóvó í Geil in that very house!

"You don't know that," Eigil replied. "No one knows that. There's no proof."

"Tóvó í Geil died on St. Olaf's in 1918, and Hjartvard was in Tórshavn on that very day," his mother said. "Besides, it was also never proven that your grandfather Gregor killed his father. Remember that. And yet he lost his mind."

"It's Nils Tvibur's house!"

"No," his mother whispered. "It's a snake pit."

"Enough," Eigil said. "I bought the house because I thought you were going to die."

"And you wanted something of your mother's? Oh, you stupid boy! Get this through your skull: A villain came from Norway. He did one good deed in his life, and that was to care for a wretched boy from Havn, and that same boy was murdered by Hjartvard a lifetime later. Our family is weak, remember that. It takes so very little to call misfortune down over our poor heads."

Two or three tears glinted in the corners of her eyes. No more than might balance on a knife point. But that point was so sharp it pierced Eigil's heart.

Since he also woke to inexplicable sounds in the house on Jóannes Paturssonargøta, he began to ask himself the uncomfortable question of whether or not he, too, might be going out of his mind.

And it did not help matters any when Kristensa gave him a neck-lace with a cross on it one day. Eigil thanked her for her thoughtful-ness, but his mother demanded he put it around his neck while she watched.

And if that was not enough, she then ordered him to go to the churchyard and clean Napoleon Nolsøe's grave.

A Wounded Sumbingur

EIGIL HAD WORN the cross around his neck for several weeks when he decided to contact the psychologist Arnfinn Viðstein. Although they did not know each other, the Viðstein folk had old roots in the city. In fact, the piano that Dia við Stein received from Napoleon Nolsøe is to this day in Arnfinn's keeping.

They met for seven sessions, but by their third meeting Arnfinn Viðstein came out and said that, in his opinion, Eigil was perfectly fine.

As for the parapsychological phenomena, he did not consider himself qualified to really address the subject. However, he stressed that during an emotionally unstable period it could be difficult to tell where to draw the boundary between old fashion ghostly visits and common paranoia.

At any rate, if he were to give a diagnosis of Eigil's condition, he would call him a wounded Sumbingur.

In his opinion, what Eigil most needed was a conversation partner to help him unravel these different cultural and psychological complexities. If Eigil regarded him as a fitting opponent, he offered to follow him down into the darkness where art remained unarticulated, where rage had no definite course, and where fear could take such irrational form that it crippled one's zest for life.

Eigil took his words to heart, and although their subsequent conversations did not alter much, it still felt like his mind expanded and his writing took off.

Eigil told the story of his great-great-grandfather's house.

The first to move in after Nils Tvibur left Havn was the soldier Jardis av Signabø. The reason Jardis moved in had to do with a violent episode that took place on board a freight yacht in 1849. Nils Tvibur had beaten Jardis so badly that he ended up an invalid and had to give up his post. To atone for his crime, Nils gave Jardis the Mosque, and Jardis lived there until his death in 1865.

Then one of Restorff's shop assistants moved into the Mosque. His name was Hansemann, but Eigil called him Dáran. He had carved his name into no fewer than three places along the kitchen walls, and as anyone knows, a moron's most identifying characteristic is the tendency to write his name everywhere.

Hansemann had moved out by the time Tóvó took over the house in 1878.

During the 16 years Tóvó sat in Vridsløselille prison, his sister Ebba managed the house, and had let an old woman and her grandson live there.

The boy was named Rikard, and although he has been forgotten today, while he lived he was something of a legend, especially among older women.

Rikard was born dumb, and around thirteen or fourteen he acquired the terrible nickname Rikard Erection. He suffered from the condition today known as priapism, which is curable, though back in the 1880s that was not the case.

The disorder involves a recurring erection, and Rikard's was of an extreme variety. He simply walked around with it protruding from his middle, and according to that day's perception of disease, it was not considered unreasonable to call him an aberrant or even demonic young man.

In one of the many hopeless letters that an aging H. P. Hølund wrote to William Heinesen, Hølund stated that Rikard was the unofficial forefather of the entire Faroese royal dynasty. Later he moderated his expression. Perhaps Heinesen had written him back to inform him that it was historically inaccurate to use feudal titles in a Faroese context.

In any case, Rikard met his benefactor in the old Leynar farmer, Skeggin Pól.

The farmer had been in Havn selling sheep, and that evening he happened upon some kids poking fun at Rikard. They had chased the boy between two houses, and each time they heard him moan in fear, they broke down with laughter. They had started to pull his pants down when Skeggin Pól was suddenly among them.

By this time Skeggin Pól was a very old man, and although his dwarfish beard was still extensive, the bloom had faded. It had turned gray, and the dry wisps fluttered around his chest and shoulders. But the voice emerging from the old, matted wool was powerful and sharp. He practically hammered out the words, telling them to take their rotten bodies to Hell or else he would call a host of iniquities upon their heads.

Rikard's grandmother was terrified when she saw the boy returning home with a dwarf at his heels, and immediately demanded to know what mischief he had gotten himself into this time.

Skeggin Pól told her to stop driveling, described what had happened, and said that everything was just fine.

Then he asked what was wrong with the boy.

The old woman said that Rikard had been motherless since two years of age, and that his father was a whoremonger from Skála who refused to recognize his offspring. The boy had been born dumb, and his father's sins had given him that terrible horn.

She pointed to Rikard's erection, crossed herself, and buried her face in her shawl.

Early the next morning the dwarf was back in their kitchen. He said that he was returning to Leynar when the tide shifted, and he thought to take the boy with him. He placed a dried mutton leg on the table, said that life was a proud song to the sun, and if she left the boy to him, she would receive two sacks of wool and a wether every year.

And it happened as Skeggin Pól wished.

Later that same morning, along with the the westwardly running current, Rikard set out in the bow of an eight-man boat, and in the following years he became the old farmer's hand.

On longer trips, for example, to Vestmanna or Kollafjørður, the dwarf took Rikard along to help, and, in the still evenings, master and servant would fish out on Steyrur or by Láturgjógv.

He tended the geese and, on his own initiative, built small hare houses up on Navahjalla and by Hvassheyggjar.

As it turned out, Amtmand Dahlerup's hares had learned to thrive not only on Sydstreymoy, but on the entire island.

The boy was also extremely dexterous with his hands. He cut the finest clog bottoms, mended tears, fashioned the wooden locks for storehouses, and also began making knife handles.

Skeggin Pól, it seemed, was correct when he argued that a farming society under Sunmen leadership was more humane than the new pecuniary society. He believed that it was uncivil and a great shame to send Faroese fools down to Danish crazy houses.

One of the first things Skeggin Pól did upon their arrival at Leynar was to give the boy a small woven belt, explaining to him that when the erection was at its worst, he should bind it against his stomach.

The good advice helped.

Otherwise, it was not uncommon for both married and unmarried women to inspect Rikard's equipment, and they could do it safely, because Rikard told no tales.

The sodomite Melkir úr Norðstovu in Vestmanna also came to inspect Rikard's equipment. He encouraged Rikard to masturbate and paid him a kroner to insert the famous erection into his asshole.

When Skeggin Pól died in the spring of 1891, Rikard had served him for five years.

With around one hundred kroner saved up in his pocket, Rikard traveled back to Havn to visit his grandmother, and, according to Hølund, that was the summer Rikard founded the so-called Faroese royal dynasty.

However, for the present story, there is another event of even greater significance.

Ebba gave birth to a late arrival, a girl named Álva after Tóvó.

One day some children were playing along Undir Kjallara on the Tinganes Peninsula when Álva slipped and fell into the water, into the forest of seaweed—and the person who dove after her was Rikard.

He knew Ebba had provided him and his grandmother with a roof over their heads and so he risked his life. He was able to save the girl, and Rikard himself was still alive when the men carried him into Henrietta Nolsøe's kitchen. But there he died. It was on Pole's old chaise longue that the courageous young man's heart stopped beating.

Eigil told this and similar stories connected with the Mosque to the psychologist Arnfinn Viðstein.

He also repeated his mother's claim that Tóvó had been murdered in his own house on St. Olaf's in 1918.

Arnfinn asked if the events surrounding the death were ever investigated, but they were not.

Eigil said that the event had the same mystical overtone as so many of the other stories his mother had told him over the years about Ergisstova and her family.

Martin, Lýðar's oldest son, inherited the Mosque, and he took everything from the house he deemed useful.

That was how the interesting sea chest made its way to Nólsoy.

Eigil mentioned the letters that the old Nólsoyingur man had left him, and he also talked about the valuable Degas painting that a clever lawyer weaseled away from Martin. In 1927, the Tórshavn Commune bought the Mosque, and now he was saddled with a haunted house and had no idea what to do with it.

Arnfinn Viðstein told him to consider following his mother's advice and selling the house, and if he could not find a buyer, then to give it away when a good option presented itself.

With that the Tvibur cabala would lift, in the sense that Eigil would be doing the same good deed that his great-great-grandfather had done one hundred fifty years ago.

The Lead Story Writer, the Torturer, and the Beanpole

THE VERY DAY that Elspa Tóra Lamhauge informed Eigil it was none other than Jens Julian við Berbisá who had written the lead article about the grave scandal, and who generally had fed the *Sosialurin* horror stories about him, Eigil left Tórshavn in his Fiat and drove north toward Kolbeinagjógv.

He inserted a Kinks tape into the cassette player, and as he drove past the dark mountains, he sang along with old hits like "Sunny Afternoon" and "Death of a Clown."

He stopped at the stone quarry in Hundsarabotnur, and while he pissed he looked up at the bright stars.

The tape played itself out on the bridge between Streymoy and Eysturoy, and for a moment he wondered at his lack of strong emotion. He felt mentally stable, and even his desire for revenge was strangely distant. It was like some foreign power had simply commanded him to carry out a violent act. The consequences were irrelevant.

The road was almost empty. It was evening and there were no birds in the sky either.

When he emerged from the tunnel on the way toward Millum Fjarða, he met a small Nissan truck, and as they passed each other, Eigil saw that the truck was loaded with sheep. A net had been spread around the wooden truck-bed, and even though it was not slaughter time, the sheep were undoubtedly headed to the slaughterhouse.

Their wooly heads stared out into empty space, and the idea that they were bound for the knife, and that no mercy awaited them, was like a shock to Eigil.

He thrust the Kinks tape back into the cassette player, turned up the volume, and hit the gas.

The new steering wheel was larger, and not leather, so it did not feel as comfortable in his hands as the previous one.

After the flat stretch of Millum Fjarða his speed reached 130 kph. The steering column trembled and the Fiat's horsepower whinnied beneath the hood.

The dark blue sky was visible above the high mountains, and when he caught sight of the full moon, hanging like a yellow evening flower, he felt his car skid off the road to the right.

He immediately took his foot off the gas, but was careful to avoid hard braking. He heard gravel hit the wheel arches and the under-carriage.

For a few seconds he fought to get the wheels back on the asphalt. He shifted the car into third and then down into second, and as his speed decreased to around 50 kph, he was able to make it back onto the road.

Devil take the moon, Eigil thought, as he pulled over at the first available spot. His hands shook on the wheel, but the tension eased as he opened the door and climbed out.

The evening air was cooler on his skin, and he wiped away some tears with the arm of his jacket, thinking that Ray Davis's nasal voice was not necessarily good for nerves of porcelain. For half a second he considered the possibility of returning to Havn and leaving Jens Julian and his fucking key ring in peace.

He stripped off his jacket and tossed it into the backseat.

Among the tapes in the glove compartment, he found Dusty Springfield's *Greatest Hits*. Already in the 70s, pop music publications were writing that Dusty was more attracted to women than men.

Who knows if there was a connection between the prying into her private life and the downturn she experienced around the same time.

Eigil, however, considered her to be one of the great pop voices of the 60s. Dusty was one of his heroes, and she had the courage to suffuse her voice with pathos.

Eigil slowly drove toward Skálabotnur, and when he heard "You Don't Have to Say You Love me," he felt the tears flow freely down his cheeks.

Although she could sound affectionate, Dusty was never ingratiating, at least not in the 60s. She was free, thankfully, of the sentimental tone that characterized her contemporaries, Tom Jones, the Everly Brothers, and the worst cream puff of all, Kenny Rogers.

Eigil burst into laughter. Purely unexpected, roaring laughter.

When Kenny Rogers really let go, he sounded like he was shitting. A pathetic idiot, that was what he was. He strained his vocal chords, tilted his head, and with those big hangdog eyes looked like he was begging for a pat. Eigil was convinced that Rogers was exactly the type who needed his plump country rump powdered at least once a week.

He saw the party chairman's house a hundred meters in front of him; two windows on the second floor were lit. He stopped his car on the south side of the house, put on the handbrake, ejected the Dusty cassette, but forgot to turn of the motor, and did not even notice the sound of it as he ran up the steps.

Jens Julian við Berbisá's front door was locked. But that did not prevent Eigil from getting inside. He simply lifted his right leg and kicked through the woodwork around the lock.

Stepping into the large, dark hallway, he spied a light beneath a door and heard a key being turned. He glimpsed a wide staircase leading up to the second floor, and where the stairs ended there were two arcades, one to the right and the other to the left. There were probably doors leading off them, but he could not see them.

Eigil headed toward the strip of light, and suddenly it was like someone had yanked his feet out from under him, and he landed with a heavy thud on the floor. He had tripped over some equipment and a stool, and he rose like a tidal wave. He threw himself at the door, and it crashed to the floor, frame and hinges and all.

Jens Julian stood behind a desk, fumbling with the telephone. He was shaking so much he dropped the receiver.

Eigil grabbed him by the neck with one hand and by the belt where the key ring hung with the other. The man was docile as a sheep, and Eigil threw him against the room's radiator with terrible force.

Jens Julian's back and neck crashed against the radiator, and the skin behind his ear was sliced open. Jens Julian vomited and remained lying there with wide, startled eyes. It was as if he was listening to the sound being transmitted to the radiator in the room above, and spreading via the pipes to every room in the house.

"I want an explanation," Eigil said.

"Go to Hell," Jens Julian groaned.

"Tell me why you wrote that article."

"Better someone like me than a psychopath from Sumba in the chairman's seat."

"Was it for mental health reasons then that you hung me out to dry as a gravepisser?"

"I was right. You are out of you mind."

Jens Julian's cheekbone must have fractured when his head hit the edge of the desk. A spray of blood splashed onto the small Olivetti typewriter, but the blow did not kill him. His throat still moved and gurgled.

"I don't want control of any party!" Eigil shouted, as he dragged Jens Julian toward the window. "Maybe you think I'm a cream puff, but to that I say, Fuck you! Vengeance's Corporal says, Fuck you! The only thing I've ever wanted is to make words grow in beautiful beds."

He opened the window and heaved Jens Julian onto the sill.

That was when he noticed how poorly the jutting lower jaw suited the party chair. His head looked like a manufacturing error. The workers at the Corpus Christi factory must have phoned it in, or perhaps they were on strike, when they saw Jens Julian's body come slowly gliding along the assembly line, and had neglected to set the lower jaw fast.

Eigil took the matter into his own hands. With his fingers beneath Jens Julian's chin and his thumbs between his teeth, Eigil tried to push the jaw back into place, but the man's jaw broke instead. In fact, his jawbone now appeared broken in several places; it was completely smashed.

The molars with their moist silver fillings resembled the Great Wall of China, the way it curved from Liaodong Peninsula west through mountainous country toward Gansu.

Eigil laughed abruptly.

Jens Julian had so often talked about protecting Faroese industry by building a protective wall around their limited Faroese production, and now that wall had collapsed.

It reminded him of how his mother had looked after her stroke. But she had not bled from the mouth, no, that she had not. It was saliva that came streaming from the corners of her mouth. And it had stunk. It was like froth. Yes. Like the froth on water violently churned up. Tears infected by rot.

Eigil suddenly remembered he had promised his mother he would tidy Pole's grave.

Several weeks ago he had bought a can of silver enamel and a small paintbrush to retouch the letters on the gravestone.

He had told Arnfinn Viðstein about his mother's advice and the psychologist thought it was a terrific idea. Such ideas were wonderfully unacademic and healthy, having grown out of ancient folkish wisdom. He had held a small informal lecture on the soul-cleansing effects of ritual, and had said that, in his opinion, the old Catholic confessional was an instrument of pure crime prevention.

Eigil heard a scraping out in the hallway, and when he turned around, he saw a tall man bending his head under the doorframe to enter the office. The man was dressed in an undershirt, and his long arms were not unlike the feelers of some large insect. He straightened up, the top of his head nearly brushing the ceiling, and then Eigil saw his face was that of a child's. He had unusually beautiful, dreaming eyes, and his chin and cheeks were covered with a light down.

It was undoubtedly an illusion, but it looked like there were berries growing amid the down.

His pants were kept up by suspenders that barely clung to his thin shoulders.

Eigil released Jens Julian.

The man with the child's face came closer, bringing with him the noticeable odor of various milk products.

For a split second Eigil considered jumping him, but then he remembered that Jens Julian had a sick boy.

The young man had reached his father and squatted beside him, and his long fingers stroked the distorted face.

Eigil crept along the wall and out into the hallway. He heard the sound of a motor outside. Could Jens Julian have called the police? Relieved, he discovered it was only the Fiat.

Halfway down the steps he turned around.

He went back into the office.

It was as if the short pause had cleared his mind.

Suddenly, he was aware that he had entered the criminal arena. In the light coming from the office, he saw that one of the doors off the corridor to the right was higher than the others, and now he noticed how the floorboards creaked.

The young man was still crouched over his father, but whether it was sobs or some other strange noise emanating from him, Eigil could not say. Even when Eigil stood right before him, the young man did not seem to notice his presence.

Eigil acted quickly. He gave the long beanpole a hard blow, and it so surprised the man that his arms and upper body jerked into the air. It was probably the first time he had ever been struck. Eigil was going to kick him, but suddenly stopped.

The young man was lying in the fetal position, and the chalk-white skin on his side and back looked so fragile.

Still, Eigil lifted him from the floor and was about to toss him against the wall, but could not bring himself to do it.

Carefully, he set the young man down and left.

The Arrest

EIGIL ROSE WHEN he saw both policemen start toward the grave. Carefully, he placed his left foot on the grave's edge, and as he shifted his weight to the other foot and was preparing to run, he saw two more policemen approaching from the Dalavegur gate. The pebbles crunched beneath their shoes, their faces were serious, and their watchfulness was betrayed by their relaxed hands, though their fingers were slightly splayed.

Kristensa had told them that her son was strong as a bear; she stood next to the gate. Apparently, the closest person to him in the world had led the police right to the graveyard.

Eigil had the insane notion of lifting the can of cleaning solvent to his mouth, two, three swallows, it would not take more to eat away his throat and intestines. And if the cops tried spraying water into his mouth, he would still be man enough to keep them away for the short time it took him to die, or at least to lose consciousness.

But Eigil did nothing.

On Napoleon Nolsøe's 185th birthday, he was docile as a lamb.

He placed his arms behind his back, felt the handcuffs close around his wrists, and the policemen led him toward the gate.

As he passed her, he smiled at his mother. He considered telling her the grave was now tidy, but it was not the right moment for words.

Before Eigil was interviewed the following day, he consulted his lawyer, Heðin Poulsen. The Writers' Association used him as an adviser, and earlier he had also advised P/F Rógv. He and Kjartan á Rógvi had both studied in Copenhagen in the 60s, and they had both been a part of the Faroese Communist movement Oyggjaframi.

This political orientation was no longer so obvious. The remains of Heðin Poulsen's old sense of proletarian solidarity was limited to the rolled cigar hanging from a corner of his mouth. His tweed jacket had seen better days, and his voice was characterized by a dry smoker's cough.

Heðin Poulsen told Eigil that, around midnight, people in the town of Morskranes had seen Jens Julian's son walking north along the road and waving his arms. He was wearing only an undershirt and jogging pants, and his face and hands were bloody. Heðin Poulsen repeated what a policeman said: that the Berbisá boy looked like someone who had escaped a horror film.

It turned out that Jens Julian's wife had been at a knitting club in Morskranes that evening and that her son had known that. He also knew the way there because it was the path he took with his mother and father on their pleasant evening strolls.

She ran out to meet her son and, along with another woman from the knitting club, was the first on the scene. They found Jens Julian unconscious and immediately called for an ambulance.

Heðin Poulsen said the matter was very serious indeed. A Faroese parliamentarian had been attacked and gravely wounded, and if he were going to take the case, he wanted Eigil to tell him the whole truth. There was no room for excuses.

Eigil said it all started during the 1992 city council election when an anonymous article in the *Sosialurin* had branded him a grave-pisser.

"I remember it well," Heðin interrupted him. "And I wondered why you never responded."

"What could I say?" Eigil said. "On New Year's Eve in 1980, I pissed on Napoleon Nolsøe's grave, and I was stupid enough to brag about it. If I'd just kept quiet, that article would never have been written and everything would be completely fine."

"And you might be the chairman of the Self-Governance Party today."

"That was never my intention."

"I was just joking," Heðin coughed.

"The article was printed on Thursday evening, and that same evening I started to experience the mental breakdown that ruined me as a politician, and that is also the indirect reason I'm no longer employed at P/F Rógv."

Eigil mentioned his car being vandalized. He also said that people had anonymously called and insulted him. Or maybe he had just gotten paranoid, he was not sure.

He also explained why he had bought the Mosque, and said that he believed the house was haunted. For this reason and others, he had sought psychiatric treatment. What had helped the most, however, was that he was writing a novel, and much of what had been plaguing him could be hung in the wardrobe that was the novel.

The day before yesterday, August 25th, he learned that the hand that had composed the damning article belonged to Jens Julian við Berbisá. What took place north in Kolbeinagjógv last evening was the reckoning for that fact.

Heðin Poulsen sat and nodded. He said that he needed to know who Eigil's source was. Not that he was thinking of using the information in a potential trial, but he needed to verify all that Eigil had told him was true.

"You mustn't misunderstand me. I'm not saying that you're being untruthful or lying, but you might have forgotten something. This matter is serious enough that there is no room for half-truths."

Eigil said that Elspa Tóra Lamhauge was the source, and that her son had worked at the *Sosialurin* during the time the newspaper printed the article.

Heðin wanted to know exactly what happened in Jens Julian's house.

Eigil said it was eleven o'clock at night when he knocked at the front door. Perhaps Jens Julian had seen his car outside, but he refused to open up, said that everyone had turned in, and that Eigil could call him in the morning. Eigil said he wanted to talk to him about the article Jens Julian had written for the *Sosialurin,* which had destroyed so much for him. The least he could do was open the door. Jens Julian told him to go away and that was when Eigil kicked in the door. Jens Julian fled to his office and locked the door, and Eigil said that he had also broken that door down.

During the conversation, Jens Julian admitted that he had written the article. He said that a political party had to maintain a certain ethical standard, and that a gravepisser was the least worthy representative imaginable. And that was when I attacked, Eigil said.

He said that he had thrown Jens Julian against the radiator, and that the blow was a hard one, but that was all. He had tried to help the chairman to his feet, and he had also apologized, but Jens Julian told him to go to Hell.

And that was exactly what he did. He drove back to Tórshavn.

Heðin Poulsen sat stroking his chin a good while.

"In other words, you're saying that the boy from the horror film was sort of an Oedipus from Kolbeinagjóv? Is a retard even capable of that?"

"What I know is exactly what I've told you."

O, Jesus, Friend
to the Melancholy

ON JANUARY 27th, 1995, Eystari Landsrættur announced its verdict.

Eigil was not present at the time.

Neither was Jens Julian við Berbisá.

The man had not spoken since the attack on August 25th of the previous year. Not even when his jaw had refused could anyone get a word out of him.

On her husband's behalf, Jens Julian's wife sent the Self-Governance Party's leadership a letter, which Jens Julian himself signed, stating that Jens Julian was resigning as chair and removing himself from all committees.

One could clearly read *Jens Julian* in the signature, but it was difficult to distinguish *við Berbisá*. And that did not bode well. The man had always been Jens Julian, but it was only as an adult that he had taken the name *við Berbisá*.

In one of the many telephone conversations Eigil had with his mother, she said that in truth Jens Julian had become his son's little brother. The man could not walk and it was unclear whether he would ever be able to walk again.

Eigil's mother seemed to know quite a bit about what was going on, and that included various small details. Yet Eigil could not bring himself to ask if she was in contact with Jens Julian's wife.

For three months, Eigil had been living in different hotels and pensions around Hordaland, Norway: in Bergen, Haugesund, Skudeneshavn, and also in the tiny town of Sveio, which lay on the peninsula of the same name.

He liked liquid comfort and he drank alone. At the hotel in Skudeneshavn, he was tossed out for being a bum and a drunk.

He was only present during the trial itself because the letter of the law required it: *The accused shall, unless under lawful exception, be personally present for the entire trial, so long as he can speak; though the presiding judge, after the hearing is finished, may give him permission to withdraw.*

That was exactly what Eigil did. He traveled to the Faroes on January 22nd, the trial took place on the 23rd, and by the next morning Eigil had already left the country.

He was worried that the *Sosialurin* or maybe Útvarpið, the radio station, would try to get their hands on him, but there seemed to be no interest.

Among the few present at the courthouse was the Writers' Association's treasurer, but it was not clear whether this was from solidarity or curiosity.

The Self-Governance Party's new chairman also showed up, and it took Eigil by surprise when the man thanked him for doing his part to get the loser from Kolbeinagjógv out of the chairman's seat.

Before Eigil left for Norway, he called his mother. He said she would be doing him a great service if she did not appear for the trial. And she fulfilled his wish.

His sisters and Ingvald were also absent.

Even though Eigil drank heavily, he was still able to write, if sometimes only for twenty minutes a day. For some strange reason, he was able to concentrate even with the pounding in his head. When his hand found its rhythm, the scratch of the fountain pen seemed to calm his mind, and sometimes he wrote an entire page that was useable.

Besides writing his novel, which was partly composed on a type-writer with large spaces between the lines, and partly handwritten in spiral notebooks, he had Tóvó's letters to Napoleon Nolsøe with him. There were twenty-nine pages, which he had photocopied. The originals he had left to the state archives. On the folder he had writ-ten: "Tórálvur (Tóvó) í Geil. Letters from 1862 to 1876."

Each letter began with the words: *Dear Pole.* Then Tóvó might write that he was sitting aboard the *Thin Lizzy*, that the weather was far too good, and that for a number of days they had been waiting on wind.

He also wrote some short descriptions of the docks in Newcastle or Hamburg. Regarding Manhattan he wrote: *On this little Island, not even as large as my birthplace Strømø, there are people of all sorts. Blacks, Chinese, Arabs, Indians, and Whites. I have no idea if they have anything to do with each other, but, in any case, they are as beautiful to see as the variety of trees in the forest.*

Even though he was a sailor, Tóvó did not write much about life at sea. Maybe it was simply too prosaic. Office workers tend not to describe office life in their letters, and letter-writing farmers do not serve up details from the stable.

Nonetheless, Tóvó did relate one occasion where he pulled a tooth from a German cook's mouth. The procedure went well and he had Pole to thank for that.

One of the letters was written in English. It filled three pages and was written in ink that once was red but had faded with time.

In the letter Tóvó cited parts of a poem by Walt Whitman.

Eigil was not too familiar with the famous American's poetry. Poet-ry as a literary genre had never excited him. He knew that Whitman was one of the most important modernists, but that alone was not say-ing much. The novel, on the other hand, was a great achievement: sty-listic, intellectual, and emotive. In Eigil's opinion, dramas and essays were also a step above poetry. People who flocked to poetry reeked of the church or of secret lodges. It did not surprise him that Tóvó was one of those people who had swooned for lofty poetic words.

Eigil had flipped through Walt Whitman's collection, and it quickly became apparent that the lines Tóvó had sent to Pole were taken from several different poems:

> Henceforth I ask not good-fortune, I myself am good-fortune,
> Henceforth I whimper no more, postpone no more, need
> nothing,
> Done with indoors complaints
> Strong and content I travel the open road.
> I am the poet of the woman the same as the man,
> And I say, it is as great to be a woman as to be a man,
> And I say there is nothing greater than the mother of men.
> I am larger, better than I thought,
> I did not know I held so much goodness.
> All seems beautiful to me,
> I can repeat over to men and women, You have done such
> good to me, I would do the same to you.
> Allons! the inducements shall be greater,
> We will sail pathless and wild seas,
> We will go where winds blow, waves dash, and the Yankee
> clipper speeds by under full sails.
> (I and mine do not convince by arguments, similes, rhymes,
> We convince by our presence.)

The most interesting letters were those in which Tóvó remembered the youthful years he spent on Tvøroyri.

Twice Tóvó visited Sumba, and the only written description of Nils Tvibur that still exists was formulated by Tóvó: *I have only seen one giant shed tears, and that was my friend Nils.* The words struck Eigil's heart.

On the way back from Sumba, Tóvó visited the poet Pól Johannis á Øgrum. He knew Pól Johannis from Tvøroyri, when the man came north for boat wood or had other errands at the Royal Danish Trade Monopoly and stopped at Pole's to buy morphine for his wife.

However, Pole, the great collector of folksongs did not value the Akrarman as a poet. Napoleon did not record a single of Pól Johannis's verses. To him, the Akrar poet was one of those Suðuroy folk who were always chuckling, *hehehe*, and who slandered respectable people.

And that was not entirely untrue. Pól Johannis was quite the comedian, a trait that emerged in his many sharp and mocking satires.

His wife suffered from melancholia and insomnia, and the only thing that calmed her down and let her sleep was morphine. In his letters to Pole, Tóvó described the woman's bed. Pól Johannis had outfitted the bed with rockers, and on the nights that nightmares and hopelessness particularly plagued his wife, he would rock her and sing to her.

Trust me, when that satirical poet's wife dies, he will make a lid for her cradle, and she will be the only woman in the world to be buried exactly the same way she slept. And I am certain that on the last day, when the earth opens up, and we are all called to Judgment, that cradle will fly up to Heaven, and on its sails will be written: Oh, Jesus, Friend of the Melancholy.

Eigil tried to find the Norwegian farm his great-great-grandfather left in 1827, and he succeeded. Or rather, he coincidentally happened upon a camping ground named Selleg's Camping. A young couple from Oslo ran the tourist business there, but he was unable to meet them because they spent the winter months in the capital.

On the other hand, he went several times to the local municipal office and police station, and here he succeeded in finding some information about his Norwegian origin.

As it turned out, by 1910 the Selleg farm was already abandoned, and the last tenant was named Gregor Selleg. That had been the name of Nils's father, and the twin brother who inherited the farm was also named Gregor. Nils's son, the patricide of Sumba, had, in other words, been named after his Norwegian grandfather.

That surprised Eigil.

Nils Tvibur had not only imported Norwegian heifer names to his new homestead, but also his father's name. Gregor had apparently been the name of the family's tenant farmers, indeed, over many generations.

The clerk at the municipal office told him that from 1825 to 1925, about a third of the Norwegian population emigrated west across the ocean, and that group contained many from Sveio. It could be that some of his relatives were among the emigrants. Another possibility was that the Selleg folk had relocated to Hordaland's larger cities. Whatever the case, today there were no Sellegs left in Sveio. One family had Selleg as a middle name, but that was it.

The woman kindly gave Eigil two addresses in town. He could contact people there who could give him more historical information.

Eigil thanked her for her advice and help.

Deep down, however, he was no longer interested in finding more information about his Norwegian origin; rather, he did not want to know any more about his violent make-up. He had ended up in Hordaland because he had avenged himself. He was a refugee on account of his psychic constitution. No matter what information he uncovered, it would not change his miserable life.

One Friday, January 27th, Eigil spent the entire day, and also well into the evening, sitting in his room at Rønnaugs Pensjonat in Sveio waiting for the phone to ring.

He had washed and shaved, and although an unopened Jameson stood on the desk, he had not tasted a drop.

He hoped and expected that he would win the case. After the successful trial on Monday, Heðin Poulsen, for one, believed the vagueness that characterized the events in this case was to Eigil's advantage. If he could escape being branded a ruthless villain, he would get his legs under him again somehow.

It was just past eight when Heðin Poulsen called, and Eigil could immediately tell by his voice that the man was moved. It could be he was also drunk, but Eigil did not dare to ask.

Heðin said that they had won the trial, but that it had been an exceptionally shitty battle. The helpless father and son, the older an invalid, the younger born an idiot—they were the real losers.

Jens Julian's son was going to be sent to an institution in Denmark for dangerous imbeciles, and Eigil was to pay Jens Julian a fine of 38,000 kroner. There were other details, but Eigil could read about them in the letter.

A coughing fit interrupted Poulsen, but when he could talk again, his voice was both hard and ruthless. He accused Eigil of being a combination of berserker and cultured villain, and he hoped that he drowned in the fucking pension's bathtub.

He said that he had known some cold devils in his day, and he himself was no ray of sunshine, but Eigil was in a class all by himself.

The lawyer took a breath. His dry cough sounded almost friendly, like he was giving Eigil a chance to ask questions.

Problem was, Eigil did not have any questions.

Three or four long seconds passed, and when Heðin Poulsen finally said goodbye, the tiny click in the receiver sounded far too loud.

Jóanes Nielsen is the author of four novels, a collection of stories, three volumes of essays, and eight poetry collections. He's been nominated on five occasions for the Nordic Council's Literature Prize.

Kerri A. Pierce has published translations from seven different languages, including *Justine* by Iben Mondrup and *The Faster I Walk, The Smaller I Am* by Kjersti A. Skomsvold, which was a finalist for the International IMPAC Dublin Literary Award.

**OPEN
LETTER**

**OPEN
LETTER**

Quim Monzó (Catalonia)
  Gasoline
  Guadalajara
  A Thousand Morons
Elsa Morante (Italy)
  Aracoeli
Giulio Mozzi (Italy)
  This Is the Garden
Andrés Neuman (Spain)
  The Things We Don't Do
Henrik Nordbrandt (Denmark)
  When We Leave Each Other
Wojciech Nowicki (Poland)
  Salki
Bragi Ólafsson (Iceland)
  The Ambassador
  The Pets
Kristín Ómarsdóttir (Iceland)
  Children in Reindeer Woods
Diego Trelles Paz (ed.) (World)
  The Future Is Not Ours
Ilja Leonard Pfeijffer (Netherlands)
  Rupert: A Confession
Jerzy Pilch (Poland)
  The Mighty Angel
  My First Suicide
  A Thousand Peaceful Cities
Rein Raud (Estonia)
  The Brother
Mercè Rodoreda (Catalonia)
  Death in Spring
  The Selected Stories of Mercè Rodoreda
  War, So Much War
Milen Ruskov (Bulgaria)
  Thrown into Nature
Guillermo Saccomanno (Argentina)
  Gesell Dome
Juan José Saer (Argentina)
  The Clouds
  La Grande
  One P...

Scars
  The Sixty-Five Years of Washington
Olga Sedakova (Russia)
  In Praise of Poetry
Mikhail Shishkin (Russia)
  Maidenhair
Sölvi Björn Sigurðsson (Iceland)
  The Last Days of My Mother
Andrzej Sosnowski (Poland)
  Lodgings
Albena Stambolova (Bulgaria)
  Everything Happens as It Does
Benjamin Stein (Germany)
  The Canvas
Georgi Tenev (Bulgaria)
  Party Headquarters
Dubravka Ugresic (Europe)
  Europe in Sepia
  Karaoke Culture
  Nobody's Home
Ludvík Vaculík (Czech Republic)
  The Guinea Pigs
Jorge Volpi (Mexico)
  Season of Ash
Antoine Volodine (France)
  Bardo or Not Bardo
  Post-Exoticism in Ten Lessons,
    Lesson Eleven
  Radiant Terminus
Eliot Weinberger (ed.) (World)
  Elsewhere
Ingrid Winterbach (South Africa)
  The Book of Happenstance
  The Elusive Moth
  To Hell with Cronjé
Ror Wolf (Germany)
  Two or Three Years Later
Words Without Borders (ed.) (World)
  The Wall in My Head
Alejandro Zambra (Chile)
  The Private Lives of Trees